SONG OF THE SWORDS

"There can be no Light without Dark
and no darkness without light.
Heed these songs well, for without them,
Alinae is lost."
~Tyranon the Artagh
Fourth cycle of the Craedr Age

SONG OF THE SWORDS BOOK ONE

THE STONES OF KALDAAR

TAMERI ETHERTON

Trudie!
Let your light
shine.
Tameri
Etherton

Merry
Christmas
2015

TEACUP
DRAGON
PUBLISHING

This book is a work of fiction. The characters, incidents, and dialogue are drawn from the author's imagination and are not to be construed as real. Any resemblance to actual events or persons, living or dead, is entirely coincidental.

Cover design and interior artwork by Carol Phillips

Library of Congress Control Number: 2014913889
ISBN-13: 9781941955000
ISBN-10: 1941955002
ISBN (ebook): 9781941955017

This book is dedicated to my fabulous husband,
David Etherton.
Not only because he loves me,
but he embraces my special kind of crazy.

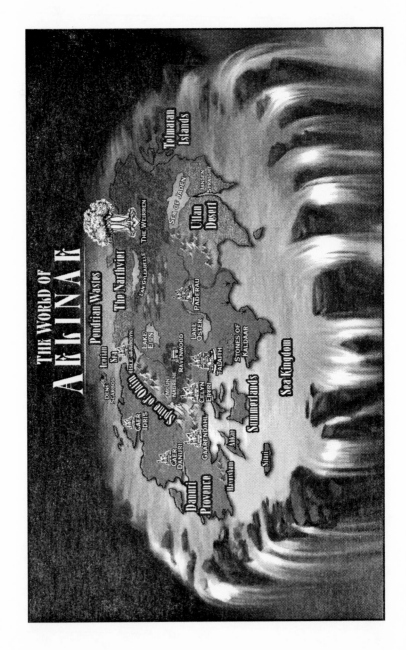

Chapter 1

IT IS time. He is waiting.

Taryn placed a finger on the page she was reading and cocked her head, listening. Voices from the pub below drifted through the thin walls of their flat. The kitchen staff preparing the day's meals. Her stomach twitched with anticipation.

She scanned the sparsely decorated room, her gaze resting on her grandfather. He sat in his favorite chair, pipe at his lips, one hand curled around a cup of tea long gone cold. Unblinking, unmoving, he remained focused on the fireplace, oblivious to his surroundings. She leaned against the window frame and shook her head. Two weeks of being cooped up was affecting her mind.

Outside, clouds, dark as pewter, blocked the sun that only an hour ago warmed the tiny room. Defiant rays struggled through the mass, but the summer storm released a torrent of rain, tamping out the last of the light.

It is time. He is waiting.

Taryn jerked forward, snagging her T-shirt on an exposed nail.

"Did you hear that?" She pinched the rip in her shirt as if the force alone could mend the frayed fabric.

Brandt continued staring into the flames. "Hear what, darling?"

"A woman. It sounded like she was standing right next to me."

"It must've been the storm."

"I guess." She rose from the window seat and stretched her long body, working cramps out of muscles more accustomed to long days of work than sitting. "Want to visit the museum today?" She had to get him out of the flat. Away from the apartment and back to work. Yet he refused every opportunity she or their clients presented. His lack of motivation perplexed her. And worried her. He was getting on in years; perhaps the constant traveling was finally catching up to him.

Wisps of white hair vibrated with the quick shake of his head. "Not today, love. Not today."

Her grandfather had loved his job, as did she. Loved the travel to far off civilizations, the discovery of long-forgotten artifacts, even loved the hard work associated with archeological digs. Then one day, without any warning, he told Taryn they were going back to London, to their flat, where he remained day after day, staring into the fire as if waiting for an answer to an unspoken question.

She rested her cheek on his head, and smoothed the tweed jacket he wore, grimacing at the lack of substance beneath. He wasn't eating well, nor did he sleep much at night.

A crack of thunder startled them both. Taryn's pendant thrummed against her skin, an insistent pulse that irritated her. She tapped the silver with her fingertips, shushing it.

A *pop* from the fireplace drew Brandt's attention, and he sat up straighter.

It is time. Awaken.

"There it is again. Tell me you heard that." Taryn scanned the room, her nerves twitching.

Brandt stood still, listening as she'd done a few minutes earlier. When he turned to face her, his eyes shone with excitement. "Aye, lass. I did."

A crack of lightning flashed outside their window, rattling the fragile glass.

"I hear you," Brandt shouted to the storm. "I hear you!" He grabbed Taryn's hands, startling her as much as the thunder had. A smile started at the corners of his lips and stretched to his cheeks, giving him a mischievous glow. "It's time, my darling girl. It's time."

"For what?" Uncertainty clipped her words. The sleepy entropy they'd cultivated over the past few weeks dissipated in the space of a moment with Brandt's sudden excitement.

"There is so much I need to explain but not here. Grab your rucksack and follow me." He spoke in the language they used in private, never around others, and as far as Taryn knew, only the two of them understood. The strange language was just one of Brandt's peculiarities. Inventing adventures was another.

"Baba, stop. This isn't funny. I don't know what's gotten into you lately." Only when alone did she use his nickname, finding it easier to call him by his given name around the men and women she worked with.

"It's time," he said, pulling her toward the door, "Come with me."

She grabbed her backpack and followed him down the narrow staircase that led to the back of the pub.

The smell of bacon assaulted her before they reached the ground floor and her stomach growled its unhappy emptiness. The sound of pots clanging and cooks yelling above the din was a comfort to her, but Brandt ignored it all as he hurried through the kitchen, its modern appliances gleaming against the ancient stones. Taryn rushed after him, swiping a scone from a nearby tray before heading through the back door.

Brandt led them down creaky steps to the cellar, where nothing more than broken chairs and leaky casks littered the earthen floor. After flipping on a single light switch, he stopped in front of a heavy oak door and motioned for her to wait. She shifted her backpack and leaned against the wall, bristling against the dampness. In the nearly twenty-three years they'd lived above the pub she'd been to the cellar twice; neither occasion she recalled with much enthusiasm.

The scone's warmth and buttery aroma did little to alleviate the cellar's mustiness. She chewed absently, painfully disappointed she didn't grab a cup of tea as well.

"Seriously, what are we doing here?" Despite her whispering, the melodic words echoed off the walls.

"I'm taking us home." His fingers danced across the edges of the doorframe, a peculiar amber light flickering beneath them.

"We are home," she mumbled through a bite of her scone. The air around them shivered, and she straightened, alert to unseen danger. "Baba, what's going on?" Her pendant flicked icy heat against her. The air thrummed with every breath, vibrated with each heartbeat as if it were a part of her. "We should go."

She reached out to Brandt, but he shook his head, sadness clear in the amber depths of his eyes. "We can't go back. You are so much more than this world would ever allow." Excitement crept into his words. "Through this doorway is a portal to our world. Our real home."

"A portal?" She snorted a laugh and choked on a bit of scone. Swallowing down her anger and the scone, she warned, "I don't know what you're up to, but I'm not a child anymore. You don't have to create distractions to entertain me."

"This isn't a game, Taryn. This is your chance to discover something wonderful. Won't you allow an old man just one more grand adventure?"

With a wink, he kissed her nose and turned back to the doorway. The way his fingertips traced around the frame and then the door itself, entranced her. There was a pattern to his movements, a staccato beat ending with him pressing his palm against the wood. A shock of searing heat flashed from her pendant, and she staggered against the pain. The air around them sighed with centuries' old longing. Amber lights blazed against the oak, and then the door was gone.

Instead of a storeroom filled with casks and old chairs as she'd expected, Taryn stared into a gaping blackness. "Bloody hell."

"Take my hand, and whatever you do, don't let go. There's no telling where you might end up."

"Where does it lead?"

"Aelinae." A mixture of wistfulness and mirth filled his tone.

"Ay-lynn-ay?" A memory teased her thoughts. Of a bright star. A man with fear etched into his features.

"Another world, another planet, actually. One of beauty and wonder. You'd be surprised what's possible if you look beyond what you think you know."

She reached out to the undulating, seductive void, stopping before her fingertips touched the darkness. Her mind raced with questions, doubts, and fears, but curiosity overrode everything. Nerves trembling, she took Brandt's hand, clasping it tightly. "Portals to other worlds? For real? You weren't kidding about it being an adventure."

"Are you ready?" Brandt's eyes glittered with unshed tears.

Not trusting herself to speak, and before she could tell him "hell no" and run back to their flat, she nodded. A thick cocoon enveloped them as soon as they stepped into the chasm. A deep, primal fear itched its way from her core, sweeping over her, suffocating in its entirety. Her breath came in small gasps that left her feeling lightheaded. Complete blackness engulfed her. If Brandt remained beside her, she couldn't see him. Nor could she see her own hand held an inch in front of her face. No sound, no brush of air indicated they were moving. She shoved down her panic, trusting that Brandt would see her safely through the abyss.

She floated in darkness, with licks of heat burning against her face and then slipping beneath her T-shirt, cutting her skin before soothing her with cool caresses. Blisters formed on her lips, then disappeared with a kiss of frost.

The sensation moved down her jeans to touch her in places no man ever had. A small moan escaped her lips, silent to all but her. Heat wrapped around her legs and bound her in its warmth. Cold thrills traveled through her, searing against the invisible flames that made her sway with desire. She yearned for the touch, opened herself to the seduction of the darkness.

An image of a man with short brown curls and eyes the color of summer moss drifted in her mind—the man from her dreams. Her submission wavered, and the void took on a prickly coldness before it shifted to a reassuring heat that wound its way over her breasts. It crept up her neck to her lips, lulling her back into sweet oblivion. The dream man called out her name, and she jerked against the stupor.

A sibilant hiss lashed against her senses. A moment later, she slammed into the unforgiving ground.

Sparks lit behind her eyes. A shock of pain ran the length of her. Ragged breaths ripped her lungs as she coughed against the dust flooding her throat. Her fingertips raked through the soft soil. After the etherealness of the void, the sand chafed against her skin.

A melody played in her mind, its tune sweet and light, hopeful. She stretched her fingertips to her pendant. "Quiet." The song lowered to a faint hum.

Each move sent a fresh spasm of pain across her forehead, trailing down her spine. Nothing felt broken, yet everything felt abused. Ignoring the protests from her scraped hands and knees, Taryn pressed up to all fours. She untangled herself from her backpack and fought off a wave of dizziness before she stood on unsteady legs. Faint light from the portal made it difficult to see where she was.

"Brandt?" Her voice died on empty air.

The portal brightened and elongated, stretching to allow Brandt to step through. "Thank the gods. I thought I'd lost you." He pulled her to him, crushing the air from her lungs. When he released her, tiny golden lights haloed his head.

The air shuddered as the portal closed in on itself until there was nothing left to indicate its existence. Brandt held her hands, murmuring beneath his breath. Several orbs lit around them, giving off enough light to see. An electric current pulsed up her arm; not unpleasant, exactly, but she resisted the urge to pull free from her grandfather's grip.

"Welcome home, my darling girl."

Fear gnawed at her belly, sharp pricks of unease heightened by the strangeness of her surroundings. "Is this—what did you call it?"

"Aelinae."

After her experience in the void, her emotions were raw, conflicted, vulnerable, and yet she was excited. "We did it? We crossed through to another *planet*?"

"Aye, we did."

His hand swept out and the light expanded, illuminating a cavern with glistening white walls and sand floors. Crystals radiating from pale white to deep purple grew in all manner of shapes and sizes. Beneath her pendant's jubilant tune, she heard a deeper strain that harmonized perfectly with her charm. The two melodies sang of a world full of light and shadow, of waterfalls and green meadows. Of temples to gods young and old, of mountains and a vast forest. They sang of a palace that overlooked the sea; they sang of Aelinae.

A world she knew without knowing.

At her back, the pull of the void beckoned her to return. Insistent. Demanding. Jealous.

"Aelinae is where you were born, Taryn." The whispered words echoed through her conscious. He didn't lie. Somehow, she knew it was true.

Taryn took a step forward, closer to the glittering gems. "I remember a star." Taryn pointed to the ceiling. "From up there."

Tears shone in Brandt's eyes. "Come with me. There is someone I want you to meet."

They wound their way through the forest of stalagmites, the crystals smooth beneath her hands. Some were as thick as her waist, their frosted coats shaggy with fingerlike growths that stretched in all directions and feathered ends blossoming toward one another.

Beyond the muted glow of the crystals, a large lake nestled in a well-lit cavern. Taryn blinked against the sudden light and instinctively headed toward the water, but Brandt stopped her with a grip on her arm that made her cry out.

She started to protest but then saw what he'd noticed first. Two men, arguing not more than twenty paces away, turned toward the sound of her shout.

Of equal height, they were opposite in expression. One dressed in clothes of darkest night with hair to match and mist-colored eyes. No warmth, no greeting entered those eyes as they traveled the length of her, bringing the slightest tilt to his tight lips. He hadn't moved from where he stood—feet firmly planted in the sand, shoulders back, head tilted just so—but his presence pressed against her, violating her space.

A breath caught in her chest, and she looked away only to meet the steady gaze of the other stranger. His eyes didn't raze her body but stayed locked on her face. Concern hid in the depths of those eyes. A tightness in his jaw and twitch to his lips made her want to reach out and stroke him, to soften the hardness beneath the stubble of beard. The idea both shocked and thrilled her. His stance wasn't as rigid as the first man's, but there was no mistaking his strength. Her gaze went from his lips, full but hard against his tanned skin, back to his eyes. They were an unmistakable shade of green.

It was the darker of the two who spoke first, his voice a low vibrato, thrumming against the empty cavern. "Greetings, Your Eminence." He bowed to Brandt, his steady scrutiny never leaving Taryn. "Well met on this day. Your absence has been too long, but I see you have returned to us that which was lost."

"What's going on? Who are these men and how do they know our special language? You told me no one else spoke it."

Brandt's chuckle did little to reassure her. "We are speaking Elennish, the oldest language on Aelinae. It was the least I could do to prepare you for your return."

Taryn stared at Brandt, mouth agape, an argument on her lips, but the handsome man stepped between them and the man in black, drawing her attention. Green lights sparked across his body.

"Zakael, this is nothing that concerns you." In contrast, his voice blended with the environment, eloquent, melodic. Safe. Comforting.

Dark, silvery flares whipped around the one he called Zakael, "I wouldn't be too certain of that." He indicated Taryn. "Who is the priest's friend? She's tall for an Aelan, but those blue eyes and that glorious, sun-touched hair remind me of someone."

The air shifted around them, electric, full of pent-up animosity.

"Stand down, Rhoane. Zakael will not harm us," Brandt warned, his anger directed at the darker of the two men. "I don't want a quarrel with you or your master. Leave this place at once."

A flash of anger crossed Zakael's face. "You have something that belongs to my lord." A bright ball of silver fire sprang to life on his outstretched palm. "Give it to me, and I'll let you live."

Taryn shrank behind her grandfather. The flame danced on Zakael's hand with a menacing ferocity, as if impatient to be released.

"Zakael," Rhoane said low enough Taryn had to strain to hear, "this cavern is sacred to the Light. Do not work your Dark power here."

"I demand that you give me what is mine." The force of Zakael's stare immobilized her where she stood.

Her mind screamed at her to run, to take Brandt and sprint to the portal, but her body betrayed her instincts and wouldn't budge.

Seconds passed in slow succession. Rhoane's jaw tightened, his fists flexed in anticipation. Then Zakael's body softened, his shoulders slumped forward, and he turned to leave. Taryn exhaled the breath she'd been holding, but Brandt gripped her hand tighter.

Zakael took a few steps and then swung around, his black cloak fanning out like wings. A silvery ball flew at Rhoane. Prepared for the attack, a web of green power consumed the fireball, dissolving it with an angry hiss.

Thick strands of Zakael's energy spiraled to the ceiling and loosened several crystals, sending them crashing to the ground. A wall of tawny light sprang up, protecting her from the glittering shards that shattered all around her.

"We need to leave. It's not safe here," Taryn urged Brandt, edging back toward the portal.

His eyes held a sadness she'd never seen before. "There is no going back for us. Aelinae is, by turns, beautiful and dangerous. You must trust this is for the best." Brandt moved them away from the fight, keeping his body between her and the men, never losing contact with her. The luminous wall of energy swirled in a frenzy, as if it longed to join the fray.

Taryn watched in stricken horror as Zakael circled Rhoane, taunting him. Their grudge went beyond this morning; that much was clear. The crystals lost their translucence, their glow vibrating in deep shades of aubergine and red.

"Do not do anything that cannot be undone," Rhoane warned.

A jag of laughter was Zakael's answer. A length of ashen energy whipped around Rhoane's legs and pulled him to the ground.

A sword appeared in his hand and he slashed through the bindings, missing several times before he freed himself. He leapt up and advanced on the other man, a murderous tilt to his features.

"Baba," she begged, "please. If we don't leave right now, one of these lunatics is going to kill us with those energy balls. Please. Now?"

Zakael held his hands out placatingly. "My quarrel is not with you this day, Glennwoods." He turned his attention to Taryn, his leaden glare cutting her soul before he settled a look on Brandt. "Priest, I will only say this once more. Return that which has been stolen."

Brandt opened his mouth to speak, but before any words were said, a bright flash of silver shot toward them.

"No!" Taryn moved to cover Brandt at the same time he threw a ball of amber flames at Zakael. A deafening explosion rang through the cavern when the two orbs collided. Sparks flared in a rainbow of color, and the impact flung Zakael backward with such force he hit the wall with an ominous *crack* before his body slumped to the ground in a motionless heap.

Waves of energy pushed over her, biting at her skin. Brandt staggered and then slid to the ground, pulling her with him.

"Brandt!" Taryn bent over him and felt for a pulse. His labored breathing echoed through the cavern. "No, no, no. Stay with me, Baba." Rhoane knelt beside her and placed one hand on Brandt's forehead, the other on his chest. "Help him, please," she begged while stroking Brandt's face. Her vision blurred with unshed tears.

Her grandfather's eyelids fluttered open, and he smiled at Taryn. "My darling girl." He reached up, cupping her cheek in his soft palm. "So much I have left to teach you. Too much left unfinished." His gaze traveled to Rhoane. *"Cael glinth aedder dia. Kulmacht vroider s'ael llynvayr khol dorn."* Brandt spoke in a language she'd never heard.

"What's he saying?" Taryn asked Rhoane. His eyes widened, but he didn't reply. "Baba," Taryn pleaded, "what did you tell him?" A wave of nausea rose in her belly, and she swallowed hard to keep the sickness at bay. A green thread of Rhoane's energy wound around Brandt, hovering above his mouth as he struggled to pull in air. "We need to take him back through the portal. We have doctors and hospitals. Someone there can help him."

"No, Taryn." The wheeze in Brandt's voice hurt to hear. "This is the only place that can help me now." The calmness in his eyes made her heartbreak more terrible. "Rhoane al Glennwoods ap Narthvier, I'm entrusting you with protecting Taryn." A look passed between the two men, and Brandt gripped Taryn's hands. "Promise me you'll stay here on Aelinae with Rhoane. Promise you won't return to Earth."

Chapter 2

WHAT could she say? It didn't matter if she was on Earth or Aelinae because without Brandt, one was just as meaningless as the other was. Home to her meant Brandt. If she stayed on Aelinae, she'd have to put her life in a stranger's care. Aelinae was not her world. It was foreign and mysterious, yet somehow familiar.

Rhoane sat opposite her, his quiet strength clear in his eyes. She stared into them, looking for answers. The tilt of his head, the quirk of his lips, brought back a hazy memory from a dream. Of a young man whispering words to her in the beautiful language Brandt had spoken. And then it was gone as if it never was.

Taryn squeezed her eyes shut for a moment, willed her heart to slow, her mind to clear. Nothing made sense.

"The adventure you seek, the life you crave, it's here on Aelinae." Brandt interrupted her thoughts with his ragged words, and she looked down at her grandfather. "Will you promise to stay?"

Tears fell on their entwined fingers, and she wiped her eyes with a shrug of her shoulder. "I promise."

"That's my girl." Brandt's eyelids fluttered, and his breath caught in his chest. "Trust yourself. I've taught you much of what you need to know, but there is more to your learning.

You'll stay with Rhoane?" His voice was nothing but a whisper.

"Yes. I'll stay with Rhoane if that's your wish." She stroked the side of his face, cringing at his rasping breaths.

Brandt placed Rhoane's right hand over her left and spoke in the lyrical and haunting language she didn't understand. Some of the words pricked her skin. The two songs of her pendant kept cadence with Brandt, silent to all but her. The lyrics blended with Brandt's words, becoming a part of his actions.

As Brandt spoke, a peculiar feeling enclosed her in a shroud of tranquility. His voice flowed around her, filling the space of the cavern and then lowering as he pulled a thin thread of amber light from the air. This, he carefully wrapped around their hands. Taryn drew in a sharp breath when the fiber disappeared into their skin. Brandt laid his head back, breathing his final words, *"Tienden dal cyrinise da gaellendale."*

"Tienden dal cyrinise da gaellendale," Rhoane intoned before kissing his thumb and placing it over his heart. With great reverence he bent, touching Brandt's forehead with his lips. A faint scent wafted over her with Rhoane's movement. Clean, crisp, with an earthiness like a mountain forest after rain. She inhaled and embraced the peace that enveloped her.

Cheeks wet with tears, Rhoane rose and curled his fingers around hers briefly before repeating his actions. After kissing his thumb and touching it above his brow, he placed his hand over his heart. "I am sorry, *Darennsai*. I had hoped our meeting would be happier than this."

His words sent a shiver down her spine and she rubbed her arms against the chill. "Were you and that other man waiting for us?"

"Zakael chose today to search the cavern. I have been waiting here for a fortnight."

"Two weeks?" It had to be coincidence. That was around the same time Brandt quit working. She shivered again and he moved as if to cover her and then hesitated.

"You are cold. Let us be by the fire."

He stood, but she hesitated. "What were you speaking to Brandt?"

"The language of my people." He held out his hand and she took it cautiously. A slight shock zipped up her arm when their palms met. The energy Brandt wrapped around their wrists brightened and then dulled in the space of a second. Quick enough she doubted what she saw.

A multitude of questions crashed through her thoughts, but they were silenced by pulsating cavern walls. They glowed with a radiance bright enough to bring day forth from night. The light swirled, coalescing into an airy star that descended from the darkness toward them. Tiny multihued rays streaked outward from the center to the far reaches of the cavern, dispelling the darkness.

A lilting female voice spoke to them. "Come here, my children." Rhoane stepped toward the light, but Taryn held back. "I have waited many long seasons to hold you once more. Come, my beloved."

Taryn put a hand over her eyes, shielding them from the brightness.

"Tell me child, why do you hesitate?"

Taryn squinted at the star. "The light is too bright, it hurts." She caught the look of surprise on Rhoane's face. "Can't you see it?" When he shook his head, she challenged, "What do you see?"

"Nadra, goddess of Aelinae and all creation."

"A goddess? As in, all-powerful, lightning bolts from the sky kind of thing?" Taryn resented the waver in her voice and the tremble to her legs.

Nadra's laughter sounded sweet and pure, like the gaiety

of children. "I've never thrown a lightning bolt, but I can if you'd like. In the lands from which you've come, I have many names that span just as many centuries, but here they call me Nadra." The star blazed brighter before settling into a muted glow that revealed a woman with flowing white hair and a round, youthful face. "Better?"

"Beautiful," Taryn whispered. Nadra hovered above the sandy ground, her bare feet peeking out from a gossamer gown. Her skin twinkled with tiny dots of light, as if she were made of all the stars in the universe.

Her soft voice bore immense sadness, her blue eyes misty as she spoke. "I am sorry, daughter, for your loss." Her gaze went to Brandt, and Taryn's chest clenched. The goddess caressed Taryn's face, warmth spreading from her fingertips. "He was ever my favorite and shall never be far from our hearts." She hovered between Rhoane and Taryn, taking their hands in hers. The thread Brandt had woven into their skin shimmered. Little pictures appeared at Nadra's touch.

Taryn traced a circular image on her wrist. The pictures faded into her skin once again and she shuddered involuntarily. If only Brandt had explained what was happening, then she wouldn't be so afraid. If only that man hadn't killed Brandt. If only.

"Couldn't you save him?" Taryn asked the goddess.

"Alas, my daughter, no. Someday you will understand why. Long have I watched over you, awaiting the day of your return. I know this is all new and upsetting, dear one. I sense your desire to return to Earth and yet an equally strong will to stay and face what may come. Earth was not your home, Taryn. Aelinae is."

"That's what Brandt said, too. Am I human?"

"No, dearest, you were born Aelan."

"Why were we on Earth? Why come back now?"

Nadra's energy flared around both Taryn and Rhoane,

giving off a soothing heat that calmed Taryn's racing heart.

"It is for you to discover your path," the goddess said, "Only then will these answers be made known to you."

Taryn pointed to where Zakael lay hunched on the ground. The slight rise and fall of his chest indicated life. "My path lies right there. Getting justice for my grandfather's murder."

"Your love of Brandt is honorable but now is not the time for revenge. I know it was Brandt's wish to see that you are cared for in his absence. These marks signify this desire." She ran a finger over Taryn's wrist, and the designs swirled before settling once more into her skin. "I would like to add my own blessings to these bonds. Will you accept them?"

"Bonds?" Taryn's voice rose an octave. She forced herself to remain calm.

"Through words and power, Brandt bound you and Rhoane in an ancient ceremony, creating a special link between the two of you. It's a very high honor."

"Are they permanent?"

"Yes, my love."

Taryn stepped away to kneel beside Brandt. She smoothed the white robe he wore, straightening the fur-lined vest across his chest. The garments looked handsome on him, dignified and regal. "These aren't Brandt's clothes. He was wearing a tweed jacket that smelled of cigar and aftershave." She squeezed her eyes against the threat of tears. "Am I dreaming?"

"No, darling. I put Brandt in his robes of office. They seemed more fitting." Nadra explained.

Rhoane knelt beside Taryn, and once again the scent of forest drifted toward her. "I can understand why you are frightened. It is not my wish to force the bonding against your will."

Taryn wiped her wet cheeks and glanced at him. "You

know what she's asking and you freely accept it, even though it means you might be stuck with me for a long time?"

Rhoane chuckled and put a hand on her shoulder. Like Nadra's, it was warm with a gentle thrumming of his power. "That is a risk I am willing to take. I gave Brandt my word that I would watch over you." A half-smile played at the corners of his lips, and he shrugged slightly. "With or without the bonds, it is you who is stuck with me."

Brandt looked peaceful as he lay against the sand. Her fingers brushed Brandt's soft cheek, smoothed a few wisps of white hair. "I made a promise, as well. I suppose I don't have a choice."

"You always have a choice, dear one," Nadra said in her lilting voice. "This must be your decision."

Taryn eyed Rhoane skeptically. "Will you help me avenge Brandt's death?"

Nadra's lips pursed at the request, but Rhoane ignored her. "I will do that and more." He touched his thumb to his heart. "You have my word."

Taryn held out her hand. "I accept. Do your thing."

Rhoane placed his hand over hers, and their bonds sparked to life. Nadra whispered words similar to Brandt's, and the lights in their skin glowed and shifted. As she wrapped a silver thread around them, new images appeared on her wrist. After a momentary burning, the glow dimmed and then settled into a discordant pattern of shapes and symbols.

Nadra kissed each of their palms. "I will watch over you, my two children, but I cannot intervene."

"Thank you, Great Mother," Rhoane said, bowing to the goddess. Unsure what to do, Taryn offered a clumsy curtsey-type bow.

With a graceful turn, Nadra scooped up Brandt's body as if he were nothing more than a small child.

"What are you doing?" Taryn moved to stop the goddess,

placing her hand on Brandt's arm.

Nadra paused, a reassuring smile on her lips. "I will take him with me to Dal Tara, where the gods dwell. It is between the worlds, a place of beauty and serenity. His selflessness and courage in an impossible situation earned him the right." A glittering tear tracked down her cheek, a moonbeam among the stars. When it hit the ground, a crystal rose out of the sand. "Be assured that he will be content. He will be with you, as ever he was."

Stupid with emotion, Taryn just nodded. Tears stung her eyes when she placed her lips to Brandt's cheek, breathing in his essence for the last time. Nadra nodded once to Rhoane and then ascended into the air, disappearing into the darkness.

When the last of Nadra's light faded from the cavern, Taryn sank to the ground, curling her fingers into the sand. It would be easy to lose herself to grief. To allow the flood of tears, but Brandt had raised her to be strong. To know when vulnerability could cripple a person.

Rhoane knelt beside her, his hand hovering an inch above her shoulder, hesitant, as if unsure how to comfort her. Despite his presence, she was alone.

In the space of a morning, she'd lost her best friend, her only family, and her world.

Chapter 3

TARYN'S belly burned with need. For vengeance and the hunger to see the man who killed her grandfather punished. There would be time for mourning later.

She sprang up, her sudden movement surprising Rhoane. He followed her angry strides until she came to Zakael's inert form. The desire to crush his skull consumed her. She gripped her fists against the impulse to cause him harm, then flexed her hands. Bloody half-moons formed in her palms where her fingernails cut into her flesh.

"Taryn?" Rhoane's voice was low, cautionary.

"He needs to pay for what he did to Brandt."

"Would you have me kill him?" A spark lit in his eyes. Challenging. Something else lay hidden there, too. Something that reached to her core and frightened her.

She glanced at the pathetic form lying huddled on the sand. "As much as I hate him right now, it wouldn't be right. There's no honor in killing an unconscious man." When she glanced back to Rhoane, there was approval in the mossy depths of his stare.

She shook out her hands, and a crystal fell from her grasp. Nadra's tear. She bent to retrieve it and studied Zakael's profile. He looked peaceful. Except for a trickle of blood from a scrape on his head, he could've been sleeping.

"Someday he'll pay."

"Yes, he will. But not today." Rhoane led her away from Zakael to the lake where she rinsed her hands and quenched her thirst. The honeyed water slid down her dry throat, and she drank as if trying to fill the void of Brandt's loss.

"Are you feeling better?"

"Yes, thank you," she lied. "What do we do now?"

"Are you well enough to travel, *Darennsai*?"

"Why do you call me that?"

"It is the name my people have given you. It is a name of respect. If it does not please you, I will not say it again."

"I was just curious." After a moment, she added, "Should I call you Rhoane, or is there another name you prefer?"

"There may come a time when you call me something else, but Rhoane will do for now."

"Okay, just Rhoane. You said travel—where are we going?" A chill ran the length of her despite the warmth of the cavern.

"To meet with some friends."

"I take it you two aren't what you'd consider friends?" She cocked her chin toward Zakael. "What was that fight about, anyway?"

Dark brows pinched above his straight nose, nostrils flared the slightest bit. "Our quarrel goes back many seasons." He turned and strode away without further explanation.

"Got it. Long standing feud. But since this *quarrel* got Brandt killed, I think I deserve to know why."

"Perhaps you do." Rhoane stopped before a thick wall of crystals. "For now, what you need to know is that Brandt's death was not in vain." He motioned for her to follow and stepped around the rocks out of sight.

Hidden behind the stones was a campsite of sorts. A small fire burned low with blankets and cooking supplies laid out in neat array. Before she had a chance to sit down, Rhoane handed her a pile of clothing.

"I have brought you a change of attire. I am afraid what you are wearing is not what Aelinaens are accustomed to."

Taryn gave Rhoane's leather pants, tunic, jerkin, and boots a long look and groaned. "I've gone back to the bloody Middle Ages. I don't wear dresses, so unless you have something like what you're wearing, I'll stick with what I have."

"Then I think you will be pleased. There is an alcove fifty paces that way where you will have privacy. Would you like me to walk you there?" He was tall, perhaps half a foot taller than her five feet nine inches, but his closeness dwarfed her. The light from the cavern cast a halo over his curls, keeping his face in shadow. His presence wrapped around her like a comfortable blanket and she had the sense she'd been there before. With him. Strange words drifted through her mind.

"Darennsai?"

His voice pulled her from the memory. "I can manage. Thank you."

She started to turn from him and paused, her fingertips stroking the soft cotton tunic in her hands. "You knew we'd be returning, didn't you? That's why you've been waiting and why you just happen to have clothes for me. But why? How did you know?"

"Yes, I knew. Nadra bade me come to the cavern and wait."

The voice from her flat tugged at her, *It is time. He is waiting.*

She shivered against the unknown and made her way to the alcove, distracted by the nagging feeling of familiarity. Rhoane, the cavern, even the fresh smell of her garments, triggered memories. Thoughts she'd pushed to the back of her mind came forward, begging to be relived. She pulled the tunic over her head and then shimmied out of her T-shirt.

The pants proved more of a problem, but she managed to strip off her jeans and pull on the leather breeches without showing too much bare leg. After several failed attempts to tie the boots, which had more eyelets and laces than she'd ever seen, she gave up and wore her sneakers.

When she returned to the campsite Rhoane was nowhere in sight. After an anxious moment where several scenarios played out in her mind—of Zakael returning to finish the fight, or Rhoane deserting her—she spied two mugs sitting on a flat rock near the fire. At least one of her fears hadn't come true. She sank to the blanket, eyeing the dark liquid in the cup. A hint of spice tickled her nose. Chilies, perhaps, but sweet like cinnamon.

Her backpack lay on one of the blankets, looking oddly out of place in the pristine cavern. Footsteps crunched against the sand, and she froze, her heart jackhammering in her chest. Rhoane stepped around the crystal wall, and she breathed out, loosening her grip on the boot she held like a weapon.

Feigning calm, she tossed the boots to Rhoane. "I can't figure out the laces on these things."

"Let me help you." He sat beside her and patiently showed her how to tie the boots, his fingers weaving the laces with practiced grace.

When he finished, she stared at the intricate crisscrossing pattern. "I'll never figure that out."

"You will in time." He handed her a mug, "Drink this, *Darennsai*. It is called grhom and will give you energy."

Chocolate, thick and luxurious, with a snap of heat from chilies flowed over her tongue and down her throat to settle her aggravated belly. "It's delicious." It was actually more than delicious; it was heaven in a cup. She emptied the mug and Rhoane refilled it. She nodded toward her backpack. "Where did you find that?"

Rhoane followed her gaze. "Where you and Brandt entered the cavern."

"Can I keep it?"

"I am afraid not." He eyed it warily, as if something horrific might be hiding inside.

Taryn inhaled a deep breath. "Figured as much." She pulled the bag toward her and started tossing items on the ground. Notebooks, pens, pencils, toothbrush and toothpaste, books—nothing of real value, but the thought of throwing them away pained her. It was her last link to Earth. To Brandt. "Can I keep any of it?" She clutched a book to her chest. It was her favorite, one she'd read dozens of times.

Rhoane took the book and flipped through it. "I am sorry, but everything from that world must be destroyed. No one can know where you have been." He picked up a small velvet pouch and held it out to her. "What is this?"

Taryn turned it over several times, examining the cloth. "I don't know. It's not mine."

"It is with your belongings. You have never seen this before?"

"Never. It looks old. See the stitching—that's by hand. The silk loop and pearl would place this somewhere in the fifth or sixth century. Brandt might have—" She stopped herself. She and Brandt traveled all over the world to recover ancient artifacts. His job was to acquire items for his clients, not keep them.

In places, the faded blue velvet was threadbare from years of handling. Whoever owned the pouch had kept it near them. She untied the delicate gold ribbon and slid out a silver disk about the size of her palm. It felt good in her hand, heavy and solid. Her pendant hummed against her skin as a ripple of energy pulsed up her arm, exciting her. When her fingertips touched the silver, etchings moved across the surface. She dropped it as if bitten. When it left her touch, the inscriptions shifted to the edge of the disk.

Rhoane made a figure eight above his head. "Nadra has twice blessed us." He picked up the silver piece to examine it. The disk gleamed in the firelight, and Rhoane muttered under his breath while covering the artifact with his hand as if to shield them from it.

"Do you know what that is? What those symbols mean?" Her fingers flexed, anxious to grab it from him, to again feel the pulse of energy.

"This is a Seal of Ardyn, lost from our world many millennia ago. How did you come to have it?"

If Brandt had hid it in her bag, he must've had a good reason. "I have no idea. Is it important?"

His eyes flicked to her and then back to the seal. "Very much so. This seal, one of thirteen total, was created to keep Rykoto locked away in the Temple of Ardyn."

"The what locked where?"

Rhoane stared at her, a shadow of contempt crossing his face. "About ten thousand seasons ago, there was the Great War between two elder gods, Daknys and Rykoto. Before the war, Aelinae was a peaceful world. Rykoto betrayed Daknys and sought to rule alone. He tried to destroy not only the elders but the younger gods, as well."

"I thought gods were immortal."

"Immortality is subjective. They do not suffer disease and cannot be killed by mortals, but one god can destroy another."

"How?"

"I am not a god and therefore cannot answer that."

"Was he able to? Did Rykoto kill them?"

"He tried, but Daknys and the others were able to seal him away before any real damage was done."

"And that little piece of silver is helping to keep him locked up? If it's so important, how did it get lost? I mean, you'd think people would keep track of that sort of thing."

"You make a good point. We must take good care of this." Rhoane placed the disk back into the pouch, securing the ribbon before handing it to her. "Keep this safe for the time being."

"Oh no. If that thing is so important, you carry it."

She thrust the pouch at him, but he held his hands up and away from her. "If you will recall, we found this in your possession. You must be the one to safeguard it."

"That's so not fair. I didn't even know I had it."

She touched her belongings with a sigh of regret for the life she left behind. Before she could change her mind, she tossed her things on the fire, ending with the backpack.

"I don't have anything to carry it in. You need to take it."

Rhoane handed her a leather satchel. "Will this do?"

Taryn took it from him, shoving the pouch inside. It looked small and utterly unimportant in the empty bag. When the carnage burned itself out, they covered the embers with sand and packed up the campsite. She was about to heft one of the bags onto her shoulder when Rhoane flicked his wrist and the gear disappeared. Energy sizzled up her arm, not exactly unpleasant, but uncomfortable all the same. Like ice held against skin a second too long. Moss green sparks lit out from where the items had been.

She gaped at Rhoane, "What the hell just happened? Where did your stuff go?"

"Where we will need it next." He said with a slight shrug and left the campsite.

Unsure if she really wanted to know how he made the equipment disappear, she followed in silence. When they neared where she and Brandt had entered the cavern, the void pulled at her, thick with desperation. She hastened her steps, ignoring the temptation to let the sweet emptiness of the portal envelop her once more. From beyond the glittering wall, a hiss recoiled in defeat. Goose bumps rose on her arms and neck. Rhoane glanced at her over his shoulder, a worried look in his eyes.

"I'm fine. Let's keep moving." She quickened her pace, matching Rhoane's long strides with her own.

The crystals dimmed behind them as they hurried along the edge of the lake until only Rhoane's glowing orbs cast small circles of light along the path. When they reached the passage leading them out of the cavern, Rhoane stopped so suddenly Taryn almost ran into him.

"Follow close. The tunnels in this mountain are treacherous. If you do not know your way, it is easy to get lost." He set off again without waiting for her to reply.

After a short distance, a flicker of light caught her eye and she stopped, calling out for Rhoane to wait. Pale green lights crisscrossed an opening off the passageway. When she peered into the darkened alcove, she suppressed a cry. In the center of the space, surrounded by purple quartz walls and a white sand floor, lay an unmoving and very naked Zakael.

"Bloody hell." She looked at Rhoane, not sure she wanted to know the answer to what she was about to ask. But she had to know. "Did you kill him?"

Chapter 4

RHOANE'S glare cut to her core. "Quite the opposite. I mended his wounds and left him with enough food and water to last the four days until the wards dissolve."

"It doesn't seem fair, does it? We showed him mercy when he gave Brandt none."

"It was the honorable thing to do. Let us keep moving."

Taryn jogged to catch up. If Zakael were to free himself and follow them—Taryn shook the thought from her mind. She didn't need to imagine what he'd do to them. Brandt's last moments were seared into her memory. "Are you sure you can't make those lights last longer than four days?"

"What lights?"

"On the alcove's entrance. Little green threads like the ones you wrapped around Brandt. I assume those are what you call wards."

"In this case, yes. Wards are constraints put upon someone or something. Their uses vary, but mine are to keep Zakael from leaving that space until we are safely on our way."

Taryn cast a last glance behind them, but the alcove was no longer in sight. She'd have to trust Rhoane and his wards. Brandt had placed his faith in the man. Thus far, Taryn had no reason to doubt his motives. Unlike Zakael.

Rhoane led them with quiet authority, directing her to

watch her head or check her footing. Some of the passageways were so narrow or shallow they had to sidle through them or duck almost to their knees to continue. On and on they walked until the darkness and silence seeped into her psyche, disorienting her.

"Cover your eyes," Rhoane whispered, his hands pressed against a sheet of rock. A jade outline created a doorway.

She stepped behind him, hands half covering her eyes. An opening appeared, and he guided her into the late-afternoon sun. She squinted against the bright light, blinking until her eyes adjusted to the sudden change.

Rhoane moved a few feet past her to where the camping equipment lay piled neatly against the mountain. She suppressed a shudder and flexed her marked hand.

"Can I help?"

He blew on some tinder until a spark flared up, nearly catching his hair. He leaned back, rubbing his palms against his thighs. "Perhaps later. Dinner will not take long, you should familiarize yourself with our surroundings, but do not go far."

They were on a ledge about a hundred feet or so from the bottom of a large mountain, one of many in a range that stretched as far in one direction as it did in the other. A river cut through the steep valley, pooling into a small lake before flowing out the other end to disappear beyond her view. Golden flowers swayed in the breeze and lush green grasses surrounded the lake. After the dank mustiness of the tunnels, Taryn welcomed the fresh air and open space.

A gust lifted her hair, swirling it around her face as she stood on the edge of the cliff. Birds chirped as they swooped and darted past her through a dazzling blue sky dotted with white clouds that moved lazily away. Everything looked clearer to Taryn, crisp and focused.

"It's beautiful." She turned toward the cave entrance,

where the rock was once again solid. "Was that another portal?"

Rhoane paused in his preparations. A small fire burned, the supplies from the cavern spread around it. "The opening is still there. You just have to know where to look. It would be best if you did not mention portals anymore."

"Why?"

He motioned for her to sit and handed her a cup of grhom. "Aelinae is a very young world. Much younger than where you came from. Based on what Brandt shared with me, less advanced than that other place, too. Only a few people on Aelinae know of the existence of portals. That is why it is important you do not mention them ever again. If the wrong person heard you talking about another world or portals to the unknown, it would put your life at risk. Many would kill or worse to learn what you know."

She could imagine many terrors worse than death. Some she'd seen with her own eyes and hoped to never witness again. "But I don't know anything about them."

"Not only have you been through a portal, you were raised on another world. You know more than anyone else on Aelinae. That is why you cannot be overheard talking of such things."

In that moment, she hated Aelinae. Hated the fact her life was ripped from her without warning. Hated that Brandt's death was the culmination of what she had lost to this new world. Hot, bitter tears streamed down her cheeks, unbidden and unwelcome. Despite her will to not show weakness, the reality of all that had happened since she'd entered Aelinae crashed upon her.

Rhoane knelt before her but did not reach out for her. There was a time she would've walked away to hide her tears, but she wasn't alone in her mourning. Later she would process all that had happened, but right then, even if it was dangerous to trust him with her vulnerability, she needed him. Needed his strength. Needed to know there was a reason to continue. She leaned into him, a silent invitation.

His arms wrapped around her, fierce, protective. "Brandt's loyalty and kindness shine through in you, Taryn. It is not a sign of weakness to show your emotions, but of love." His whispered words brought her comfort. His body trembled against her; his voice became raw. "I shall miss my friend dearly, of that be certain."

For the longest time she stayed in the safety of his embrace until there were no more tears to shed. Even after her cheeks dried, she lingered. "Sorry," she mumbled into his shoulder.

"No, Taryn," he said in a gentle but firm voice. "You have nothing to be sorry for. Brandt was taken from you much too soon. You cannot be expected to get over that loss in less than a day."

It wasn't just Brandt's death, but she couldn't explain to Rhoane the mixture of emotions that churned through her—sorrow for the loss of her best friend, distress for what she left behind, and fear of the unknown. Beneath it all, guilt at the excitement Aelinae presented.

"Thank you." She pulled away from him and ran her fingers through the tangled mass of hair that fell over her shoulders. "You wouldn't happen to have a brush, would you?"

A silver hairbrush with white bristles appeared on his palm. "Will this do?"

"How did you do that? Is it magic?"

"ShantiMari is a power far beyond magic. It exists in everything around us. Is there no ShantiMari where you came from?" She shook her head, and his expression grew distant, as if he were listening to something far away. A flicker of doubt crossed his face. "You should rest while I finish dinner."

She stared at the brush in her hands, half afraid to use it. The only thing special about it was the etching on the silver. At least when she touched the designs, they didn't move. With more than a little apprehension, she pulled the brush through her hair. When nothing happened, she continued until her hair hung down her back tangle-free. She tucked the brush in the leather satchel beside the disk and then twined her hair into a thick braid.

The aroma of Rhoane's cooking made her stomach growl. She wasn't certain how long she'd been on Aelinae, but it had been a long time since breakfast. Rhoane set a plate of fish and vegetables in front of her, and she looked at him in surprise. "Did you magically make these appear, too?"

"Not at all. The fish are from the river. The roots I brought with me."

"But you never left the ledge. How did the fish get here?"

He studied her a long moment and then sighed as if he'd made some sort of decision. One he wasn't happy with. "Those lights you see, they are a part of ShantiMari, a power found in all living things. Just as there is no light without dark, there can be no Shanti without Mari. They are the male and female opposites of the same power."

"This ShantiMari, it allowed you to make our camp gear appear here and get fish from the river?" The awful fight with Zakael bubbled to the forefront of her thoughts. "And other things."

"Yes, and other things." Sadness hung from his words.

"When you say Shanti and Mari are the male and female opposites of the same power, does that mean everyone has Shanti and Mari?"

"Not everyone has the power. Of those that do, men have Shanti, women have Mari. There are three strains to the power: Light for Mari, Dark for Shanti, and Eleri."

"Eleri?"

"The Eleri are Aelinae's oldest race. They were here before most of the world and helped nurture the planet to what it is today. They are caretakers, of a sort."

"So, Eleri men and women have both Shanti and Mari?" Her head swam with the information he was giving her.

"No, they have Shanti or Mari, but it is different from Light and Dark. More tied to nature, or the terrarae, if you will."

"Terrarae." She knew the word. Brandt had used it on several occasions to refer to the earth.

"Mari pulls energy from the night sky. The moon, specifically. Shanti, from the sun."

"That makes no sense. If Mari is Light, why doesn't it get energy from the sun and vice versa?"

"Because there can be no Light without Dark and no darkness without light." Icy pricks started at her crown and cascaded down her back. She knew those words. Had heard them before, but she couldn't recall when or where.

"How does this power work?"

"The key is to understand what it is you want from your ShantiMari." He stretched his arms and showed her his empty hands. With a flick of his wrist, he held within them a small pig. Another flick and the piglet disappeared.

"It is easier to produce something that already exists, but if you understand what it is you want, you can create it from your mind. ShantiMari can create and destroy in the same breath; one must be careful with one's ability. ShantiMari is first and foremost always to be respected." She opened her mouth to speak, but he put a finger to her lips. "No more questions for tonight. You have had a long day and will need your rest for tomorrow."

Frustrated and a little annoyed he was babying her, she stalked to the farthest blankets, not caring if they were hers or not, scuttled beneath and pulled them to her chin, her back to Rhoane. For a long time she lay quiet, welcoming sleep, but it didn't come. Too many unanswered questions raced through her mind.

A rustling to her left startled her and she stiffened, hoping it wasn't Zakael with his terrible fireball. She craned her neck to see Rhoane shuffling around the edges of their small campsite, muttering beneath his breath. An intricate network of lights spread over and around the camp, enclosing it in a fine web of protective ShantiMari.

When finished, he stood outside the lights, staring into the distance. Giving up on sleep, she went to the barrier. With a tentative finger, she reached out to touch it, but Rhoane's low voice stopped her.

"You may cross through. You will not be harmed."

His power caressed her skin when she stepped gingerly into the lights. She stood beside him on the ledge, listening to the comforting sounds of the night.

"Tell me, *Darennsai*, how is it you can see my ShantiMari?" Rhoane kept still, his focus on the mountains in the distance.

"I thought you said no more questions," she joked. Her marked hand itched, and she flexed her fingers. "I don't know. I just can. Can't you see it, too?"

He gave a slight shake of his head. "I have never heard of anyone who can. What is it you see?"

"Just strands of light. Brandt's were amber, Zakael's grey, and yours are green. What do you think it means that I can see them?"

"I am not certain." Dim moonlight turned the top of his brown hair silver. It highlighted his cheekbones, giving him an angelic, ethereal look. When he spoke, his voice was strained. "It might be best if you do not mention this to anyone else just yet. It is a feeling I have, nothing more, but something tells me this information should be kept between us."

"Is it bad I can see your ShantiMari?"

"No, just different."

"What's it like? To have that power?"

His jaw tightened and then relaxed. "I have nothing to compare it with, so I could not say."

The underlying tension in his tone unnerved her, and she shifted nervously, looking at her hands. The silver and amber threads danced in the moonlight. When she moved her wrist, the tiny pictures reappeared. Fascinated, she turned her hand back to front, front to back, watching the images fluctuate with her movements. "Do yours do that?"

He held his hand out for her to see. His markings caught the light, moving in the same way as hers. She placed her arm just under his, mesmerized by the shimmering figures. "What are they?"

"Ancient runes." Rhoane indicated the image of a mountain on her wrist, and then his. "This is Mount Nadrene, where we are right now, and this," he pointed to a picture of a large tree, "represents the Weirren of the Narthvier."

"Oh. What's a Narthvier?"

"The great forest to the north. It's where the Eleri live and the Weirren is a vast city in the trees where the king resides."

The runes shifted until she could clearly make out their shapes.

"Why are only some of yours the same as mine?" Taryn held his hand, comparing the images. Mount Nadrene and the tree were there, as well as a star superimposed on a circle. She traced another image, and it came into sharp focus. A laurel wreath with two gems, one above, the other within its embrace. The threads glittered in the moonlight as if the diamonds were real. She dropped his hand. "That's my pendant." Her fingers went to her throat as if to protect her necklace.

"*Cynfar* is the proper name." He reached toward her neck

and hesitated.

A flutter of insecurity passed and she released her grip on the charm, giving him a nod.

He took the *cynfar* between two fingers, rubbing his thumb over the delicate leaves and then tapping the middle stone. "This represents Aelinae. And this," he brushed his finger over the smaller stone, "is the place from which you came."

"And the wreath?"

"That is the world between worlds."

"How do you know so much about it?" She looked at the pendant in the moonlight, as if seeing it for the first time. The leaves rustled in the breeze, and she drew in a sharp breath.

Rhoane's gaze returned to the valley where night creatures hunted and dark shapes ghosted through the sky. The mountain peaks were nothing more than silhouettes against the starlit night. "Do you know how you came to have this pendant?"

"Of course. Brandt gave it to me."

"Did he ever tell you where it came from?"

"I never asked." Unconsciously, she stroked the gemstone, trying to recall whether they ever discussed its origins. "Do you know?"

Even as she said the words, a memory drifted in her thoughts. She saw Rhoane as he was, young and handsome, with brown curls falling over his face as if he were bending over something. Fear edged his eyes. He whispered words in his mystical language and then kissed the pendant before placing it around her neck.

"You! You gave it to me." She rubbed her forehead, trying to recall the details. "It was here, I think. In the cavern? Brandt was there." She paused, letting the memory unfold. "And Nadra. We were in a hurry. You," she met his eyes and saw in them the same lingering fear, "you were worried about us. About me." It was as if the fragments of memory that haunted her as a child coalesced into coherence at last. "I remember you."

Rhoane raised a hand toward her, but stopped midair before dropping it to his side. *"Darennsai."* The word was nothing more than a whisper. "You were so young."

"All these years I assumed I was half mad for having an enchanted pendant. It sings to me, you know."

By the look on his face, he hadn't known. "It was made to be your companion and, if need be, to keep you from harm."

"I have so many memories—strange ones—that I never understood." Tears streamed down her cheeks, and she brushed them off with her fist. "God, you must think I'm such an idiot."

Rhoane didn't move as he studied her with the same moss-green eyes that plagued her memories. Finally, he put a hand over hers, saying, "In time, all of this will make sense. *Nyath minas, ninyeh, Darennsai.*"

Taryn swallowed hard and stared at him, disbelieving what she'd heard. "What did you just say?"

"You need to give it time."

"No, not that part—the other thing you said."

"Nyath minas, ninyeh?"

"Yes, that. What does it mean? I've heard it before."

His look was questioning. "It is an ancient saying of my people. It means, 'You are one with this world.'"

She thought for a moment, absently nodding her head. "There's more to it. *Taen das laerl. Dinyath allundrel kneesh awl hap teergartn.* What does that mean?"

"It is a blessing. Again, a very old saying from my people."

She smiled at him through her tears. "You said that to me, didn't you? When you gave me this." She tapped her *cynfar.*

"You were just a few days old. How is it you remember?"

She laughed, but it came out more like a sob. "I don't know. In my dream, or memory, you look the same as you do now, but you can't be more than a few years older than me and it's been almost twenty-three years since we left."

"I am much older than I look. And you have been gone nearly thirty-five seasons. Time in the other world and here must move at a different pace."

"Brilliant. Now I'm middle-aged. This world of yours isn't looking too good right now."

"Thirty-five is still considered very young. You are just maturing into an adult. Tomorrow, I can explain it all, but I think we should try to sleep now." His gaze scanned the dark landscape. "Myrddin will have gotten my message by now and be on his way."

The name tugged at her memory, another hazy image lost to time. Taryn made her way back to the pile of blankets and snuggled deep in the soft fabric, suppressing a yawn. "Thank you for trying to save Brandt from that man."

Rhoane's silence stretched into the night. Taryn was about to roll over for sleep when his words came to her on the breeze. "I am only sorry I could not do more. Brandt will be missed."

"I would like to hear about your friendship with my grandfather."

"And I would like to know of your life beyond the cavern."

Taryn propped her head up with one hand. "Really? I thought you didn't want me to talk about it."

Rhoane lay on his back, his profile stark against the light of the fire. His skin held a slight sheen, as if the glittering crystals of the cavern left an indelible mark on him. "I said I would prefer you not mention names and places, but of your experiences, that I am curious."

Taryn yawned and stretched, rolling to her back. "Sure, but tomorrow, okay? I'm exhausted." She stared into the blackness above them, trying to follow the threads of light. Several creatures, owls or bats, she wasn't sure, drifted close to the barrier and she shuddered. Their silent wings reminded her of Zakael's black cloak. She was used to men making rude or suggestive comments—it came with the territory of her job—but Zakael's scrutiny was like that of a predator to his prey. He possessed a power she didn't understand. Not only that, he showed he could kill with little to no consideration.

Unsettled by the thought, she adjusted herself to where she could see Rhoane without being obvious. For a long time she watched him. Watched the steady rise and fall of his chest. Watched him as surely as he'd always watched for her. The day she left Aelinae with Brandt he'd been there in the cavern, and he'd been there again the day she returned. It couldn't be a coincidence.

Her bonds burned beneath her flesh—not an unpleasant feeling, but a constant reminder she and Rhoane were connected. Connected by more than just an oath.

Chapter 5

THE crown princess perched on the thick banister built to keep dimwitted fools from tumbling off the empress's balcony to the sea far below. Marissa heard neither the crash of waves behind her nor the cry of seagulls above her. Her focus was on the two writhing figures on the bed in the next room.

They thrashed atop the silken sheets, unaware of the small petrel that watched from a short distance away. She hopped from one claw to the other, impatient for her mother to be done with the gorgeous stud. Marissa chose the tiny bird over her usual feiche for just that purpose. Spying on the empress was not an easy task, even for her daughter.

The young Geigan groaned his pleasure, arching away from the empress. Lliandra trilled a reply and raked her nails down his back, leaving streaks of blood in their wake. Marissa fought off the surge of jealousy that pumped through the bird's heart. Another growl from the bed, a cacophony of moans and whimper. Then it was finished. The stud collapsed beside the empress as Lliandra adjusted herself on the pillows, her hair fanning around her.

It was something Marissa had watched her mother do a hundred times, and with every fluff of Lliandra's shimmering golden hair, Marissa wanted to hack it off.

When snores came from the man beside her mother,

Marissa flew to the empress's sitting room and transformed back into her womanly form. A startled servant scuttled from the room, and a moment later, her mother arrived, eyeing her with suspicion.

"Is there a reason you're interrupting my afternoon?"

Marissa gave the briefest of nods toward the servant. When they were alone, she shared the reason for her visit. "I've not heard from Zakael. When I try to reach him, there is only silence."

A frown creased her mother's marbled features. "You assured me we could trust him, that the timing was right. What if he took the girl to Valterys instead of killing her?"

"To her father? He wouldn't do that." Marissa desperately hoped he hadn't done exactly that. Her orders had been clear: intercept Brandt with the girl and kill them both. No one could know of her involvement in the scheme, or that Brandt tried to return to Aelinae with the Eirielle. "Something must have happened."

"I'll send Myrddin to the cavern. He's near enough. It will only be a day out of his way."

Marissa kept her face calm. Either her mother or Myrddin had lied to her. "I thought he was in Paderau. Why is he near Mount Nadrene?"

Lliandra waved her hand to dismiss the ridiculous notion. "Duke Anje needed him at Ravenwood for the gods know what. His note was cryptic, to say the least. Keep trying to reach Zakael. If you hear from him before dinner, alert me." Lliandra traced a finger around the edge of Marissa's dark curls. "Did you enjoy watching, my feathered beauty?"

Marissa swallowed hard, willed her heartbeat to slow, and stayed silent.

"His ShantiMari is weak, but his bloodline is worth it." Lliandra pressed her fingers tight over Marissa's face, scrunching her cheeks together, hurting her. "I might be carrying his child right this moment. Another heir to solidify my rule." Lliandra released Marissa with a hostile push. "Find Zakael and the Eirielle. Kill them both."

"Of course, Mother. But wouldn't you rather the Eirielle survive and be aligned with the Light Throne? Why destroy a thing of such power and beauty when you have the opportunity to cultivate and harness that power for yourself?"

Lliandra's eyes narrowed in thought. Marissa could imagine the argument being played out in her mother's mind. She'd do anything for the empress, except kill Zakael. That, she could never do.

"I'll have Myrddin take her to Paderau. There, we can study her. If she has any value to us, then she lives. If not, then I expect you to dispatch her without question before we return to Talaith."

"With pleasure, Your Majesty." Marissa curtsied, sweeping the floor with her gowns. Zakael was safe, for the time being.

Marissa hurried to her rooms, anxious to find Zakael. The plan was simple. The plan should have worked. The plan had gone entirely awry somehow, and Marissa had to find out why.

Lady Celia burst into her rooms before Marissa had a chance to send her maids away. With a forced smile, Marissa greeted her favorite lady-in-waiting.

"Your Highness." She bent to one knee, which alerted Marissa that they needed privacy.

She led Celia to her sitting room and enclosed them in a web of Mari too powerful for even Lliandra to penetrate. "What is it, my darling?"

Celia pressed herself against Marissa, her soft lips seeking the crown princess's. Irritated, Marissa pushed Celia from her. "You came here for a tryst? I told you never to abuse your privileges with me."

"I haven't. I wouldn't." Celia dabbed at the corner of her

mouth with a delicate fingertip. Her pink tongue licked her lips. "I missed you. It won't happen again." Once composed, Celia said in a breathless torrent, "The empress finally approved our trip to Paderau. We leave at first light tomorrow, which, as you know, means midday for the empress. Who, by the way, will not be traveling with us, but a few days behind. I think she wants more time with her latest acquisition. I hear she won't be bringing him with us, though, because of a feud between his family and Duke Anje's. No matter, we'll be going, and I will be your traveling companion."

Marissa's thoughts spun in a tempest. Gossip traveled fast at court, but not in the space of her walk from her mother's apartments to her own. Which meant Lliandra was already making plans to travel to Paderau.

Celia tugged at her hands. "I haven't told you the best part." She lowered her voice despite the wards. "Your mother is considering Lord Herbret's petition to court Princess Sabina."

"No!" Herbret had been trying for the better part of a season to win over Lliandra, but for some reason her mother played coy with the disgusting runt. The petition wasn't absolute approval and Lliandra could revoke it at any time, but, if approved, it opened the door to betrothal negotiations. "Does Sabina know?"

"Not a wink. I will bask in delight when Herbret claims that stuck-up bitch on her wedding night. She's probably frigid beneath that Summerlands sun-kissed skin."

Sabina had no ShantiMari, which made her less than worthless in Marissa's opinion, but Herbret's determination made her curious about the exotic beauty. On more than one occasion, Sabina had rebuffed Marissa's subtle invitation to her bed, which stung. She, too, would like to see the haughty Summerlands princess brought down a rung or two.

"Celia," Marissa cooed, knowing her favorite had also

tried to bed the lovely Sabina, "that is not behavior befitting a lady of your rank." She stopped herself from stroking the girl, instead choosing to punish her by refusing affection.

Heat filled the room, and for a moment, Marissa wavered in her decision, but there were more pressing concerns to be dealt with.

"My darling, wicked girl." Marissa breathed against Celia's lips. "We must find new ways to amuse ourselves on the journey to Paderau."

Celia shuddered against her. "I am yours, my lady. Body and spirit."

Marissa tweaked her lady-in-waiting's nipple. "Yes, and you must remember that. Always. Now, go. I have matters to attend."

As the girl was leaving her room, a pout to her pretty lips, Marissa called after her, "Tomorrow, wear the jade gown." A smile broke across her lady-in-waiting's face, and she skipped from the room.

Once certain Celia was gone, Marissa hurried to her vanity where she retrieved her supplies. She arranged a flint and strip of fabric beside the small crystal bowl and took three deep breaths. With her mind calmed, she lit the fabric and dropped it into the bowl. Smoke drifted up, then across the mirror, composing her message to Valterys. Short and to the point, the vaporous threads read: *Zakael silent. Concerned.*

Within the space of two heartbeats, his reply formed in the mist: *Silent here as well. Not to worry. Ravenwood?*

Marissa hesitated. She'd done as he asked to ensure Duke Anje wouldn't stand in their way, but with Myrddin on his way to Ravenwood, she wasn't sure if her plan had succeeded. Valterys needn't know that until she was certain.

Success. The sword is yours to claim.

Be safe.

Marissa smiled wryly at the suspended words. *Always.*

She pressed her hand against the cool glass of the mirror, imagining Valterys doing the same in his room at Caer Idris. She didn't regret telling him of the secret child Lliandra sent away moments after her birth, nor did she regret the plans they'd made to destroy the empress. What Marissa regretted most was the anguish she'd caused Valterys when he learned of her relationship with Zakael.

No one could understand the bond she had with Valterys. Certainly not Lliandra, who, when Marissa was but five seasons old, had beheaded her father. After that, a succession of lovers walked the halls of the Crystal Palace until one day Valterys came and stayed. In him, Marissa found the father figure she'd been seeking, and his attention filled the emptiness she'd lived with since her father's death.

With Valterys came his son, Zakael. Marissa was only ten seasons then, Zakael twenty-five. Despite his being an eligible bachelor, Lliandra forbade him from courting any of the ladies that roamed the palace. Marissa became his near-constant companion. A playmate to pass the lonely days and nothing more. But to her, he was the world. Smart, charming, and full of wicked ideas that often got them into trouble. For Marissa, it had been immediate love. Heartbreaking, life-changing, desperate love. She'd never told a soul about her feelings for Zakael, nor did she ever give any outward indication. She'd understood enough about court life to know that if she did, he'd be taken away from her, possibly forever.

So she'd waited. Even after Lliandra destroyed her relationship with Valterys and had taken Zakael into her bed, Marissa waited. Then, one day, when she was a child no longer, she sought him out. Now fifty seasons, Marissa had been Zakael's lover for half her life.

Marissa blew gently against the smoke, dissipating Valterys's message and ending their connection. A terrible excitement rushed through her, one that wouldn't be satisfied until Zakael's Dark Shanti penetrated her entire being.

On impulse, she sent another message to Zakael. Silence. The sick thrum of fear she'd been pushing to the back of her consciousness crept forward until it cloaked all her senses in a feeling of helpless foreboding.

"Your Highness," a soft voice said beyond the closed door, "it's time to ready you for dinner."

Marissa waved the smoke from the mirror and snuffed out the fabric before putting the bowl in its cupboard. "Enter," she commanded as she released the Mari barrier around the room.

Two bells later, Marissa was in the ballroom dancing with her sisters. To all the court, she appeared carefree, a young woman enjoying herself. Inside, she was a tempest of emotions. Lliandra had refused to tell her if Myrddin found Zakael, and that stud of hers was giving her serious cravings of the illicit kind.

Herbret pranced by with a delightful young lady in his arms, smiling to Marissa as he passed. His feeble attempt to make Sabina jealous didn't work, as the Summerlands princess's attention was elsewhere. Marissa almost felt sorry for Herbret.

"Sabina, you've been here almost a season, have you decided on a proper suitor yet?" Marissa asked the gorgeous creature.

"Not yet, but I've been assured I haven't met every worthy bachelor in the kingdom, so there is still hope."

"I told her she needs to wait until we get to Paderau. There will be more men to choose from, and not just from the East," Tessa, Marissa's youngest sister, assured them. "If only she had ShantiMari, she would be a perfect match for our cousin Hayden, don't you think?"

Sabina didn't flinch at the mention of her worthlessness.

Nor did she smile, but a flicker of indignation in her deep brown eyes caught Marissa's attention.

"Hayden is the most sought-after bachelor in the East. As third in line to the Obsidian Throne, he must choose his bride carefully," Eliahnna, Marissa's other sister, said in her quiet voice. "There is protocol to follow."

"You and your rules. They're so boring!" Tessa stood up with a sweet pout to her lips. Her blonde curls refused to stay pinned in place and swirled around her head. "I want to dance. Who will be my partner?"

"I would be delighted." Sabina took Tessa's hand and led her to the center of the room.

Tessa loved to dance almost as much as she loved to fight. For certes, she would someday make a grand general for Marissa's armies. Her gaze swept over the ballroom, settling on the young lover at Lliandra's side. Back straight, hands on knees, he watched the proceedings with a slightly terrified look. Lliandra was notorious for beheading her lovers if they didn't produce an heir. The idea sent a tremor of excitement through Marissa.

He bent to whisper to Lliandra, and after her nod of approval, he slipped quietly from the room.

Marissa excused herself from the group and dashed around the dancers to follow him. She needed to have him. To take something precious from her mother. She didn't think of it as treason, but survival. Lliandra was withholding information from her and should be punished.

She stood alone on the veranda, breathing in the heady scents of the summer night. Jasmine mingled with a briny tang from the sea. Rose bushes, heavy with their charges, drooped around the columns and lattices. The smells intoxicated her, and but for her mission, she might have lingered. She scanned the area, but the young man had disappeared.

The most obvious place to find him would be the orchards,

where privacy was afforded by the lushness of the trees. She practically skipped through the dimly lit gardens in the hope she'd locate her prey. Several times, she had to stop and greet a courtier or minor noble before continuing in her search. The desire to have him burned through her, culminating in an anxious need nestled at the apex of her legs.

At the farthest end of the castle grounds, he stood with his back to the orchard, facing the ocean. Silhouetted by the crescent moon, he looked like an apparition. A catch in her breathing brought her up short, despite her bravado. Lliandra could have them both hanged if they were found together.

When she stepped out from the trees, he turned toward her, a frown creasing his brow. "Princess." He bowed low. "I sought some quiet. Forgive me if I'm intruding on your peace."

Marissa put out a hand to stop him from leaving. "Stay, please. I confess I am seeking solitude, but you are a welcome distraction."

He bowed again but not as low. Then, turning back to the ocean, he said, "There is an element to the sea that beckons my soul."

"Oh? I suppose it has its purpose, but I've never felt especially drawn to water." Marissa moved beside him, closer than etiquette allowed.

"I suppose there are other wonders of the world you've seen that call to you. I am not much traveled, and the sea is all I have."

"There is one place," she admitted, "far to the north, where volcanoes meet with ice."

His body trembled slightly, and Marissa swayed into the tremors.

"They say the fires of Dal Ferran were started with those volcanoes. Surely you've never been?"

"Not only have I been to the volcanoes, I've seen the fires

for myself."

"You jest, Princess. Only those consumed in Hell have seen Dal Ferran's fires. I would think you're destined for the starlit nights of Dal Tara."

"So you think I should be a goddess? I should reside with the most venerated of Aelinae? Tonight, I am simply an Aelan." She looked up at his profile, at the strong jaw and commanding brow. He was lovely. She could see why Lliandra wanted to breed with him. "Is it awful being here?"

A slight smile broke the line of his lips. "Not all of it." He glanced down at her, sadness wrought across his features. "But I admit, I didn't think it would be quite like this."

"You mean you didn't know you'd be a slave to my mother's appetites? Oh come now, certainly you've heard the rumors?"

"Rumors, as you know, have some basis in truth, but still, I had hoped it would be different." He waved a hand as if to dismiss his last comment. "Don't get me wrong, anyone would be thrilled at such an opportunity."

"But you wish you had a choice in the matter, is that it?"

Again, the little smile. "Yes." He turned toward her, keeping a discreet distance between them. "I was sent here by my parents in the hope I could bring honor to our family. If I don't produce an heir, I might as well move to the deserted islands off the Ullan coast. They have no need for me since I'm the third born. But my ShantiMari is strong, and Valterys is my uncle, so they had hoped I'd be the one to create the Eirielle. It's ridiculous, really. Everyone knows that's just a myth."

The missing pieces clicked into place for Marissa. Lliandra hadn't picked this man on a whim. She was trying to make another anomaly. One Nadra wouldn't take away. One she could control. She'd tried with Zakael and how many others?

"You poor lamb," Marissa cooed, pressing herself against

his chest. "How terrible it must be." Her pelvis tilted up, meeting the erection beneath his trousers. A low moan escaped his lips. "I wish those prophecies had never been made. Light, Dark, what does it matter? We should live together in harmony and combine our power to better the lives of all the people of Aelinae."

"Yes! That's exactly what I told my parents, but they insisted I come here to be the empress's concubine. It's humiliating." A look of fear crossed his stern features. "I apologize, Princess. I didn't mean to imply that I was ungrateful."

Marissa shushed him. "You have nothing to apologize for. Please, always speak freely with me. I value your insight." With a slight tilt of her head and lift of her breasts, she looked both consolatory and alluring.

Indecision flicked behind his eyes before he sighed against her. "Thank you. I could use a friend." His gaze traveled from her eyes to her bosom, resting there for several moments. She inhaled deeply, bringing her breasts closer to him, and watched the bob of his Adam's apple with silent triumph.

When his gaze returned to her face, a look of hunger clung to him.

"Princess," his voice was low, full of wanting, "since I've been here, serving the empress, I can't stop thinking about you."

"Me?" Marissa fluttered her lashes and put a hand to her lips. "But we've hardly spoken."

"I know. I was too nervous to say anything to you, and being that I was commanded to share your mother's bed, I didn't think you'd find me attractive."

She feigned surprise, her voice a sultry taunt. "Surely you're not telling me what I think you're telling me?"

He stroked her face with a fingertip, leaving a trail of hot desire in its wake. "I know it's treason, but when I'm with her, I think only of you." His lips touched hers, tentative at first, until she swooned into him.

His Shanti snaked around them, pricking at her skin, fanning the flame that already threatened to burn out of control. "This is wrong. We shouldn't be here," Marissa whispered when he paused for a breath. Her hands expertly fumbled with his trousers, untying the strings and pulling them loose. "We could be hanged."

His cock jumped at the word, and he shivered. "Then perhaps we should stop."

Her hands wrapped around the deliciously smooth hardness of his shaft. "Should we?"

A deep growl was his answer. His head sank to her bodice where he nipped at her breasts through the fine fabric of her dress. Her Mari dug into him, eliciting a delightful cry from his lips. Tired of the game, she drew him to her. "Take me as you've been imagining."

He spun her around until she was perched upon the seawall, her skirts a billowy cloud of silk and cotton. The rough stone cut into her skin, exciting her further. She leaned back until her head dangled over the edge of the wall, with nothing between her and the sea. A rush of adrenaline pounded through her in pace with the crash of waves. He cradled her head in his hand, pulling her up to a half-sitting position.

"Careful, Princess. You don't want to tumble over the edge."

"Oh, but I do. Bring me there, my darling. Push me over the edge," she replied a bit too coquettishly, but he didn't seem to care.

His lips, harsh and deliciously brutal, found hers. She opened her mouth, inviting his tongue to dance within the depths. Like a man starved, he devoured her mouth. She moaned and wriggled, her legs wrapping around his waist.

With a solid thrust, he entered her, sending sparks of fire and ice throughout her overexcited body. Each touch was a smooth caress followed by a tantalizing slap.

Her mother's lover was well versed in the art of lovemaking. He knew how to bring her to the brink of desire and leave her there, dangling, yearning. His free hand plunged inside her bodice and released her breasts to the warm night air. Her traitorous nipples hardened to chiseled nubs. She needed more. Craved more, always more.

She grasped at him, pulled him closer, deeper. Their mouths locked in a frenzy of desire, their ShantiMari swirling in a tempest around them. With each pump, she pressed her legs against him, harder, harder, harder, but he was still too gentle. The stone wall allowed for little movement and she was at the mercy of his pace. It wouldn't be enough.

Like most men, he didn't know what she needed. Would never understand her cravings. Would never give her what she sought. Only one man had ever satisfied her.

The concubine's body trembled against hers, then stiffened with his coming release. It was too soon. "Wait," she panted and pushed against him.

With a strength few would guess she possessed, she twisted both their bodies until he was stretched on the wall, her legs straddling him. His grin sent wicked shivers through her, and she ground against him, pressing her pelvis hard, trying to find her own release.

He gripped her waist and thrust as much as he could in his position, moaning loud enough the entire palace could hear. Marissa returned the moan, her head lifted to the night sky. So close. Just another moment more. But he cared not about her pleasure and emptied his seed with a satisfied yowl.

He rose up to kiss her, and his rank breath assaulted her senses, the scruff of his beard grated against her delicate skin.

"Princess," he huffed as if he'd run a league, "you do me a

great honor this night. I look forward to our next encounter."

"I'm afraid, my dove, that will never happen."

Confused, he searched her eyes. "But I thought…"

Before he could finish, Marissa tightened a thread of Mari around his throat. His eyes bulged and he made gasping sounds that delighted her. "What? That I would help elevate your position? You should've thought less about your own ambitions and more about satisfying my needs. You'll not make the Eirielle with the empress or with me." He was an idiot like all the rest who thought he was special enough to make the Eirielle. Poor lambs, they were nothing without their delusions.

Marissa tugged on her Mari, loving the way it cut into his skin. "Your ShantiMari is nothing. You are nothing."

He struggled beneath her, trying to find purchase on the seawall. His arms flailed to the side before swinging wildly toward her, his hand wrapping around her neck.

The wild gyrations, coupled with the loss of air from his strong grip, sent her over the edge and she trembled with her own release. His eyes, so full of life a moment before, stared at her with silent horror. His hands went slack and dropped to his side. Pinpricks lit her vision as oxygen flooded her brain.

The lovely violence he'd inflicted on her was overshadowed by his inconvenient death.

She pulled the remaining dregs of his Shanti around her. In his power, she sensed his connection to the water. Taking another's ShantiMari without their consent violated everything she'd been taught, but it wasn't as if he would need it. Besides, the effects only lasted a short while.

Slowly, she removed herself from his lifeless body and stood panting as she stared at the churning sea. Her tryst with Lliandra's lover could never be discovered. She would've found a way to silence the man, with bribery or blackmail, but now he'd put her in a difficult position.

She paced a semi-circle, tapping her nail on her bottom lip, every so often scraping hard enough to draw blood. Moving quickly, she pulled his breeches up and retied them. Next, she arranged his hair and vest, tucking in his frilled shirt.

With a swirl of her Mari, she flung his body over the wall, regarding it coolly as it bounced down the cliff to land with a satisfying *thwump* on the rocks below. With any luck, he wouldn't be found and if he was, the empress would think he'd slipped.

It took her several minutes to straighten her skirts and arrange her mussed hair. Satisfied that no evidence of her mother's lover remained on her person, she returned to the palace where she danced and drank until the morning rays touched the ballroom windows.

Chapter 6

THE air clung to the ground in a dewy crispness that belied any hint of the heat the afternoon would bring. Sunlight had yet to make its way above the mountains as birds awakened to greet the day with song. Rhoane listened with keen interest, but they sang of nests and food. Nothing untoward lurked nearby. When he and Taryn reached the small clearing where he'd corralled the horses, Rhoane felt her fear as if it were his own. Not of Zakael, which he still sensed, but of the beasts themselves. Anxiety clung to her like a thick cloak, but she said nothing as they readied the horses.

He took his time saddling her horse, instructing the mare to be gentle with her rider while making certain the cinch wasn't too tight. Cynda was young enough to challenge Taryn's abilities, and the last thing Rhoane needed was for the *Darennsai* to break her neck from a fall.

Glowing orbs of his ShantiMari bobbed ahead of them, lighting a little-used trail that hugged the mountainside. Cedars with gnarled trunks bent into grotesque shapes arched over the trail. Thick limbs dangled like fingers, ready to grasp unsuspecting riders. Taryn shivered as they stepped around a wayward branch. Fallen needles from giant pines crunched beneath the horses' hooves, filling the air with an earthy scent. Taryn inhaled a deep breath and then another before her shoulders relaxed a fraction.

"You are smiling," Rhoane said to her.

She lifted her face to where the light broke through the branches. "It feels good to be out of the darkness."

The sun's rays danced across her hair, making it even more golden. The desire to reach out and stroke it, to pull her face closer to his, rushed through him. She glanced at him and held his gaze. Despite the tragic events of the previous day, there was a subtle confidence in her he found immensely attractive. Her beauty left him breathless, even though she didn't seem to realize the effect she had on him. Nor did she realize the Eleri garments he'd given her clung to her curves, enticing him with wicked thoughts.

"You're staring."

Rhoane cleared his throat and reluctantly turned away. Every so often, she glanced behind them until Rhoane assured her there was no danger from Zakael.

"Are you sure? I just thought I saw something."

Rhoane scanned the area but could see nothing amiss. "In time you will learn to trust in ShantiMari and our ways. There is no danger."

A drerfox darted across their path, and Taryn's mare pitched to the side. She sat frozen in the saddle, white knuckles buried in Cynda's mane. Her frightened stare went past him, and her breathing sounded in deep, even breaths. When he placed his hand over hers, her rapid pulse strummed beneath his touch.

A memory—hers—pushed into his mind. She was young and Brandt stood next to her, telling her she must learn to ride horses. Taryn resisted. When he placed her in the saddle, the horse spooked, taking off at a full gallop. The memory vanished as quickly as it had come. Once again, Rhoane struggled to keep her thoughts from his.

Since her arrival in the cavern, he'd been deflecting her

thoughts and emotions as much as he could. Whether it was her *cynfar* or their bonds, he knew not, but trying to keep his mind free of hers was a constant struggle.

"I am sorry, *Darennsai*, I did not realize your fear of horses was so deep."

Taryn blinked as if she'd forgotten he was there. "I'm not afraid." She shook her shoulders and straightened in the saddle. "I just don't like being surprised."

Her fingers relaxed beneath his, her pulse calmed. For a moment longer he rested his hand on hers, letting her warmth seep into him, fill him. Before she could pull free, he removed his hand. "If you are ready, we should continue."

They rode a short way before Taryn spoke again. "When I was little, I was thrown from a horse. Brandt made me get right back on, but I never forgot how it felt to hit the ground. I could never understand why he insisted I take lessons. I guess now I know." The youthful honesty in her face included a twist of defiance, as well.

"Do you prefer to ride in carriages?"

Her laugh echoed across the valley. "Not in the sense you're thinking." Bit by bit, she told him of the world she came from and of her life with Brandt. Some of it Rhoane understood; other parts of her story made little sense to him. Images shuffled through his mind of contraptions and buildings that defied his imagination. Emotions swept over him—Taryn's longing for what lay beyond the cavern, her love for Brandt, and her fear of Aelinae. He should shut her out, but he lingered even when he knew it wasn't safe.

Several stories she shared made them both laugh, and in time, her mood lifted. The dark anguish she held on to faded until he could sense no more than a dab of her anxiety.

They stopped for lunch, letting their horses roam while he unpacked a sparse meal and heated up some grhom. Taryn took delicate bites of her food, eating little more than she had the night before, which concerned him. Their ride to Talaith would be difficult, and she would need her strength.

He handed her a cup of grhom, saying, "You and Brandt shared a good life. It is clear that you loved him very much."

"He was all I had."

"It must have been lonely for you."

"At times." She stretched her back and grimaced. "How much longer will we be riding today?"

He wanted to tell her she was home now, among friends who loved her. That she would never be lonely again. Instead, he pointed away from them. "We will follow the river until we reach the glens. We should be there by nightfall. Myrddin and the others will meet us in the morning."

A momentary look of apprehension crossed her features, and it struck him once more how young she was. "Then what?"

"We will just have to see what the day brings, will we not?" His light tone belied the heaviness in his heart from thoughts of the coming days.

The horses grazed near the river while he and Taryn relaxed, both happy to be out of the saddle. Their conversation centered on their surroundings with Taryn asking questions about the names of trees or animals she saw, shaking her head each time.

"It's like a fantastical version of where I'm from. The plants and animals are similar but also different. Like that fox we saw earlier—his fur shimmered and his fangs were much too long."

"A drerfox, more dangerous than his cousin the fox. Those fangs are coated in a poisonous sheen that immobilizes his prey."

She stood on tiptoe, reaching toward the sky. "Everything is clearer, more focused here. I feel as if I could just stretch and tickle the clouds."

Rhoane reclined on his elbows while she inspected the area. It has begun; her sight was sharpening, and soon she would be able to hear what Aelans could not, even her own blood as it pulsed through her body. She was becoming *Darennsai*.

If only Brandt had prepared her for the changes, for what was to come. Lliandra shouldn't have sent her away when she was nothing more than a few moments old. He shook his head to clear the dangerous thoughts. If Taryn had stayed on Aelinae, she'd most likely be dead. Zakael's presence in the cavern confirmed Valterys knew of her existence. How he'd found out and for how long he'd known were the questions that distressed Rhoane.

A flash of fur darted beneath a bush. "See that over there?" He crept near Taryn, pointing to where a winged catlike creature crouched low, her tail whipping behind her. "Watch how she hunts."

Taryn stared in fascination as the animal's haunches twitched just before she leapt forward, snatching a squirrel from the trunk of a tree. Her iridescent wings beat fiercely, lifting her into the air as she flew off with her catch dangling from her mouth.

"She's beautiful. What's she called?"

"A carlix. She is as ancient as these mountains she calls home. Only *darathi vorsi* are older than her kind."

"What's a *darathi vorsi*?"

"The Aelans call them dragons."

A light sparked in Taryn's eyes, her dark brows arched. "You have dragons here?"

The ache of loss seared through him. It was a physical pain that never truly went away. "They disappeared several ages ago. No one knows why, but one day they were simply gone." He lifted his face toward the sky, hoping to see the magnificent beasts flying overhead. "My people had been their caretakers since the beginning of time. It was a period of great mourning for us when they left."

"I'm so sorry, Rhoane." She took his hand in hers, and their runes sparked to life, glowing in the afternoon sun. "Are they going to keep doing that? It's a little annoying."

Her touch eased his pain, making his sadness float away on the wind. "They will quiet down in time."

"You make it sound like they're alive."

"In a way, they are."

"Because they're made of ShantiMari, right?"

"Exactly. The runes will evolve and change as does your path."

Her laugh came out more of a snort followed by another laugh that caused a cascade of even more giggles until tears were streaming down her cheeks. She rolled on the grass, holding her sides, and convulsing with suppressed laughter. "Oh God, I'm so sorry." Taryn wheezed between hiccups.

Rhoane held himself in check, not wanting to laugh at her expense, but amused by her gaiety. A snicker escaped his lips and she smiled up at him.

"Laughter is good medicine. That's what Brandt always said."

"I remember. It was one of his favorite sayings."

She flung her arms out to the side and gazed at the cloudless sky. "I don't have a path. I can't even avenge Brandt's death. At least, not against someone with ShantiMari when I have nothing." Fresh tears slipped beneath her hair.

"You have many things, *Darennsai*, you just do not know them yet."

They packed up their lunch and rode on, their easy banter returning but more subdued. At length, Taryn asked, "That war you told me about, with Rykoto and Daknys, what started it?"

Rhoane rode beside her, surrounded by trees on the

mountainside, the river several paces to their left, but if he so desired, he could close his eyes and be on the battlefield where his ancestors had fought alongside their goddess, Verdaine. It was the way of his people to share a collective memory of every event that occurred.

On that day, with the sun warming his face and Taryn riding beside him, he chose not to relive the horrors of the wars.

"When Nadra, the Great Mother and Ohlin, the Great Father created the planet of Aelinae, they assigned four gods to rule over the land: Kaldaar, Rykoto, Daknys, and Verdaine. We call them the elder gods. Each was beholden to his or her respective territories. Rykoto the Northwest, Verdaine the Northeast, Kaldaar the Southwest, and Daknys the Southeast. For many seasons, they ruled in peace, benefitting from the people who worshipped them. It was a glorious time for Aelinae. All races lived in equal prosperity.

"The elder gods flourished, as well. They created younger gods to rule the emerging minor kingdoms and often mated with their people, strengthening the bond between race and god. These children carried the blood of gods, what we now call ShantiMari."

He glanced at her profile. She was watching him with curious intensity. "Is this a tale you have heard before?"

"Not exactly, but it sounds vaguely familiar. Continue, please."

"Daknys had a daughter with Rykoto, Julieta, who ruled over the Summerlands. Her people adored her, and she never chose favorites. Or lovers. They say she remained unspoiled."

"A virgin goddess?" Taryn grinned. "Interesting."

"Truly, since the gods were well known for their love of pleasures of the flesh. It was this virginal quality that attracted the attention of Kaldaar. He became obsessed with the workings of Light and Dark ShantiMari, but he took his curiosity too far. He is the father of the Black Arts."

"I'm going to go out on a limb here and guess that his followers weren't nice people."

Despite himself, he chuckled. "There will always be men and women, of Light and Dark, who abuse ShantiMari, whose hearts are not pure, but practitioners of the Black Arts have no soul. They are devoid of goodness of any kind. The Blackness consumes them until they are but a shell of their former selves." He suppressed a shudder. It was Kaldaar and his minions who nearly destroyed Rhoane's people in the wars. Black ShantiMari was an insidious, destructive evil that lurked in the shadows of every living spirit, waiting to be coaxed out of hiding.

"So, what did this Kaldaar do to piss everyone off?"

"He manipulated Rykoto, convincing him that Julieta was destined to be his sole concubine. The mother of all future Black Arts practitioners. A high honor to some."

"You mean sex slave. Not such a high honor if you ask me."

"I agree. Part of the problem with the Black Arts is that any woman who practices them becomes barren. Without progeny, the bloodlines would thin and eventually become extinct. Kaldaar found a way around this by taking a virgin sacrifice and suffusing her with the seed of his strongest devotees. With that one offering, she would bear him many offspring until she died."

"That's kind of disgusting." A cloud passed in front of the sun, and she looked over her shoulder as if the shadow trailed them. A moment later, sunlight broke through, and she turned her attention back to Rhoane.

"So, Rykoto gave his daughter to this creep so he could rape her and use her as a brood mare?"

It was a brutal way of saying it, but that was how it happened. "When Kaldaar was finished with Julieta, Rykoto took a turn, believing his seed mixed with Kaldaar's would create a more powerful supplicant. No one is certain why Rykoto wanted to support his brother in his Black Arts, but you can imagine her anger when Daknys heard of the ordeal."

"If that was my daughter, I'd cut off their balls and kill the bastards. You don't fuck with family."

Rhoane blanched. He had no doubt that was exactly what Daknys had wanted to do. "And they would deserve nothing less. Daknys, however, did not kill them. She took her daughter away, hiding her from the two gods for many seasons. When Julieta finally returned, it was without a child. Some say Daknys destroyed the seed within her daughter, others say she allowed the birth of one child and then cleansed Julieta's womb. What we do know is Daknys begged Nadra and Ohlin to intervene. They banished Kaldaar to the edge of nothingness. Exiled from Aelinae, without a world, without his followers, without sanity. As for Rykoto, he fought back. Before he could be exiled, he brought his armies to war."

Taryn whistled a long breath, her braid swishing with each shake of her head. "Your gods are insane, you know this, right?"

"They are not immune to the same capriciousness that drives some men to commit selfish acts."

"Why didn't they exile Rykoto, too? Why did he get to stay?"

"Because when he lost the war, he claimed he had found humility and promised Ohlin he would serve out his sentence, whereby he would become a better god once released. Ohlin showed compassion for his son and agreed to confine Rykoto in the Temple of Ardyn."

Taryn stretched her back, again looking behind them. Rhoane followed her gaze, seeing nothing. A frown pinched her brow, her lips pursed into a tight little bow.

Her emotions roiled over him. Fear of Aelinae remained,

a bit heightened now, but another feeling, one of distrust, or, more specifically, repulsion, settled heavy upon her.

Rhoane remained quiet while Taryn absorbed what he'd told her. It was important to her to make sense of his tale; that much he could decipher from her conflicting emotions.

Giant trees gave way to junipers and bristle cones as they made their way out of the mountains to a flat plain that stretched in every direction. The Narthvier hovered at the farthest edge of the horizon. He turned his horse away from the vier, but the tug of his homeland continued.

Rhoane stopped their travel for the day and while he set up their camp, Taryn took the horses to water at the river. By the time she returned, a fire blazed with a pot of grhom bubbling on a rock. After tethering the horses, he took her to the meadow, where he showed her how to make a rabbit snare.

She watched everything he did. From brushing the horses to stringing a trap, she studied him. The attention thrilled and unsettled him at the same time. They set several traps before setting off to forage in the bushes for root vegetables and berries. He took special care in instructing her which were ripe and which to avoid because they were poisonous.

"I never realized how spoiled I've been," Taryn joked as they gathered several handfuls of cockleberries. "Even on our remotest digs, we had tents with cots and food cooked for us. Do you always find your own dinner?"

"Only when necessary. I imagine there will come a time when you are sleeping on a fine down mattress and eating rich foods covered in thick sauces, you will long for air this pure and berries this sweet." He tossed her a plump, golden-orange cockleberry, and she caught it in her mouth. "A hidden talent, *Darennsai?*"

"It's a game Brandt and I would play."

He relished the sound of her voice. Her silence during

the afternoon had left him unbalanced.

He tossed several more, with her catching each one. "Impressive. Any other talents you would like to share?"

She looked away with a smirk on her lips. "Maybe someday."

After their meal, Rhoane lay on his blankets, hoping for a dreamless night. Taryn paced the edge of camp, pulling his attention to her. She stopped before his protective barrier and glanced back to where he lay. Apprehension crossed her features before she stepped through.

He sat up, watching as she made her way to the river and climbed up the side of the cliff. She never slipped, placing each foot carefully before grabbing hold of the rock above her. A waterfall flowed over the cliff, and Taryn cautiously avoided it and the spray that dampened the rocks around her. There was definitely more to the Aelan girl that he wanted to discover.

When she pushed herself over the top of the plateau, he debated with himself only a moment before following. By the time he reached the cliff top, the sun hung low over the horizon, its last rays stretching across the land. Several stars glistened like pale silhouettes in the still-lit sky.

Taryn reclined on her elbows, her face turned toward the sunset. "I thought all day we were going east, but I must've been turned around. The sun is setting over there."

Rhoane stretched out his long legs and rested beside her. "Yes, in the east, and tomorrow it will rise in the west."

"Where I come from the sun rises in the east and sets in the west. No wonder I feel backward." She glanced to her left. "Is that north?"

"Of course, and there is south." He motioned to his right.

"At least your compass isn't messed up."

The visions he'd had of the world she came from made him shudder with unease. "In a few days you will get acclimated to life on Aelinae."

"I hope so." She looked over the unblemished landscape. "It's so quiet here. Where are all the people?"

"At home, most likely."

Her laughter startled him in the still night. She lay back, looking up at the stars. "I mean, villages and towns. There isn't a single light for miles."

The last of the sun's rays dipped below the horizon, and the sky turned from dusty hues to deep indigo, casting shadows across their bodies as they lay on the warm rock. His runes flared to life, igniting the heat he'd been trying to stifle since she'd arrived in the cavern.

His hand twitched closer to her as he replied. "We are no more than a day's ride from the nearest village. It is not so remote here as you might think."

"Where I come from there are several *billion* people."

"I do not know this word, *billion*. Is that many?"

She squinted up at the night sky. "Yeah, it is. Maybe as many as those stars up there."

The idea of living in such a place, with so many people, sent a chill through him. "It must be terrifying, where you came from."

She shrugged against the ground. "It's what I knew. The quiet here is almost more frightening to me."

A swirl of indecision flashed through her and then disappeared. Whatever she'd been going to say, she changed her mind.

"I don't recognize these constellations."

Sections of the sky in misty nebulae of pinks and purples ranged above them. Rhoane could name every star and its creator.

"Do you think Brandt is up there somewhere?"

Rhoane pointed to their left. "He is just there, below that cluster."

Taryn followed his outstretched arm. "That's pretty specific. How can you be sure?" As if in answer, the star blinked. "Oh." It came out less like a word and more like a catch in her throat. "I miss him," Taryn said to the twinkling star. She held up her hands, making a heart shape with Dal Tara in the center. "We've never been apart. I'm not sure I know how to live without him."

A tear slid down her cheek, and he wiped it away with his thumb. "You have to trust yourself, Taryn. Brandt's death will not be in vain, but you must move forward with your life and remember you are not alone."

"I know."

The conflict he sensed in her stayed him from reaching out to comfort her. She was like a newborn darathi vorsi, timid and frightened, unaware of its grace and beauty or the immense power it would one day wield.

The oaths he took as a boy and the double bonding made his connection to Taryn a near torment. To tell her of her purpose would ease the burden to be sure, but it would frighten her as well. It was a risk he couldn't take. Not until he was certain she understood all that was involved. Not just for Aelinae, but him as well. He swore an oath before his goddess to protect Taryn, and to know only her, but Taryn gave no such promise. If she came to him, it would be of her own desire, not out of obligation. On that he would not yield.

A night creature ghosted above them, and Rhoane stood reluctantly. "We should not be so far from the fire."

They made their way back to camp, and Taryn crawled beneath her covers while Rhoane checked his barrier. Satisfied it would keep out man or beast, he settled into his bedroll.

"Rhoane?" Taryn asked in a sleepy voice. "Are you sure you didn't see anyone following us today?"

Prickles of apprehension plucked at the back of his neck.

"No, I did not. Nor did I sense anyone. What did you see, Taryn?"

"Just shadows, I guess. If you didn't sense anything then it was probably nothing." She snuggled deeper into her covers. "Good night, Rhoane."

"*Derth gayledd,*" he said to her in Eleri.

"What does that mean?"

"May your dreams be light."

"What language is it?"

"The ancient tongue of my people."

"It's beautiful."

"Indeed it is. Good night, *Darennsai.*"

"*Derth gayledd,* Rhoane."

Rhoane stared at the night sky. His dreams would be anything but light. If Taryn sensed something in the shadows, Zakael was the least of their dangers.

Chapter 7

SUNLIGHT filtered through the trees surrounding the campsite. Taryn rolled to her back, looking up through the hazy barrier to an endless blue dome. The previous night she'd found a simple tranquility in sharing the night sky with Rhoane. She'd hoped it would last, but her dreams were filled with Julieta's cries and a Dark god's laughter.

During Rhoane's recounting of the events that led to the Great War, Taryn kept thinking of the void and the seductive pull it had on her. Kaldaar had been sent to the *edge of nothingness*, as Rhoane called it. What if the void was, in fact, the space between worlds? Then the touch she'd felt, the seductive caresses, they'd come from Kaldaar.

If Aelinae had frightened her before, her feelings bordered on terror now. A gentle breeze tickled her face, whispering words that sounded much too much like her grandfather.

"Trust in yourself, dear one. Trust in Aelinae." A soft chuckle, followed by the scent of cigar tobacco and cologne, left her trembling.

She untangled herself from the blankets and shuffled to the fire, where a cup of grhom sat on a rock waiting for her. It and her bedroll were the only items that suggested they'd camped there. The rest of the gear had been packed and removed, leaving the area scrubbed of their very presence, void of anyone else but her. Taryn ignored the tremor of panic that roiled in her gut, sipped her drink, and waited.

Voices drifted to her from beyond where the horses snuffed and pawed the ground. Rhoane's protective barrier caught the light, and she hesitated a moment before stepping through. Even with Rhoane's assurance it would take several more days before Zakael could leave the mountain passages, she was cautious. Without a weapon or the power others in this world had, she was vulnerable. It wasn't a pleasant feeling or one she was accustomed to having.

Taryn stepped around a thicket and saw Rhoane with a small group of people. A renewed flutter of apprehension soured the grhom in her belly. Two men and a woman stood with Rhoane, listening intently while he spoke. His voice was too low for her to hear, but by their faces, Taryn could tell they were upset. The woman openly cried. One of the men, tall, with skin the color of molasses and braids brushing his shoulders, wrapped an arm around her and she sank into him. Taryn looked guiltily away, as if she spied upon something she was not meant to share.

The shorter of the two men caught her attention. Blue ShantiMari flared around him, illuminating his grey hair and clipped white beard. He looked to be about her grandfather's age, with a lifetime of cares worn on his face. Handsome but not overly so, he dressed in clothing similar to the other men but with subtle differences—a shorter tunic, gloves that reached his elbows, and he didn't wear a sword.

He watched her with an inquisitive grin for several minutes before alerting Rhoane to her presence.

Rhoane jogged to her, a smile on his face. "Good. You are awake."

"They don't look happy."

"I have just told them of Brandt's death."

An all too familiar dip in her gut slowed her pace. "Did

they know him?"

"As well as you or I. They are friends who loved Brandt very much. You can trust them."

The woman stepped forward, folding Taryn into an embrace. A delicate floral scent filled her nostrils. "My dear girl, it is good to have you home."

"Thank you," Taryn replied automatically. The woman's silky hair caressed her cheek, and for one curious moment, Taryn could've sworn Brandt's arms wrapped around them both. Dismayed, she pulled away, breaking the connection.

The tall man—taller than Rhoane by at least a hand— bent at the waist, his black braids falling forward and jingling with the sound of bells. "Welcome home."

Then the older man approached and regarded her for a long moment before scratching at his beard. "It's good to have you returned to us, Taryn."

"I hope you'll forgive me, but if we've met before, I don't remember," Taryn said.

The woman laughed, easing the tension in the air. "I would imagine so. You were naught but a babe when you left. I hope you don't mind if we remember you."

She was breathtakingly beautiful, with auburn hair that cascaded in loose curls down her back and framed a face the color of fresh cream. Her eyes, similar in shade and shape to Brandt's, blazed with intelligence. She held her petite frame with poise and moved with a grace that Taryn, with all her gawkiness, admired.

She took Taryn's hand, giving it a squeeze before turning to the men. "Let me introduce you. This fine gentleman you already know. Rhoane, please." He bowed low, his hand over his heart. "And here," her voice softened when she indicated the giant man, "is Sir Baehlon de Monteferron."

His almond-shaped eyes never left her as he inclined his head. Unsure how to respond, Taryn waved awkwardly.

"Hello."

The woman turned to the older man and with an unladylike grunt said, "Here we have Alswyth Myrddin. Scoundrel and knave to be sure, but he's a kind soul, so please have pity on him."

Myrddin gave a curt nod in Taryn's direction. "Aren't you going to tell her who you are?"

"Oh, yes, I almost forgot." The woman curtseyed. "I am Faelara Kaj Endion."

Taryn's pendant hummed against her skin as she appraised the group. "You were all friends of my grandfather?"

Tears shimmered in the woman's eyes, giving them an alluring translucency. "We were much more than friends. Brandt was very dear to us." She folded Taryn into another hug, holding her a moment too long before releasing her. "Now, we should be going."

The abruptness of their parting startled Taryn. When she tried to catch Rhoane's attention, he was already halfway to the horses. The men followed Faelara in the opposite direction, and Taryn hurried after Rhoane.

When they finished loading the horses, she touched his hand. Their runes instantly sparked to life. "What do I do?"

A look of confusion crossed his face. "With what?"

"Them." She jerked her head toward the trees.

"Keep up. They will set a faster pace than yesterday."

"That's not what I meant and you know it." Taryn snapped her reins at him.

"Be yourself and listen." His voice was low as he watched the others, who in turn watched them. "As Fae said, they are friends."

His advice did not go unheeded, but she would do more than listen. If they were friends of Brandt's, they might be willing to help her see that Zakael was punished.

Her backside rebelled when she pulled herself into the

saddle. She was fairly certain she had blisters in places that weren't polite to mention.

"How much longer do you think we'll be riding?" She adjusted her position, finding little relief.

"At least a sennight." Rhoane said before clucking his stallion to join the others.

A week. She groaned and kicked her mare forward. With all of its power, she didn't understand why the people of Aelinae employed primitive resources. The least they could do was invent comfortable saddles.

As they moved through the meadow, her stomach growled, and she put a hand over her abdomen. When Faelara gave her a concerned look, Rhoane held back his stallion to hand her a pouch containing dried bread and cheese, along with meat from their meal the previous night.

Growing discontent settled in Taryn's thoughts. She didn't like depending on Rhoane, or anyone, for food, for shelter, for anything. Fields and grasslands sprawled in every direction, an unfamiliar landscape with unknown horrors. Until she knew her way around Aelinae, she would be exactly that—dependent on him or one of the others for her survival. The depressing thought weighed heavily on her.

Faelara moved beside her, saying in her gentle voice, "Do you see those trees over there?" She pointed in the distance. "That's the southernmost border of the Narthvier. And over there," she indicated to their left, "is the Spine of Ohlin. Those mountains stretch all the way from the Summer Seas to the Temple of Ardyn in the far north."

At the sound of the familiar name, Taryn shot Rhoane a glance. "Is that where we're going, to the temple?"

"No, darling," Faelara looked away from the mountains toward the north, "we're headed to Ravenwood, the country home of Duke Anje. He sent an urgent message, so we're going to offer assistance."

"Is that what you do? Wander around helping people?"

"It does seem that we travel much more than I'd like. The world is a curious place lately, and we go where we're needed. Today, that just happens to be a day's ride north." Faelara reached over to pat Taryn's leg. "This will give you a chance to see some of the countryside. When we get to Ravenwood, you'll meet Hayden, Duke Anje's son and heir. Very pleasant boy and your age."

"Which age is that?" Taryn mumbled, distracted by the shadow that had tormented her for most of the previous day. She'd hoped it was a fluke, but its presence once again set her on edge. Each time she tried to look for it, the shadow would dissipate, but if she kept her focus straight ahead, she was able to keep the blot in her peripheral vision. Whoever or whatever it was, it was keeping pace with them but at a discreet distance.

Faelara gave her a strange look. "The only one you are."

"Which is thirty-five in a few weeks?"

"Yes, that's right. You and Hayden were born two days apart."

Taryn studied her riding companion. Faelara wore a deep green riding jacket with matching hat and split skirt that allowed her to sit astride her horse. Taryn admired how graceful she looked upon her mare and shuddered at how she must appear to the regal woman. Dirt smeared, disheveled, disoriented. Never before had she given a thought to how she looked to others, but being near the elegant woman made her self-conscious. Grimacing at the state of her hands, she picked at a cuticle, tearing the skin.

Faelara took her hand in her own. "Let's see if we can't get you more familiar with your surroundings. Make you feel more at home."

The tone of her voice, and slight upturn to her lips, suggested she knew where Taryn had been all those years, but she dared not confirm her suspicions. Rhoane had warned her to keep her past hidden and that's what she would do.

She listened with quiet intensity as Faelara explained the topography of the land they traveled. They rode through meadows of thick grasses and past fields gone fallow, the pace faster than the day before as Rhoane had promised. Every so often Rhoane would range ahead to scan the area or Baehlon would hang back to ride behind them, but neither seemed to see the shadow. After a while, she stopped looking for the flicker at the edge of her vision.

With every rut or mud-filled road they crossed, more knots formed in her shoulders and backside. Her knees were numb from gripping Cynda, and she was certain she'd forever lost all feeling in her hands from clutching the reins too tightly. They stopped briefly for a midday meal and to rest the horses but were back in the saddle much too soon. Myrddin pushed them faster as the afternoon wore on. When dark tendrils stretched across the road and the sun's rays slanted beyond the trees through dusk, Baehlon turned them down a treelined drive. Too weary to see straight, Taryn barely registered their location until Faelara touched her shoulder.

"Ravenwood," she whispered.

Taryn jerked in her saddle and straightened her posture, her exhaustion a nagging memory. Ravenwood meant a bed. Possibly a shower. Definitely a break from the pounding of riding.

She followed Fae's outstretched hand and whistled low in her throat. "That's a bloody castle."

"Manor house."

"Whatever." Taryn took in the turreted corners and delicate battlements. Though built for show, it still managed to appear imposing perched upon a hill. The group made their way up the gravel road, past landscaped borders and decorative hedges.

Too busy admiring the scenery, Taryn didn't notice Myrddin had slowed, his hand outstretched in a silent signal to the others, until she was even with his horse. He placed a finger to his lips, his glare boring into her.

Rhoane and Baehlon drew their swords.

Nervous energy rippled over her in waves, making her palms moist, her throat dry.

Instinctively, Taryn moved closer to Faelara. Gravel crunched with each hoof their horses placed on the ground. Myrddin reined in his gelding, and the others followed, quietly dismounting. Within several yards of the manor, Taryn paused in her step.

The front door stood wide open, without a soul in sight.

Taryn tapped Faelara's arm, but the woman shook her head and motioned to the manor. Streaks of ShantiMari circled everyone except Baehlon and Taryn, which did not instill her with confidence.

Myrddin felt around the doorway and then stepped into the house. The men moved from room to room looking for signs of life or a struggle, finding neither. With each new room, Taryn's heart thumped harder, threatening to burst from her chest.

They moved up the stairs to the first landing, and Myrddin motioned for her to stay with Faelara while the men crept up and down the hallways, checking each room. Halfway up the next flight of stairs, Taryn's pendant burned against her skin. She stifled a gasp, causing Rhoane to look back. When she pointed to her *cynfar*, his eyes narrowed for a moment, and then he continued up the stairs, saying nothing. They stopped on the upper landing, where, again, the men crept down the hall.

Taryn moved away from Faelara to follow Rhoane. When he stepped from an empty room and nearly collided with her, he frowned, but she put a finger to her lips, motioning for him to follow.

At the last door, Taryn stopped. "In here."

Rhoane flinched when he touched the wood. He waited until the others joined them before slowly opening the door. Taryn was last to enter the dimly lit bedchamber. Furniture crowded the large room, and in the center rested a huge four-poster bed with heavy curtains tied to the posts. Beside the bed, a man sat hunched, the sound of his soft cries filling the space. Faelara and Myrddin went to him while Baehlon and Rhoane continued to check the perimeter. A fetid odor like the scent of pork left out overlong assaulted her senses.

Help me, a voice whispered.

Taryn spun around to see who had spoken, but no one was near. She stepped around a chair and covered her mouth to keep from crying out at the ghastly sight before her. Atop the bed, uncovered but clothed, lay a young man. A glowing sword hung suspended above his heart.

The stench increased the closer she moved to the bed. It infiltrated her nostrils, her throat, her mind until she felt as if maggots crawled through her thoughts. Bile burned from her belly to her tongue. She gagged, dizzy all of a sudden.

No time. Please, the voice begged.

"Who are you?" she whispered aloud to the empty air.

Bed. Help. Now. Desperation choked the voice.

Lavender strands of ShantiMari enclosed the man's body, with the thinnest of threads holding the sword aloft. Even as she watched, the sword moved a fraction closer to piercing his shirt. "Oh my God."

Hurry.

His anguish permeated her mind to her very core. She swallowed down the bile and took a deep, calming breath. "What do you want from me?"

Sword, the voice rasped. There was no pain in his tone,

just a sense of panic and fear.

She had to do something before the sword broke free. Rhoane prowled the opposite side of the room, his focus away from her.

"Hang on." Before she could change her mind, she sprinted toward the bed. When she'd nearly reached it, she jumped as high as she could, kicking out. A cacophony roared through her mind when her foot connected with the metal. Shards of ShantiMari tangled around her leg, and a burning sensation shot up from her heel. Rhoane stepped out of the way a split second before she crashed to the floor, the sword landing with a heavy clang beside her.

Time slowed as the ringing continued. Vomit roiled in her gut. Images, flashes of light and dark, tore at her thoughts. Shouts and cries echoed in her mind. Julieta's screams. Kaldaar's banishment. Rykoto's laughter as he raped Julieta.

Rhoane was speaking to her, helping her up. She stared at his face, focused on that one reality. A gasp from the bed pulled her attention back to the young man and the threads of ShantiMari tightening around him. He couldn't breathe. She moved without thought and grabbed the sword that lay at her feet.

When she touched the handle, a shock ran up her arm. Not like the one in her leg, which felt as though it were on fire, but a soothing feeling, as if the handle welcomed her touch. The voices stopped. Her mind cleared. Her stomach calmed. Gripping the hilt with both hands, she raised the sword and brought it down over the man, slicing the lavender cords.

"Taryn, no!" Faelara cried out. Amber streaks of Mari shot toward her, but they were blocked by Rhoane's Shanti.

"Hold, Faelara." Rhoane's voice was like iron. "She will not harm him."

Taryn ignored the strange tingling of her skin as she cut

the threads. When they were too small for the sword, she tossed it aside and broke apart the remaining bits with her fingers, digging through them until the man inhaled and his chest heaved with the rush of air.

The stink of death lingered. "Open the windows," Taryn commanded. Baehlon moved with silent swiftness, opening first one and then all of the windows, letting in the last of the sun's rays and fresh, pure air.

After a few minutes of coughing and sputtering, the man took several deep breaths. Taryn stepped back, allowing Faelara to fuss over him. Myrddin's scowl was her last sight before everything went black.

Chapter 8

MEN argued in the hall. A man, not Zakael but of similar height with the same black hair and grey eyes, wanted the sword. Needed it. Taryn watched from above, as if she floated among them. Rhoane and Myrddin restrained the man with their ShantiMari while Baehlon pointed his sword at the man's chest.

Valterys, they called him. He was arrogant enough to think he could defeat the three of them. Taryn drifted closer.

Valterys looked to where she was and was not. He saw nothing and so looked through her. Pulling shadows over himself, he raced down the stairs.

Myrddin swore at the suddenly empty air. "I wish I knew how he did that." He spat at the ground where Valterys had stood.

Taryn found it curious Myrddin didn't know such a simple trick.

Searing pain bit at her leg, bringing her back to her body. Gritting her teeth, she fought against the onslaught of fire that raced through her veins.

"Lady Faelara," a voice whispered above her. "She wakes."

Faelara's cool hand felt good against her skin. "She's burning with fever."

Rhoane came into focus.

"My leg hurts," Taryn groaned.

"Hayden, help with her boots," Faelara told the young man from the bed. They tugged at the laces, pulling the boots off in seconds. Faelara gasped, and Taryn struggled to sit up.

"Stay still," Rhoane commanded.

Faelara ran a finger along Taryn's leather pants, tearing them all the way up to her thigh. "Poison. There must've been a spell woven around the sword."

Another shot of fire tore through her. "Get the sword," Taryn breathed. "It wants to help."

Rhoane and Faelara exchanged a look before she motioned to Hayden. He darted from the room.

"Why does he want the sword? The man in the hall?" Taryn stuttered through gritted teeth.

"Don't you worry yourself with that," Faelara said with another glance at Rhoane.

Taryn arched against the burning that engulfed her leg, biting back a whimper. Hayden returned a minute later with the weapon wrapped in a heavy blanket. Very carefully, he set it on the bed and then stepped back as if it were a viper set to strike.

Taryn's fingers itched as if she'd been pruning poison ivy. They reflexively twitched toward the blade, curling her fingers around the pommel and pulling it out of the blanket.

"Are you certain, *Darennsai*?" Rhoane asked. "We do not know that the poison is gone."

Hazy fever thoughts crowded her mind. Images of the Great War. A woman with skin like warm chocolate and hair the color of deepest night. The sword sang a song of forgiveness. For her. With a shock, Taryn realized the other melody she'd heard since the cavern came from the sword. All those years, every song her pendant sang to her, had come from the sword.

The woman smiled and then drifted off through the

clouds. *Learn the words*, she whispered. An inscription, written in the same ancient text as on the Seal of Ardyn, ran down the center of the blade. Taryn traced the words with her fingertips. They rose and fell beneath her touch. Slowly, she set the sword beside her leg until it rested against her skin. When nothing happened, the others let out a collective sigh of relief.

"Use the sword to get rid of the poison." Taryn explained, "I'll be fine. Trust me."

Faelara's eyes narrowed, then she said to the group. "Hayden, you and his grace will keep Taryn steady."

Taryn glanced to where an older gentleman had entered the room. She hadn't seen his face in Hayden's room, but his red-rimmed eyes marked him as the man who was sitting beside the bed. He shuffled to stand beside Hayden, nodding to Faelara.

Rhoane pressed his hands against Taryn's thigh. "Keep your thoughts focused on healing your leg. This might sting a little."

Taryn swallowed her apprehension and closed her eyes. "Do it."

At first, she felt only the sword and their hands on her. Then heat ripped up her leg. Her thoughts scattered. She reined them in by focusing on her kata, specific karate moves that required leg strength. Sweat ran down her face, pooling in her hair as bolts of agony tore through ligaments and sinew, muscle and bone. Rhoane's and Faelara's ShantiMari pulsed through her, heightened by the sword's power to work out the poison. Again and again, they gripped her leg, sending their ShantiMari into her.

Their worry and frustration lingered in her thoughts. The sword sang to her in dulcet tones of healing. Beside her, the duke whispered, and his Shanti pricked her skin. The poison especially disliked his power. Taryn invited his ShantiMari into her, coaxing the sword to accept his healing. She didn't know why or how, but it was necessary to cleanse her blood.

The sword pulsed with a blinding light that shot around the room in a whirlwind, and their healing webbed through her to find every last drop of poison. She arched against the pull of energy and then sank onto the bed, drained. As quickly as it came, the light vanished.

Faelara stumbled from the bed, her brow drenched, her pale face nearly translucent. The duke offered her and Rhoane each a chair and then stood between them, hovering like a concerned mother. Rhoane, too, looked exhausted. His hands shook a little when he took the glass of water the duke offered.

The young man from the bed, Hayden, wiped her brow with a cool cloth. Her throat scratched when she tried to speak, and Hayden dabbed water on her dry lips with the utmost care. He was handsome, the duke's son. Sandy-blond hair and hazel eyes. Full lips that looked as if they smiled more often than frowned.

"Thank you," she croaked.

Baehlon and Myrddin entered the room, their features mirror images of displeasure. Faelara asked, "Did you find any signs of Valterys?"

"None. The bastard just disappeared." Baehlon snarled.

"We'll keep vigilant, just in case." Faelara stood, shaking out her skirt. "I suppose I should see what's left in your pantry. Paderau can wait a day if necessary."

Rhoane put a hand on her arm. "Are you recovered?"

"Well enough, thank you. I'll send up a sleeping draught for Taryn. I think we should let her rest." She checked Taryn's forehead before kissing it lightly. "Sleep, my darling."

She left the room, and the others followed. Except Rhoane. He pulled his chair closer to the bed, leaning back as if he might sleep, as well. Taryn moved the sword aside before snuggling under the heavy blanket, facing him. He was snoring lightly by the time Hayden returned with Faelara's potion, and Taryn motioned for him not to disturb the man. She drank the foul-tasting liquid with a grimace. Instead of leaving, Hayden sat in the chair Faelara had vacated, watching her until her eyelids grew too heavy and she slept.

WHEN she woke, the sky held the last vestiges of night, with a few stars stubbornly clinging to the pale dawn sky. She stared at the ceiling, willing night to hasten as she tracked the shadows that made a slow progression toward the light. Brandt would know what she was supposed to do. He would make sense of everything that had happened. Her heart pinched with the reminder he was gone. A lone tear slid silently down her cheek to rest in the cradle of her neck.

"Are you in pain?" A voice cut through the darkness.

Fear, raw and primal, paralyzed her body and her tongue. The man had returned for the sword. Possibly to kill her.

"Taryn." A softness entered the rich baritone and she recognized Baehlon's voice. She forced herself to look in his direction, chastising her wild imagination. He stood over her, a hand resting on her shoulder, warm and comforting.

Slowly, her heart rate evened and she found words. "You scared the crap out of me." The tightness in her voice matched her nerves. "What are you doing here?"

"Watching over you."

"I don't need a babysitter."

Even in the dim light, she could see the slight wince, the narrowing of his eyes. "Of course you don't. I, however, wanted to make certain there was no threat of another spell or more poison causing you harm."

"I'm sorry, you startled me."

"No apology necessary. You've had an exciting few days. I would be jumpy as well."

Shadows slithered across the ceiling, and Taryn subconsciously moved for the sword.

"It is there, just beyond your reach. You should get used to having it close at hand. When you're feeling up to it, I'll teach you how to properly handle the weapon."

She itched to touch the hilt, to feel its weight in her hand, its power coursing through her. A little too much. "I think I'd like that." It was a step closer to avenging Brandt's death. "Who was that man and why does he want the sword?"

Baehlon stiffened, but then said in an even tone, "Valterys, The Overlord of the West, and if I knew the answer to why he wants the sword or what it was doing hanging over young Hayden's chest, I wouldn't be sitting here watching you sleep."

"I don't have the answers, either." She scooted to a sitting position, wincing at the slice of discomfort that shot from heel to thigh.

"Is it bad?" Baehlon's large hands hovered above her leg. "May I?"

She nodded and pushed the blankets off her body. He gently prodded the mottled skin around her heel. "You'll be sore for a few days, nothing more." His glance flicked to the weapon. A slight tightening of his full lips and a twitch to the corner of his mouth marked his reticence.

"You don't like the sword, do you?"

"It's a mystery to me, and that makes me nervous. I make it my business to understand weapons, but this, I just don't know."

The metal called to her still. A song of yearning playing constantly in her mind. She had to forcibly shut it out.

"I've never met a knight before."

"What makes you think I'm a knight?" The velvety softness of his tone held a hint of humor.

"Besides Rhoane, you're the only one with a sword, and Faelara called you, 'Sir.'"

"Just because you can't see their weapons, don't think they are unarmed."

"You mean they have special powers, right?"

"ShantiMari? Yes, they have that, but never assume that kind of power will protect you. There's something to be said for a nice bit of steel." He glanced warily at the blade, distrust dancing at the edges of his irises. "Faelara has at least six daggers hidden in her skirts, and Myrddin never travels without two throwing knives up his sleeves."

"I'll remember not to piss them off."

"If that means not vex them, then that might be for the best."

"It does," she said with a weak laugh. "You're pretty cool for a knight."

His mouth quirked in question.

"Where I come from that's a compliment."

"Ah. Then you're pretty cool for an Aelan."

She played with the lace edge of the sheet. "You're not Aelan?"

"Of course not. My mother was Geigan and my father Danuri."

"Ah, right," she pretended to understand.

His chuckle was like a chimney billowing puffs of laughter. "In a few moonturns this will become second nature to you. Can you walk?"

She swung her feet over the side of the bed and stood, placing most of her weight on her good foot. "I think so."

"We should break our fast. Faelara would like to leave for Paderau today."

Taryn stepped around him, swallowing down the ache that swelled up her leg to twist in her gut.

"Taryn." Baehlon stopped her with the single word.

"What possessed you in there?" He cocked his head toward Hayden's room.

"He asked for help."

"Who? Rhoane?"

"No, the guy. Hayden."

"Ohlin's teeth. Did it occur to you that you might get hurt?"

"Yes, but he was going to die."

Baehlon stared hard at the sword before turning back to her. "The next time you're feeling heroic, alert us first, okay?"

"Sure thing. Not a problem." It wasn't likely she'd find another young man with a sword hanging over him, after all.

Baehlon moved in step beside her and placed his fingertips at the bend of her elbow. That slight touch, barely felt through her blouse, held immense strength, and a silent promise that he'd never, ever let anything happen to her.

Chapter 9

RHOANE stood with his back to the room and watched the couple as they strolled along the formal gardens below. Through the open window, he caught phrases of their conversation. Each time he heard Taryn's rich laugh, he flinched. Dressed in the late duchess's clothing, she looked like her aunt's twin. If Hayden saw the similarities, he didn't show it, but then, Rhoane didn't think the young lad saw much beyond Taryn's golden beauty.

"Ready?" Baehlon's deep voice startled Rhoane.

His friend stood in the doorway with a crossbow dangling from one hand, Rhoane's longbow held out for him in the other. "You convinced Faelara to leave tomorrow, then?"

"Taryn could use a day to recover. Plus, it gives us time to refresh our stores."

Baehlon held something back, but Rhoane didn't press. Whatever Faelara's reasons for delaying their journey, he was thankful Taryn had one more day before the inevitable. For today, she was just a girl strolling the gardens with a boy. In a few weeks' time she would be a princess with the future of Aelinae resting on her royal shoulders. Rhoane took one last look at the garden before turning from the window and taking his bow from Baehlon.

They passed Hayden's room on the way to the back stairs,

and Rhoane had to suppress his gag reflex. Baehlon didn't flinch at the stench of stale poison and vile ShantiMari, but to Rhoane's acute olfactory senses, it was overwhelming.

"Seems a bit odd Valterys would poison the sword, don't you think?" Baehlon asked, taking two stairs at a time.

"He is desperate. I have found those are the most dangerous types to encounter."

"Something's not right here, but I can't figure out what." Baehlon shook his head, his braids flailing in every direction, a chorus of bells tinkling. "Why now? Why Hayden? If he wanted the sword, he only needed to find someone of the Blood to take it."

"Not just of the Blood. The stipulations are not clear, but the sword would only accept a bearer it felt worthy," Rhoane reminded him.

"She really doesn't know, does she?"

They reached the kitchen door, and Baehlon held it open for Rhoane, piercing him with a look that begged to be defied. Rhoane stepped through to the outer courtyard, shaking his head.

"When Faelara told me Taryn had no idea of her identity, I thought she was jesting."

"What changed your mind?" Rhoane asked, unconsciously scanning the gardens for Taryn.

"The sword. The girl would have to be mad to attack that thing like she did. When she held it…" Baehlon exhaled slowly. "Rykoto's balls, I'll never forget that sight. She fairly glowed with power."

"She will be needing you to instruct her how to use it."

"Aye, that she will. And happy to do it, I'll be, but I don't suppose her learning will stop at swordplay."

Rhoane gave a curt nod in agreement and led them toward a thick forest north of the house, away from the gardens. "That is where it will begin. Myrddin wants me and

Faelara to show her how to wield ShantiMari once we are in Talaith."

Baehlon boomed a spurt of laughter. "I think I got the easier of the tasks. Has she told you anything of where she's been all these years?"

"Not much, but I have had glimpses, and I do not mind telling you, the place looks terrifying."

"You've eavesdropped on her thoughts?"

"Not exactly." Rhoane held up his hand, and the runes shone bright in the morning sun. After a few moments they faded back into his skin. "I try to block the images, but they come too fast. She has no idea."

Baehlon nudged his friend in good-hearted ribbing. "About the eavesdropping or what those fancy pictures on your hands mean?"

Rhoane blanched at the forthright question. "Either."

"I hope I'm not around when she finds out. That girl's fearless and reckless. You better watch yourself."

"Yes, I know. Thank you for your support."

Taryn's laughter drifted on the breeze to where he and Baehlon stood. Hayden and Taryn were a perfect couple. Both tall with shining hair. Hers long and hanging loose down her back, his shoulder length in the latest fashion. Rhoane tried to stop the nagging thought, but it entered his mind like a worm all the same. Taryn was young and beautiful—she could love anyone she pleased—and she wasn't bound by an oath. Wasn't bound by a promise not only to her goddess but to her very soul. If she desired, she could choose Hayden to be her life mate.

A spike of jealousy pinched his heart, and he turned toward the trees.

"She watches you when she thinks you aren't looking," Baehlon said in a somber tone, his eyes serious and full of concern.

"Yes, I know. She suspects I am withholding information from her."

"You are, and it isn't just who she is. You could tell her how you feel about her."

Rhoane sighed and motioned to the garden. "She has enough to cope with at the moment. What she needs now is friendship and people she can trust. Anything more will come with time."

Baehlon clapped him on the back. "I don't know if I'd wait too long, my friend. Young Hayden doesn't seem to think the same as you. When we get to Paderau, it will only get worse. All those lords with nothing to do but find a wife. Once they learn who she is, she'll be more sought after than a Danuri hildgelt."

Baehlon had managed to uncover Rhoane's deepest fear. "If the gods will it, then I have nothing to worry about. I will not have her come to me out of obligation."

"Suit yourself. I'm just saying a word or two of encouragement might not be a bad thing. Ignoring someone generally doesn't foster romantic feelings."

Damn the man and his honesty. It was true; he had been avoiding Taryn. His feelings for her were too raw, and he needed space and the normalcy of his friendships with the others. When he was around Taryn all he could think about was the soft curve of her neck or the way her hips moved when she walked. The sound of her voice sent sparks through him like volcano flares. When he first saw her in the cavern, all doubt of whether he could fulfill his part in the prophecy vanished. His heart was hers before she ever spoke a word to him.

"It is complicated, as you know."

"Look, man," Baehlon said, turning to face him. "I'm the last person you should take romantic advice from, the gods only know, but you and Taryn are the future of this world.

Whether you want to accept that or not, it's true. She needs you. More than you'll ever understand."

"To instruct her, I know."

"I've read Verdaine's prophecy. I know damn well it's more than instructing her."

Rhoane let his thoughts brush against Taryn's for the merest moment. The desire to eavesdrop was too great. He cut the connection and blocked her from his mind, leaving a shallow opening for her protection.

"We should see about catching our dinner," Rhoane said, trying to change the subject. But Baehlon put out a hand to stop him.

"You're my friend, Rhoane. You know I support you in everything, but if Valterys infects her mind with his Black teachings—"

"I know my duty," Rhoane interrupted. No one knew the prophecy as well as he did. "If it comes to that, I will kill her."

Chapter 10

NEVER in her life had Taryn longed for modern conveniences as much as she did that night at dinner. After spending much of the day wandering the gardens with Hayden while he talked nonstop about people she didn't know and places she'd never been, all she wanted was a tumbler of whisky, a hot shower, and some painkillers. Her heel throbbed with a devious constancy that distracted her just enough to be bothersome. She had to be careful how she placed her foot to avoid the point of impact or a slice of fire would ravage her leg.

"You're not eating," Duke Anje whispered. "Faelara will not be pleased." A smile crinkled the edges of his dark eyes, giving him a softness she liked.

Taryn forced several forkfuls of the delicious meal down before pushing a root vegetable around on her plate. The others weren't interested in what she ate, at least not at the moment. They were too concerned with other things she should or should not be doing. Things like learning to dance and using the sword. Or not wearing the torn leather pants Rhoane had given her; instead, she'd wear some of the late duchess's clothing. Above all, she must appear proper.

Taryn stabbed a ruddy looking vegetable. "Wear this, say that, blah, blah, blah. I'll wear what I damn well like, thank you very much. And live where I choose, not in some bloody palace."

Of them all, only Duke Anje heard her. "Don't let them upset you. Once in Paderau, we'll get you fitted for clothes that are your style. As for lodgings, I hope you'll stay in the palace as my honored guest."

She couldn't refuse his kindness. "Of course I will. I didn't mean to sound ungrateful."

"Not at all." He motioned to the others who continued speaking as if she and the duke weren't in the room. "They have your best interests in mind, do not doubt that."

Beneath their words existed an undercurrent of another, secret conversation, one she was not privy to. The looks they gave one another did not match the spoken discussion, and the death grip Rhoane had on his fork gave away the ruse. Despite Duke Anje's fatherly scowl, Taryn pushed away from the table. Rhoane glanced up, but she avoided his look as easily as he'd avoided her the entire day. The slice of misery had nothing to do with her foot as she walked with forced steadiness into the library.

Once certain she was alone, she slouched into a chair, rubbing her heel absently as she took in all the books amassed on the shelves. It would take her two lifetimes just to read them all.

"If your foot is bothering you that much, you should have Faelara make you a concoction for the pain," the duke said from behind her.

Caught, Taryn turned to face him and smiled her best can-we-keep-this-between-the-two-of-us smiles. "And here I thought you liked me."

His chortle made his belly jump, which in turn made Taryn giggle. "They're dreadful, aren't they? Let's see if I can't ease your burden a bit." He sat in the chair opposite and took Taryn's foot in his hands. After several minutes of his massaging, a sharp prick burned her heel. Instinctively, she flinched, but he kept a hold of her.

"This is odd," he mused. "There doesn't seem to be any more poison, but I can feel something…just here." He gently pressed with his thumb. "Hold onto the chair, this might sting."

Before she could protest, the duke ground his finger into her flesh, mumbling indecipherable words with a set cadence to his speech. Hot turned to cold that blurred into pins and needles before finally settling into a comforting warmth. A smattering of sweat on his forehead caught the candlelight, deepening the frown that cut between his dark brows.

"What was it?" Taryn asked, her voice unsteady.

"I don't know, and that concerns me." Remembering himself, he said to Taryn, "Nothing for you to worry about, though. I believe I got the last of it. Here," he placed her foot on the floor and stood with his hands held out to her, "let's give it a test."

Taryn took his hands in hers and rose slowly, still placing most of her weight on her good foot. Gradually, she eased more weight to her right until she stood balanced on the two. No ragged shots of pain raced up her leg, no throbbing from her heel—only a slight tenderness remained.

"Oh, your grace, thank you." Impulsively, she leaned forward and kissed his cheek.

"Please, call me Anje." His eyes clouded as he gazed at her. Again, she sensed there was something more happening, something she wasn't invited to share. A breeze swept through the room, rustling the pages of a nearby book, and Anje cleared his throat.

"You don't happen to have any *whisky*, do you?" Taryn asked, hopeful for at least one comfort from home. "It's a drink, strong, burns your throat in the most delightful way."

"I think I have just what you need." He moved to a

sideboard and poured a dark liquid into two glasses. "To you, my brave and beautiful friend." He handed her a glass and smiled at the *clink* the crystal made when they touched.

"To you," Taryn raised her glass, "my healer."

The drink slid down her throat with a satisfying burn. It wasn't her favorite scotch, but it would do.

"Well?" Anje asked when she finished her glass.

"Just what I needed."

"Would you like another?"

She did, but she politely declined. "I can barely ride a horse as it is. Being hungover won't help." She thanked her host before heading upstairs.

The faint scent of roses lingered in her room, and she stood for a long time at her open window, gazing out at the lovely garden and hills beyond. If she'd had a choice, she would've asked that they stay there, at Ravenwood. From what Hayden had shared, life would be quite different in Paderau, and Taryn had had enough change already.

When she closed her eyes to sleep, a dark face with a blood-soaked smile and hair the color of a raven's wing teased the outer edges of her dreams. The night passed in a fitful attempt at rest.

WHEN Faelara came to wake her, dawn was just breaking over the mountains. Exhausted, crabby, and out of sorts, Taryn met the others in the stables where the duke presented her with a gorgeous white mare named Ashanni. Gentler than the frisky Cynda, Anje assured her the ride would be much smoother.

His generosity touched her. "Thank you, but you didn't have to. Cynda was fine."

"Perhaps now you will have a second glass of dreem

with me." He gave her a wink then led his gelding out of the stables.

Hayden stood nearby, a question in his eyes.

"What?" Taryn demanded.

"You drink dreem?"

"Yes, I drink dreem. Is there something wrong with that?"

A wide smile broke over his face. "Not at all. You are certainly a curious one, my new friend." He left the stable shaking his head.

As Rhoane passed, Taryn asked quietly, "What's the deal with dreem?"

"Not many ladies like such a strong liquor."

"Good thing I'm not a lady then."

Rhoane stifled a laugh as he led his horse to the courtyard. Taryn stared after him, completely perplexed.

"We'd like to leave sometime today, if you don't mind." Myrddin's chiding spurred her to clamber into the saddle and join the others as they rode away from Ravenwood.

The horse's hooves squelched with each step on the road made muddy from storms that had raged throughout the night. Mist hung about Taryn's ears, tickling them. Drops of chilled water ran down her skin, soaking through layers of clothing. She pulled her cloak tightly against her, but the moisture found a way in despite her best efforts.

The group rode quietly; when they spoke, it was in hushed tones, as if the trees themselves might give them away. Her night of fitful sleep dragged at her, but she fought to stay upright and alert. Myrddin once more led the group, staying away from the major roads and skirting any villages or homesteads they came upon. His flimsy explanation for the clandestine route—that the duke rode without an escort—only heightened her suspicion something was not right. The same something they refused to discuss with her. A nattering at the back of her mind told her to be wary.

Tension from the previous two days touched them still. The burden of their fear lay wrapped in a blanket tied to her saddle where the sword sang a gentle melody about the days of Aelinae before the Great War. Taryn's hand twitched, and she had to keep herself from taking the weapon from its coverings.

Truth was she liked the feel of it in her hand. The leather grip, secured with decorative silver work and studded with gems the color of a tranquil sea, warmed and molded to her touch. Exquisite dragons flanked the pommel with wings flared, talons gripping a large ruby. Crushed jewels of every color created the illusion of scales and diamonds glittered in their eyes. The imposing piece thrilled her each time she held it. More than that, it infused her with a sense of belonging. Of purpose.

"These trees were planted by my great-great-grandfather on the eve of his wedding to his bride. Their marriage lasted two hundred seventy-nine seasons." Hayden's words interrupted her thoughts. "This part of the road is referred to as the 'Lovers' Tunnel.' See how the branches join above us?"

A line of trees stretched far into the distance, their verdant cover stretching from one side of the road to the other, twining in the middle. Sunlight peeked through, dappling the ground and warming her chilled skin. Too consumed with thoughts of the sword, she'd not noticed the tunnel of trees or the valley dotted with daffodils beyond the sturdy trunks. Sparrows sang sweet songs to them as they passed.

"It's lovely. They must've loved each other very much."

"Theirs was a love match from the first moment they met." His eyes caught the light and glowed as brilliantly as the backlit leaves. "Would you like to hear the story?"

Her brief nod was all Hayden needed to launch into the tale. When he finished with his great-great-grandparents' courtship, he segued into Duke Anje and Duchess Gwyneira's romantic endeavors. The song of the sword kept distracting Taryn, but when Hayden mentioned his mother was the empress's sister and his father was the cousin of Valterys, her attention snapped fully back to him. Anje had the same dark hair and grey eyes as Valterys, but not the height or the hard edges. In fact, Anje's gentle manner reminded her of Brandt.

Hayden, the only living child of the duke, had inherited his looks from his mother. From the paintings Taryn saw at Ravenwood, Gwyneira was a beautiful woman with flowing golden hair, the same as her son, but with dazzling blue eyes. Anje's firstborn was killed in an accident three seasons past, and six moonturns after that, his newborn daughter died in her mother's arms only moments after birth and Gwyneira of a fever a few hours—or bells, as they called them—later. Luck did not favor the duke where his family was concerned, a fact he attributed to his severed relationship with Valterys's family.

Hayden skirted the issue, but Taryn heard the pain in his voice as he spoke. Anje put a reassuring hand on Hayden's shoulder, giving a slight squeeze.

"So, you're related to the empress and the, um, king?" Taryn asked.

"Overlord. There's never been a king in the west, only an overlord," Anje said.

"It's Rykoto's way of repressing us mortals," Hayden joked, but there was a bite to his words.

Myrddin led them off the road to a clearing. "We'll sup here then continue our travels. Don't dawdle, I'd like to be in Midvale before sunset."

"There's so much to remember," Taryn mumbled as she slid from the saddle. Names, places, customs—it overwhelmed her.

"There will be plenty of time for you to absorb it all, my dear," the duke promised. "Don't concern yourself with memorizing everything in one day."

She stroked Ashanni's muzzle, choosing her words with care. She didn't know how much Anje knew, how much anyone knew for that matter, about where she'd been her whole life. "It's very different where I was raised."

Anje took her hand, patting it the way Brandt used to. "I imagine it is, but you're not alone, Taryn. We're here to help."

They kept saying that. *We're here to help.* But she wasn't sure exactly what they meant. There was an unspoken sense of expectation, as if she was supposed to be doing something but somehow had missed the memo.

Their meal consisted of dark bread, cheese, and meat, with cockleberries and a banana-like fruit that Faelara called a skirm. Simple fare, but delicious. Taryn ate enough even the duke approved, and she lay back to relax before she had to get in the saddle again. But Hayden had other plans, declaring it time to begin her dance lessons. Taryn groaned and took his offered hand.

The first dance Hayden taught her was simple enough, but when they moved on to the delante, her feet lost all coordination, finding each other more than the ground. Every so often, her heel would rebel with a sting of pain, but for the most part, whatever Anje had done the previous night had helped. To Anje, she would be eternally grateful. His son, not necessarily.

With forced patience, Hayden instructed her on the steps of his chosen dance. When she had the basics down, he showed her three others, each of which had Taryn swearing off dancing forever.

"This is bloody ridiculous," she complained after yet again tangling her feet and ending in a heap on the grass. "I'm not a freaking princess, and I don't need to dance!"

"Ohlin's blood, Taryn. It's not that difficult."

"Hayden." Anje warned, his voice low.

His son took a deep breath and dropped the aggressive tone. "You don't have to be a princess to enjoy a turn around the ballroom. It's a civilized way of interacting with one another. Besides," he reached down to help her up, "many a secret is revealed in the way one dances. You just have to know what to look for."

"I'm pretty sure the only secret I'm keeping is that I have no patience for this kind of stuff. Can't we just play *football* and end this torment?"

"That's enough for today," Myrddin said. "Give the girl time. She'll come around." He caught Taryn's eye and winked. "Let's load up."

Taryn mouthed a thank you to him before retrieving her cloak and heading to the horses.

Rhoane moved in step beside her, surprising her. "What is *football*?"

She glanced at him, a smile on her lips. "It's a game we play where I come from. Lots of running, kicking a ball—it's fun. If you want, I can show you when we get to Paderau."

"I would like that." They reached the horses, and he stroked Ashanni's neck, his head bent close to the mare. "She says to relax and sit farther back in the saddle. You will not be so sore if you do."

"You talk to horses?"

"Would you like me to teach you?"

"Sure, right after my dancing lessons and just before Baehlon destroys me with the sword. I'll pencil you in."

"You say the most curious things." He patted Ashanni's neck and helped her into the saddle.

"Welcome to my world." It felt good to banter with him again. Since joining the others, he'd kept Baehlon company most of the time, and she missed him.

They rode at a quicker pace but not too harrowing or difficult for Hayden to instill every facet of court life into her brain. At first, she tuned him out, but eventually she realized his information would help her. If she was going to blend into Aelan society, she needed whatever knowledge Hayden could give her. What he knew could fill volumes.

As they rode, she listened with renewed interest, asking few questions. The more she heard, the more she felt like an interloper. Paderau was about as far from the life she'd lived as she could get.

She could only hope she didn't make a fool of herself and embarrass the others.

The sun sat low on the horizon when Myrddin led them to a grove of trees not far from the road where they would camp for the night. Hayden took the horses while Baehlon and Rhoane went to gather wood for the fire. Duke Anje and Myrddin busied themselves with setting up sleeping rolls, which left Taryn to help Faelara prepare their meal.

Faelara hummed softly as she went about her tasks, every so often stopping to tap her finger upon her lips. Then she'd snap her fingers with a nod and return to whatever it was she was doing. Taryn sat on a rock peeling potatoes and watched the peculiar woman. Pots sat on an open flame with ShantiMari enhanced spoons lazily stirring the contents. Faelara dug through a leather satchel, pulling out more items than the satchel could physically hold. Pale amber Mari rolled off her in waves.

Taryn leaned in to the power, anxious to feel Faelara's warmth. A sharp jab pierced her skull, shattering her thoughts. Her shoulders bunched against the assault, and she groaned. Another stab was followed by yet another, more insistent. She grabbed her head with a small cry.

"Taryn, what is it?" Faelara knelt before her and gently removed the knife Taryn held in her hand.

"My head. Shit!" A fierce blow made her reel with dizziness, bile rose up the back of her throat, and she gagged against it.

Her pendant flared heat across her chest, followed by a stinging cold. From the edge of her vision, she saw Rhoane burst through the trees, his sword drawn. Baehlon followed a step behind.

A roar, like the clamor of a powerful hurricane, rushed through her, drowning all other sound. Rhoane knelt beside Faelara and placed his hands alongside Taryn's head as searing pain ripped through her. She flinched, and Rhoane held her tighter. A wavering darkness just beyond the trees teased her sight. Not human, but a shadowy presence. When she tried to make it out, it vanished.

The torment stopped. Warmth flooded her. Rhoane's Shanti. She angled into it like a sunflower seeking light. Gradually the throbbing lessened until her vision cleared and she could make out their voices.

"Should be warded."

"Don't want to inflict more harm."

"A danger to herself and others."

She wasn't sure who said what, but fragments of their conversation stuck in her mind.

"Taryn?" Rhoane's gentle tone pulled her attention to him. A tiny dimple she'd never noticed before quickened her pulse. She reached to touch it, and a surge of emotion swept over her. Rhoane's thoughts and feelings—not hers.

Alarmed, she jerked her hand away. "I'm fine. Really, it was nothing." She brushed him off, afraid of what would happen if she touched him again.

"You should rest, girl." Myrddin commanded and the others parted so she could lie on one of the bedrolls he'd laid out.

"No, I need to work." She picked up the knife Faelara had taken from her and began peeling another potato.

They hovered over her for several minutes until Duke

Anje shooed them away. He sat beside her, stroking her hair while the others went back to their chores. A wall of his ShantiMari rose around them, hovering above Rhoane's but not touching his power.

Curious, Taryn thought as she finished the potatoes. Within the strains of ShantiMari existed a form of etiquette. A code of respect, perhaps.

Rhoane kept close, finding tasks to complete that required his presence. By the time supper was eaten, she'd recovered completely, which meant Baehlon thought her fit enough to begin sword lessons. Despite the fact she was exhausted from riding all day, had danced through her lunch, and had a seizure before dinner, Taryn was excited to take up the sword.

When she touched the hilt, a ripple of power traveled through her. The exhaustion she'd felt a moment earlier disappeared, leaving her feeling alive, refreshed.

Orbs bobbed around them, giving off muted light by which to see.

"You hold your sword so," Baehlon instructed.

She copied his grip on the handle, her fingers wrapping around the leather, becoming one with the weapon.

"Your foot position is just as important as your sword." Baehlon moved through transverses and passes, side steps, advancing and retreating, all the while adjusting the angle of his blade.

"It's like a dance," Taryn said, breathless from the constant action.

"But more deadly. Never let your guard down, young one." He thrust at her, narrowly missing her side. She swung a clumsy parry, knocking his sword away. "You'll have to do better than that." He swung low and smacked her bum.

"What the hell, Baehlon! That freaking hurt." She rubbed her backside, glaring at him.

Baehlon twirled his weapon in his hand, a wicked grin

spreading across his face, showing straight white teeth.

"Oh my God. You're kind of cute when you smile," she teased. "You should do it more often."

Immediately, she regretted the witty comment when Baehlon advanced on her with devious precision. Taryn followed his every move, mimicking him as best she could.

When the light had faded to dark shadows and they were both drenched in sweat, Baehlon called a halt to their lesson. "I think that's enough for one night." Baehlon clapped her on the back. "You did well. I'm serious, Taryn. You have the talent to become a warrior."

"What if I don't want to become a warrior?" She envisioned herself on a field of battle, armed with the sword and wearing garments of leather and steel. The image unsettled her.

"You either are or you aren't. There is no choice." He sheathed his blade before joining the others.

No. She wrapped the sword and placed it under her bag. *I have a choice.*

She took a seat by the fire and listened as her traveling companions discussed the lesson she'd had with Baehlon. It dawned on her that all of them saw her as something she wasn't. They were each, in their own way, moving her toward some unseen goal. A warrior or a courtier, she wasn't sure. But she wouldn't be a doll for them to dress up and orchestrate to their whims. Who she would be was *her* choice. If they didn't like it, well, that was *their* choice.

Chapter 11

TARYN quietly made her way through the trees to train before the others woke. For as long as she could remember, she'd been in one martial arts class or another. It kept her grounded, Brandt had said. Taught her self-defense while focusing her mind.

She'd hated it at first, but after a few years, she'd found the forms, or katas, meditative. No matter where they were in the world, Brandt sought out a master to train her. Her mixture of varying styles frustrated many teachers, but the constant learning stimulated Taryn.

For the better part of an hour, she moved through her kata. Despite the chill air, her shirt clung to her skin from the exertion. The way she flowed from one move to the next was much like the sword work she'd done the night before. Of all the disciplines she'd studied, she'd never trained in kendo, but as she trudged to the stream to wash up before the long ride ahead, she was already planning how to combine her sword work and karate, making it her own.

The bracing water sent goose bumps over her skin. Standing with her chemise tucked between her thighs, she did her best to rinse herself without offending her modesty as she bent at the waist and poured handfuls of water over her scalp. It wasn't much, but it would have to do. With a flip of her hair, she stood, pulling it into a sloppy knot. Her gaze went to the shore, and she froze.

Rhoane stood a few feet from the water, sword drawn, a bemused smile on his face.

"What are you doing here?" She sloshed to the shore and pulled her pants over clammy skin then jerked her arms through her vest. Rhoane didn't even have the decency to turn around. "You're staring."

"I know."

Those two words sent shivers through her and she flushed with embarrassment. And excitement.

Rhoane adjusted his stance and said in a low voice, tinged with huskiness, "When I saw your empty blankets, I wanted to make sure you were safe."

"I like to get a fresh start to the day. Riding a horse is one thing. Smelling like one is entirely different."

"You slept well, then?"

"As well as can be expected." She stretched her back and legs. "I keep hoping I'll get used to riding, but it hasn't happened yet."

"In time, *Darennsai*." They'd walked a few paces under the cover of trees when Rhoane turned to her. "There is something I need to tell you."

His ominous tone set her on edge. "That doesn't sound good."

"I should have done this sooner." His hand rose as if to touch her forehead and then stopped in midair. "May I?"

"What are you going to do?" She struggled not to flinch.

"I believe last night someone was trying to access your thoughts. I could not discern who, but I can prepare you against any more attacks."

"Read my mind?" It hadn't occurred to her it was possible. Hayden speaking in her mind at Ravenwood was a fluke, somehow tied to the sword and her heightened sense of danger. "It felt like someone was making an ice sculpture with my brain. Does it always hurt?"

"Only when they wish you harm. Which I do not." When Rhoane's fingertips touched her forehead, a familiar warmth spread through her. Recollections and images swirled into a blurred mess and then came in sharp focus. A woman of immeasurable beauty stood beside a huge tree in the center of a forest. Her dark, waist-length hair blew in the slight breeze.

"She's gorgeous. Who is she?"

Rhoane glanced at her, surprised. *My mother, Aislinn. Would you like me to teach you how to keep others out of your head?* His words whispered through her mind.

"Yes, please. The idea that someone can get to my thoughts and memories is more than a little disturbing."

Communicating with your mind is more efficient. If you do decide to let someone in, all you have to do is invite him or her. Even so, you can control how much access they are allowed. Now, speak to me without words.

How? She tried to think the word instead of using her voice.

Exactly, but you do not have to shout.

Sorry. She pictured Brandt, as she liked to remember him, in his smoking jacket, reading in his favorite chair. She sent the thought to Rhoane.

Some things never change, I see.

When the connection ended, emptiness enveloped her. "Now, try to enter my thoughts again," Rhoane said aloud.

Confused, Taryn reached out to him with her mind. "There's something blocking me."

"Do you feel what I have done? Recreate that." He pulled the barrier away so she could sense his actions.

"I think I've got it." She imagined an impenetrable wall, shutting out her thoughts.

"You do not need to be so fierce. A gentle block will

suffice, but you have the idea." Sadness clouded his eyes. "You are a fast learner."

She wondered whether he felt the emptiness, as well. They stood close enough she could smell his scent of a forest after a rainfall, but there was something different, a subtle tang of apple. She breathed him in, let his Shanti and essence linger over her. Calm enveloped her, and she sighed into the morning air.

Rhoane sought her gaze for a moment, holding it. He was about to speak when suddenly he turned and stalked off. The warmth left her, cold snapping against her like a lash. A violent shiver shook her to the core as she stared after him. Unsure what had happened, she grabbed her sword and headed to the campsite. When she arrived, the others were starting to awaken for the day.

Hayden looked as if he'd gotten no sleep, Myrddin even less. Rhoane returned as they were putting out the fire and spoke to no one as he readied his horse. Having worked with men her entire life, Taryn had thought she understood them, but as she studied Rhoane, she realized they were as foreign to her as Aelinae. She didn't know what she'd said to upset him, but if he wanted to talk, he knew where her mind was. She giggled at her little joke.

"You seem merry this morning," Hayden said with little enthusiasm.

She gave him a sly grin, kicking her horse to join the others.

"Am I to guess at your good mood, or will you share it with me?"

"I'm here. You're here. Life is good. What more do you need?"

He arched his back and twisted from side to side. "A decent bed. I'm afraid my experience with road travel is not what it should be, but you seem adept at sleeping on the ground. What is your secret?"

"My grandfather and I traveled a lot."

"What is it you did to travel so much?"

Rhoane glanced at her, apprehension woven though the tightness of his features.

"I suppose you could say we were collectors. We traveled to distant lands finding treasures for people."

"That sounds exciting. Did you enjoy the work?"

"Very much. But what I liked most was being with Brandt. He was such a character, and everyone loved him. There was this one time," she started to laugh at the memory, "at a dig in some rainforest, I forget where exactly, but there was this monkey—" She stopped suddenly, the weight of her words falling heavy upon the hush that had settled over the group.

She'd forgotten they were Brandt's friends and she was the reason he was no longer with them.

Faelara broke the silence. "I hope we can prove as entertaining as your grandfather."

"Oh, trust me. You are. But, really, if you want to tone down the excitement a bit, I won't mind."

Hayden rubbed his chest where the sword had nearly pierced his heart. "Do you mean to say you didn't rescue young men from poisoned swords before you met us?"

"Not hardly! I also had never met a knight or a duke. Which reminds me, don't you have more to teach me about, uh, what did you call it? The Crystal Court?" She deftly changed the subject.

"Empress Lliandra's palace at Talaith? If you'd like. Or, I could tell you about Caer Idris, the home of Lord Valterys. The place is positively steeped in mystery." Hayden launched into a story about his predecessors and how they came to build the great castle that overlooked the Western Seas. The entire place was made of stone brought down from the north by men who were half monster and lived on fields of ice. Taryn would've believed only half of what he said, crediting his imagination for the rest, except no one challenged him.

In fact, every so often someone would chime in to add details to Hayden's story or to tell a tale of their own. Baehlon and Myrddin took turns spinning a yarn about the older man, the details of which Taryn wasn't sure she quite understood since both men were laughing too hard to form coherent sentences. Something about Myrddin mistaking a goat for a nymph. Large amounts of alcohol had been involved, of that much she was certain.

By the time they stopped for lunch, her sides ached from laughing so hard she almost fell off her horse. The light mood continued through their meal, and when Hayden suggested another dance lesson, Taryn didn't object. Running the steps through her mind, she sashayed to where Hayden waited for her. A fleck of black caught her attention. When she looked up, a huge bird careened through the trees, heading straight for her.

"What the—"

One minute she was standing, the next, Rhoane knocked her to the ground.

"Bloody hell, Rhoane," she wheezed from under him, all the air having whooshed from her lungs on impact. She pushed him off and rolled to a kneeling position to catch her breath. Another creature swept toward her.

"Taryn, stay down," Rhoane warned before unsheathing his sword. The sky had darkened with scores of the flying menaces.

Ignoring Rhoane, she ran to Ashanni and grabbed her sword. Myrddin raised a hand, sending fireballs at the birds. They banked, missing the flames by a feather. Hayden stayed at his father's back, slicing at anything that flew too close while Baehlon covered Faelara's flank. Taryn ran beside

Rhoane, using him as a shield as she fought off the incoming beasts.

Dozens of birds tore at their clothes with sharp claws while others grabbed at their hair with ugly, gnarled beaks. To her left, Baehlon swore as he swung his sword again and again, cutting into one and decapitating another. Taryn dodged thick talons while trying to hit the birds with her sword. For their size, they were fast, darting in and around the group, forcing her to spin and duck to avoid getting cut.

All around her was chaos. She spied the others through the melee, while trying to keep the pests from attacking her. The birds danced around Faelara's deadly flames, and she quickly changed tactics, throwing a net of ShantiMari toward the flock, capturing them in a web of power. Still, it was useless. For every bird they killed, five more flew down to torment them.

Nearby trees whipped their branches out to strike at the birds, causing momentary disarray within the flock. Taryn glanced at Rhoane, whose concentrated stare toward the woods answered to her unspoken question. The trees gave the group only a moment of reprieve before the attack resumed, harder and faster than before.

Duke Anje cried out as a vicious-looking bird caught him on the shoulder, tearing through his jerkin. He impaled the creature with his blade, spitting out several curses as he flung it to the ground.

Rhoane kept close to Taryn, warning her when a bird approached from her blind side and protecting her flank, much like the others were doing for each other. Rhoane swore as a beak nipped his arm, and Taryn smelled the sharp tang of his blood. Panic gripped her, but there was no time for fear. It was a luxury they did not have.

Another feathered creature angled toward Taryn and she steadied herself for its attack.

Die, you filthy fucking birds, every last one of you!

She heaved her sword up with both hands. As the steel met bone, a loud *crack* stuttered across the clearing. The blade cut into the bird's rib cage, slicing clean through, sending feathers flying in every direction. A revolting stink assaulted her nostrils. An all-too-human scream came from the beast before it fell to the ground.

Taryn spun around for the next attack, but Rhoane and the others just stared at her, swords paused in midair, hands held up to an empty sky. All around them birds lay on the ground, each cut in half exactly as the one she'd slain.

Adrenaline pumped through her veins, even as her stomach soured. "What happened?" The sight before her made no sense.

"Good question. Would you care to enlighten us?" Myrddin stepped to the bird closest to him, kicking it with his boot. "How is it you managed to slay all these feiches at once?"

"Feiches?"

"Yes, these birds. How did you do it, Taryn?" Myrddin's face was a storm cloud.

"I didn't. I mean, I don't think I did." Taryn stared in dull shock at the feiche carcasses. "Does it matter? They're dead."

Faelara tread between them, avoiding the birds. "Let's get away from here before something larger comes to feast." She looked pointedly at Myrddin. "We can discuss this later."

He grunted and shot Taryn a withering glance. "It might be best if you didn't swing that thing around any of us until you learn to use it."

Stung by the recrimination in his voice, she gaped at him. She hadn't expected applause or accolades, but she hadn't expected a rebuff, either. Biting back a retort, she turned from him to clean the blade on a patch of moss before sheathing the sword behind her saddle.

Hayden approached as she tightened Ashanni's girth.

"What?" she snapped.

He placed his fist over his heart and inclined his head. "My lady."

Her answering snort made him wince. "Lady, my ass. It's this damned sword." She pulled herself into the saddle, turning her horse toward the road. Each time she recalled the scene with the dead feiches, her stomach roiled and the taste of bile teased her throat. Outwardly she remained impassive, but inside was a mixture of excitement and frenzied action, countered by a calm that came from her martial arts training. There was more—a sense of purpose to the killing.

Taryn, Rhoane said in her mind, *do not let Myrddin upset you. The sword and your* cynfar *were protecting you. You did nothing wrong.*

Thank you. Taryn appreciated his saying so, but Myrddin was right. She had to learn to control the sword before she hurt someone she cared about. Or worse.

Chapter 12

THE dark sea glittered like a jewel-encrusted gown, beckoning. How often had he stood on that very balcony and wished for nothing more than to explore the vast wonders that lay beyond the dazzling expanse of ocean? Too often for a man of his privilege, his power. Valterys watched the seagulls hunt for their dinner, dipping into the waves and surfacing with their catch. They were scavengers and hunters. Not too unlike himself.

At the polite sound of a throat clearing, he turned from the temptation of flying with them, of seeing blood stain their feathers as his sharp talons bit into their feathered flesh. Of hearing their screams as they died.

A servant stood in the doorway, and Valterys motioned him forward.

"Have you located Zakael?" Concern laced his words. The man had been gone well over a fortnight.

"He entered the city not more than a half bell past. The sentry at the eastern gate sent the message, my lord."

"Was he alone?"

"Indeed, my lord."

"Very well. Let me know the minute he enters the castle walls." Valterys returned to his position on the balcony, the sea lost from view as his thoughts clouded.

He'd placed his trust in Marissa and sent Zakael to Mount Nadrene. All of his plans hinged on the arrival of the anomaly. So far, Marissa had never given him false information. He had no reason to doubt her. Not once in all the past seasons had Lliandra given him hope that his child had lived. With his own eyes, he saw the infant corpse, and yet Marissa claimed there was another, secreted away moments after her birth. A girl. Not the son he'd wished for.

For near on thirty-five seasons he and Zakael had searched every kingdom on Aelinae, save for the Narthvier. The Eleri allowed very few to cross their borders, but no matter. Valterys had spies everywhere. If the Eirielle was hidden in King Stephan's forest, he would've known.

Valterys allowed himself a rare moment of speculation, and a surge of power flowed through him as he dared hope it was true—his and Lliandra's child, the one of prophecy, was alive and among them now.

He would restore Rykoto's freedom and, in return, be granted immortality. With his rise, all of Aelinae would bow to him as their one true leader. Valterys smiled to himself. As soon as he had the girl, he could set about destroying Lliandra.

Zakael swept through the doorway, ignoring protocol to grasp his father's arm in greeting.

"What kept you? It has been too long since your last missive." Valterys kept his tone even, not wanting to alert Zakael to the fact he'd worried about him. "What in Ohlin's name are you wearing?"

"I had some difficulties." Zakael rubbed the back of his head. "I will tell you all, but let me first refresh myself. I'm afraid my horse will be useless for a sennight. Order us dinner. I will meet you here in three-quarters of a bell."

The peasants' garb he wore bespoke of more than a few difficulties. Zakael was nothing if not vain.

His son arrived moments before the food and poured himself a large glass of wine without bothering to offer any to Valterys. He kept his anger in check. His son was getting too bold, too full of his own importance. He would need to set Zakael straight soon enough, but not before he got what information he could. When they were seated, Valterys leaned eagerly toward the younger man, prompting him to tell of the events at Mount Nadrene.

"Glennwoods was there, as was Brandt."

"Truly? The Eleri prince and Lliandra's high priest? But what of my daughter? Did you see her?"

"Aye, she was with the old man. Very fair of face and dressed in strange garments. I could not discern where she'd been all these seasons, but if I had to guess, it would be with the Eleri. Perhaps with a lesser clan, on the outskirts of the Narthvier."

Valterys leaned back, thinking. "We will have to assume Stephan knew nothing of the girl. For now. I don't want war with the Eleri until the end."

"This can be a huge bargaining tool, if necessary." Zakael ate his food between sentences, taking care not to spill anything on his tunic.

Valterys looked away, it was a habit that irritated him. "What happened in the cavern that you did not return with the Eirielle?"

Zakael started slowly, spinning a tale about his confrontation with Rhoane, the arrival of Brandt and the girl, and the subsequent fight. "They were gone before I recovered. There's more, Father. The Shanti Brandt used against me... it felt wrong. I know the priest. He would not willingly kill. She didn't use her power, but I suspect the girl had a hand in helping the old man defeat me. The raw strength of his attack was clumsy."

"Marissa tells me the priest died in the cavern."

"What?" Zakael looked genuinely flustered. "Not by my hand. My Shanti was enough to stun, nothing more."

Valterys took a long drink of his wine, savoring the delicate taste of Geigan blood in the mixture. "No matter. Brandt was an inconvenience, that's all. While you were otherwise indisposed, I went to Ravenwood to retrieve the sword."

A flash of excitement crossed Zakael's face. "Where is it?"

"Myrddin was there with that giant knight of his. Come to think of it, Glennwoods was there, as well. He must've met up with Myrddin after the cavern." Valterys thought hard, his mind racing over the events at Ravenwood. "I didn't see the girl, but there was a presence that I could not explain."

"And the duke's heir? Is he dead?"

"Myrddin blocked my way, but if it is as Marissa claims, the boy is dead."

"Do not doubt her powers, my lord. Or her loyalty."

Valterys snorted. What Zakael didn't know about the crown princess could fill volumes. "Time will tell. For now, I'll trust in your judgment and hope Myrddin does not possess the sword."

"Impossible. Only one of the true blood can wield it." They looked at each other in alarm, Zakael voicing their shared thought. "Nadra's tit," he swore. "If the Eirielle is at Ravenwood, that means they are in possession of the blood and the blade."

"Now that we know she is out of hiding, we can proceed with our plans." Valterys went to the balcony, resting his arms on the railing. "She will be of age soon—that is why Lliandra has chosen to reveal her now. Very cunning. It must be a public declaration, but when?"

"There is the duke's ball, but I doubt she would present her there. She will wait until they are at the Crystal Palace and the seat of her power before announcing the return of her long-lost daughter."

Lliandra needed the sword to convince the court the girl was her true daughter, yes, but if she wanted them to believe she was the Eirielle, Valterys must also acknowledge the girl. Even though his daughter could not inherit the Obsidian Throne, he needed her to further his plans, which meant he had to publicly claim her.

He slammed his glass on the stone railing, sending tiny shards spraying in every direction. Blood seeped from several cuts on his palm.

"If I'd known she was at Ravenwood, I would not have left so quickly." Valterys cursed under his breath. "Still, I could not fight them all, not alone. We must make haste to Talaith. If Lliandra plans to present my daughter to the world, I should be there."

"Give me a day to rest and see to my work, and then we'll do as you wish. But first, we should pay your cousin a visit." Zakael's eyes glinted like polished granite in the firelight, his lips curled in a wicked smile. "What better way to observe the Eirielle than at a masked ball?"

Chapter 13

AFTER the attack, Baehlon increased not only the length of Taryn's sword training but the intensity. Each night, she crawled beneath her blankets exhausted and sore from his ministrations. For the next seven days, they encountered no further assaults but stayed wary as they traveled. The dark shadow tracking her movements had vanished after she killed the feiches, the flicker at the edge of her vision gone, as well. Its absence should've made her feel better, but it only added to the many questions she had about her home world.

On the last day of their ride to Paderau, Taryn awoke before the others and trekked a short distance to a secluded spot. Each morning, she rose early to practice her kata. The hour or so alone became her solace, a time of quiet she learned to value with so little privacy afforded by the group.

She moved through her forms, reflecting on her promise to Brandt. At the time, it had been difficult, and her first few days on Aelinae a trial, but being with the others taught her to see the beauty of this world, not just the monstrosities. Given the chance again she would willingly give her word that she would remain here.

Her longing to avenge Brandt's death thrummed just beneath the surface of her thoughts, making the hard work she put in every day more bearable. Her constant travels with

Brandt meant she'd never had lasting relationships, but the others had accepted her, giving instant friendship. Each day, she felt more a part of the small group, and with that came a sense of loyalty to them. It was important to her that she not disappoint them.

She was so completely focused that when a heavy hand gripped her shoulder, she acted on instinct, seizing it, then twisting and pulling as she thrust her hip into the intruder. He flipped over, landing on his back with a *thunk*. Heart racing, knees trembling with the rush of adrenaline, Taryn placed her foot at his throat, hands up in a defensive stance. It took a moment for her to register the face of Baehlon as he stared up at her, his dark eyes huge with a mixture of anger and curiosity.

Taryn blinked down at him. "What are you doing here?"

He moved slightly, but her foot prevented him from getting up. "Do you mind?" He indicated her leg. Taryn removed her foot and held out a hand to help him up. He eyed it warily. "You won't flip me again?"

"You surprised me."

Baehlon stood, rubbing his backside. "A mistake I will not make again." He stretched his long body and rolled his head from side to side. "Faelara is looking for you. She wants to go over last minute details before we ride into the city."

"I'm sorry, really. It was reflex. If I'd known it was you, there's no way I would have, you know…" She rolled her hands to indicate him flipping.

"All is well. But Taryn, why didn't you tell me you could fight?"

"You never asked."

His laughter boomed through the trees, frightening several birds into flight. "Can you teach me what you just did?"

A tickle of excitement fluttered in her belly. "Now?"

"And risk Fae's wrath? Not on your life. Once you're settled in Paderau will be soon enough."

When they reached the camp, the others were dressed and packing the horses. Faelara's instructions were simple things Taryn didn't need to be reminded of but she listened out of respect. *Stay close. Speak to no one except those she rode with. Keep the sword hidden.*

Faelara kissed Taryn on the cheek, holding her close. "I've enjoyed our time together. You are a treasure, to be sure." Tears shone in her eyes when she pulled away.

"Are you okay?"

"I'm fine, sweetling." She squeezed Taryn's hand before pulling herself into the saddle.

Taryn glanced at Rhoane, who sat on his horse a few feet away. A similar look was etched across his face, not necessarily concern but a resignation of sorts. She climbed into the saddle and patted Ashanni's neck, ready for the next leg of her journey.

Beyond a large grove of trees, the road opened up. They stood on a hilltop, looking down at a valley of rolling green meadows. Nestled between two rivers, Paderau sparkled like a pearl set in a dazzling sapphire choker.

"Well?" Hayden said beside her.

"You told me your city was beautiful, but—wow."

The closer they got to the city gates, the pull of ShantiMari, its multi-colored lights glistening above the walls and around the thick wooden gates, dazzled her senses. Guards stood at posts near the west entrance and even more walked along the battlements. Myrddin rode forward with the duke, and the guards snapped to attention, saluting them as they passed.

Paderau defied Hayden's descriptions. Taryn followed the others, taking in the sights. Wooden buildings flanked the street, some with signs hanging above doorways, others with windows that offered everything from wineskins and cooked turkey legs to cotton tunics and boots.

Taryn had to keep from gawking at the sheer number of people who roamed the streets. Hundreds of inhabitants moved about their day. On more than one occasion, she spied soldiers patrolling the streets or standing outside pubs, keeping a close watch on everyone.

At the first bridge they crossed, Taryn leaned over to get a glimpse of the river. Clean, clear water flowed to the south. Farther down was another bridge, and after that, the river disappeared. The duke turned the group off the main street onto a small residential avenue lined with trees. The two- or three-story homes were solid and simple. Some had ornamental gates and paths leading to attractive porches.

The avenue opened to a square with stalls surrounding a huge fountain. Hawkers called out their wares, adding to the din. Pelts hung from the booth of a petite man with a flamboyant hat. Next to him, chickens pecked and scratched in a tiny enclosure. The square had an earthy smell to it—of sweat, dirt, and livestock. Comforting smells.

They rode along two more avenues, each more opulent than the previous one. As their horses clomped along the cobblestone streets, the tension from the long days of traveling drifted away from the group. Their voices rose with excited anticipation. Hayden gestured ahead, and Taryn held her breath at the sight of Paderau Palace.

The four-story palace was even more magnificent than it had looked from the hilltop, with arched windows and columned terraces. An intricate ironwork fence surrounded the gardens and buildings, with thick cords of ShantiMari snaking around the perimeter dissuading anyone who hadn't been invited from entering. Each corner boasted a tower with discreet arrow slits, and the roofline effectively hid battlements capable of holding several platoons of the duke's guard.

All those times you quizzed me about castles and palaces, now I know why. Taryn kissed her fingertips and looked up to the sky, hoping Brandt could hear her.

She followed the others into the courtyard, where a massive magnolia tree blossomed in the summer heat. She barely had time to grab her things before a groom led Ashanni away. They entered the palace through a side door, and Taryn almost tripped over herself staring at the opulence around her. The room was half the size of a football pitch, with perhaps sixty people seated on fragile-looking couches and chairs. Gold filigree edged the elaborately painted ceiling and walls. Before she could take it all in, Faelara led her away from the others.

They went up several flights of stairs and down more hallways than Taryn could remember. "Here we are. My rooms are down the hall." Faelara pointed to a set of large doors. "If you need anything, come and find me."

A rush of panic seized Taryn. "What am I supposed to do?"

"I'll send a maid to run a bath for you, and I'll have a tailor come by for measurements, as well." She plucked at Taryn's shirt. "You've been wearing this so long, I fear we'll have to burn it." She gave her shirt a sniff, crinkling her nose. "Mine, as well, I'm afraid. Not to worry, love, all will be well."

The older woman led her into a room with two long windows opening to the gardens. The scent of jasmine drifted up to greet her. The smell reminded her of a time not long past in another world. She inhaled the sweet fragrance with a pang of homesickness. "It's lovely, Faelara."

Everything in the area matched in varying shades of yellow, from the soft-butter walls to the floral fabric of an overstuffed chair and small couch. Vases of fresh flowers adorned the tables. It was at once homey and unfamiliar. Taryn wandered to yet another room, where Faelara *tsk*ed to herself while opening several cupboards and drawers. Her slim fingers danced along the wall until Taryn heard a slight *click*.

The secret compartment hinged open without another sound. "Taryn, dear, get your sword, please." She brought the weapon to Faelara. "Put it in here. Now, I'm going to place some wards on the sword and the cupboard. If anyone besides you tries to open it or touch the sword, they'll get a nasty shock." She eyed Taryn. "Do you understand what a ward is?"

"I think so. Will it hurt me?"

"Not you, but everyone else." Faelara whispered under her breath while Taryn followed the flow of ShantiMari as it wound its way around the sword and through the door. When she was done, Faelara closed the compartment with a final command. "It would be best if you don't disturb the sword, but if you should need to, make certain you close this door when you're done. Otherwise, the wards will unravel."

Taryn placed her hand on the cupboard. A buzz of power ran through her and then back to the sword. Faelara's Mari had a gentleness to it. Reluctantly, she took her hand away from the sweet feeling.

"Come," Faelara's voice called from beyond the bedchamber. Taryn almost swooned when she saw the next room. A large claw footed tub sat in the center of a bathroom. "I'm sure you will appreciate a nice bath after our ride."

"Oh yes, please." Much to her surprise, there was plumbing for the tub and sink.

Faelara led them back into the sitting room. "His Grace and Hayden have rooms on the top floor. Myrddin likes to stay in the eastern tower. Rhoane's rooms are on the floor above us. Baehlon, I imagine, will stay in the barracks with the soldiers." Her eyes drifted to the window, and her expression grew distant.

"Why do you all have rooms here?"

Faelara blinked at her question. "What?"

"Do you stay here that often?"

"I have a suite in every major castle or palace in all of the East. It comes with being one of the empress's ladies." She touched Taryn's cheek. "You'll have your own apartments, too."

"Why? I don't work for the empress."

Faelara's expression was soft, but her words held a hint of steel. "In time, you'll understand. I'll send in those maids. I'm sure the other girls will wish to meet you." Again, she heard the steeliness. "Be polite, but please, do not tell them anything about where you came from. Just remember everything Hayden taught you, and you'll be fine."

After Faelara left, Taryn sat on the windowsill, breathing in the scent of jasmine, hoping it would calm her nerves. All it did was dredge up memories she couldn't share about a life she was compelled to forget. More alone than ever, she sat and watched without seeing the people who moved along the garden paths.

A young woman dressed in a plain blue dress with a white apron tied around her waist entered with a small curtsey. "I've come for your bath, miss." Another girl dressed in a similar fashion followed her. They looked to be in their late teens, but with Aelinaen years, she wasn't sure.

Their giggles floated above the sound of running water, and Taryn idly wondered what they found so amusing. Probably her dismal appearance. One of the girls appeared in the doorway to ask quietly whether she would like to bathe. Taryn had to keep herself from jumping straight into the tub fully clothed.

"Do, uh…do you usually stay here while I undress?" She asked when it was clear the girls weren't leaving.

They held up a large towel for privacy, and she slipped

out of her dirty clothes. Before they could stop her, she sank into the bath, doing her best to hide under the bubbles. Every ache she'd accumulated on the road started to melt away in the hot water.

"What are your names?" Taryn asked.

They were sisters, Mayla and Lorilee. More than the slight resemblance in their faces, their dark hair and sturdy frames marked them as kin.

"I'm Taryn." She tried to keep herself submerged as much as possible. "I don't normally bathe with others in the room."

"Lady Faelara said you might be shy." Lorilee applied a heavenly scented shampoo to Taryn's hair and began massaging her scalp.

A small moan escaped Taryn's lips, and she lay back against the tub, more relaxed than she'd been in months. When Mayla turned her slightly to wash her back with a sponge, Taryn gave in to their ministrations, her inhibitions forgotten.

After bathing her, they rubbed scented oil into her roughened skin before wrapping her in a robe and sitting her in a chair. Taryn must've dozed while they brushed out her hair because a knock at the door startled her awake.

As Faelara promised, the seamstress arrived to take her measurements. Margaret Tan was a large woman who brooked no nonsense and made Taryn stand still while she measured every inch of her body. All the while, she made little clucking sounds before writing on her pad of paper.

After Margaret Tan left, Mayla finished Taryn's hair and handed her a silver mirror. Taryn stared at the intricate mass of braids and curls. "Oh my God. It's beautiful."

Lorilee and Mayla smiled at her while curtseying together.

"We're glad you like it, miss," Lorilee said for both of them.

Taryn kept touching her hair, amazed at what they

did with the rat's nest it had become since she'd arrived on Aelinae. "Like it? I love it."

The girls giggled and curtsied again. The older one, Mayla, said, "Your hair is lovely, like gold silk. We'll be back before dinner; if there is anything else you need before then, just ring the bell." She pointed to a tasseled bell pull discreetly placed by the window.

Hayden arrived as the maids were leaving, and Taryn fidgeted with her robe ties, feeling vulnerable in her undressed state.

The plain brown tunic and breeches he wore on their journey were long gone, replaced with tight-fitting trousers and a brocade jacket that skimmed his hips. His blond hair gleamed in the sunlight. The effect was stunning and a bit unsettling.

He deposited an armful of rich fabrics on a couch. "These should last you a few days."

Taryn sifted through the beautiful gowns, the desire to wear them causing an unfamiliar thrill. "What's wrong with the clothes your father gave me at Ravenwood?"

"Those are fine for a country manor, but at Paderau, the dress is more formal." Hayden picked out an emerald green gown for dinner and a pale blue dress for her to wear until then. "I like your hair up. It suits your face."

His compliment caught her off guard. "Lorilee and Mayla work miracles." She paused. "Why do I have to change for dinner? Can't I just wear one dress all day?"

Hayden's glare could cut stone. "Ohlin's beard, no. Day clothes aren't suitable for dinner."

"I'm not sure this is suitable to be worn out of the bedroom." Taryn fingered the blue gown. Little more than rich silk draped to the floor, bits of lace accented the bodice and sleeves. Pearls dotted the empire waistband.

"You say the most curious things. I'll leave you to dress,

but don't take long. There are some people I'd like you to meet."

She hesitated a moment before calling after him. "Hayden?" When he turned back to her, she blushed. "Thank you for being so kind to me."

"You saved my life. I will forever be in your debt."

"Is that the only reason?"

"Of course not. If I may be so bold, I consider you a friend and hope you might see me as such, as well."

"I couldn't think of a better friend in all the world." She held him tighter than she'd meant. His arms wrapped around her, hesitantly at first, and she sank into him. Raw emotions— gratitude, relief, loneliness—swept over her. She took a step back, wiping a tear from her eye. "God, I'm sorry. I don't know what's come over me." She swiped at her tears with the handkerchief he handed her. "About that whole lifesaving thing—do you think we could keep it between us?" She waved a hand around the room. "This is more than I can take right now, and having people think I'm some sort of hero would be way too much."

"Of course. I'll respect your wishes."

"Can you make sure the others don't say anything? It might be too late, but we can ask."

"Done. Now, if you've no other requests, I'll wait in the sitting room." He closed the door behind him, and she changed into the dress, feeling exposed beneath the soft fabric. She took a deep breath before joining Hayden in the other room.

"You are a dream, Taryn."

She curtseyed as he'd taught her. "Thank you, Hayden. I mean, Lord Valen."

"Very good. You remembered." He held his arm out to her. "Are you ready?"

"No, but let's go anyway." Remembering a title was one

thing, recalling everything else he taught her was something else entirely.

Chapter 14

THE princesses gathered in the garden room of Paderau Palace, as they always did when visiting the duke. A meeting place of sorts, guests could linger over tea to hear the latest court gossip or play games, if that was their inclination. Marissa sat with her sisters but only half listened to what they said. Her attention was drawn to Duke Anje's son, looking very much alive, and the girl who stood nervously beside him.

An unpleasant tremble ran through her as the couple approached. Like pins and needles from a sleepy limb, her nerves twitched, unbalancing her carefully constructed composure. The bewildered feeling was unnatural for Marissa, and she pulled her power around her like a cloak, keeping her face calm, her senses alert.

Hayden bowed low to them. "Your Highnesses, I would like you to meet a dear friend of mine. Taryn, these are the Princesses Marissa, Eliahnna, and Tessa, all daughters of Empress Lliandra." He faltered a bit when he came to the dark haired beauty who sat slightly apart from Marissa and her sisters. "I'm afraid we haven't formally met, but you must be Princess Sabina." He turned to Taryn to explain. "She is visiting from the Summerlands."

Sabina held out her hand to Hayden, a demure smile

teasing her delightful lips. "It is my pleasure, Lord Valen. The princesses have told me stories about you, and I must confess I was rather looking forward to our meeting." Her lush lashes beat once, twice and then rested prettily on her cheek a moment before fluttering open.

Hayden's lips pressed against her skin, and Marissa looked away only to meet the curious stare of Taryn. She inclined her head in greeting.

Taryn executed a perfect curtsey. "I'm honored to make your acquaintances."

Marissa couldn't place Taryn's accent, but it sounded rough, unrefined like an Offlander. "Where are you from, child?" Marissa asked when it became clear the girl wouldn't speak unless spoken to.

Taryn's shoulder twitched with a suppressed shrug. "No one location. My grandfather and I traveled from place to place most of my life."

Hayden indicated they should sit, and Taryn took a seat, her back straight, palms pressed against her knees. She was nervous, that was certain. When a servant brought her tea and cakes, Taryn gave him a grateful smile. Her hand trembled when she lifted the cup to her lips.

Faint inscriptions circled Taryn's wrist. A tug from deep inside pained Marissa, as often happened when something one longed for is lost for all eternity. Earlier, she noticed Rhoane wore similar marks on his hand, which could only mean one thing. The Eirielle had returned.

Since Taryn's birth, Marissa had dreaded this day. Her Mari flared for an instant, and Taryn looked at her with doe eyes filled with something akin to recognition.

Tessa pelted Taryn with questions, only pausing long enough to let her give a quick response. She was unfailingly polite, if a little stiff in her replies. Her easy manner charmed the younger princesses, nonetheless. Twice, Marissa tried to enter her mind, but the girl had it sealed shut. What Marissa couldn't determine was whether Taryn knew who she was and toyed with them or if she was truly ignorant. Pretending to be what you were not was a game Marissa excelled at and, as she studied her, she gauged how skilled Taryn might be, as well.

"I've heard your palace is quite remarkable. Is it really made of crystal as everyone says?" Taryn asked Tessa with a guilelessness Marissa found insulting.

Only an Offlander would be dense enough to ask such a tactless question. Perhaps her innocence was genuine, and if so, it would make Marissa's objectives that much easier to obtain.

"Not really," Tessa explained, "but Mother likes to tell everyone it is. They call it the Crystal Palace because of the rock it's made from. When the sun hits it, it shines like polished diamonds. There are whole walls made of rock so clear you can see through them, but unlike glass, it is impenetrable. Even to ShantiMari. Perhaps someday you can visit and I'll show you."

"I would like that very much, but I'm afraid I don't know where my travels will take me next." She looked at Hayden, who shrugged in answer. "I suppose I could ask Faelara."

Tessa nodded enthusiastically, sending her fair curls bouncing and bobbing around her head, fighting against the pins meant to keep them in place. "Please, do."

"Have you met many princesses on your travels?" Eliahnna asked in her quiet voice. "I am ever so keen to learn about the other kingdoms. Princess Sabina has been very kind to help me with the Summerlands. She's been telling me about a sea king whose citizens are merfolk. Have you ever met a mermaid?"

"I'm afraid not. The closest I've ever come is reading a story about a mermaid named Ariel," Taryn offered.

"The Eirielle is not a mermaid," Sabina protested. "That's just a tale mothers use to frighten their children into good behavior."

Marissa enjoyed the heat coming from the Summerlands princess. Like Eliahnna, it was rare to see her angry or upset. Tessa's outward show of discomfort at Taryn's statement, followed by Sabina's angry retort, genuinely confused Taryn.

"I'm so sorry. I, uh, it was a fairy tale." Again, her hands trembled slightly.

Marissa sipped her tea with quiet contemplation. If Taryn was playing them, she gave a skilled performance. The game became immensely more interesting with the dawning understanding Taryn knew nothing about herself or the others. Marissa traced a fingertip around the rim of her cup, wondering idly what her mother would think of the pretty girl. Moreover, what would Taryn think when she found out her companions were her sisters?

A shadow teased the edge of Marissa's vision, and she turned to see the disgusting little weasel, Lord Herbret, standing to the side of the group. He cleared his throat, pulling their attention to him. Lady Celia followed a step behind, a smirk on her lovely face. Marissa studied the pair, not at all liking the thoughts that scampered through her mind. There would be time for questions later, when she had Celia alone in her rooms.

"Herbret, don't be droll. This isn't the Crystal Palace. You don't need an official invitation to join our group." Marissa gave him her most beguiling smile, the one she knew made his cock jump and his knees weaken. As expected, he shifted uncomfortably, adjusting the front of his trousers as he took a seat opposite Sabina.

Introductions were made with Herbret lingering overlong on Taryn's fingertips. The girl vibrated with suppressed anxiety, which further intrigued Marissa. She was a puzzle, for certes. Unsure of herself, and yet carrying a confidence Marissa admired.

An unbidden memory seared her thoughts, yanking Marissa back to the storm ravaged night Taryn was born. The stench of death, the bright light when Nadra placed the baby's hand on the sword, were as real to her now as they'd been thirty-five seasons earlier. She could hear the sound of Lliandra's sobs for the exiled princess and the dead prince. Tears Lliandra did not share with Valterys the next day when she had so callously told him his son was dead, never mentioning another child.

Hidden in the shadows, no one saw Marissa that night nor did they notice when she began investigating why her mother would lie. By accident, she discovered the prophecy and the reason her mother was frightened enough by the child to send her away. And then to order her death upon her return.

Hayden stood, jerking Marissa from the past. Making his apologies, he excused himself from the group, but not before a long glance at Sabina.

"Well, that was rude," Celia quipped to Hayden's retreating back.

While she was reliving the past, Marissa had obviously missed something important. She fixed her thoughts firmly on the present. "Hayden? I don't think he knows how to be rude. Something must've upset him," Marissa offered, hoping her comment hit the mark.

Herbret leaned closer to Sabina and whispered words that made her go pale, which, considering her sun-kissed complexion, was remarkable.

"Indeed," Celia said, her gaze lingering on Herbret as he pawed Sabina's gown, a dribble of spit making its way down his chin.

Marissa stifled a shudder. Once again she thanked the

gods she could decide who her lovers would be and didn't have to rely on the generosity of the court to appoint her a husband.

"Would anyone like to take a walk in the gardens?" Taryn asked and half rose before Celia interrupted her movement.

"Please, stay a bit longer. The sun is so harsh this time of day, I can't possibly tolerate it." When Taryn resumed her seat, Celia continued, saying in complete innocence, "It is my understanding you are here as a special guest of the duke. Might I inquire how it is you are acquainted?"

"The duke is an old friend of my grandfather's."

"And what House does your grandfather hail from?"

"House? I don't understand."

"All noble families have a House name." Tessa explained. "Was your grandfather titled?"

Taryn glanced at Celia and then Marissa. Again, that look of recognition crossed her face. Marissa instinctively pulled her power close. "I'm not really sure." Taryn said, "He never mentioned it if he was."

"I've never known a nobleman to not to associate with his House, so he must not have been titled." Celia said knowingly.

Taryn shrugged, "Then I guess he wasn't." She glanced yet again at Marissa, a frown creasing her youthful brow, "Your eyes are lovely, Princess Marissa. Such an unusual color."

"I take after my father in looks. His eyes were a deep aubergine. Mine are more lavender in shade, which is much more becoming, don't you think?" She tossed her black curls over her shoulder and blinked to catch the light.

Taryn started to reply when Tessa interrupted them. "I heard you were attacked by a band of thieves on your way to Paderau and Prince Rhoane fought them all by himself."

Marissa corrected her little sister. "It was a gypsy gang. And Myrddin was the one who held them off while the others made their escape."

Taryn looked from one to the other, her eyes widening. "Rhoane is a prince?"

"An Eleri prince," Tessa offered. "He's so handsome! I told Mother that if I were older I should marry him, but she told me that he's been betrothed since before anyone can remember."

Marissa watched the interplay of emotions cross Taryn's face. So, Rhoane hadn't told her who he was... Curious.

"I didn't know," Taryn said in a small voice.

"I've heard Offlanders are ignorant of many things; I shouldn't be surprised that court etiquette is among them," Celia said in a cheerful voice.

"Lady Celia! Don't be so horrid to our guest. If Prince Rhoane didn't feel the need to tell her he's royalty, he probably had a reason for it." Eliahnna gave her older sister a scathing look before turning to Celia. "Apologize to Taryn."

Eliahnna was right, of course, but Marissa couldn't help the surge of delight Celia's teasing brought.

Her friend gave a dramatic sigh. "I suppose that was ungracious of me. Won't you please forgive me?"

Eliahnna would not back down. "Mother won't take it well if I tell her you've been rude to Duke Anje's personal guest. Taryn's ignorance of court politics is not to be demeaned, but perhaps, gently reversed."

Her sister rarely stood up to anyone. If Lliandra found out Celia had treated Taryn poorly, there would be serious repercussions.

Marissa nodded her agreement and said with an imperious tone, "You're absolutely right. We've no reason to criticize your upbringing, Taryn. Not everyone is as fortunate as we are. I hope you don't think we share Lady Celia's opinion."

"Of course not," Taryn stammered, clearly unsure what had just happened. "It's fine, really."

Herbret snorted something about "ignorant Offlanders" then tried to cover it up with an obsequious display of gratitude toward Eliahnna. All the while, his hand reached closer and closer to Sabina. The Summerlands princess sat frozen in place, a look of terror etched on her beautiful features.

"Sabina," Taryn said, standing so suddenly the others jumped in surprise. "You look like you don't mind the sun. Won't you please join me in the gardens? All this sitting makes me anxious to stretch my legs."

Sabina sprang from her place on the couch, almost knocking over Herbret in the process. "I would love to. Thank you."

Eliahnna cast a quick glance at Tessa before the two of them followed the older girls from the room. Left with just Herbret and Celia, Marissa let out a low chuckle. "Herbret, what ever did you say to poor Sabina. She was positively death-struck."

Herbret reclined into the chair, his paunch clearly visible beneath his waistcoat. "I simply mentioned some of the pleasures she and I would share once we are betrothed."

"Did my mother give you permission?"

"Not yet. We're still negotiating." A sly smirk made him even less attractive. Beneath the smile were horrors Marissa doubted even she could bear.

"Until you have it in writing, you must be more discreet. The wrong word from one of my sisters," silently Marissa included Taryn in the list, "and you'll find yourself without a bride."

"I'll take that into consideration." His simpering annoyed Marissa. "Since when do you allow Offlander trash in your company?"

Taryn made a huge mistake by protecting Sabina from Herbret. He was not a man who forgave easily, and he never forgot a slight.

Marissa ignored him and stood. "I think I'll take some fresh air before retiring to my rooms. Herbret, I'll see you at dinner. Lady Celia?" She didn't wait for a reply, knowing Celia would follow.

When certain no one of consequence could see, she slipped into an alcove with her lady. Her lips sought her friend's with a hunger women rarely aroused in her.

"You are a gem, my sweet Celia. Come to my rooms tonight, and I will reward you further." She pinched Celia's breast before leaving the woman gasping in her absence.

Marissa hurried to her rooms, clearing her mind of Celia, focusing on what must be done. Whatever happened at Ravenwood, Valterys needed to know that Hayden lived and Taryn traveled with Myrddin. Sparks of her Mari shot from her fingertips as she cursed that fool Zakael and, to a lesser extent, herself. How Hayden had survived the poisoned sword, she couldn't understand. No one should've been able to undo her spells.

The sword.

Marissa spun to her left, heading to the wing where Taryn was sure to be staying. It took a few inquiries, plus a touch of her Mari to compel the servants to forget they'd told her where to find Taryn's quarters. It was in a part of the palace she remembered well. A delicious courtier had once stayed on the very same floor as Taryn. A thin smile broke across her face. She could traverse every secret passageway hidden behind the walls. If Taryn had the sword, she would find it.

The secret door swung open with a slight creak. She paused in the darkened hallway, unsure whether Taryn's maids were in the chamber beyond. When no sound came to her, she pushed aside the heavy tapestry, leaving the door slightly ajar.

The bedchamber was small but adequate for someone

of Taryn's supposed rank. To Marissa's trained eye, nothing looked out of place. She felt along the walls for a place large enough to fit a sword. A set of three cupboards lined the wall opposite the bed, two of which opened at her touch. The third remained locked. When she sent a thread of Mari through it, a shock of cold ran over her skin. Someone had placed wards on the cupboard.

She had set about untying them when voices in the outer room disturbed her progress. A moment before Baehlon— the giant knight her mother favored—and two girls came into the bedchamber, she slipped into the corridor. The secret door clicked shut, and she stood for several moments, breathing heavily.

When certain Baehlon could not hear her footsteps, she raced to her rooms. Two of her maids from Talaith and two the duke had lent her jumped when she entered the suite, flushed and out of breath. She gave orders to the duke's girls that would keep them occupied elsewhere. To her ladies, she gave a gold crown and bade them to find any information they could about the duke's special guest. They were to discern who Taryn spoke with, where she went, what kind of food she ate—anything at all. When her maids had gone, she locked the door, placing several alarming wards on it for good measure. She needed complete privacy, and although her maids were accustomed to her peculiar entertainments, it was best if they weren't there for what she needed to accomplish.

She called forth her seeing bowl and several strips of fabric. Before she struck the flint, a funnel of smoke issued from the bowl, snaking its way up her mirror, coalescing into words.

Will be in Paderau by the twin moons.

Marissa stared at the mirror before blowing the words into the air. Would it be just Valterys, or would Zakael join them, as well? The all too familiar jag of lust ran the length of her. The last time she and Zakael were alone, he'd wrapped her in his Dark Shanti, giving her the most exquisite pleasure; it was almost better than their lovemaking. Almost.

But there was no time to think about her physical needs. There was much to do to prepare for their arrival.

Chapter 15

DINNER at Paderau Palace did not mean sitting at a quiet table, partaking of a meal with one's immediate family. The event was orchestrated, timed perfectly to His Grace's wish. A hierarchy existed in the seating arrangements, and when the duke led Taryn to a table with the princesses, she tried and failed not to notice the stares of the other diners. He held a chair out for her between Sabina and Tessa, both of whom seemed pleased to have her as a dining companion.

Duke Anje signaled the start of the meal, and servants in fine livery brought out dishes on stunning silver trays. Exotic birds Taryn didn't recognize were cooked and then reassembled to look as if they were still alive, their feathers so meticulously placed Taryn didn't know where to cut. Freshly caught fish stared up at her, while other dishes—she hoped they were beef—glared at her with dead eyes. It was most unappetizing.

Servants roamed the tables, cutting through the masterpieces and serving slices of succulent dishes. More food than Taryn had ever seen in one place drifted through the hall, balanced on the servants' fingertips. They drank wine and toasted the duke when he stood to give thanks to his guests. He welcomed them all to his hall and bade them good fortune. When he confirmed the rumors Empress Lliandra would be at Paderau to celebrate Hayden's birthing day, as he called it, the room vibrated with excitement.

Hayden rose to thank his guests for honoring him by attending the masques. They held their glasses aloft, toasting the young marquis. When he winked at Taryn, Sabina pouted until Hayden looked her way, raising his glass.

Throughout the meal, performers walked among the tables, juggling knives to the astonished cheers of the guests. A group of tumblers entertained them with gasp-inducing tricks while minstrels strolled the room, singing jubilant tunes. The dazzling display of pomp surprised Taryn. On their journey to Paderau, the duke seemed low key, but the spectacle of wealth at his palace, and the extravagance of the evening reminded her that people weren't always as they appeared. Sometimes they came with a title.

With effort, Taryn avoided looking at Rhoane, who sat at the high table beside Marissa. Although she couldn't say why, she was bitterly hurt and angry with him for concealing not just his betrothal but that he was a prince. Not that it should matter, but it did. The rational part of her mind argued that a title did not change who he was, but somehow Taryn felt *less than* because of it. When he was just Rhoane, he was like her. Regular. Ordinary. Not a prince betrothed to a princess.

When dinner concluded, Hayden offered to escort her and Sabina on a walk through the gardens. He was uncharacteristically quiet as they meandered through the sculpted hedges, surrounded by the heady scent of summer blossoms. Taryn made idle chatter while the other two would comment or nod but made no effort to offer conversation of their own. It was as if they both had forgotten how to speak.

They sat on a bench beneath trees laden with ripening sargots, a fruit that looked like an orange but tasted more like a mango. Taryn loved them from the first bite she'd taken at Ravenwood. After Taryn expended herself of topics, she stood to leave.

"What are you about?" Hayden asked, a note of alarm in his voice.

"I'm exhausted. It's been a long day, and I can't help but think of that wonderful bed in my room." She plucked a sargot from the tree. "Enjoy the rest of your evening."

"I'll come with you," Sabina said, standing slowly.

"Stay here with Hayden. There's no reason you shouldn't enjoy such a lovely evening."

Taryn wove her way through the garden room with its glass ceiling and tall windows that afforded grand views. Several clusters of people milled about, and Taryn kept her head down to avoid being snagged into conversation. She slipped through the door and wandered down a darkened hallway before she realized she'd made a wrong turn. Voices a few feet away made her pause.

Marissa's throaty words floated toward Taryn. Instead of leaving, she kept near to the wall, inching closer. "Mother misses you, as do we all. You really should spend more time at the palace, Rhoane."

Taryn's heart jerked in her chest.

"I have been busy, Marissa. You know that."

"Yes, but it doesn't make it any easier. Tessa practically announced your betrothal today. Mother will be here tomorrow. You could make it official then."

"Do not start with that again." A cut of anger sliced his words.

"But Rhoane," fabric rustled against fabric, "if not now, when?"

Taryn spun to leave, catching her foot on a chair. The room twisted for a brief second before her head hit the floor with a resounding *thud*. Marissa muttered a curse, and then Rhoane was standing over her.

"Taryn? Are you all right?" He looked more concerned

than angry.

"I was trying to find my room, and I got lost." Ignoring Rhoane's outstretched hand, she pushed herself up. "I'm sorry to have disturbed you."

Rhoane called her name, but she ran from them, not stopping until she reached her room. She slammed the door behind her and turned the key in the lock with a savage twist. Her breath came in jagged gasps as she leaned her head against the wood.

When she turned around, Lorilee and Mayla stared at her. "What are you doing here?" Her tone was much harsher than she'd meant.

"We're to help prepare you for sleep, miss."

Taryn kept silent while they unpinned her braids, but when they tried to help her into a nightdress, she drew the line. They were getting too familiar with her, and boundaries needed to be set.

THE next morning, Taryn woke early and slipped from her room before Mayla or Lorilee could arrive to help her dress. She wasn't accustomed to having someone assist her with things she'd been doing her entire life. After wandering lost for a while, Taryn finally asked a servant to help her locate the kitchens.

She knocked on the open doorframe, but the busy workers ignored her. Two steps into the interior, however, drew the attention of a woman Taryn's height with dark curls and a pretty, heart shaped face.

"Can I help you?" she asked, her gaze locked on Taryn's face. A hum of voices tickled her mind, and her pendant thrummed pleasantly.

"I don't mean to be a bother, but I'd like something to

eat."

"And you thought you could walk into my kitchens and help yourself, yes?"

"Well, kind of. It seemed a bit silly to have someone bring me food when I'm perfectly capable of getting it myself."

The cook bit her cheek, making a hollow below her lovely green eyes. "And who shall I tell the duke is an impertinent guest?"

Taryn grinned at the cook's brashness. "Taryn, and I'm sure he won't be surprised."

The humming heightened and then lowered to a hush. A subtle change came over the cook. "Ah yes. The mysterious guest of the duke. Sit here while I have a meal prepared for you."

She sat alone at a table while she ate, ignoring the strange looks and barely tempered whispers. They could say whatever they wished, she was not, nor would she ever be, one of the stuffy courtiers upstairs, and the sooner everyone realized that, the better.

Meal finished, she called out her thanks to the cook, who gave a quick nod, adding, "You are welcome to dine in my kitchen anytime you wish." A few maids looked up in surprise.

Taryn inclined her head, hiding a smile. "I hope you can join me sometime." The look on the women's faces kept Taryn grinning wickedly all the way to the yard.

After an especially brutal training session with Baehlon, Taryn sought refuge in her room but was waylaid by Margaret Tan. She bustled into Taryn's suite, giving directions to her assistants and ordering Taryn to strip, all in one breath. Mayla and Lorilee scampered out of her way while she set up equipment in the sitting room. When Taryn saw the pile of clothing her assistant held, her stomach dipped at the growing debt she owed the duke.

Taryn stood self consciously, wearing what Margaret Tan called 'small clothes', which were nothing more than a few strips of fabric, and willed the minutes to tick past. The seamstress and her assistants didn't care if Taryn wasn't accustomed to undressing in front of people. When one of the assistants stood to adjust her blouse, she blanched. Shorter than her by half a head with a face prettier than some of the girls at the palace, she'd mistaken him for female. She sucked in a breath as he tucked the fabric around her waist, certain he could hear her racing heart.

Margaret Tan slapped her leg, commanding her to stop squirming. "Don't mind Tarro. He doesn't like girls."

The pretty young man looked up at her and nodded. "All of this," he waved at her breasts and privates, "is wasted on me."

Despite his claim, she was mortified he'd seen her naked. She rushed through trying on each outfit. But when Margaret Tan held out her dress for the masque, Taryn's breath caught. Brandt would have been overjoyed to see her in the beautiful creation.

Ice blue gossamer folds swept the ground, with tiny rhinestones dotting the skirt, giving the gown a starlit radiance. The silk bodice hugged her form, accentuating her curves in just the right places. Tarro handed her matching silk slippers and a mask made of silver with light blue feathers.

"It's gorgeous. I feel like a princess."

Margaret Tan nodded. "You look like a princess. Now, take it off before you ruin it." Tarro carefully hung it in the dressing room.

As the seamstress arranged her supplies in a basket, Taryn surreptitiously looked through her fabrics.

"Is there something in particular you're looking for?" Tarro's vibrato voice whispered beside her.

Taryn jerked her hand away, blushing. "I was um, looking

for leather."

"Leather?" A wicked smile lit up his face. "For what?"

"Well, pants for one, but also I want to make a ball. You know, to kick?"

He shook his head, the smile growing wider. "You are a mystery. I like that." He glanced quickly at Margaret Tan, "Let me see what I can do. Is there anything else you'd like?"

Scribbling quickly, Taryn sketched out a ball and several items she wouldn't mind adding to her wardrobe. Decent small clothes topped the list. Tarro took the paper and tucked it into his pocket with a wink and quick shake of his head toward Margaret Tan.

After they left, she stared at the dress for a long time, wondering how much something like it would cost. She needed to find a job if she were ever to repay Anje. The only problem was she didn't know what she was qualified to do.

The warmth of the summer day beckoned, and she rooted through the clothes in her armoire until she found loose-fitting slacks and a deep-blue blouse. They were the closest things she could find to shorts and far more comfortable in Paderau's heat than the fragile dresses Hayden had selected. She avoided the garden room and skirted the orchards to the river where she walked along the shore and mulled over her predicament. Her archeological skills wouldn't help her unless Aelinae had a need for such a person, which she doubted. She could certainly learn a trade, but what and where?

Rhoane moved in step beside her, startling her. "For gods' sake, Rhoane. You scared the crap out of me." The black court doublet and leather pants gave a dangerous edge to his look. As always, he wore Eleri boots polished to a high sheen.

"I did not tread lightly. I thought you heard my approach."

"I was distracted."

"I spoke with Baehlon this morning. He says your sword work is coming along well and you taught him some of your fighting techniques. He is impressed with your speed and dexterity."

"He's too stiff. He needs to do stretches to loosen up. Some of the other soldiers were watching and want to join us." She glanced sideways at him. "Do you think Duke Anje would mind?"

"I think he would be most grateful. A soldier can never be too skilled." He took her hand in his, tracing the runes on her wrist. "I owe you an apology, Taryn. I should have told you I was a prince."

"Why didn't you?" She cursed herself for the hurt that sounded in her voice.

"It was, and is, important to me that you know me as a man before you see me as a prince." His eyes sought hers. There was an emotion and meaning behind his words she didn't fully understand.

"I have to admit, if I'd known you were nobility, I don't know whether my perception of you would've been different. I'd like to think not, but who's to say?"

"I appreciate your understanding." He kissed her fingertips, holding them against his lips a moment too long before she pulled them free.

They walked along the shore to where the massive Kiltern River split in two, making a natural moat around Paderau. Boats floated up and down stream, bringing goods from Ulla to Paderau and then on farther south to Talaith.

"As for the other matter," Rhoane said in a quiet voice.

"Your betrothal to Marissa?"

"I am not betrothed to Marissa."

"I heard you talking last night." Taryn absently traced the runes on her hand.

"Marissa and I have been friends since she was a young girl. I have never once looked at her in any other way."

"So you're not betrothed?"

"Not to Marissa, no."

"Someone else then?"

He glanced out over the river toward the north. "A betrothal is an agreement that two people will be married at some time in their lives. It can be broken, and I believe it should be if the two do not love one another. When I was born, it was foretold with whom I would mate. Eleri mate for life with only one partner, and I have known about this match my entire life. But the woman in question is as yet unaware. I will not force her to be my partner unless she loves me and agrees to the conditions set forth by the Eleri."

He stopped, and she turned back to him, not wanting to hear more about his betrothed and yet needing to know every detail.

"Do you love her?"

Rhoane took her marked hand in his and traced the runes with his thumb. "Tell me, *Darennsai*, why is this so important to you?"

She liked the way her hand felt in his, the flow of his Shanti over her skin. She liked it a little too much. She forced herself to withdraw her hand, the words heavy on her tongue. "I've decided to ask the duke to help me find Nadra so that we might undo our bonds. I thought you should know before I leave Paderau."

"Where will you go?" A thrum of panic lifted the undercurrent of his words.

"When I promised Brandt I'd stay with you, it was mostly so you'd help me avenge his death. But now, I don't know, everything's changed."

"Nothing has changed, Taryn. Not me, if that is what you are implying."

"I didn't know you were promised to another. Not that I mind, but it wouldn't be fair to her to have me hanging around. It will just be better if I go and leave you to your life while I make my own."

He took her hand again, rubbing his thumb over her runes. "I never meant to hurt you. If I had thought for one moment that someone's loose tongue would cause you pain, I would have told you everything on that first day in the cavern."

"Brandt told me I could trust you. And I want to with all my heart."

"I will never lie to you, Taryn."

"You kept a couple of important details from me—that's like lying."

"No, I was trying not to frighten you. I have lived a long time, and there is much to tell of my story. I did not want to burden you with everything at once. If we are to be friends, you will have to learn to trust me implicitly. I will have to do the same."

"You have no idea how much I'd like that, but I don't like secrets."

"Neither do I. However, there might come a time when you will have the choice to tell me something that could hurt me or to keep it to yourself to save my feelings. I will understand, should that ever happen."

He kissed the insides of her wrists, and white heat twisted her gut. "Exactly how old are you, anyway?"

"One hundred eighty-seven this past harvest."

"Seriously? How long do the Eleri live?"

"Several thousand seasons if one is lucky."

"That's a long time." His betrothed was probably an Eleri princess, and they would live a long and happy life.

"Will you postpone your plans until we reach Talaith? I know the duke enjoys your company and would be vexed if you left. Just until Talaith, and then we can send for Nadra, if you so desire."

She was close enough to feel his body heat, smell the

scent of forest and loam that intoxicated her. "How long will that be?"

"A fortnight or so." He put his hand against hers, and the runes sparked to life. A tremor ran the length of her, igniting a flame that burned low and deep. A small moan slipped from her throat to her lips.

Rhoane pulled away so suddenly she reeled back. "What's wrong?"

"I must go."

"Rhoane." Taryn's voice was low, needy. She reached for him but did not touch him. "I'll wait until Talaith."

They stood apart for several moments, waves of heat pulsing from him to her and back.

"Promise you will never doubt me again?" Rhoane said at last, his voice a raw whisper.

"I promise."

He closed the space between them and held her face in his hands. His lips brushed against hers, tentative. Unexpected, but not unwanted. She gave in to the sensations of hot and cold that teased her nerves, making her knees give way. Rhoane pulled her against him, steadying her. His lips pressed harder, urgent in their need. She should stop him, remind him he was betrothed, but she let him kiss her.

He tasted of crisp green apple and mint. Her hands scraped over his silk tunic to the base of his neck. When her fingertips touched his skin, searing heat pulsed through her, blocking out all thought save for Rhoane. He was ice and fire, love and death, lust and longing. His hands roamed over her back to her hair, stroking her braids before pulling them taut. His lips stayed on hers, his tongue exploring, probing, teasing until she buzzed with an impatient hunger.

When he lifted his head, she swooned with the sudden release. *"Tan rael danlith, Darennsai."*

"What does that mean?" Through the fog in her brain,

she could still feel his lips on hers.

"It is an Eleri custom to wish one good fortune on their birthing day. Today you are thirty-five summers." She was touched he remembered. For the better part of the day, she'd been trying to forget.

"Best birthday gift ever." She grinned, pushing aside the slice of guilt that nagged her happiness.

"Today, you have reached your majority."

"My majority?" She tore her gaze away from his lips, from the slight redness and swelling she knew she'd caused.

"For those with power, it is when their strength is fully realized. For those without it, is when they are considered adults and have no more allegiance to their parents. Although the latter is more a technicality because familial honor is strong on Aelinae."

His words sobered her. She had no family on Aelinae. No honor. No allegiance. A wave of sadness almost crushed her. "I wish Brandt were here."

Rhoane wrapped his arms protectively around her, and she resisted the urge to snuggle into him.

"He is, Taryn. Every day he is with you; you just need to know where to look."

"Why did he have to leave Aelinae? Was he banished?"

Rhoane's chest rose and lowered with his deep inhales, his heart beating a fierce rhythm echoed by her own. The song of her sword played mournfully in her mind.

"Banished? No. Brandt held a position of great importance to the empress. When we reach Talaith, I am sure she will explain everything to you."

No good would come of speculation, so Taryn pushed aside thoughts of Talaith and Brandt and the empress. It was her birthday; she didn't want to be sad. Lifting her face to his, she asked, "Will you dance with me tonight? Margaret Tan made me this dress and Hayden taught me all those steps—it would be a shame to waste all their hard work."

His eyes sparkled with mischief. "I will dance with you if you let me train with you tomorrow."

"Deal."

He turned to leave but hesitated, his gaze razing the slacks and blouse she wore. "And to think you told me you do not wear gowns."

"I'm full of all kinds of surprises, *Your Highness*." Her curtsey, reserved for the highest ranking rulers only, skimmed the ground.

His chuckle drifted in his wake as he walked away, his footsteps crunching on the gravel. When they faded completely, she exhaled the breath she'd been holding.

The kiss was for her birthday. It meant nothing.

He wasn't hers, could never be hers.

Chapter 16

THE ceiling of the grand ballroom had been painted in painstaking detail to resemble the night sky. ShantiMari stars twinkled against the midnight background, and misty nebulae of pinks and purples scattered across the cosmic space. With the enhanced lighting, it looked magical, enchanted. It took Taryn several minutes to accustom her sight to that much ShantiMari, but eventually she was able to mute the threads until they were barely noticeable.

The gems in Taryn's gown caught the light of every candle they passed, winking in and out, casting rainbows of color across the floor. She fidgeted beside Baehlon, who looked resplendent in a crimson doublet and hose. His mask of gold feathers rested atop his braids, which he'd adorned with golden bells for the evening.

"Don't be nervous," his deep bass whispered.

High ranking men and women from all over Aelinae came to Paderau for Hayden's masques. It was a tradition started after the birth of the duke's firstborn, and it continued with his only surviving child. For the partygoers, it was a chance to reconnect with friends, discuss business, and of course, to mingle with nobility.

Every style of clothing was represented, from the loose-fitting slacks of the Ullan men, to the tight, almost suffocating, leather corsets of the warrior women known as Sitari. Their scarred faces and blue, tattooed bodies were a stark contrast to the pale Aelan women. Feathers adorned masks, some covering faces but most resting atop dramatically styled hair. Jewels of every shape and color bedecked throats, arms, ears, and wrists—even ankles for the Summerlands women. The glittering array of wealth exposed Taryn's plainness, assured her insignificance.

Baehlon led her through the room, nodding in greeting to several people. Curious stares followed wherever they went.

"See? They know I'm not one of them."

Baehlon's soft chuckle caressed her battered nerves. "Thank the gods you aren't. Pompous arses, every one. If you ever become like them, I'll take a switch to your backside."

"You do, and I'll do more than toss you on your back."

"There it is! Keep that fire, girl, and ignore what the court thinks."

She straightened, pulling her shoulders taut. "I will."

A smile broke across his face, lessening the deep creases between his brows.

"There it is! That's the smile I've been waiting for," she teased. "Seriously, though. Thank you for everything. The scabbard, the advice, your lessons—I truly appreciate it."

Two bells earlier, Baehlon and the others had surprised Taryn with gifts for her birthday. Even the young princesses, which humbled Taryn. She'd been surprised Rhoane remembered it was her birthday, but to have Faelara and Myrddin, as well as Anje and Hayden, celebrate her day, affected her. It made her decision to leave all the more difficult.

"You best take care of that sword. Keep it in the scabbard at all times unless you're using it."

"It's not bespelled, is it?"

He shook his head, creating a tinkling cascade of bells.

"Always so suspicious."

"I think I have reason to be, don't you?" A low growl came from her abdomen. "Can't we eat yet? I'm starving."

Heavenly smells drifted from tables set along the walls, laden with food. Sumptuous delicacies nestled next to spiced meats on one table; on another frothy confections drizzled with honey competed for dominance with puff pastries covered in what Taryn hoped was chocolate.

"Not until the empress arrives."

"Stupid rule." Taryn grumbled at the same time trumpets played a fanfare, signaling the arrival of the empress and her daughters.

They made their way to the center of the room and stood beside Faelara. Taryn bounced on the balls of her feet with pent-up anticipation. When the chamberlain called out Rhoane's name, a small shiver of excitement traveled up her spine. Dressed in a silvery blue tunic with a delicate leaf motif embroidered along the edges, he looked every inch a prince with his silver coronet resting in his curls. The princesses were introduced one by one. Each wore a charming tiara that matched her lavish gown. Taryn snuck several glances at Rhoane, remembering the kiss they shared.

Only when the empress was announced did she fully pull her attention away. Lliandra's glorious hair cascaded over her shoulders to a dress of pale green chiffon. A large gold crown encrusted with jewels caught the light, sending sparks of color throughout the room. An etherealness surrounded the empress, as if she had stepped down from the enchanted ceiling.

"They are magnificent, are they not?" Faelara whispered to Taryn.

She watched the princesses take to the dance floor with their partners. "They seemed so normal yesterday, but to look at them now with their tiaras and fancy dresses…" She sighed, "I feel like I'm in a fairy tale."

Duke Anje escorted Lliandra to the dance floor, passing them on their way. The empress nodded to Faelara and Baehlon. Her deep blue eyes took in Taryn with a glance, and then she was gone without a hint of acknowledgment. The rebuff stung for reasons Taryn didn't quite comprehend.

Throughout the night, her pendant sizzled and snapped at her with no clear reason. Each time Taryn would search the room, she found nothing amiss. She spent most of her time with Sabina, enjoying several desserts while her new friend gave an informal summary of the guests. After Sabina's fourth dramatic sigh, Taryn faced the exotic beauty and asked what was troubling her.

Sabina sulked, sniffing at the puff pastry on her plate. "All Hayden talks of is *Taryn did this* and *Taryn said that*. According to him, you are the most interesting girl he's ever met."

Taryn shrugged. "Then he hasn't met many girls, I'd think."

"See? You're funny, whereas I'm not, and I'm afraid Hayden finds me boring."

She was a sweet enough girl, but Sabina *was* boring. All the princesses were. As far as Taryn could tell, their lives consisted of playing cards, embroidery, and gossip.

"Besides, I have no ShantiMari. The empress would never grant her consent for us to wed."

"So? I don't have ShantiMari, either. That shouldn't define your worth, and if anyone lets it, then they don't deserve you."

"That is very nice of you to say, but you are quite mistaken."

"Come with me." With Sabina close behind, she made her way to where Hayden was talking to Rhoane.

"You taught me all those dance steps," she said to Hayden.

"It would be a shame to waste that time and effort."

"Indeed it would." Hayden held out his arm to escort her to the dance floor.

"Not me." She pulled Sabina up behind her. "My friend." He looked surprised but not unhappy.

"Princess, it would be my pleasure to have this dance with you." Sabina wrapped her arm around his, and they made their way through the crowd.

Taryn turned to Rhoane. "You did promise me a dance, if I recall correctly."

"That is a very nice thing you are doing." He gestured to Hayden and Sabina.

"Am I that obvious?"

"Not to Hayden."

He placed his hand on her lower back and directed her into the dance. Her focus shifted from the warmth of his touch to the dance steps with no small amount of effort. When the song ended, she was delighted he kept his grip on her for another dance. It called for them to switch partners, and Taryn left Rhoane's embrace grudgingly. On her second pass, Taryn spun into the arms of the one man she never thought she'd see at Paderau.

He wore a mask, but Taryn would know Zakael anywhere. He pulled her to him with a devious grin and a glint to his steel eyes. "You dance remarkably well."

Taryn's throat constricted with each beat of her racing heart, cutting off much needed air. "What are you doing here?" she managed to wheeze.

"Dancing. I thought that was obvious."

Taryn tried to break free, but Zakael held her fast. "Let me go or I'll scream."

"And then what?" He moved close so only she could hear. "I didn't kill Brandt. The Shanti I threw at him was meant to stun, nothing more. His heart was old, but that's no fault of mine."

Taryn struggled against the firm grip he had on her wrist.

He pressed against her, his lips at her ear. "Gods, but I admire a girl with strength. Imagine what we could do together, Taryn." An unholy growl came from his throat. "We would be unstoppable."

Taryn jerked away but not before Marissa grabbed her by the upper arm, her nails cutting Taryn's flesh. Rhoane was suddenly beside her. Jaw tight, eyes narrowed, power circling him with controlled restraint.

"Marissa, is there a problem?" His glance went from Taryn to the masked Zakael.

"Of course not, Your Highness. The duke's guest looked pale and I was concerned for her safety, but her color's returned so all is well." She smoothed a hand down Taryn's arm, caressing the skin with blistered fingertips.

"You seem to have burned yourself, Princess," Rhoane said, reaching out to inspect Marissa's wounds.

She snatched her hand back. "It's nothing but a trifle. Clumsiness on my part. I thank you for your concern." She turned to Zakael and inclined her head. "Sir, I believe there was a remarkable young woman who wished to dance with you, if you'll come with me?"

They left before Rhoane or Taryn could say another word. "What the hell is he doing here?"

Rhoane stared after the couple. "Who?"

"Zakael." Taryn almost spit the word.

"You must be mistaken. He would not dare come here."

"He told me so himself. Even went so far as to tell me it was Brandt's weak heart that killed him, not his Shanti."

A storm raged over Rhoane's features in an instant and then dissipated. The swiftness of his emotions rocked Taryn nearly as much as seeing Zakael.

Rhoane beckoned Hayden from the dance and ordered

him to take Taryn outside and stay with her. Then he disappeared into the crowd.

Hayden hadn't seen Zakael or the confrontation with Marissa, so quickly was it over. Since Rhoane had given him no reason why he needed to stay with Taryn, he didn't realize there was a threat, and Taryn wasn't going to be the one to tell him.

He swiped two glasses of wine from a passing servant and chatted about Sabina as he steered Taryn to the balcony. She drank the wine in one long gulp, willing her heart to slow, her breathing to normalize. Whatever she and Hayden discussed, it was lost to the blur of chaotic thoughts running through her mind.

Rhoane returned at some point, thanked Hayden for staying with her, and then Hayden moved off. Her pulse beat in her ears, the rush of adrenaline making everything jumpy and out of focus.

Rhoane's hand covered hers. *Breathe, Taryn.*

She inhaled until the warm night air tickled the back of her throat, filled her lungs. A few more deep breaths brought the calm she needed.

She entwined her fingers in his. "Is he gone?"

Rhoane leaned against the balcony, looking up to the night sky. "It would appear so."

Taryn followed his gaze and blinked at the two moons she saw. "Were those always there and I missed them?"

"They are only visible at midsummer and midwintertide. The rest of the time you can only see one moon."

"I wonder where the other one goes."

Sabina rushed up to them, panting and bouncing on her toes. "Hayden has promised to teach me to ride. I've never been on a horse, and I'm terrified." She squealed and rushed back to the dance floor.

"The princesses are very taken with you."

"I'm honored to call them my friends," Taryn said simply. Zakael's appearance had drained her, but she wouldn't let him ruin her night. "Can we stay here for a few more minutes and then dance again?"

Rhoane squeezed her fingertips. "Of course."

Taryn danced with Rhoane and the younger princesses until the two moons were low in the eastern sky. When her eyes could barely stay open, Hayden offered to escort her to her rooms. They stumbled through the halls, having drunk a little too much wine. At her door, Hayden bowed low, his palm pressed against his chest.

"Good night, fair maiden. May your dreams be sweet and the morning light late. Or something. Retreat?" He shook his head and laughed at his dreadful attempt at poetry.

Taryn giggled and pushed him down the hallway. "Thank you for a perfect birthday, my friend."

Hayden saluted her and swaggered off, disappearing in the darkness.

She fumbled with the doorknob and then tumbled into her room, sobering the instant she saw the spectral form of her grandfather.

He drifted close, greeting her astonished stare with an airy hug and kiss.

"How is this possible?" She touched his cheek, feeling warmth beneath her fingertips.

"My spirit dwells on Dal Tara. It is because of your love for me that I am able to manifest myself to this degree."

"But, you're... I saw Nadra take you away."

"Did you think I would forget what today is?" He indicated the table where a wrapped box waited.

Taryn gently opened it, saving the paper. Inside, nestled on a bed of blue satin, was a small stone. "It's lovely." She held it up, squinting in the candlelight. Tiny flecks of silver sparkled within the cream-colored rock.

"It's a moonstone. It will provide you with comfort when the darkness becomes too much to bear."

A small cry escaped her. "Thank you, Baba. I will keep it with me, always."

"I'm pleased you've made friends." He touched the book of fairy tales Eliahnna had given her, then the dagger from Tessa. He picked up Myrddin's gift—a large clear marble that he'd called a looking glass.

Brandt rolled the ball between his fingers with a somber chuckle. "One of Myrddin's favorite inventions, this. I'm sure he told you how to call forth an image of those you love, but did he also tell you that it is useful to see what has been?"

Taryn shook her head. She didn't fully understand how the marble worked. Brandt demonstrated by asking the ball to show Taryn the entrance of Lliandra and the princesses to the masque. Taryn watched, enthralled, as they entered the Great Hall. The procession was as exciting as the first time she saw it.

"That's remarkable."

"Yes, it is, really." Brandt replaced the clear orb in its box. "But don't let on how impressed you are. Myrddin's ego is big enough already." Warmth suffused his words.

"You and Myrddin were close?"

"Like brothers." A wistful smile lit up his face. "We used to terrorize the empress, driving her to distraction. Not Lliandra, mind you, but her mother. We practically raised Lliandra and Gwyneira."

When Brandt started to fade, Taryn reached toward him. "Please, stay a little longer."

"My time here draws to a close. I love you, darling girl."

"I love you, Baba." But he was already gone.

She stayed rooted where she was, in the hope he would reappear. When it became clear he wouldn't return, she shuffled through the empty rooms. Apparently, the best way to avoid having maids fuss over you was to stay out late enough. As she made her way to the dressing room, a glimmer of ShantiMari caught her attention.

The wards on the cupboard were tattered wisps. Taryn carefully opened the door to make certain the sword and seal remained untouched. Relief flooded through her at the sight of them. In the morning, she'd have Faelara strengthen the wards. After taking care to close the compartment, Taryn retrieved the looking glass.

"Show me who entered my rooms," she commanded the ball.

A slight figure dressed in a dark cloak lit up the clear marble. Taryn couldn't tell who it was, but the person roamed her suite with authority. At the secured compartment, the figure flinched from a flare of Faelara's ShantiMari. A minute later, the intruder left Taryn's rooms.

It was then she remembered Marissa's scorched fingertips.

Chapter 17

CANDLES in glass vases hung from branches, giving the gardens a misty glow. Ladies and lords strolled the gravel paths, talking in hushed tones as if not to disturb the ambiance of the night. Valterys kept himself cloaked in shadow, mingling through the crowds, careful not to disturb anyone. Marissa's suggestion that they attend the masque was originally met with disdain, but the temptation to be near Lliandra, to possibly learn something of her plans, swayed his opinion. If what Marissa said was true, the Eirielle would be there tonight, which only made the evening more enticing. Valterys pulled the darkness tight around him while making his way closer to the empress.

Lliandra sat in an elaborate chair—the best they could find to resemble a throne, most likely—looking stunningly regal and beautiful. Even after many seasons, she still excited him in ways no other woman could. When she bent to speak with a courtier, Valterys saw the tiny pulse flutter beneath the creamy skin of her throat. He edged closer still. Close enough that he could reach out to place his hands around her delicate neck and squeeze the life from her if he so desired.

For the briefest of moments, he allowed himself to imagine her face as she took her last breaths. A delicious warmth spread from his groin, and his fingers flexed in anticipation. Myrddin stepped beside Lliandra to whisper fervently in her ear, altogether destroying Valterys's fantasy.

A commotion on the dance floor drew his attention and he looked up in time to see Zakael storming off with Marissa. In their wake, a striking girl, tall with golden curls and piercing blue eyes, was led away by the duke's son. A memory seized him of a time long past when Lliandra was carefree, before her crown became a weapon, when she would smile and dance through the night. The girl he saw on the balcony with young Lord Valen could have been her twin. He had no doubt she was Lliandra's missing child.

His daughter.

If memory served, tonight was her birthing day, and yet Lliandra did nothing to acknowledge the girl. Not even a glance or discreet wave. Whatever the woman was planning, he needed to find out.

Prince Rhoane approached Lliandra, and, to her hearing alone, told her of Marissa's guest. Despite the mask, Zakael had been identified. The empress remained calm, but her pulse quickened ever so slightly. Myrddin was sent to find the errant princess, and then, as if nothing had happened, Lliandra rose from her chair, and held out her hand for Rhoane to take. They joined others on the dance floor, blending seamlessly into the crowd.

Valterys hurried from the ballroom and found Zakael with Marissa in the farthest corner of the garden. They argued in tense, whispered tones.

"Rhoane saw the blisters. I doubt he'll believe my excuse of clumsiness," Marissa hissed.

"He doesn't know you tried to undo the wards. Act as if nothing is wrong. You're too emotional. You must learn to control yourself."

"Me? It was you who demanded we get near enough that you could see the girl. If not for you, we wouldn't have been discovered."

Valterys let the shadows fall away, and Marissa jumped at his sudden appearance. "What are you doing here?"

"Your mother has sent her watchdog after you. Perhaps you shouldn't be seen with my son."

Marissa's lovely lavender eyes flashed raw anger for a moment before she inclined her head. "Thank you, my lord." She turned to Zakael. "We will speak more of this on the morrow." She stormed away, the gravel path crunching beneath her delicate slippers.

"Did you accomplish what you came for?" he asked Zakael.

"I would not have thought it, but by her own admission it is the same girl as in the cavern. Blood's oath, what a difference a gown makes."

"Stay away from her. Get to the inn, and do not be seen. I must go see to something before we reach Talaith."

Zakael quickly transformed into a levon, rising into the air, beating his slender wings hard to catch an updraft. He flew away from the palace toward the city.

At least the boy had the good sense to listen to his father. For once. Valterys saw the desire in Zakael's eyes when he spoke of Taryn. The fact she was his half-sister meant nothing to him. If anything, it made her all the more enticing. Their offspring would be more powerful than any mage or sorcerer in all of Aelinae.

Valterys also changed into a levon and rose high into the air, gliding on an undercurrent while he considered the possibility of Zakael siring Taryn's child. Rykoto would never allow it. He had plans for Taryn that didn't include Zakael, or Valterys for that matter.

Before the sun rose in the west, he circled above the temple. The instant his talons landed on the snow-covered ground, he shook out his wings, transforming back into a man. Summer's warm breezes never touched the frozen north, leaving this part of Aelinae perpetually in wintertide. He shivered against the cold as he entered the temple, sending flames dancing around the pillars. Next, he went to the altar and knelt, his fingertips touching the ground.

"Great lord, feel my flames, hear my words. Show me thy face that I might know your bidding." While he spoke in the ancient tongue, tiles rose in the floor, making a labyrinth leading to a hole about the width of a gold crown. Through that tiny opening, Rykoto could stretch out to taste the world denied him.

An image of a man, black hair streaked with flames and lips of blood, appeared against the flames. "My son, what have you brought for me this night? It is midsummer and two moons shine on us."

Damn. "My lord, it is not time for your feeding."

Flames touched the ceiling, scorching it. "You come here without a sacrifice? My hunger knows no bounds. Be gone with you. Disturb me not until you have fulfilled my desire."

"Great Lord Rykoto, the Eirielle has returned."

"So my dreams were correct. I've sensed his presence this past moonturn. Where is he now?"

"She is with the Lady of Light in Paderau." That Rykoto could only sense Taryn, and not even accurately, disturbed Valterys. Nadra must have concealed her well.

Rykoto's dark eyes danced with flames. "A girl?" His forked tongue flicked over his lips, smearing blood across his chin. "How sweet she will taste." The flames quivered against the air.

Valterys suppressed a shudder. "She will be yours, I promise this." He placed his fist over his heart, bowing his head.

"Show her to me." An image materialized in the fire, and Taryn's face danced before them. Rykoto moaned in ecstasy. "My desire grows even now." His black eyes turned on Valterys. "And my queen?"

"She looks forward to her union with you." He worried for Marissa only a moment before casting aside his concern. It was what she wanted. She understood the risk.

"When I possess the steel of Ohlin, the milk of Nadra, and the tear of Aelinae, then you will have your prize. You will be a god with a world to command as you wish."

Valterys could hardly breathe, his heart pumped hard against his chest into his throat. "Thank you, Great Lord. I am ever your humble servant." He bent and kissed the floor, feeling the heat rise from Rykoto's prison.

The god's face dissolved from the flames. "Fulfill my desire. Bring me the girl."

Chapter 18

VALTERYS stood over Taryn, holding the Seal of Ardyn in his hands. Slowly, he broke it apart, unleashing a flood of evil across the lands of Aelinae. Hordes of creatures charged through towns, killing people and ravaging the landscape.

Taryn raced to the palace, where she found Marissa standing over Rhoane with the Sword of Ohlin in her hands. When her eyes met Taryn's, she plunged the sword through Rhoane's chest. Taryn cried out, but a thread of lavender ShantiMari snaked its way toward Taryn, wrapping around her neck until she couldn't breathe.

Marissa's manic laughter throbbed in Taryn's head as darkness closed around her. Zakael stooped to pluck Rhoane's heart from his open chest. With a twitch of his fingers, the still-beating heart burst, spewing blood over Zakael. He licked at his fingers, an ugly grin on his face.

Taryn awoke in a pool of sweat, her hair matted to her head, heart racing from the nightmare. The scent of Rhoane's blood lingered in her nostrils.

Rhoane! Her limbs trembled as she repeated to herself that it was only a dream. Rhoane was safe. Most likely sleeping. Unharmed. Her pendant sent flicks of cold against her chest. A tune heavy with drums beat in her mind. A death march.

She threw the sheets off and stumbled to the cupboard where Faelara's wards still hung in tatters. With clumsy hands, she opened the door, and there, shining in the dim light, was the sword. The seal was tucked behind the weapon.

Tears—from gratitude or fear, she wasn't sure—stung her eyes.

The door to her rooms banged open then slammed shut, and she froze, eyes wide, alert to the tiniest movement. Someone was in the outer room, heading her way.

She grabbed the sword and pressed herself against the wall. Heavy footfalls sounded just outside her bedroom. Hands slick with sweat gripped the hilt. She lifted the sword, ready to attack. Rhoane stepped through the door, and Taryn stopped mid-swing.

"Rhoane? What are you doing here?"

He took a step back, eyeing the sword half a foot from his head. "You called me." He tapped his temple. "There was distress in your voice."

Her body shook with the release of adrenaline. She lowered the sword, feeling more than a little stupid. "I did? I, uh, I had a nightmare." Part of his nightshirt hung loose from his leather pants, and his disheveled hair looked very un-Rhoane-like. "I didn't mean to call you. I'm sorry."

Relief at seeing him alive flooded through her with chilling speed. An involuntary shiver brought Rhoane's attention squarely on her. "Are you sure you are well?"

"Yes. I think. Mostly, maybe." She replaced the sword and carefully shut the cupboard door. "If you wouldn't mind adding a ward or two, I'd be grateful."

Rhoane said nothing as he knelt beside her and placed several wards over the closed door. She followed his strands, mentally mimicking what he did. The song her sword sang shifted as he worked. The heavy bass changed to an up-tempo tune similar to one she had danced to last night. With

Rhoane. Her fingertips touched her pendant, and the melody quieted.

When he finished his warding, he stood, leaving Taryn in the awkward position of kneeling before him, her head level with his groin. Distracting thoughts pulled her mind where it shouldn't be. With effort, she pushed them aside and stood to face Rhoane.

"Again, thank you." She glanced at the cupboard, debating whether to tell him about her suspicions. Since that's all they were, she kept quiet.

"It will be light soon. You should send for your maids, get something to eat before you meet with Baehlon." A twinkle of mischief danced at the edges of his eyes. "You want to be at your best today."

"I'll be fine." She answered his challenge with a grin. "It's you I'm worried about."

After he left, she dressed in leather pants and a loose blouse. Instead of calling for her maids, she hurried to the kitchens, losing her way twice before she found the small doorway that led to the cavernous rooms.

The main area was a hive of activity with servants scurrying in every direction. Taryn stood to the side, not wanting to get in the way, while at the same time trying to catch someone's attention.

A young woman ran past with a tray of heavenly smelling rolls, followed closely by a man carrying a salver overflowing with crocks of cream and butter. Her stomach groaned in appreciation.

"You can't be here." A young fellow, not more than twelve by the looks of him, stared Taryn down. "Get back to the performer's tents. You'll get your grub soon enough."

"I'm not—" Taryn started to explain, but was interrupted by a lilting voice that came from behind her.

"She is not with the performers." The duke's cook

stepped into Taryn's vision. The first time they met, Taryn had thought her pretty but, on seeing her again, realized she had truly underestimated the woman's looks. Eyes the color of green sea glass missed nothing.

Taryn again heard the incessant buzzing, like that of a thousand voices speaking at once. The woman shooed the boy and he left. But not before giving Taryn a warning look. With another wave, the buzzing faded and then stopped completely.

The cook clapped her hands together, making puffs of flour that floated in the air between them. "We did not properly meet yesterday. I am Carga, the duke's head chef."

"Taryn." She held out her hand, but Carga didn't take it. Instead, she looked questioningly at Taryn. "Where I come from, you shake hands when you meet."

"Ah." Carga took her hand. "It is a pleasure to meet you, Taryn."

"And you, Carga. Do you mind if I breakfast here again? I hate to bother my maids."

Carga pulled out a chair and indicated Taryn should sit. She called orders to the boy and settled into the seat beside Taryn.

The boy brought them two steaming cups of grhom and a plate of food for Taryn. "Thank you, Gris," the cook said.

He gave Carga a smile, followed by a scowl to Taryn.

"I don't think he likes me."

"Gris does not trust the upstairs folk. Too many nobles think they are above the rules."

"And here I am breaking them." Taryn watched the boy for a few minutes, noting the slight limp in his walk, the way he favored his left hand over his right. "What happened to him?"

Carga regarded her for a long breath and said finally, "He was abused. Not for pleasure. For sport. Some nobles think servants are nothing more than chattel, put here to entertain them. Gris was popular in the hunt."

"The hunt? Like horses and dogs chasing him?" Her stomach churned, spoiling the few bites of food she'd eaten and souring the grhom she'd drank.

Carga studied her reactions with calm scrutiny. "I am afraid so."

"That's disgusting. The duke doesn't know, does he?"

"I would hope not." She pointed to Taryn's meal. "Eat. You will need your strength today, yes?"

"Yeah. But how did you know?"

A smile transformed the woman's face. Gone was the sadness in her eyes. It was replaced with a hint of mischief. "There is nothing that happens in this palace that we do not hear. You are the girl everyone is talking about. The one who trains with a sword and dances with princes, and yet no one knows where you come from or what House you represent. You are quite the curiosity."

"Seriously? That's just great." Taryn stabbed a sausage with her fork. "These people need a hobby," she mumbled around a huge bite.

Carga slid from the stool and placed a warm hand on Taryn's sleeve. "*You* are their hobby. They delight in rumor and intrigue. My advice would be not to give them anything to gossip about. I will let you finish your meal in peace."

Taryn ate her meal in silence, unsure how to handle the unwanted attention. If she confronted the courtiers directly, that would encourage them to dig into her background. Since that wouldn't end well for anyone, the best course of action was as Carga said—do nothing. At least not as far as the gossipers were concerned.

She arrived at the training ring just as eighth bell tolled. Baehlon trailed a few minutes later, followed by twenty or so soldiers. They were well into their warm-up when Rhoane arrived, looking slightly less disheveled than he had earlier.

The lesson went better than she could've hoped. The soldiers, all trained in fighting and weaponry, caught on to the forms quickly. After two bells, she called an end to the training with the promise of another lesson in two days' time.

Rhoane caught up to her halfway to the palace. Rivulets of sweat coursed down the sides of his face, and his tunic was stained from his exertion. "What is it you are fond of saying? That kicked my ass."

A little thrill trumpeted through her. If Rhoane found it difficult, she'd taught it right. "You did well today. I'm impressed."

"I will be feeling my age later, I am sure."

"Yes, you will, old man." She glanced at the courtiers who mingled throughout the room. "I need to talk to you. Do you have a few minutes?"

"Of course. What is it?"

"Not here."

She rushed through the hallways with Rhoane beside her. Once they were in her rooms, Rhoane ensconced them in a ward for privacy.

"At Ravenwood," she began, not certain how Rhoane would react to what she had to say but certain he needed to hear it, "I saw Valterys in the hallway with you and the others. Don't ask me how because I'm not sure. Anyway, he was demanding the sword, so everyone thought he put the damned thing over Hayden's chest. But he went to the room you were standing in front of, not Hayden's room. I didn't think about it at the time because I was in too much pain, but this morning I realized that if he had been the one to put the sword over Hayden, wouldn't he remember which room it was in? Hayden's room was down the hall in the opposite direction." She waited for him to process what she'd said.

"If not Valterys, then who tried to kill Hayden?" Rhoane

paced around the room, stopping in front of the windows.

Taryn shifted uncomfortably in her seat. "I think it was Marissa."

His hands gripped the windowsill until his knuckles turned white. "It cannot be. She is heir to the Light Throne."

"And that means what?"

"She is the crown princess and when Lliandra dies, she will become the next empress, the Lady of Light and sit on the Light Throne."

"Is it really made of light?"

Rhoane chuckled. "Not of its own accord."

"Okay well, Light stuff aside, Marissa has the same color ShantiMari that was holding the sword over Hayden."

"Is it not possible for someone else to have the same as her?"

Taryn did her best to explain the subtle nuances she saw. "From what I can tell, the color of one's ShantiMari is tied to the shade of their eyes. I first noticed it in the cavern, remember, when you asked what lights I saw? Well, Brandt's Shanti was amber, like his eyes, yours pale green, Zakael's grey, etc. Then I started to notice everyone's power has a certain feel to it, like a signature. Faelara's is nurturing, Myrddin's cool, yours protective. What I felt in my dream was the same as the ShantiMari at Ravenwood and, again when I met Marissa the first day in the garden room. It wasn't until this morning that I put everything together."

Rhoane stood facing her, his face pinched with discord. "You must understand. I have known Marissa her whole life. She can be petty at times, but what you are suggesting is beyond treason."

"I know, and I'm sorry, Rhoane. I didn't want to believe it, either. Everyone loves her. But if she's the one who did that to Hayden, don't we need to know?"

"I cannot in good conscience call into question the

motives of the crown princess. Still, you make a valid point that if she is involved with Valterys somehow," he paused, shaking his head, "I hate to even think it, but we should watch her."

"We need someone on the inside, like Sabina."

His look told her he didn't like the suggestion, but after a few moments, he nodded. "We must be discreet. Are you certain you can trust the Summerlands princess?"

"No, but then again, I don't know that I can trust you, either. That's why it's called faith. You need to have some in me right now, and we both need to have a little in Sabina." Taryn pointed to her bedroom. "Someone broke in here last night trying to steal the sword. Tell yourself that it wasn't Marissa all you want, but my money's on the woman who had suspicious blisters on her fingertips. My guess is, she's playing both sides, and she's the one who can't be trusted."

"Unfortunately, right now that is all you have—a guess. Until we have proof, we cannot do anything to cause alarm."

A timid knock at the door startled them.

"Are you expecting someone?" Rhoane asked, a hint of annoyance in his voice.

"I don't think so."

Taryn opened the door to Margaret Tan's assistant Tarro. "I have your gown for tonight. And this…" He held up a wobbly looking blob of leather.

"Oh my God, you didn't?" At Tarro's sheepish look and slight blush, she threw her arms around his neck. "Thank you! I don't know how I can ever repay you." She took the leather sack from him and bounced it on her foot several times while Tarro hung her dress in the other room.

"What is it?" Rhoane asked, his head cocked to the side.

"A football. It needs air, though." A mischievous smile crept up to her cheeks. "Do you think you could, you know, add a bit of ShantiMari to the ball, and make it airtight?"

"Is this for the game you told me about?" Rhoane took the leather from her, rolled it in his hands, and examined it from all angles.

"Yes. And if you give the ball some bounce, we can have a game later. Can you do it?"

Rhoane pressed his hands together, squishing the ball. Slowly, it began to inflate until filled. Taryn squeezed it a few times before bouncing it on the floor. Satisfied it would do, she dribbled the ball around her room before kicking it gently onto a love seat.

"Brilliant. Can you find Hayden and see if he wants to play? We'll need at least ten people."

Rhoane looked unconvinced. "If that is your wish, I will seek out players." His glance took in Tarro and returned to her. "As for the other issue, we will continue our discussion later."

"I'm breathless with anticipation."

He left with a chuckle and shake of his head. When the door clicked shut, Taryn turned to Tarro. "I need shorts, a T-shirt, and shoes. What have we got to work with?"

Chapter 19

THE empress and her daughters sat beneath a small pavilion as they watched Taryn's spectacle on the grass. Once word spread that the Offlander wished to partake of a ball game, Lliandra insisted her brood attend.

Marissa fanned herself against the afternoon heat and stifled a yawn. Thus far, Taryn's game consisted of twelve young lordlings dressed in breeches and hose, running across the lawn chasing a lump of leather. At least the lords were shirtless. That gave her something interesting to watch. She fixed her gaze on Rhoane; he alone wore a cotton tunic over his leather breeches. Damn him and his sense of propriety.

Taryn trotted past wearing a ridiculous costume of short pants, a loose-fitting black top that did nothing for her figure, and work boots. She called out instructions to the men on the field, waving her hands to emphasize her words.

"She's rather remarkable, don't you think?" Tessa asked in her breathy little girl voice.

"She's odd." That was Eliahnna. Honest. Blunt.

Lliandra remained silent, her eyes tracking Taryn's every move.

"What is the purpose of this game?" Marissa asked no one in particular.

"Does it need a purpose?" Sabina answered, her gaze

fixed on Lord Valen's bare chest.

"Hayden seems rather adept at it," Marissa teased. To her right, Herbret twisted the ring he wore on his pinky finger. If he worried it any harder, he might cut off the appendage. Marissa derived a small amount of satisfaction at seeing him upset. He'd taken the empress's silence regarding his betrothal request as approval and had been far too lax in his comportment. Herbret's money meant he could afford to offend Marissa, but his lack of royal blood and lesser title meant he needed her on his side. Something he'd forgotten in the last few weeks.

Their eyes met, and Marissa's smile dripped treacle, it was so sweet. Herbret looked momentarily nervous, then sat up straight and met her smile with one of his own. Acidic enough to burn through the sugar.

Defiance wasn't like Herbret. He was a coward when it came down to it. She doubted he acted alone, which meant someone had to be coaxing him. Whoever it was, Marissa would find him and destroy him. No one took what was rightfully hers, and Herbret had been her pet for too long. He knew enough about her indiscretions to make him dangerous but not enough to derail her plans.

Marissa licked her lips, a slow turn around the fullness with her tongue, making certain Herbret watched. Slowly, so as not to draw attention to herself, she stroked Sabina's long locks, bending over to whisper in her ear. "You deserve a man as virile as young Hayden. I don't know what mother is thinking letting Herbret petition for your hand."

Sabina's huge brown eyes fluttered up at Marissa, a look of cautious terror brimming in them. "She what?" A slight tremble started in her hands, working its way to the rest of her body.

"Shhh, now. Don't worry so. I'll speak with mother and sort everything out."

Gratitude, raw and unabashed, glowed on her face. "I don't know how to thank you."

Marissa continued stroking Sabina's silky hair, delighting in the closeness it afforded. "Don't say another word. You're like a sister to me." From above her dark curls, Marissa met Herbret's uneasy stare. Accepting defeat, he blinked and looked away, but not before Marissa saw unbridled hatred burning in his eyes.

"Blood and ashes! Did you see that?" Tessa paced along the edge of the tent, her little hands balled into fists. "He missed the ball!"

"It's only a game, Tessa. There is no reason to get so worked up," Lliandra chided.

The players ran in a group, kicking the ball to each other. Marissa didn't think any of it warranted the excitement Tessa showed. When the ball was kicked to Taryn, she gracefully ran a short distance, keeping the ball between her feet and then kicked it between two posts that had been erected at the far end of the lawn.

The lords cheered and circled her, talking in exaggerated tones that reached those sitting in the shade. Whatever she'd done, the men thought it worthy of praise. Heaps of it, by the sound of their voices.

The group gathered in the center of the lawn where someone dropped the ball. Several men converged on it, trying to get it away from the rest. One lucky man managed to capture the ball, and ran, less gracefully, several paces, before kicking it to another player.

A crowd had gathered on the lawn by now. Soldiers and servants stood shoulder to shoulder cheering and yelling taunts to the players. With each turn Taryn took, the spectators called out her name. Marissa watched the interplay between Taryn and her teammates with increasing interest. The court's favor was fickle at best, but that afternoon, Taryn was the definite favorite.

If it were anyone else, Marissa wouldn't give her a second thought, but Taryn posed serious problems if she became too popular. Marissa sent a strand of her Mari toward Taryn. Instead of tangling around her ankles, Taryn leapt over the Mari as if it were nothing more than a stick. Bewildered, Marissa sent another, stronger thread toward the girl. Again, she dodged the Mari, snuffing it out with the heel of her boot.

"See how she deftly handles the ball," Tessa began. "I hear she is equally skilled with the sword. Today she taught the soldiers hand-to-hand combat." There was a dreamy quality to Tessa's voice that grated on Marissa's nerves.

"She is a treasure, to be sure," Marissa offered, putting as much enthusiasm as she could into her tone. "Would you like to join them?"

Tessa's face lit up with eagerness. "I would indeed. Do you think I could?"

"Tessa," Lliandra began, using the timbre she reserved for special disappointment, "I don't think it would be proper."

Tears filled Tessa's eyes. "Yes, Mother." She took her seat beside Eliahnna, pulling her knees to her chest and resting her chin on her crossed arms.

The ball dropped, the players raced after it. They ran, they kicked, they cheered. Marissa was bored of it all. She sent one last charge of Mari at Taryn. Her power wrapped around Taryn's legs, taking her down with a satisfying *thump*.

A collective gasp came from the crowd.

As graceful as a carlix, Taryn rolled to her feet and brushed off her legs. When she jogged back to the group, Marissa noted a slight limp in her gait and smiled to herself. She cast a lazy glance over the crowd before turning back to those seated in the tent. Her gaze fell upon Herbret, who watched her with troublesome intensity. He gave a small salute and pivoted, leaving her to stare at his ample backside as he left the tent.

A short while later the game ended with congratulatory remarks and cheers for Taryn. The geniality lasted well into the evening, giving the second masque an air of excitement. The lords who had played with Taryn enjoyed their elevated status, with ladies lining up to dance with them. As for Taryn, she stayed close to Sabina much of the night, danced only with Hayden or Rhoane, and left well before midnight bells.

At second bell, Marissa excused herself from the party, wanting nothing more than to return to her rooms and curl up in the blankets, sleeping until tea the next day, but she'd promised Zakael she'd meet him at the inn. For half a heartbeat, she debated whether she should beg off. The pull of his Dark Shanti was too strong, though, and she headed toward the gardens, avoiding as many courtiers and servants as she could.

The party would continue for several more bells until the morning light, even into the next day if Hayden wished it. Three masques over three nights, each themed and outlasting the previous party. Marissa scoffed. It was a ridiculous display of Anje's wealth, but if the stupid man wanted to waste all that gold on his only son, who was she to argue?

"Your Highness, may I speak with you a moment?" Herbret's clammy hand wrapped around her wrist with a familiarity she resented.

"Not now, Herbret." She withdrew her arm from him, ignoring the need to wipe it on her gown.

"Please."

Marissa stopped short. Herbret did not beg. Ever. "What is it?" She kept her tone neutral, but inside, she thrilled at the neediness she saw in his face.

"You have to help me gain your mother's support for my petition."

"I don't have to do anything, especially not for someone whose loyalty has waned of late."

His beady eyes, set too close together and making her think, not for the first time, he had descended from trolls, shifted from side to side with nervous energy. "You're right. I apologize for my behavior. I don't know what came over me. Love, perhaps. This union with the princess—I need it."

"Why, Herbret? Why her? She has no ShantiMari, and you don't need her coin. What does she offer you?"

His eyes darted to the left, then right, and then to her breasts where his gaze lingered. "She has ties to the southern shipping routes. I need those merchants in my favor. There have been increasing pirate attacks in the southern seas that have nearly crippled my fleet."

Plausible, but not the whole story. Marissa took a deep breath, lifting her breasts to just below his nose. "Losing your ships would be tragic. I'll speak with Mother. But Herbret…" She waited until he pulled his gaze to her face. "I need to know you will never defy me. If we're to have a partnership, we must trust one another." She ran a finger down his sweaty cheek, pausing to rake a nail over his lower lip. "We make such a good team, you and I." She ran her fingers through his hair and Herbret shivered into her touch, his body vibrating with suppressed pleasure. "There's something I need from you, but I can't tell you now. Come to my rooms tomorrow, and we'll chat."

His reply was a low moan punctuated with an elongated, "Yessss."

"Your Highness." A youthful voice sounded just behind her, and Marissa turned to see one of the duke's servants bowing low.

"Yes?"

"Your mother would like a word. If you'll come with me."

Marissa yanked a few strands of Herbret's hair and patted

his cheek. "Be a good boy. All will be well."

She followed the servant in silent fury. If she hadn't stopped to deal with that twit Herbret, she'd be in Zakael's bed this moment. Not on her way to see the empress.

Lliandra beckoned her forward when a maid announced her arrival. Her mother wore one of her more demure sleeping gowns, which covered little of the woman's voluptuous curves. The years had been good to her mother, Marissa admitted grudgingly. Still beautiful, with a body men craved, Lliandra ruled with as much strength and passion as she put into her lovers. To Lliandra, mating was nothing but an extension of her duties as an empress.

"Leave us," Lliandra commanded her maids. When they'd gone, she handed Marissa an ornate silver brush and settled into her chair.

Marissa dutifully began combing her mother's luxurious tresses, being careful not to snag the bristles.

"I called you here to discuss your plans with Zakael. Is he still in Paderau?"

Marissa kept the brush moving, not wanting to give Lliandra reason to doubt her. "Of course not. He left after the debacle last night. I don't know what possessed him to come here."

"Good. We don't need any further distractions. Taryn has gained too much favor, it would be impossible to eliminate her now without questions, therefore, I want you to ingratiate yourself with the girl. As yet, she knows nothing, and I'd like to keep it that way. At least until Talaith."

Lliandra's eyes, deep blue pools of glass that shone whether there was light in the room or not, met Marissa's gaze in the mirror. "We can't expose her until we're in the capital city. Valterys knows this, which is why, I believe, he sent Zakael. To force our hand. Taryn must be accepted at court."

"She's never used power. Are you sure she is the one?"

Lliandra winced as the brush caught a snarl, and Marissa tensed, waiting for the expected lash. "I am sure. ShantiMari or not, she is the Eirielle. Tomorrow is the last masque. We'll return to Talaith a few days later and then I'll publicly declare her in front of the court."

Marissa's mind spun with the implications. "You can't possibly arrange everything while you're here. Why don't I return to Talaith now? That way, I can have the ceremony in place for when you return." A fortnight alone with Zakael at the Crystal Palace—it was almost too good to be true. "That would give you nearly two weeks to get close to her, study her, learn her weaknesses."

Lliandra tapped a finger on the vanity, her nail making a *tick* sound with each tap. "Yes, that might be for the best. You would do that for me? I know how you hate planning these things."

Marissa bent and kissed her mother's cheek. "I would do anything for you."

"I know you would, my love." She pointed to her head, and Marissa resumed her brushing. "Have you decided on a husband for Sabina?"

"I think the Danurian would be to our best advantage." Marissa said with genuine enthusiasm. She wanted the handsome man for herself, and the quickest way to get him to Talaith was a betrothal to Sabina.

"Lord Aomori?" Again, the *tick, tick, tick* of her nail on wood. "I thought perhaps he would make a good match for Eliahnna. She's coming of age in a few seasons, and we need a strong ally in the west."

"We don't have the time to wait for her to mature. We need strength in the west now."

"Lord Herbret has petitioned for Sabina's hand." Lliandra said without much enthusiasm.

Marissa kept her face blank. "Has he? What does he hope

to accomplish?"

Lliandra waved as if swatting an irritating bug, "I'm not sure, but keep an eye on him. He's planning something, and I need to know what." Lliandra reached back and took Marissa's hand in her own. "They found Liago's body, by the way."

Marissa frowned. The name meant nothing to her. "Who?"

"My lover. By the marks of ShantiMari on his throat, it appears he was strangled."

"I'm sorry, Mother. I know you enjoyed his company. Do they know who killed him?"

Lliandra's eyes bore into hers. Her mother knew. Knew she'd been the one to murder her lover, but Lliandra had no proof. "No."

Marissa wound her arms around Lliandra and gave a comforting squeeze. "Perhaps you'll find a new concubine here. There is a delicious looking Ullan who's been shadowing you. I hear they are wicked healers. He could help mend your broken heart."

Ullans were notorious for their alternative ways, often employing pleasures of the flesh in their healing rituals.

"Perhaps I will." Lliandra stood to embrace her daughter. Her soft lips covered Marissa's, her tongue sought the warm comfort of her mouth.

Marissa returned the kiss, moaning against her mother as Lliandra's fingertips pinched between her legs, finding that little button of pleasure and rubbing hard. Her body jerked in response, releasing the pent-up energy she'd been saving for Zakael. Wetness pooled between her legs. Her body trembled.

Lliandra pulled back slightly, a triumphant smile lighting her face. The hard slap across Marissa's cheek stunned the younger woman. Heat flamed from her neck to her temple, but Marissa kept herself steady as best she could.

"Liago was dispensable, yes, but when you killed him, you betrayed me. I will not suffer your vanity again." Lliandra smoothed Marissa's hair, cooing the words she spoke. "Be careful with your heart, my love. Zakael won't be so easily disposed of, or forgotten. Now go."

Shaken from her mother's words, and her touch, Marissa left the empress's rooms, mentally listing what needed to be done. First was to put that Ullan in Lliandra's bed. Marissa needed her mother distracted, and a good lover always did the trick. Next was to speak with Sabina. There had to be a reason Herbret was willing to risk his favor with her for a worthless girl.

Chapter 20

TARYN stood outside the duke's rooms debating whether to knock or leave before she made a fool of herself. The door swung open, and Oliver, Hayden's valet, gasped at seeing her, then ushered her inside.

"I was about to go looking for you. Come in," he said, a hand to his heart.

"I didn't mean to startle you." She placed a hand on his arm, balancing the cake with the other.

"That's all right, dear. I'm getting on in seasons, is all."

They walked down a long hallway to the duke's private dining room where Sabina and the younger princesses were already seated. Duke Anje sat at the head of the table, with Rhoane to his right and Baehlon his left. Faelara chatted with the giant knight and looked up when Taryn entered.

"There you are. We were beginning to worry." Hayden greeted her.

Taryn held out the small cake she'd made. "This is for you. Carga said it's your favorite."

Hayden took the cake from her, admiring the decorative frosting she'd painstakingly applied. "Apple spice?"

"Yep. I made it myself."

"You can cook?" Faelara asked, surprised.

"Technically, this is baking. But yes, I can cook. Before

I ran around with you lot, I used to cook for Brandt all the time. He could barely boil water." She snort-laughed. Then laughed at her snort.

"I will remember that for the next time we travel." Faelara promised.

Taryn sat down beside Sabina and held up her glass for some wine. "As long as someone else gets to peel potatoes. But first, a toast to the birthday boy."

They ate a light meal and laughed at the duke's stories about Hayden's childhood—everyone except Hayden. His mischievousness wasn't as humorous to him as it was everyone else. Myrddin stopped by as the meal concluded to give Hayden a leather-bound book of ancient myths and legends. When the rest of the gifts were given and well wishes for a prosperous season were made, they drank cups of spiced grhom.

"I'm sorry I don't have anything else to give," she said with a sheepish grin. "Not that I'd know what to get a marquis anyway."

"This," Hayden said, holding a forkful of cake, "is the best present I've ever received. And it's delicious." He plopped a piece in his mouth and chewed with exaggerated delight.

"There is one other thing Taryn can give you," Anje said cryptically. "Fighting lessons."

Taryn stared at the duke, unsure if he was joking. "But you said no."

"I've changed my mind."

Hayden whooped and caught Taryn up in a hug, spinning her around the room. When he set her down, he kissed her full on the lips. Silence clung to the air as Hayden stepped back, aware of his actions and their audience. He bowed first to Taryn and then to Sabina, muttering an apology. Then, to Taryn's horror, Hayden bowed low to Rhoane. The Eleri prince waved him off with a shrug. Faelara broke the awkward moment, congratulating Hayden, and fussing over him to be careful in the training yard.

Taryn moved away from the group, ostensibly to examine some portraits hung on the wall but more so she could clear her thoughts. Hayden's kiss was nothing like Rhoane's. There was no weakening of the knees and certainly no swooning. The kiss was nice but lacked spark. She touched her lips and recalled the strength of Rhoane's lips on hers.

"I have a surprise for you," Sabina whispered, and Taryn jumped. She'd not heard the girl approach.

"What is it?" Taryn said hesitantly, hoping her friend wasn't angry with her for Hayden's kiss.

"Marissa has left Paderau." At Taryn's look of shock, Sabina continued, "I've made a few inquiries, and I'm fairly certain her guest the other night is a visitor she's had at the Crystal Palace."

"You've seen him?"

Sabina shook her head. "They are too clever for that, but I've known she was sneaking a lover into the palace for a long time. My maid heard him arguing with the princess in the garden and recognized his voice. She wasn't near enough to make out words, but she is certain it was him."

On impulse, she kissed Sabina's cheek. "Thank you, my friend."

Sabina giggled. "No offense, but that's not the kiss I had hoped for tonight."

Taryn squeezed her friend's fingers. "Nor I."

At the third and final masque, guests dressed in either black or white with feathers and flowers attached to stylized masks. That night's ball was themed a *setante cuir*, or hidden secret, the stark black and white meant to represent Light and Dark ShantiMari. As Taryn surveyed the room, and the ever more elaborate displays of jewels, she was glad she hadn't grown up on Aelinae. A world where every lord or lady tried to outdo the other with a grotesque display of wealth. She shuddered at the thought.

Taryn didn't wear any jewels to the final dance, not even the exquisite sapphire and diamond necklace the duke had given her for her birthday. Her gown consisted of little more than a tight white corset and a flowing semi-sheer skirt split to her hip. She didn't need to add jewelry to draw attention. She pulled her mask farther over her face to hide her blush and moved through the crowd, looking for her friends.

The sound of her name made her pause.

"Princess Marissa would never admit it publicly, but she knows that girl is an Offlander. The duke took pity on her because she's an orphan," Lady Celia said knowingly.

"The princess says a lot of things," a male voice replied. "Have you spoken to her?"

"Once. She's tiresome and ignorant. From what I hear, she's just as powerless as that Summerlands slut."

Angry heat rose up Taryn's neck, but she kept listening.

"The princesses seem rather fond of her. Perhaps the crown princess was mistaken."

"Aomori, you are such an innocent. Those girls are nice to her because the empress commanded it."

Pain sliced through Taryn's heart.

"Once they leave for Talaith, they'll forget all about that trash," Celia added.

"Your fangs are showing."

"I have claws just as sharp," she purred to her friend. "Would you like to come to my rooms to discover them for yourself?" Her voice dropped in husky tones as she added, "No one needs to know. It will be our own *setante cuir*."

"As much as your offer tempts me, I'm afraid I must decline. I see your mother approaches. I will leave you two your privacy." Aomori passed Taryn without noticing her.

Taryn glanced around in time to see a majestic being,

clad all in black, bearing down on Celia. She slipped away, only to be stopped by one of Lliandra's courtiers.

"Taryn," he drawled, "it's nice to see you out of those men's breeches you so favor."

"Thank you, Lord Herbret." She tried to move past, but he blocked the path. "If you'll excuse me, I'm looking for my friends." The corset was too tight, and her breath came in short gasps. She needed to escape the heat of the room.

From the opening of his mask, his little black eyes wandered to her legs before settling on her chest. "Quite an improvement, yes." A slug-like tongue made its way around his lips before darting out and back in with alarming speed.

A slow thrumming started within her, shallow at first, barely perceptible until it made its way to her ears, pulsing against her skull. The room grew warmer, and she tried to step around him again, wishing for nothing more than sweet, fresh air.

A sweat-slicked hand wrapped around her arm, pinching her. Herbret's acrid breath assaulted her nostrils as he hissed, "I don't know where you came from, Offlander, but I've dealt with your kind before. If you think for a moment that any of these nobles will accept you and your tainted blood, you're mistaken." A crack of lightning flashed just outside the windows, startling the guests, but Herbret was too intent on her to notice. "I don't know how you've managed to charm the duke, but your witchery won't work on me."

"Is there a problem, Herbret?" Rhoane removed the man's hand from her shaking arm, bending low to whisper in his ear, "Touch her again and it will be the last thing you do."

Herbret backed away, making apologies and claiming he was just trying to be friendly. Rhoane pressed his palm against the small of Taryn's back and propelled her out to the garden.

Dark storm clouds marred the peaceful summer night.

Air, thick with unspent energy, stirred with an electrified current. The pounding in her ears was either her heartbeat or her pendant, she wasn't sure, nor did she care. Rhoane's Shanti spread across her skin, dulling the clamor, easing her rage. Even after her breathing settled, she couldn't muffle the sound of Herbret's taunts and Celia's cruel words.

"Thank you," she said at last.

"I am sorry for that, Taryn."

"I've dealt with worse."

They strolled through the garden in silence with Taryn stopping every so often to enjoy the fragrance from blooming roses. They reminded her of the pub's small garden below the London flat she'd shared with Brandt. On the rare occasions they were home, Brandt would spend hours tending the flowers, coaxing them back to life knowing full well they would wither again once he and Taryn had to leave. She bit back a sob and crushed her nails into her palms until the homesickness passed.

Gradually, she and Rhoane made their way to the orchard where they sat on a bench under sargot trees.

"Tell me, what is *pizza*?" Rhoane asked at length.

Taryn looked at him in surprise. "How do you know about that?"

"It is in your thoughts often tonight."

"We agreed we weren't going to read each other's minds without permission," Taryn said, an edge to her voice.

The river lapped by in gentle waves, and Rhoane said, "I have not been entering your thoughts. You seem to be dwelling on this thing. It is difficult for me to avoid."

"It's food from back home. Delicious and cheesy, and oh God, I so wish I had some right now. I could probably make it for you if Carga will let me use her kitchen again."

Rhoane took her hand in his and traced the lines of her runes. "Do you regret coming here?"

She leaned against the bench, looking at him from the corner of her eye. "By 'here' do you mean Paderau or Aelinae?"

"Either. Both. You know what I mean. Do you wish you had stayed where you were?"

"There's no point in looking back. This is my life now. I can either accept it or fight it. There's more drama here than I'm used to, that's for sure." She plucked a leaf from a nearby tree and rolled it between two fingers. An acridness filled the air around them. She tossed the leaf aside and stared at the clear sky. Stars twinkled against a bed of deep purple.

"Brandt and I had a simple life. We traveled all the time, which made it hard to make friends, but we had each other. That just sort of made everything okay. Still, I always had this sense that I didn't fit in, like I was an observer in other people's lives." She glanced at him. "Does that make sense?"

"And now? Do you feel you belong here, Taryn?"

Celia's words stung anew. "I want to, but it's been difficult learning all the rules and customs. I don't know what I'm supposed to be doing or where I belong."

He stroked her arm with his forefinger. "Do not try too hard to find an answer. In time, I am sure it will find you."

The thrill his touch brought was tempered by a wave of guilt. She gently took her hand from his. "I think I should be getting back."

"Have I said something to upset you?"

"You're betrothed, Rhoane. We shouldn't be here."

He leaned back, exhaling and stretching his arms behind him. For several long moments, he stared ahead without speaking.

Taryn shifted, impatient to be away from the pull of the water and romance of the night. "I saw what Hayden did today. In the duke's room when he kissed me and then bowed to you as if apologizing. I won't be your mistress, Rhoane. If that's what everyone thinks, then they're wrong."

He gave a curt laugh. "My mistress? Taryn, you have no idea what you are talking about."

"Don't pretend, Rhoane. I know I'm an Offlander. You're just being nice to me because the empress commanded it."

He stood before her, his eyes a dark mystery. A spark of green ShantiMari flared away from him, and he took a deep breath. "Taryn, the empress did no such thing. You are not an Offlander." His finger traced her jawline; his thumb pressed upon her lips.

Taryn shivered against the night's warmth. "Please don't." With all her will, she kept from pulling him close.

"If that is your wish. I will escort you back to the ball."

They walked along the path in silence, Taryn not trusting herself to speak. Despite what he'd said, she was an Offlander and would never be his equal in status.

When Taryn returned to her rooms, she waited until Lorilee and Mayla finished readying her for bed before checking the looking glass. Nothing had been disturbed. She asked it to show her Brandt, and his smiling face appeared in the ball. Wherever he was, it was peaceful. Unable to sleep, she sat in a chair by the window, staring at the shifting sky.

Movement in the garden caught her attention, and she spied two lovers tangled in their ShantiMari. Streaks of ebony and gold whizzed around them. She leaned forward, resting her chin on her fist. She and Sabina were the only people she knew without power. Even Baehlon was able to perform simple tasks with his limited amount of ShantiMari.

The lovers finished their tryst and ambled off, a soft orb drifting behind them. Taryn resented their love and their power. It wasn't fair. But then, life never was. She blew out a deep breath, and the orb blinked out.

A surprised male voice asked his partner if he'd extinguished the light. He hadn't. Another light appeared, floating close to the man's face. Taryn recognized him as

Celia's friend from earlier in the evening—Aomori. She didn't recognize the other man.

Taryn blew a kiss to the men. The orb blinked out yet again.

"Tinsley." Aomori's terse whisper came from the darkness. "Stop playing games."

"I'm not. Perhaps you aren't focusing enough." They ducked under a tree and were lost to her sight and hearing. She wished them much happiness in their endeavors. A blaze lit forth from the trees several yards from where she last saw them. The sound of angry footsteps, followed by hurried shuffling was the last she heard of the men.

She sat straight in her chair. The realization that she'd blown out their light as clear to her as the starlit night.

It wasn't possible.

She didn't have ShantiMari.

She held her palm in front of her and took a deep breath, exhaling slowly.

"Glowing orb," she commanded. Nothing happened. Next, she concentrated all her thought on the empty space above her palm. "Ball of light." Still nothing.

The crushing truth that she wasn't gifted with power flooded over her. As much as she hated to admit it, she'd wanted to be like the others. To be special.

She sighed the last of her hope and whispered, "Light."

A faint spark flickered in her palm.

She jumped, nearly knocking herself out of the chair. "Light," she said with more confidence. A near-transparent flame danced above her palm. Taryn's heart beat with such ferocity she feared it would burst.

She wanted to run shrieking down the halls, showing everyone what she could do, but stopped herself. Before she told anyone, she needed to be certain it wasn't a fluke. For most of the night, she practiced making flames, and eventually floating orbs, sending them out the window to hover in the garden. Several times, she almost dropped one on an unsuspecting passerby and had to duck beneath her window to keep from being caught.

When she was too tired to keep her eyes open, let alone the balls aloft, she fell asleep with her palm flat, an orb of light dozing silently upon it.

It was the perfect ending to an imperfect night.

Chapter 21

NOT only did Carga agree to let Taryn use the kitchen, on the condition she teach the cook how to make this mysterious *pizza* dish, she offered to accompany Taryn to the market. They left the palace grounds by a side gate, and Carga steered them through the shoppers with trained efficiency. Despite her slim form, she muscled her way around the crowds, her short hair bouncing with the effort. Taryn's *cynfar* kept up a constant buzzing while they shopped, annoying her. Once they had all the items Taryn needed for her pizzas, they went to a tavern for their midday meal. They were nearly finished when her pendant sent an angry zap against her skin.

"Shit," Taryn swore under her breath, rubbing her chest. "What the hell?"

Carga's concerned look was more of the have-you-lost-your-mind kind of expression. Taryn took a sip of her mead and glanced around the tavern. When her gaze settled on a man sitting in a booth not far from them, she had the odd sensation she'd seen him before, even though he wore a dark cloak with the hood pulled low over his face.

"What's with him?" Taryn motioned to the man.

She looked where Taryn indicated. "Who? I see no one."

Icy chills slithered down Taryn's neck. "There's a man sitting right there. He's wearing a dark hood." The cook shook her head. "He's right there, watching us. I can feel him."

Carga quietly slid her dagger from its sheath, then lifted her mug and called out, "To the duke!" Everyone in the tavern raised their cups, echoing her cry. Without warning, she threw the dagger straight into the man's chest.

Taryn watched in horror as it went through him, plunging into the wood. He slid from the booth, grinning at them, his yellow teeth catching the light from a nearby candle. When he brushed past her chair, she shuddered at the frigid air.

"Did you feel that?" Taryn challenged Carga.

The cook's face paled. "Yes." She retrieved her dagger from the bench and tossed several coins on the table before grabbing Taryn's sleeve. "We must return to the palace."

Taryn clutched her basket and hurried after her. There was no sign of the shadowy man on the streets, and even if there were, she wouldn't have known because Carga nearly sprinted to the palace. When they passed the stables, she slowed to a walk until they reached the kitchens.

Panting, Taryn grabbed her arm. "Who was that man?"

Carga brushed her aside. "He is no one. Nothing. You do not need to worry about him. He is my problem."

"What did he want from you?"

"What does every man want from a woman? Now, we have work to do, yes? You are going to make something delicious for us to eat. No more talk of what happened at the tavern. He cannot come here, so you need not worry." After she unpacked her basket, she wrapped an apron around her waist before handing one to Taryn. "Work, yes?"

Taryn kept herself too busy to think about the shadow man while they made dough and sauce. The sounds and smells of the kitchen were intoxicating. She loved the dynamic between the cooks and scullery maids, like a dance performed to the tune of spoons stirring and pans clanging.

By the time the pizzas were ready to go into the bread

oven, the sun was dipping low in the east. Carga sent a page to gather Taryn's friends while they set a table in the kitchen garden. At first Carga objected, but Taryn assured her that where she came from, eating outside was perfectly fine.

They were just setting the food down when her guests arrived. Hayden brought two additional people with him, Lords Tinsley and Aomori. Taryn greeted them without any hint she knew of their rendezvous the night before.

When everyone was seated, she stood at the head of the table, indicating the food before them. "This is my small way of showing you how much I appreciate everything you've done for me." She looked at the duke. "Back home, we call this pizza. It isn't as fancy as you're accustomed to, but it's one of my favorite meals. I wanted to share it with you. Enjoy." No one moved as she helped herself to a slice.

Tessa stood and leaned over the pizza. "It smells divine, but it looks unfinished."

"Just take some and try it." She served herself salad and breadsticks before passing them to the duke. "Here you go, Your Grace." She indicated a bowl. "You can eat them plain or dip them into the sauce." She dipped a breadstick and took a bite.

Rather than making her homesick, the tang of the tomatoes and garlicky dough evoked in her a feeling of being among friends. When no one else moved to eat, she gave a snort of disgust. "Okay, listen up, people. Tonight, we don't have any servants. It's feed yourself or go hungry. You are all too spoiled."

At that, Baehlon reached out and took two slices. He folded one in half before devouring a large bite. A wide grin broke across his face. With two more bites, the pizza was gone. Bolstered by his approval, the others piled their plates with food. Duke Anje declared Taryn's pizza his new favorite while Tessa thought it must've been sent from the gods.

"What we really need is some good ale," Taryn suggested.

Carga hopped up from the table. "I have a barrel in the back. Brewed it myself." When she returned with the cask and several mugs, the men cheered the cook. Carga gave a pretty curtsey and blushed. "It is nothing much. Just a recipe I stole from a merchant on his way to the Danuri Province." She looked pointedly at Aomori, who laughed.

"If it's a Danurian blend, then how can it not be excellent?" Aomori's family was apparently one of the wealthiest in the province. He was fostering with Lord Tinsley for the season to teach him about winemaking, although Sabina argued the Summerlands produced the best vineyards in all of Aelinae.

"Perhaps you should visit my homeland and see for yourself," Sabina said, with more than a little flirtation in her voice.

Aomori blushed, his olive skin shining in the dusky night, making Hayden's and Tinsley's pale faces look bland in comparison. He was more than just pretty, he was gorgeous. High cheekbones, slender nose that met full lips and a sturdy chin—he could've been a model.

"Does the ale displease you?" Aomori asked when she'd stared at him too long.

The ale was as good as any Taryn had had before. "No, it's great. Perfect for our meal *al fresco*," she stammered.

"Al who?" Tessa asked around a mouthful of breadstick.

"It means *outside*."

"What language is it?" Eliahnna asked.

Shit. Aomori's good looks and the ale had muddled her thoughts. "Just something I made up when I was a kid. I didn't have many playmates, so I was forever making up my own languages." She prayed Eliahnna would accept her crap answer.

"How creative you are!" Sabina came to her rescue. "Perhaps someday you can teach me one so we can communicate in secret."

"Why don't you just, you know…" Tessa said, tapping her forehead.

"Tessa," Eliahnna hissed. "Don't."

"Thank you, Eliahnna, but there's no need to save my feelings," Sabina said. "I can't mind-speak, Tessa. Not only am I lacking in ShantiMari but I don't seem to possess the ability to converse with my thoughts."

"Oh." Tears brimmed in Tessa's cornflower blue eyes. "I'm terribly sorry."

Duke Anje patted his stomach, breaking the tension. "I didn't think something so insubstantial could fill me up, but you have succeeded, my girl. I hope you've taught Carga how to make this heavenly dish."

"I watched everything she did." Carga gave Taryn a direct look. "And I know every spice she used."

"Thanks for reminding me." Taryn left them to retrieve the small pouch that Tabul, the spice merchant, had given her as a gift for Sabina. When she returned, she handed the bag to Sabina. "The spice merchant said you would like this."

Sabina opened it, inhaling the scent. "Oh, he's right. These are from my homeland. I've not smelled this in a long time." She carefully tied the pouch before tucking it into her dress. "Thank you, Taryn. You have indeed brought me a precious gift. I would like to see this merchant and thank him myself."

"I can take you tomorrow," Taryn offered.

"I am sure Prince Rhoane would be happy to escort you," Carga offered. A strange look passed between her and Rhoane, one that gave Taryn pause.

"I'd like to go," Tessa piped in, followed by Eliahnna's plea to join them.

"The more the merrier," Taryn agreed.

"We should be plenty merry now," Baehlon grumbled.

"Why don't you just invite the whole bloody palace?"

Taryn served dessert, a modified version of her favorite cookies. Chai spiced snickerdoodles with ice cream sandwiched between. Every last bite was devoured by her guests. They passed the evening in genial conversation, and Taryn listened as they discussed everything from politics to the ripening of sargot trees in summer.

Each time the topic of Talaith was brought up, an excited buzz went through the group. Of them all, only Taryn and Aomori had never seen the capital city.

Duke Anje pushed himself away from the table and gave Taryn a warm hug. "Again, my thanks for a wonderful meal." He looked at the sky above them, glittering stars stretched across a dark canvas. "We should dine *al fresco* more often." He kissed Taryn's forehead, lingering for a moment. The heady scent of musk and sweat tickled her nose. "You are quite a surprise, my young friend."

"I'm glad you liked it. You've been so kind to me; it's the least I could do. Maybe I could stay here and work for you?"

The duke chortled, shaking his head. "I don't think that would be the best use of your talents."

He said his good-byes and the others followed, drifting off into the night. Taryn busied herself clearing the dishes, but Carga stopped her. "You have been in the kitchen all day. I will have someone come do that. Go enjoy the evening."

"What about you? I'm sure you deserve a night away from the ovens. Will you join us?"

Tears sparkled in Carga's eyes. "You have already given me a much needed break. You allowed me to sit at your table with the duke and princesses. I feel blessed this night."

Taryn embraced her new friend. "Me too." Murmurings from hundreds of voices buzzed in her head. "Did you hear that?" Carga only smiled and shooed her away.

Rhoane moved in step with her. "What are *cheeseburgers*?"

he asked. Taryn looked at him in surprise before laughing.

"Baby steps, Rhoane. I don't know whether you're ready for those quite yet."

They roamed the formal gardens, talking about things some people might consider inconsequential, but when Rhoane took her hand in his to lead her through the orchard, she didn't remind him of his betrothed.

To the shadow man from the tavern, she gave not another thought.

Chapter 22

THE small alcove off the kitchen barely fit both of their bodies, but it was the only place afforded any privacy from the kitchen staff and courtiers with nothing better to do than create scandal. Rhoane pressed himself against the wall, making as much room for the duke's cook as he could. Still, they were close enough that he could smell lavender and ash, the scents he'd known since his childhood.

Carga smiled up at him, enjoying his discomfort, he was sure. "Are you certain you do not want to sit and enjoy some grhom?"

"I would love nothing more and you know it. But this conversation cannot be overheard." He noted a tightness in the fragile skin around her eyes, a slight dullness of her irises, the sadness that dwelled in their depths. Her eyes had always captivated him, had been filled with more wisdom than mirth, but of late they bore the weight of her sheanna.

"As you desire." She tickled up his sternum and grinned at his unease. "Although, if we are found here alone, that will set their tongues to wagging more than an innocent chat in the kitchen."

"What more can you tell me about what happened yesterday? There was a man following you? Can you describe him?"

Carga dropped all pretense of playing her little game, her face serious. "I did not see him. Taryn said there was a man, but I sensed nothing. Until it moved past me. A chill like none I have ever known crept into my spirit."

A buzzing touched his thoughts and Rhoane shut out the murmurings of his people. "How can you bear their constant chatter?" The Eleri shared a collective consciousness, one that he could delve into if he so wished, but rarely did. The whisperings were irregular to him, but for someone like Carga, the ancients never ceased speaking.

"I am used to it. They want to believe I am still their high priestess. I have told them several times that is not the case, but they linger. Some have questions. Some have answers. All of them wish to help." Her eyes grew distant for a moment, and Rhoane heard the rush of conversations. With a leaden sigh, she opened her eyes. "Even they do not know what tracks the Darennsai."

Her short curls danced around her face as she shook her head. Two Eleri, exiled from their homeland. Sheanna to his people. He tried to see her as often as he could, but even those visits he kept short. The less attention he drew to them, the better.

"You are certain he was after Taryn?"

"I am sorry, Rhoane. She is in great danger, but I do not know how to find this apparition. There is evil in this world we cannot see, a force that beckons to be released. If it should come to pass, not even she can save Aelinae."

"Can you name it?"

"Nay. My sight is limited. Once my sheanna is lifted, perhaps then I will know more, but for now, know that my dreams are shrouded in blackness."

It was not the news he was hoping to receive, but unsurprising nonetheless.

"I will do what I can to protect her while she is in Paderau, but once she leaves this city, my power is useless."

Rhoane pressed his lips against Carga's forehead, hearing again the stirrings of his people. "That is all I can ask." A yearning swept over him, and he tamped it down to the dark place inside where all his disappointments dwelled.

"You are going to search for him." It wasn't a question. "Be safe, *mi carae*." She rested her forehead against his. "When next we meet, may it be in sweetness and not sorrow."

"When next we meet." Rhoane brushed her cheek with his lips and slipped from the alcove, checking the area before he left from a side entrance.

THE garments he wore, a rough linen poncho over a tunic and breeches of the same fabric, helped him blend into the crowd of the busy marketplace. He trailed Taryn and the princesses, keeping a discreet distance, as they stopped at stalls every so often to barter with the merchants and purchase items. Aside from several rambunctious children, all was in order.

Taryn cast furtive glances around the square, her eyes always seeming to find where he was hiding. When she looked closer, Rhoane disappeared into the crowd. At least he hoped.

Baehlon and a half dozen of the duke's guard watched over Taryn and the younger princesses. A few of them cut curious stares his way, but made no move to initiate contact. When finally the group left the market and returned to the palace, Rhoane roamed the area, using his ShantiMari to search for any abnormalities.

At twelfth bells, he made his way to the tavern where Carga said Taryn saw the man. Several patrons watched him with apprehension. A peasant of his stature would have enough coin to visit such a place, if only once a moonturn.

Rhoane tipped his weatherworn straw hat at them and entered the darkened building. Nearly all of the tables were crowded with the city's inhabitants escaping the heat of the day and enjoying the coolness of the tavern.

A quick scan of the room produced nothing alarming.

"Are we looking for anyone in particular, or just out for a stroll?" Baehlon's baritone rumbled beside Rhoane. He must've followed Rhoane from the market, or returned after seeing the princesses safely to the palace.

"We are searching for someone who is not there. I should not be seen with you." Rhoane moved away from the big knight to sit at a vacated booth.

A serving maid approached, hands on hips, a grimace marring her otherwise pretty face. "You got money to pay?"

He placed a few coins on the table, and she snapped them up before returning the way she came. A few minutes later she brought a tankard and trencher of food. "You're far from home, lad. What brings you to Paderau?"

"Work. How'd you know I wasn't from here?" He worked his mouth around the contractions, trying for a Southern accent.

"No one from around these parts wears a hat that tacky. Even the peasants have their pride." Rhoane hastily removed the offending garment, a sheepish grin on his lips. "You eat your sup, and I'll see if there's anyone who needs a hand. You good with a blade?"

Rhoane suppressed a laugh. She didn't mean a sword. "A little."

She adjusted her bodice and skirts, cringing slightly. "Gods, but it's hot today. You menfolk are lucky, what with your loose breeches and all."

"Whyn't you wear 'em? Or is there a law 'gainst women being comfortable?"

"You're a cheeky one." Her warm smile hinted at

flirtation. "Only soldiers wear trousers, and I'm better at loving than fighting." She winked as she moved away, her backside sashaying beneath her heavy skirts.

Two men sat at the table behind him, voices lowered, their words spoken in a rush. Rhoane ate his stew and eavesdropped. His heightened Eleri hearing made their voices as clear as if they sat with him. One of the men, the spice merchant Taryn had mentioned the previous evening, gloated to his friend about the Summerlands princess's visit that morning.

"I told her about the embargoes on our goods. She had no idea."

"Or she knows but is protecting the empress. Tread lightly, Tabul. She might be a countrywoman, but she's been with the Talaithian whore long enough we should question her loyalty."

Rhoane stretched his body, twisting his back and head until his muscles cracked. The movement allowed him a brief glimpse of the speaker. He returned to his ale before drawing attention to himself, mentally marking the man's features.

"She's no more loyal to the crown than my dog. I spoke to her at length over tea. She's homesick and desperate for any news of the Summerlands. I've sent word to my brother in Talaith. He will find a way to ingratiate himself to her. Perhaps with her help we can lift the taxes."

"That harlot is bleeding us until there will be nothing left. Did you see her daughters in the market? Wearing fine silks while we must squat in the dust for pittance." The man spit on the floor. "The lot of them should be put to the blade."

"Shush!" Tabul warned. "You'll draw the attention of the guard. I have a nice business here and don't need your radical ideas making trouble."

"Wishing that woman and her misbegotten spawn would stop stealing my money is not radical. Forcing the lot of them to suck my cock while I sit on the Light Throne? That's radical."

"Hold your tongue, man! That's treason, and I'll have none of it."

Rhoane slid from his seat and stood at the men's table. "I am certain you did not mean what you just said, my friend." Rhoane's quiet voice held the strength of steel.

"What's it to you, peasant?"

Tabul stammered an apology, saying to Rhoane, "Don't listen to him. He's not right in the head. Words come out that he doesn't mean."

The other man stared at Tabul with a look of murder in his eyes. "I meant what I said. The empress and her lot are worthless bitches. Aelinae would be better off without them."

Rhoane grabbed the man by the collar and dragged him from the booth. The first punch connected with his nose in a resounding *crack*. A thick stream of blood flowed over his lips. The second jab landed in the man's midsection, rendering him breathless and on his knees.

"Enough!" Baehlon's voice broke through the crowd. His huge hand pulled Rhoane away before he could strike again.

A sickening wheezing came from the man. He stood with the help of Tabul and regarded Rhoane with skepticism. Then his fist lashed out, hitting Rhoane square on the temple.

The blow dazed him, and he staggered against Baehlon before righting himself. Another punch aimed at his sternum had Rhoane gasping. Tabul pulled his friend toward their table, apologizing over and over again for the trouble.

"I stand by my words, *peasant*," he asserted, the last word said with contempt.

"Then you shall die by them." Rhoane reached for his sword, but it wasn't there. He'd left it at the palace. Before Baehlon could hold him back, Rhoane lunged at the man.

The tavern erupted at once with tables being overturned,

chairs broken across backs. Rhoane attacked the man, each punch aimed at restoring Lliandra's honor. His fists bled with the beating he gave the other man. Baehlon called for order and was ignored by most everyone in the tavern. When finally the duke's guard arrived, it took them several minutes to break up the fighting.

Rhoane breathed heavily beside Baehlon, his split lip swelling and blood dripping from a nasty cut above his eye. For every two hits he'd connected, the other man had made one. *At least he looked far worse*, Rhoane thought.

Baehlon gave the tavern owner several gold coins to pay for the damage and dragged Rhoane out to the street.

"Blood and ashes, man. What was that about?"

"He insulted Lliandra and her daughters."

"And so you thought you'd give him a bit of justice, is that it?"

Rhoane shuffled alongside Baehlon, his head throbbing from the fight. "Yesterday something unseen stalked Taryn. Today, a merchant wished, in public, for the death of the empress. Yes, I sought justice. Is that so wrong?"

Baehlon didn't answer. He didn't need to. Rhoane knew his actions were unnecessary. His frustrations had gotten the better of him.

"Tell the guard to keep watch on him. And the merchant Tabul. If there is an uprising, we need to be forewarned. Also, we should look into something Tabul mentioned. He said Lliandra has placed embargoes on the Summerlands products. If this is true, she is breaking the law."

Baehlon grinned as they passed through the palace gates. "Aside from a potential riot, did you discover anything useful?"

"Yes. Women envy our breeches."

"Well, I thought that was obvious." Baehlon rumbled a low chuckle.

Chapter 23

ON THE morning they were to leave for Talaith, Taryn made one last visit to the kitchens to give Carga a bouquet of wild flowers.

The cook's eyes misted when Taryn handed her the small arrangement. "It was very sweet of you to remember me."

"You let me breakfast with you every morning, it was the least I could do. I'm only sorry I don't have anything of real value to give."

"Nonsense, you gave from your heart, and that is richer than all the coin in the world."

"I hope to see you soon."

Carga held Taryn's face between her hands, touching their foreheads together. "You will." More murmuring swirled in Taryn's mind, and dizziness rocked her. The voices trailed off when Carga pulled back. "I am glad to have met you, Taryn."

Taryn took the stairs two at a time and ran into Rhoane at the kitchen door. His bruises were healing, but they still looked ghastly. The last thing she ever thought Rhoane would be in was a bar fight, but according to Baehlon, that's what happened. Rhoane simply said he was teaching a man a lesson.

"Saying your goodbyes?" He asked, holding open the door for her.

She stepped through and shielded her eyes from the bright sun. "I'll miss her. Do you think we'll come back?"

"One never knows where their path will take them."

"Don't start with that again. I finally got my runes to stop glowing. You might get them all excited." In the morning light, the runes looked like a ghost tattoo on her skin. Less than a month since she arrived on Aelinae, the world was becoming familiar to her, like home. Like she'd always lived there. On the way to the stables, Taryn greeted several soldiers, who waved in return. "You were right, you know. I have acclimated to being here. I feel alive, almost as if over there I was just going through the motions."

He helped her onto Ashanni, resting his hand on her thigh. "Life is precious, Taryn. Never take it for granted or waste a moment of it."

"I won't. Not ever again." When he removed his hand, she longed for its warmth.

She distracted herself by checking her bags. The sword was once again wrapped in a blanket and tied to her saddle. Protected in the gorgeous scabbard Baehlon gave her for her birthday, he'd stressed the need to keep it hidden until they reached Talaith.

Hayden pulled his horse up to hers. His handsome leather jacket of burnished brown set off his hazel eyes, giving him a devilish look. "The empress has granted Father and me permission to stay in Talaith until after Harvest."

Taryn suppressed a grin. "Really? So I'm stuck with you for, what, three more moonturns? Does the empress hate me?"

Hayden snapped his reins at Taryn. "Her decision, I'll have you know, had nothing to do with you."

Of course it didn't. It had everything to do with Sabina and they both knew it.

The captain of the duke's guard called out, and the

caravan slowly made its way off the palace grounds. A wave of excitement mixed with apprehension washed over her. Once they reached Talaith, she had to make a decision about her future. Stay with the others, or forge out on her own. Either way, she couldn't keep listing through life without a current to carry her. She would avenge Brandt's death in time, but until then, she needed something to *do*.

Duke Anje refused to let her stay at Paderau, either as a cook or a soldier, and so she set her sights on finding employment in Talaith. Faelara kept dropping hints that Empress Lliandra would have a position for her, but that wasn't a life Taryn wanted to live. Being cooped up in a palace wasn't for her. She needed her freedom far too much.

It took the caravan eight days to travel from Paderau to Talaith. They rode through landscapes that changed from forested hills to vast meadows. At the beginning of their journey south, they followed the Silden River, keeping close to its banks until it turned into Lake Oster. In the evenings, Taryn often saw Baehlon and Rhoane head away from camp with long poles in hand, returning later with a string of brightly colored fish.

The empress traveled in style, which made for shorter rides each day and a longer trip overall. Every afternoon, large tents were set up for her comfort, only to be taken down the next morning. There were well more than two hundred in the group, including Lliandra's and the duke's guards, as well as courtiers, nobility, servants, and the like. Taryn longed for the simplicity of travel she'd had on the journey from Ravenwood to Paderau.

Most days she rode with Hayden, often dividing her time between the soldiers and the princesses. Since the empress refused to let her daughters ride, they were stuck inside a musty carriage. Perhaps in defiance of what Celia had said, Taryn made it her mission to earn their friendship. Even so, she never forgot that they were Marissa's sisters and their loyalty would always be first to their family.

Sabina, on the other hand, didn't share that bond. She was more than willing to spy on Marissa, which caused Taryn to speculate that perhaps there was more to the Summerlands princess than everyone gave her credit for.

On the afternoon of the eighth day, Talaith hovered in the distance. Perched on a cliff, the Crystal Palace loomed like an overprotective mother, the city walls her all-encompassing embrace. Sunlight glanced off the rock, turning the palace into a great diamond whose light blazed like a beacon welcoming them home. Paderau looked like a village in comparison.

Hayden rode beside her, quiet for the first time she could remember. When she turned to see what held his tongue, she met his even stare. "What?" His look unnerved her, as if he were studying her under a microscope.

His smirk gave a hint of mischievousness she'd come to recognize as a sign of trouble. "Nothing. Here comes the Empress's Household Guard. They will escort us to the palace."

Two dozen men dressed in crimson and gold led the procession through Talaith. Their sleek black horses pranced in perfect unison, hooves clacking a staccato beat on the cobblestones. Hordes of people came out to see their empress and her beautiful daughters. The girls waved from the windows of their carriage, trying to catch the many flowers thrown to them. Taryn rode a short distance behind, watching the proceedings with curiosity and envy.

They passed under several walkways made of lacy stonework that appeared to float from one building to the next. People dressed in an array of colors and fashions were crowded on the bridges and Taryn feared they would collapse. Each home they rode by looked equally magnificent to those in the richest quarters of Paderau.

If Talaith had a slum, she didn't see it on the way to the palace. From what Taryn *could* see, the capital city had no shortage of coin. The men and women wore expensive fabrics of silk or linen. Some even braved the heat while wearing their best velvet. Every now and then, Taryn spotted someone with intricate designs drawn on their hands or faces. They were a rainbow, the inhabitants of Talaith. From palest white to deep ebony, their skin and hair was as varied as their clothing.

When the caravan crested a road that curved around a square, Taryn drew in a deep breath at the sight of a vast ocean stretching before them, broken only by tiny dots of islands far in the distance.

"Behold, the Crystal Palace." Hayden's voice cut through the cheering crowd. Taryn looked away from the ocean and stared in wonder at the massive building.

"I thought your palace was big. This place is huge." The palace stood six stories high, spreading far to the left and down to the beach below. "How many people live there?"

"Perhaps a thousand, I would imagine."

Taryn shuddered at the thought. "I could barely find my way around Paderau; how will I ever manage?"

Hayden laughed. "I'll draw you a map."

"You know the palace that well?"

"I used to summer here with my mother." He looked to the sparkling blue sea. "We'd play down at the beach and swim in the warm water."

"Perhaps you and I could go there sometime."

"I'd like that." He gave her a curious smile. "Do you think Sabina would care to join us?"

"You have feelings for her then?"

"I find her intriguing. Yes, I like her."

"Then I'm happy for you." She took his hand in hers. "I'm really glad we're friends."

"So am I." His Shanti slipped up her arm. It was warm

with a hint of precision to it.

Imposing statues lined the drive, staring down at them as they rode into a courtyard that surrounded a fountain with water flowing from the mouths of cherubs and unrecognizable creatures. Gryphons, or lions, or elephants, she wasn't sure. Perhaps a mix of all three.

Large doors, the height of three men, stood open, and many of the empress's staff waited on the steps. Taryn's gaze traveled up the gleaming walls, past the many windows, to the top of the palace. Pennants embroidered with the royal crest whipped in the wind. Several birds raced across the blue sky, their cries lost amid the din of the travelers.

A page showed her to a suite of rooms, leaving her alone as soon as she entered. Taryn wandered from room to room, reminding herself not to become too attached to them. In the space of ten minutes, she was doomed. She'd take whatever job she could for the chance to stay in Talaith. To live in this spacious, expensively decorated apartment.

After meandering through several rooms, including an office area with a desk and two chairs flanking long windows, Taryn found the bedchamber. She threw her leather satchel on the bed and went in search of a compartment to hide the sword and the seal. Finding nothing suitable, she gave up and tucked the items under her wardrobe, adding several wards to deter any unwanted attention. Since discovering her power, she'd practiced every night, making flames, warding objects, toying with shadows. Always at night. And always in secret.

Two maids wearing Lliandra's House colors entered the rooms, directing porters where to put her trunks. They introduced themselves as Cora and Ellie before asking after her needs. When Taryn said all she required was a hot bath and some tea, they disappeared before she could tell them her name. They returned promptly and began unpacking her belongings in complete silence. Their politeness and quiet efficiency was a harsh contrast to the open friendliness of Paderau.

A messenger arrived and spoke with Cora for several minutes before she returned, informing her that the empress requested Taryn dine with her the following evening. At Taryn's stunned muteness, Cora repeated the message.

"I heard you. I'm just a little surprised, is all." Taryn paced for a few minutes before turning to Cora. "Do you know where Hayden, I mean, Lord Valen, is staying?" *Too many damned names.* Why couldn't they just pick one?

After her bath, she piled her hair into an inelegant bun, much to Ellie's distress, and dressed simply. The maid led her through the palace to Hayden's rooms. Along the way, Taryn made polite conversation and discovered, with a small amount of surprise that without Cora's stern glare directed at her, Ellie was enchanting.

Hayden's valet opened the door and greeted her with a warm smile. "Miss Taryn, how lovely to see you. The ride was not too tiring, I hope?"

"Hello, Oliver. Not overly so. Of course, having you to converse with only made it that much sweeter."

He pinched her cheek. "Charmer. I'll get Lord Valen for you. Please, wait here." He disappeared into a room, leaving Taryn to look around at the sumptuous apartment. Several portraits hung on the walls and one in particular caught Taryn's eye: the duke's late wife, Gwyneira, posed with her family.

Taryn recognized Ravenwood in the background, and Gwyn's graceful features and long blonde hair looked very much like her sister's. Taryn wondered if Lliandra missed Gwyneira as much as Hayden and the duke did. For the briefest of moments, she imagined the girls as young princesses running through the Crystal Palace. The image made her chuckle.

"Did I miss something humorous?"

Taryn spun around at the sound of Hayden's voice. "I was just picturing your mother and the empress as young girls, terrorizing the palace."

"I do believe you have it right. From what I've been told, they were quite the troublemakers. For what do I have the honor of your presence?"

"I was hoping you could give me your famous tour."

His eyes lit up. "I'd love to."

She waved at Oliver. "Good night, thank you." He bowed in return. "He reminds me so much of Brandt. I do miss him so."

"You're starting to sound like the princesses. 'Oh, however will I survive, I do miss him so.'"

Taryn slapped his arm. "You're mocking my pain."

"Never—just your speech." He pushed at her with his shoulder. "I think you need a distraction, and I've just the cure." He put a finger over his lips before moving aside a large tapestry that hung on the wall. Hayden pressed himself close, his deft fingers dancing over the wood. After a soft *click*, a hidden door swung inward. Hayden produced a glowing orb, and Taryn was tempted to do the same but she wasn't ready to tell anyone her secret.

They walked along the darkened passageway through various galleries. Hayden showed her where the throne room was and how if she were to lie on her stomach and put her ear just so, she could hear the proceedings in the room below.

"I used to hide here as a young boy, listening to Lliandra holding her audiences. I learned a great deal from her. She never belittles her subjects. Every claim, whether legitimate or false, is heard with an open mind, and her justice is nearly always fair."

"She wants to dine with me tomorrow in her private rooms. Do you have any idea why?"

His gaze drifted away. "None at all."

"I'm nervous about meeting her. She never once spoke to me at Paderau, you know."

"I wouldn't worry about it if I were you. If it were something serious, she'd call her court to the throne room and you'd meet with her there."

She tried not to think of the empress while they continued their tour. Hayden wasn't lying when he said he knew this palace as well as his own. Hunger beckoned, but Hayden wanted to show her his last special hiding place—the small room where servants often slipped away when they wanted to have some privacy, usually with another servant.

"We shouldn't. If it's for the servants, leave them their secrets," Taryn objected. But Hayden ignored her, pressing on through the corridor.

When they approached the room, Hayden stopped so suddenly Taryn ran into his back. He turned quickly to shush her, his orb blinking out. The hushed tones of conversation drifted to her. A lazy orb hovered at the far end of the room, giving scant light to the space, leaving the couple in shadow. Hayden crept along the wall to hear better but Taryn tugged on his shirt, trying to get him to leave. She could just make out a shake of his head in the dark.

"You can't stay here. Mother will find out, and then everything will be ruined. We've dawdled long enough as it is. You must leave at once."

Cold dread congealed her blood when she heard Marissa's voice. She tugged on Hayden's shirt again, but he shrugged her off, moving forward. When Taryn heard Marissa's companion, her insides recoiled.

"You worry too much. I've managed to keep my presence hidden this long. A few more days won't matter." The sound of kissing filled the small space, and Taryn tried once more to pull Hayden back.

"Tell me again you want me to leave," Zakael whispered in a silky voice.

Moaning, followed by more kissing sounds, came from the darkness. Zakael and Marissa's ShantiMari swirled close enough to Taryn that if she reached out she could touch it. Zakael had Marissa against the wall, her skirts around her waist. To Hayden, everything was shrouded in dusky obscurity, but for Taryn, the couple's ShantiMari illuminated them as if they stood beneath a streetlight.

Panic whipped up her spine. They should leave, but if they moved, the pair might hear them. Instead, they stood as still as possible while Marissa and Zakael continued to moan and grunt. Zakael moved against her, his breath coming in heavy gasps as his pace quickened. Skin slapped against skin, and Taryn averted her eyes to keep from seeing them. Hearing their lovemaking was mortifying enough. With shuddering cries, they finally stopped.

Zakael breathed into Marissa's ear, "Find out what you can. I don't like this sneaking around. Tonight, come to my room at the inn." He gave her a loud kiss on the lips before leaving in the opposite direction, the lazy orb bobbing after him. After a few moments of adjusting her skirts, Marissa left the same way as Zakael.

Neither Taryn nor Hayden spoke until they were far from the secret room, and when he did, he sounded excited. "Do you know who that was in there?"

"I couldn't see anyone. Could you?"

"No, but the woman in there was Marissa, I'd swear to it."

"What about the man?"

"His voice was familiar, but not enough to say for certain."

"What should we do?" Taryn's nerves spasmed down her back. They'd been too close to being discovered.

Hayden rubbed his chin. "I suppose if the princess has a

lover, then it's none of our business."

She wanted to argue with him, to point out Zakael was the person who killed Brandt, but Hayden didn't know the details of Brandt's death or her suspicion Marissa had placed the sword above Hayden's own chest. If she told him about Zakael and the cavern, it would open a whole host of questions she couldn't answer. "I guess you're right. Strange, though, that they had to hide. I wonder who her lover is."

"It doesn't matter, really. Not unless she gets with child. Then it becomes a case for the realm to handle. I'm famished. All that exploring has worked up my appetite. Let's get some dinner while we can."

Taryn was shocked he could think of eating after what they'd witnessed. They needed to tell Rhoane, to warn the empress. Her gut wrenched with the terrible understanding she couldn't say anything to Rhoane until she had proof. Without Hayden's corroboration, he wouldn't believe her.

Rhoane had to see it for himself, which meant catching Marissa unawares. Something told Taryn skinning a carlix would be easier.

Chapter 24

TARYN'S calm expression belied the mass of nerves that twitched periodically, heightening her anxiety. Her skin, still warm from the sun, glistened with the oil Ellie had used to combat the salty dryness of the sea. Sabina and Hayden had done their best to keep her mind off her meeting with the empress by taking her to the small private cove beneath the castle.

Over the course of her day, Taryn ran through several reasons the empress might want to see her and could only come up with two. She either found out about her role in saving Hayden or she wished to discuss Brandt. Either way, Taryn wasn't looking forward to dinner with the most powerful woman in all Aelinae.

Rhoane arrived to escort her to dinner, a happy surprise to be sure, and relief washed over her. She didn't have to endure the ordeal alone. They arrived at Lliandra's door much sooner than Taryn expected, and her stomach dipped as a guard opened it for them. They waited in an entrance hall with floor-to-ceiling mirrors and a huge chandelier. Everywhere she looked, reflections of her reflection repeated in an infinite array of mirrors.

"Creepy," Taryn murmured, trying to find a single place to stand where she wouldn't have to stare at herself.

"I find the floor immensely fascinating," Rhoane intoned, eyes lowered.

A footman escorted them to Lliandra's sitting room where entire walls of crystal allowed views of the beach and ocean beyond. Striations of color, from pale jade to turquoise and finally deep denim, marked the various depths of the sea.

Rhoane leaned over to whisper, "Welcome home, *Darennsai*."

"You said that in the cavern, too, you know."

"That was to welcome you back to Aelinae. Now you are truly home." His eyes shone with intensity as he watched her.

She started to ask him what he meant when the empress swept into the room, radiant in a frothy gown of pale blue. Lliandra greeted Rhoane in Eleri and then in Elennish said, "Prince Rhoane, I'm so pleased to see you returned to Talaith. It has been much too long since you've graced our court with your charm and wit."

Rhoane bowed low. "It is I who has missed your company, Great Empress. It is my sincerest hope that my travels will abate for a long period and I can continue to enjoy your generosity at the Crystal Palace." An underlying tension marred their words, which did nothing to dispel Taryn's anxiety.

Threads of ShantiMari crisscrossed Lliandra's face, giving the observer an impression of a youthful complexion. Taryn tried not to stare at the empress, but the face beneath the veneer held the look of someone either very old or very sick. Dark circles stood out against her pallid, almost jaundiced skin. Taryn checked herself in time to smile when the empress took her hands, kissing her cheeks. At Lliandra's touch, her pendant hummed in her mind. The woman's Mari slid over her skin, cold with a touch of tension.

"Welcome, Taryn. I've heard many wonderful things about you. I hope you don't mind I put off our formal introduction until now." To Rhoane she said, "She is as lovely as they say."

"Yes, she is." A look of something close to pride danced in the depths of his eyes, unsettling her even further.

Taryn curtseyed to the empress. "Thank you, Your Majesty. I'm honored to make your acquaintance."

The empress studied her face before turning to Rhoane. "My darling prince, give us some time alone. I'd like a chance to get to know Taryn better."

A shot of panic ran through her. She had no desire to be alone with the empress. Rhoane paused a moment to touch Taryn's cheek, and in that small gesture was all the strength she needed.

Lliandra bade Taryn to sit while a servant brought them a dark red wine in crystal glasses.

"Have you ever heard of the Eiriellean Prophecy?" Lliandra asked casually.

"No, ma'am." Her pendant fluttered at her neck, distracting her thoughts.

Lliandra took a long drink before she began. "Several hundred seasons after the Great War, an oracle from the West foretold a schism in the world. A child would be born of this world, but not from this world. One who would usher in a new era for Aelinae, restoring the balance that Kaldaar had upset. For eons, the oracle's words were laughed at and discarded, but then events began to happen on Aelinae that made scholars believe the oracle might have seen something after all.

"The Master mages scoured the countryside looking for the child. Then, in the seventy-fifth season of the Sylthan Age, another oracle had a vision. It was different from the first. She spoke of an Eirielle who would destroy all that lingered of the old regime, bringing forth a terrible and frightening future for Aelinae."

Lliandra's voice was distant, as if she were back in time with the sages of old. "Once more, mages searched every kingdom looking for the child, this time so they could destroy the one of prophecy. After a thousand seasons of searching, the mages once again discounted the oracle's vision and gave up."

The empress paused in her recounting and stared into her empty wineglass. Taryn waited patiently for her to continue but Lliandra sat silent with her thoughts.

"Your Majesty?" Taryn hoped to prompt the rest of the story.

A servant announced dinner, and Lliandra beckoned Taryn to follow.

A massive table, large enough to sit twenty people comfortably, was set with two places at one end. Fragile plates and glasses made of rose-colored crystal rested on a tablecloth of gold filigree. Knives and forks, trimmed in gold and embedded with pearlized shells, fanned out from the plates. One servant filled their goblets with more of the rich wine while another brought out several dishes of various sea creatures. Purplish lobster-looking things rested atop toast; legs, from what Taryn hoped were crabs, oozing butter were placed before her. Doughy rounds stuffed with white fish and smothered in cream sauce came next. Despite its unusual appearance, the food smelled delicious.

Lliandra turned to Taryn. "I hear I must thank you for saving the life of my nephew."

"Hayden? That was nothing."

"So you are as humble as I've heard. What you did was not 'nothing.' That took bravery."

"Or stupidity." She smiled at the empress. "I think I lack the former and have too much of the latter."

"Nonsense." *The sword would not have chosen you if that were true. Do you have it—the sword?*

The last she spoke in Taryn's mind, startling her. Rhoane had told her no one could enter her mind unless invited.

I don't need to know where it is, only that you have it.

"Yes," Taryn said, gently nudging the empress from her thoughts.

"No one else must know of it, and I'm afraid the walls have ears."

Lliandra's midnight blue threads of ShantiMari interlaced throughout the room. Other colors lingered from past empresses; their threads frayed but still powerful.

"I wanted to thank you for the lovely apartment. I don't know how to repay your kindness." Taryn said, changing the subject.

Lliandra took dainty bites of her food before replying. "You have quite captured my daughters' hearts and imaginations. According to them, there is nothing you cannot do."

"They're sweet but mistaken." She quickly added, "I like them very much. They have been very gracious to me."

"That is nice to hear, thank you," Lliandra said sincerely. "And how do you fare with my eldest daughter?"

Taryn took a bite to stall her answer. "I haven't had the opportunity to get to know Princess Marissa as well as your younger daughters, but I hope my stay here will reverse that."

Lliandra laughed, a throaty sound that belied her delicate frame. "Well said. You might make a politician yet. I was led to believe you speak from your heart, but it seems you also have a brain that works equally as well."

"Your Majesty?"

"There is so much you cannot possibly understand, and I am sorry for that, but as Marissa is my heir, it would serve you well to stay in her good graces. The next few weeks will be trying for you, to be sure."

Lliandra started a new story, one that involved the Overlord of the West. "The first man I ever fell in love with lived on the other side of the world. I saw him often at court, but he was nearly a man, and I was but a child. That didn't stop him from charming and beguiling me so completely that I dreamed of one day marrying him so we could rule our kingdoms together."

"Did he return this love?"

"He did. Valterys and I shared a bond not many lovers have." Lliandra's eyes glossed with unshed tears. A longing fluttered beneath her words. "I was inconsolable after the death of Marissa's father—he was beheaded for trying to poison me. Some say he wanted to seize the crown for his daughter, but she was neigh on five seasons. Still, I forced her to watch her father's death as a reminder never to cross me."

Taryn swallowed a sip of wine with difficulty.

"Don't think too unkindly of me, please. To be a great ruler, you must be willing to make sacrifices. Marissa understood that and is now my worthiest ally."

Taryn nodded her agreement, surreptitiously checking the room for exits.

Lliandra continued without pause, "Valterys came to me out of friendship. By then, Zakael's mother was long dead and because I had never truly stopped caring for him, we became lovers." Taryn couldn't imagine the angry man she saw at Ravenwood with the fragile empress. "Despite my continued pleas, Valterys refused to marry me and co-rule our kingdoms. For ten seasons, we were together. Most of that time I opened my bed to only Valterys, but my appetites are many and I admit, I had others that satisfied my needs."

Taryn squirmed in her seat, mentally counting the egg-and-dart pattern around the ceiling to keep from hearing all of the empress's lurid details. When a servant brought dessert and Lliandra persisted in her tale, Taryn blushed furiously and kept her head lowered, her focus on her plate. The frothy concoction might've been delicious, but it settled on her tongue like sand.

"I loved Valterys with every fiber of my being. I would've given him my throne if he'd but asked." Lliandra finished at last.

Taryn nodded, seriously doubting Lliandra would *give* her throne to anyone, including her daughters.

With dinner concluded, they moved to the sitting room, where another servant brought them sweet wine in tiny glasses accompanied by a shot of something that smelled like sewage and tasted even worse. Lliandra held her glass aloft, giving a silent toast before tossing it back. Taryn had no choice but to follow suit. The disgusting sludge burned down her throat to her already unsettled belly.

After knocking back another shot, Lliandra picked up the thread of her story from dinner. "For most of our time together, Valterys was loving and kind. He doted on me and Marissa. Zakael would visit from time to time, but he mostly kept to Caer Idris." Lliandra signaled for another shot of the soupy liquid. "This is my favorite blend of trisp. Have you had this before?"

"No, Your Majesty," Taryn said, stifling a shudder and declining the servant's offer of another. The smell alone was enough to make her gag.

"It wasn't until I got with child that Valterys's personality changed. I had no idea what the man planned for our unborn baby."

Lliandra stood so suddenly that Taryn jumped. She went to the window, rubbing her arms as if cold. A minute passed in silence as Taryn waited for Lliandra to continue, all the while debating if protocol allowed her to comfort the empress. The woman looked frail and alone as she stared at the unchanging scenery. She might be hanged for it, but Taryn couldn't just watch her shiver. Compassion won out, and she wrapped a blanket around Lliandra's shoulders.

"You are kind." Lliandra's breath emptied in a sigh. "That just might be enough." She pulled the blanket tight over her shoulders.

"Might be enough for what?"

Lliandra ignored her question. "Valterys used me to give him a son who would hold both the power of Light and Dark. He'd discovered an ancient translation of the Eiriellean Prophecy and was certain our child would be *the one*."

Taryn brought Lliandra another glass of trisp, mentally making the connection between the two stories.

"Drink this, Your Majesty. I see this is difficult for you. Please, don't continue on my behalf."

"It's all on your behalf, little one." Lliandra took a sip before continuing her story. "On a night ravaged by heavy rains, I delivered a stillborn son. My heart ached for the death of the little prince, but a part of me rejoiced that Valterys would never be able to take him from me and corrupt him with his vile Dark teachings." She turned misty eyes on Taryn. "You've met his son Zakael, you've witnessed the cruelty he's capable of, but trust me when I say I know all too well how he can beguile you with an endearing smile while simultaneously ripping out your heart with his bare hands."

Taryn shuddered at the empress's words. That was exactly what Zakael had done to Rhoane in her nightmare.

"While we were mourning the death of the prince, the midwife cried out that there was another child. It was bittersweet I gave birth to a baby girl that night. A girl that showed all the signs of having both Shanti and Mari. An anomaly. The child of prophecy born from Light and Dark."

"What did you do? Did Valterys find out and take her?"

Lliandra's voice dropped to barely a whisper. "Valterys never found her. I sent her away with a trusted advisor before anyone knew there had been a second child. The midwives were compelled to forget about the girl."

"What happened to her?" Taryn's pendant vibrated with alarming force. She could taste the wine she drank in the back of her throat. Details and memories were coalescing in a most disturbing way.

"She and her guardian escaped, but somehow Valterys found out about the second child and has been looking for her ever since."

Taryn recalled Zakael in the cavern, demanding Brandt return something to his father. Her stomach roiled.

"Taryn, that baby girl was you." Lliandra watched her face, studied her reaction.

Her pendant burst into song as if finally released from its tethers.

Taryn's knees buckled, and she swayed dangerously close to the wall of glass. With surprising strength, the empress caught her and settled her in a chair.

"It can't be. I'm not that girl. I'm nothing—a nobody." The jubilant song drowned out all sound. She grabbed her head, demanding quiet in her mind. Her thoughts scattered and then swirled around the muted tunes. The glass of sweet wine shook when she brought it to her lips. "It isn't possible."

"It is, Taryn. Nadra and I sent you to live far away where Valterys could not find you. I never knew where you went, but I watched as you grew into a lovely young woman."

"Why? How?"

Lliandra pulled a looking glass from her pocket. "With Nadra's help, I was able to see you from time to time." Tears spilled from her eyes. "I missed so much of your life, Taryn. Now that you've returned, we can be together."

"Brandt," Taryn said with an ache that burned clear to her soul, "is he my grandfather?"

"In blood, no. But his love for you is real. Never, ever think for one moment that he isn't what you know him to be in your heart."

Brandt was not her grandfather. Lliandra and Valterys were her parents.

She went numb. Memories of her childhood with Brandt raced through her mind alongside images she didn't yet understand, as if her past and future blurred into one and then winked out. The flimsy fabric of her dress suffocated her. Through a fog of confusion and tears, Lliandra spoke to her, but the words drifted away unheard. Without asking permission, she paced around the room until her heart quieted, and the rest of the story unfolded before her.

"If Brandt took me away to protect me from my father, why did he bring me back? Why now?"

"You are an adult, Taryn. Your power is fully realized."

"Why didn't you tell me at Paderau? Why make me wait?"

Lliandra avoided looking at Taryn, her hands clasping and unclasping several times before she replied. "You needed time to understand this world. I also wanted you to have a chance to meet your family without the obligations of a title." Lliandra's features softened, "You were raised far from home. I thought it best you eased into your new life."

Suddenly the realization hit her. "Oh my God, I have sisters!" And then, "I have a brother. Holy fuck, I have a twin. Had." She dropped into a chair. "This is a lot to take in. I went from an orphan to having an entire family in two minutes."

Lliandra knelt before her and pulled Taryn into her arms. Odd details crystallized in her mind. Lliandra smelled of lilacs and roses. And even though Lliandra was slight, her frame was strong as she held Taryn. The ShantiMari she saw crisscrossing Lliandra's face faltered for a moment and then snapped back in place.

"My daughter, you always had a family, and now you are finally home."

"That's what Rhoane said. Does he know?"

"Of course. So does Myrddin, Faelara, Baehlon, and Anje. They were sworn to secrecy, even from telling you."

"What about Hayden and the princesses?"

"No one else but those few know who you truly are. They are my most trusted friends and have known about you since your birth."

"I don't know what to say, or do. This is a total shock."

"Tomorrow, I will present you to the court. My seamstress, Margaret Tan, tells me your gown is ready."

Just the thought of a formal presentation to the court, where Taryn would be acknowledged by Lliandra as her daughter, overwhelmed her. Paralyzed her.

"We'll keep the ceremony simple. There's no need to elaborate as to where you've been for thirty-five seasons. We'll focus on your return." Lliandra rambled aloud about the details of the ceremony, but Taryn barely heard.

She had a family.

"I've asked your father to be here, as well."

Valterys.

Taryn's insides quailed with a deep trembling.

The more Lliandra spoke, the farther away her freedom slipped. Leaving Talaith was no longer an option. The betrayal stung. Brandt should have told her. Or one of the others. Royal command or no, they could've given a hint or two to prepare her for this.

"What if I don't want to be a princess? Can I say no to this anomaly thing?"

"You are who you are, Taryn. You cannot deny that."

Taryn massaged her temples, wincing against the throb in her head. "I don't know who this person is that you think I am. What if I'm not her?" She looked up at Lliandra.

"I can sense your power from here. You are the Eirielle. You are my daughter. Whether you choose to accept this or not, it remains so."

Taryn moved to look out the windows. The surf glowed white in the moonlight. If only Brandt had told her.

As if reading her thoughts, Lliandra said, "Brandt did as he was told. He raised you without any knowledge of Aelinae or your birthright to protect you. He is your savior, Taryn. He gave up his life to keep you safe. Do not mistake his actions." Lliandra's voice was stern, but Taryn heard the love she had for Brandt.

"Faelara." Taryn turned to look at the empress. "Brandt was her father?"

"She knew the risks involved and wouldn't have it any other way."

Taryn's chest tightened as a wave of emotion swept over her. She wanted to weep, to scream, to rail against Lliandra, to run to her sisters, to see Rhoane. "What do you want from me?"

"Does this mean you accept who you are?"

"I don't know what to think right now."

Lliandra put her arms around her, resting her face against Taryn's cheek. Sudden images flared in her mind: a dark night, Lliandra's screams of pain, the first baby, born dead. After that, it was a blur of faces and figures rushing around the birthing chamber.

Then there was Brandt, younger and more fit, but the man she knew as her grandfather. He stood with Nadra as Lliandra cried out in joy at the birth of the second child. A bright light shone forth from the infant.

Lliandra's face crumbled into tears when Nadra took the baby from her mother's arms, and placed a tiny hand on the pommel of the sword. Songs burst inside Taryn's mind as if she were there again, touching the sword. Nadra kissed the infant before giving her to Brandt.

He bent low over his empress in farewell and then left the room with the tiny thing in his arms. Rhoane, looking as handsome and young as he did that very evening, followed close behind.

The scene changed, and Taryn saw Valterys stride into the chamber. Upon being presented with his stillborn son, he raged at Lliandra, vowing revenge. The violence he inflicted on her that morning wasn't physical, but much longer lasting.

Lliandra pulled away. "That was the last time I saw you until the ball at Paderau. You can try to deny this or you can embrace it with all the power you possess. I warn you, denial will not make it so."

Taryn searched Lliandra's eyes, seeing in them the heartbreak she suffered when Taryn was taken away. "I'll bring the sword tomorrow. Is there anything else I need to do?"

Relief spread across Lliandra's face. "Nothing more than carry yourself with dignity. I will announce to the court that my long lost daughter has returned, and you will be home, finally, as my daughter and a princess.

"Faelara will help you in the morning. Right now, I want to discuss those marks on your hand." Taryn instinctively hid her hand beneath her gown. "I know they're there; you cannot hide them from me." Lliandra studied the runes. "They are incomplete. Tell me, Taryn, do you understand the meaning of these bonds?"

"I know they mean Rhoane and I are connected in some way and that we can read each other's thoughts, but beyond that I'm not sure."

A discreet knock at the door interrupted Lliandra's next words. Both women looked up to see Rhoane enter with the footman. "Ah, Rhoane, exquisite timing. I'm afraid I've given our dear Taryn much to think about this evening. Will you see that she gets to her rooms safely?"

"Of course, Your Majesty."

Taryn touched Lliandra's arm. "You were going to tell me

about these bonds."

"Rhoane can tell you what you need to know. I've burdened you with enough for one evening. Sleep well, my darling daughter. I'll see that your rooms are moved while we are at the crowning ceremony."

"Why do you have to move my rooms?"

"Because you will be a princess. Your apartments must reflect this change in status."

Taryn shook her head. "I don't think I'll ever understand court politics."

"I sometimes wish I didn't understand them so well." Lliandra turned to Rhoane. "Thank you for taking care of my little girl." She tapped Taryn's *cynfar*. "I felt your presence with her, always."

Taryn wrapped her fingers protectively around the pendant. "What do you mean?"

"Even before the bonding, you and I were connected through your *cynfar*. While you were away, I could feel your happiness and your sorrow. I never knew what you were doing, but I knew what you were feeling," Rhoane explained.

"Don't you think it's a little disturbing how all of you could spy on me and I had no idea you even existed?" She walked to the door and turned back to Lliandra. "I'd appreciate it in the future if you'd grant me the courtesy of privacy."

"You are a princess now. Privacy is a rare commodity for us all." Lliandra's voice was soft and full of sorrow.

Instead of going to her rooms, Taryn asked to walk while she processed everything Lliandra had told her. They strolled through the vast gardens, Rhoane keeping the conversation to a minimum, speaking only to point out a certain flower or plant he thought Taryn might like.

They passed fountains and hedges cut in ornamental shapes. Their steps crunched on crushed seashell paths, echoing in the quiet night. Eventually they made their way through a tall maze at the outer edge of the garden, where they stood beside a low wall overlooking the ocean.

A soft breeze cut through the summer heat, and Taryn shivered. Rhoane moved close behind her, skimming his hands down her bare arms, wrapping them around her waist. It would be too easy to give in to the delicious feel of his embrace, to sink back and drown in the familiar scent of him.

Reluctantly, she pulled away to face him. "Rhoane, don't. You're promised to another."

"Taryn," he whispered, "*you* are my betrothed."

The words hung between them, Taryn not trusting herself to speak.

"Does this displease you?"

"It pleases me very much." If he could feel the rapid pace of her heart or the tightening of her chest, he wouldn't have had to ask. "I never thought I'd hear those words said to me."

His lips touched hers, gentle, inquisitive. Sound vanished as her blood pulsed in her ears. Taryn surrendered to the kiss, letting go of the control she'd fought to hold on to for so long.

Thrilling sparks of fire blazed through every nerve, pooling in a knot below her belly button. Lliandra's words were a distant memory as Taryn sloughed off her disquiet and allowed herself to be in the moment. Rhoane's kiss deepened, and she opened herself to him.

He pulled back, eyes lidded, and left her breathless, wanting more. "How? I'm not Eleri."

"You are much more than either Eleri or Aelan." He traced a finger along her jaw, running his thumb over her lips.

A jag of excitement rippled beneath her skin, alighting her senses.

"When I was born," Rhoane continued, a shiver echoing

in his words, "the Eleri goddess Verdaine prophesied that I would leave my people and live among the Aelans. I would be an exile, a *sheanna*, among the Eleri. I would live as an outcast in both my land and that of the Aelans, never fully accepted by either, but it was also said that one day a child would be born of the Light and Dark. A very special child who would need my help if she were to succeed in her quest to bring balance back to the world."

"You left your people? That must be awful."

"It is for a purpose greater than my own." He smiled, and it melted her insides as surely as a flame to chocolate. "You, Princess Taryn, are the one Verdaine prophesied when I was born."

"So you believe I'm this anomaly—the Eirielle."

"I do."

"You gave up a kingdom for me…" She spoke more to herself than to him, her words trailed away on the breeze.

"What I gained is worth more than all the crowns in the world."

Everything Lliandra had told her, coupled with Rhoane's revelation, was too much for Taryn to bear. The responsibility settled heavy upon her with crushing permanence. There had been signs—the cavern, Rhoane's cryptic words about his betrothed, Baehlon's insistence she learn to master the sword—all of it threatened to drown her.

Tiny lights blinked on the ocean, a ship sailing into Talaith's harbor most likely, and for one impossible moment Taryn saw herself running from the palace and stowing away. Except, she had never run from a challenge in her life and wasn't about to start now. She needed time. Time to sort through her feelings for Rhoane. Time to understand what it was Lliandra expected of her. Time to accept her fate.

Of everything she'd been given, time was the only luxury she was denied.

Chapter 25

TARYN stood outside the throne room, wearing the gown Margaret Tan had brought to her that morning. When she moved, the fabric changed color from silver to ice blue to pale pink. Tiny diamonds glittered and winked with each swish of the skirt, sending rainbow prisms dancing along the walls. More exquisite than anything Margaret Tan had made for her, it was fancier by far than any of the gowns she'd seen the princesses wear. A silver robe trimmed in white fur and dotted with more diamonds trailed several feet behind her. Taryn gripped the sword under the robe.

Faelara stood with the others, speaking in muted tones while they waited to be announced. She'd arrived at Taryn's rooms early to help with the preparations, overseeing everything from how Taryn wore her hair to what she ate for breakfast. Taryn was grateful she'd had the time with her. It had given them an opportunity to talk about Brandt. At Taryn's attempt to apologize for being insensitive, Faelara waved her off. But Brandt gave up his family for her; her guilt ran deep.

The pounding of the chamberlain's heavy staff brought Taryn back to the present, making her tremble. In a matter of moments, she would be presented to the Crystal Court. Trumpeted fanfare heralded Lliandra and her daughters into the throne room. An eternity later, when the crowd quieted, the empress spoke eloquently to the gathered nobles, calling the occasion "auspicious" but saying nothing about her missing daughter. She flattered them and joked with Myrddin about the passing of time.

Beads of sweat trickled down Taryn's back. After yet another eternity, the doors opened. In a booming voice Taryn was certain they heard in Paderau, the chamberlain announced her companions. Sir Baehlon de Monteferron escorted Lady Faelara, followed by Duke Anje and his son, and finally, Prince Rhoane of the Eleri. The chamberlain offered no explanation why they were accorded a special entrance, nor did he announce Taryn. She fidgeted, uncertain if she should follow the group. When she took a step forward, the guard motioned for her to wait. The soothing tune of her sword did little to quell her racing heart or alleviate the feeling of insecurity that paralyzed her.

She clutched the sword with both hands, willing herself to stand tall and have courage. The others made their way to the dais, bowing low to the empress. Lliandra stood before the court, resplendent in a gown of glittering gold, welcoming Taryn's companions. Myrddin stood to her left, looking regal in a deep blue doublet and black leggings and watching her with a mischievous sparkle in his eyes.

Lliandra descended the dais to kiss the cheeks of each of Taryn's friends. When she finished, she motioned for them to join the princesses. She returned to the raised platform and spoke in a soft voice amplified through ShantiMari to the back of the throne room.

"As most of you know, a little more than thirty-five seasons ago I had a son who died in childbirth."

A murmur of condolences spread through the crowd with several figure eights traced in the air above their heads.

"But only a few knew that I also had a daughter that

night." The crowd quieted. Heads turned toward Taryn, who stood frozen in the doorway, trying to ignore the stares. "Because of certain information I acquired about this child, it was decided that she would be raised innocent of her birthright. My most loyal subject and trusted advisor, the High Priest Brandt Kaj Endion took the child to raise as his own."

Lliandra's voice caught, and she put a hand to her lips. "It is with profound sadness we have learned Brandt was tragically killed upon his return to our great kingdom." Mutters and nervous twittering bubbled from the crowd. "He died protecting someone he loved as much as Aelinae—my daughter."

A sob rose in Taryn's throat, and she blinked back tears.

And in that same instant, the sword in her hands vanished.

One second she held the hilt with a death grip, the next it was gone. Not wanting to cause alarm, but panicking all the same, she searched around her as much as she could without actually turning. The guard's scowl was sharp enough to cut leather.

She took a deep breath, smoothed her gown, and clasped her robe closed just as Lliandra announced, "Lords, ladies, nobles of Aelinae, today we have gathered to bear witness to the return of Princess Taryn Rose."

Trumpets blared from the gallery, startling Taryn. The guard motioned for her to move forward, but her body wouldn't obey. It took all her will not to turn and bolt from the palace. Just when she thought she might, she looked straight ahead and met Rhoane's even gaze. A resignation of sorts rested in his eyes, the cautious look of worry she first saw in the cavern, but beyond his fears, she saw his belief in her. Taking one step at a time, Taryn made her way up the long aisle.

Her empty hands clutched the robe as her mind taunted

her. *The empress is going to kill you.*

Two songs played in her mind—one a festive refrain, the other harmonizing in dulcet tones. Two songs meant the sword was near. That was enough to calm her for the moment.

To her right, Lords Tinsley and Aomori beamed their pleasure and clapped politely as she passed. She smiled at them, grateful for the friendly faces. She glanced to her left and saw Lady Celia's pale face, looking as frigid as a marble bust, hostility clear in her hazel eyes. Beside her, Lord Herbret stood just as immobile, but his glare looked past Taryn to Marissa.

She pulled her robe tighter, pushed her shoulders back, and walked with her head held high, as Faelara had taught her to do.

When she reached the dais, she stopped before the empress to curtsey low, almost to the ground.

"Arise, daughter of Aelinae." Lliandra motioned for Taryn to join her on the dais. When she turned around to face the crowd, her stomach pinched at all the faces before her. Some of them were delighted, others confused, and even more bore outright hatred. Her confidence faltered.

Breathe, Taryn. You have every right to be here. Rhoane's melodic voice soothed her spinning thoughts.

The sword's gone. It just vanished. She chanced a glance at him and saw in his mossy eyes the reassurance she needed. A wicked half-smile teased her.

It cannot have gone far. Be still. It will return when needed.

"If there is anyone who doubts my claim that this girl, Taryn Rose, is indeed my daughter, let him or her come forward now and state his or her case."

An excited twittering rustled in the crowd. Taryn held her breath, waiting for an objection that did not come. "Very well, let it be known that all nobles in attendance accept this child as my daughter and one of my legal heirs."

Nadra drifted slowly to the floor then, her radiance illuminating the throne room. The audience lowered as one, their heads bent in supplication. When they rose, several of the angry members of court looked at Taryn anew, mistrust slipping from their features.

Nadra greeted the crowd with gracious words and a loving glance before turning to Taryn. "It is with a happy heart that I see the two of you reunited. On that day so long ago when our paths separated and the fate of this land hung in the balance, it was most difficult to let you leave our side. But now that you have returned, balance will be restored."

A crown, the likes of which Taryn had never seen, with radiant tips covered in gems and swags of diamonds, materialized in the air above Taryn's head.

"Daughter of Light and Keeper of the Stars, I bestow upon you this crown, made of moonstone and stardust so that all will know your birthright."

The crown settled on Taryn's head, harmonizing perfectly with her *cynfar* and, thankfully, her sword. Perhaps Rhoane was right. It would return when needed.

"As you have witnessed, Nadra, Great Mother of all Creation, has accepted Taryn as my child. Her gift of this crown is proof that she is the Child of Light. Ohlin has also accepted Taryn as the daughter of Valterys, Overlord of the West and Lord of the Dark.

"When she was but a few moments old, her palm was placed upon the very sword Ohlin crafted for his own daughter, so that when she returned, it would know her and reveal her true identity. We have asked the Lord of the Dark to join us today, but I see he has declined." Sadness echoed in her words. She whispered for Taryn to produce the sword.

Panic surged through Taryn. "I don't have it," she said through a tight smile.

"What?" Lliandra hissed.

"It," Taryn began, unsure how to explain, "just vanished."

A storm raged across Lliandra's features, visible to none but Taryn. The ShantiMari that concealed her age cracked, then smoothed like the surface of a lake. Lliandra opened her mouth to speak and stopped short, her gaze drifting upward to where a sphere of light descended from the glass ceiling.

The gathered nobles rustled anxiously, their apprehension palpable as Taryn stood on the dais. The light elongated, and she struggled to make out the figure manifesting from the brightness.

A man stepped forward and embraced Nadra.

"My dearest Ohlin." The goddess brushed her lips across the cheek of her eternal mate.

He cupped her face in his hand, a wistful smile on his face. Then he addressed the crowd. "As you know, I prefer to remain neutral in your affairs. But there are times when I feel compelled to intervene." He took Taryn's hand in his, pulling her to stand beside him and Lliandra. "This girl before you is as Empress Lliandra says. She was born in this very palace thirty-five seasons ago. She was raised without any knowledge of you," he swept his gaze over the nobles, "or her role in your future." Ohlin nudged her, and she swallowed hard, trying to recall the short speech Faelara had written for her.

"Friends," she began, hating the screech of nerves in her pitch, "for many long seasons, I lived outside the customs and traditions of your great kingdom. Despite this, I am committed to learning all I can so that we can keep the peace and balance on Aelinae. I ask that you find it in your hearts to accept me as one of your own."

"What about her father?" a voice called from the crowd. "Does he, in truth, accept her as his heir?"

Lliandra answered in a soft voice. "I should hope he does. Perhaps we should ask him, *Lord Zakael.*" The crowd gasped and moved aside to let him through. A hooded figure followed closely behind. A thrum of ShantiMari flowed over Taryn, and she shuddered against it.

"You are too bold, Your Majesty," Zakael said, the sneer on his lips flowing to his words.

"Am I? For presenting my daughter in an open court? Should I slink around beneath a cloak like Lord Valterys?"

A ripple of nervous confusion floated through the audience as the hooded figure took off his cloak. Valterys stood not more than ten paces from Taryn. Rhoane stepped forward, but Nadra put out a hand to stop him.

"My dear Valterys, I was hoping you could be here for today's ceremony. Do you wish to make a claim on this girl?" Nadra asked.

Taryn willed herself to stand tall. He wouldn't dare try to hurt her with so many people around.

"If she is my daughter, as I'm sure you believe, I want proof." Valterys glared at Lliandra. "I only knew of one child born that night. He was quite dead when I saw him."

Lliandra's voice dripped sugar thick enough to sweeten the sourest lemon. "Lord Valterys, you, of all people, should understand why I had to make the decision to send Taryn away."

Ohlin stepped down to face Valterys, putting a hand on his shoulder. His dark hair and hazy grey eyes were a softer shade of the Lord of the Dark's. "The girl is indeed your daughter. Judge her not, for she is innocent in this. Love her as you do your son."

Valterys bowed to the god but not before a brief scowl crossed his face.

Ohlin returned to the dais and stood in front of Taryn. For a long time, he merely looked into her eyes. She met his gaze, feeling light and free. Finally, he inspected the runes that glowed faintly against her skin.

"When you are ready, come to me that I may add my blessing."

"Yes, sir."

The skin near his eyes crinkled when he smiled. "I believe this is yours." With a flourish of his wrist, the sword materialized, causing a murmur to ripple through the crowd. "I am pleased the sword has chosen you."

"Thank you." She knelt before the god, her legs trembling enough to make her crown rattle. She kept her eyes focused on his boots and steadied herself.

"It is with great honor and lightness of heart that I bestow upon you this sword as a symbol of your birthright. Arise, daughter of Valterys, Lord of the Dark, and Lliandra, Lady of Light. From this day henceforth, you shall be known as Princess Taryn Rose of House Galendrin, Keeper of the Stars, Eirielle, Child of Light and Dark, *Darennsai* and betrothed to Prince Rhoane of the Eleri, as prophesied by Verdaine, our daughter."

The gathered nobles were silent as he handed her the sword, and she stood to accept it. "Thank you, Great Father, for this gift." She turned to Nadra. "And thank you, Great Mother, for your gift of my crown. I will do my best to prove worthy of them both."

Taryn shrugged back her robe and held the Sword of Ohlin aloft. A shaft of white light lit from the tip, piercing the glass ceiling before disappearing into the sky. Her sword burst into song, joined by the pendant and crown, and filled the throne room with a triumphant melody. ShantiMari coursed through her to the sword, casting a rainbow of light over the walls and gathered guests. Some ducked, others stared in wonder. Taryn looked to the heavens where she hoped Brandt watched with pride.

A cascade of stars rained down on them, glittering motes settling upon bare skin before dissolving. She lowered the sword and stood, shivering. The sheer force from not only the sword but herself terrified her. The audience stared at her in wild-eyed incredulity. Her heart beat in her throat, and she fought to swallow.

Finally she found her voice and, after a low bow to the assembled nobles, said the final line of Faelara's speech, "Let it be known I serve all of Aelinae."

Applause broke out, and Taryn choked on a lump of emotion that wedged itself between her heart and her lips.

Ohlin touched her cheek and whispered, "We are very proud of you, Taryn." From the corner of her eye, she thought she saw Brandt's spectral form hovering above his old friends, a wide smile on his face. Hot tears stung the backs of her eyes, but she refused to blink them away.

Ohlin gave Nadra one last embrace before ascending into the cloudless sky.

Valterys stood before them, false geniality oozing from his clenched smile. In much too loud a voice, he announced, "It is with a happy heart that I accept into my life a daughter." He addressed Taryn, "Being a woman, of course it is fitting you are presented on the Light Throne, but do not think that means you are unwelcome in the West. There will forevermore be a place in my heart for you, so, too, will there be in my home."

He bowed to Lliandra, "It appears, Your Majesty, that you and I both have something to celebrate this day."

Lliandra nodded in a gracious gesture. "Yes, my lord, we do. Welcome, Valterys. Welcome, Lord Zakael. You are honored guests."

Baehlon moved forward and asked the empress to grant him the honor of serving as Taryn's champion and protector, surprising everyone, especially the empress. Lliandra made a show of granting his request, even going so far as to produce a scepter out of nothing. Taryn babbled something about being honored, and it was done. Baehlon's House was forever sworn to hers.

Next, Myrddin stood before her, his head inclined in supplication, although he didn't swear fealty to her. The princesses were next, curtseying low to their sister, whispering a few words of encouragement before kissing Taryn's fingers as they rested on the Sword of Ohlin. Each time their lips touched her skin, a shock of power rushed through her.

When Marissa bent over her, Taryn flinched but Marissa's lips did not meet her fingertips. When she rose, there was an open challenge in her lavender eyes, and Taryn winked. A flash of Marissa's Mari whipped out, but stopped short of harming her. Taryn then shocked everyone, including herself, and bent low, kissing Marissa's fingertips. Her sister yanked her hand away and stormed to where the other princesses waited. Taryn hid a smirk beneath a mask of confusion.

Lliandra watched the interplay between her daughters with cool disinterest before addressing the gathered crowd. "Today is a day of celebration and joy. I wish you all much of both. After the parade, there will be feasting until dawn." She glided down the steps, taking Valterys's hand in hers. "My dear lord, would you be so kind as to escort me to my carriage? I'd be honored if you would accompany me for the parade."

Taryn fidgeted on the dais, not quite sure what to do. Nadra put an arm around her and said, "Welcome home, Taryn." The goddess brushed her cheek with her fingertips. "Are you well?"

"This is all very confusing."

"You will figure it out. You always do."

Lliandra and Valterys were already making their way down the aisle, and Nadra gave her a nudge. "Your turn."

"But shouldn't the princesses go first?"

"Taryn darling, you are a princess. Now go."

Marissa and Zakael strode down the aisle together, followed by Taryn and Rhoane with Tessa and Eliahnna a half step behind them. Rhoane leaned over to whisper in her ear. "You are truly one of us now." At her puzzled glance, he said, "You, too, have several names." She smiled in reply, still not quite sure what to make of it all.

After the parade, Sabina escorted Taryn to her new rooms, talking excitedly the whole time about what they could do now that Taryn's rank was elevated. When Sabina mentioned Taryn was higher in position than Marissa, and possibly even the empress, her interest piqued. Sabina promised to research the ramifications of Taryn having her own House as well as the newly made position of Keeper of the Stars. Not wanting to appear ungrateful, Taryn thanked her friend, even though she had little interest in the title or crown she wore.

Exhausted from the morning, she just wanted a chance to relax before being ushered to the garden, but when she reached her rooms, they buzzed with activity. Cora and Ellie stopped unpacking her belongings long enough to change Taryn from her coronation gown into a simpler dress of deep blue. She argued that she'd like to dress casually in trousers and a blouse, but the girls held firm that the empress would not approve.

"Well, I don't approve of all these dresses." Taryn sulked as they rearranged her hair to fit a smaller, less elaborate crown. When Taryn objected, Ellie ignored her, affixing it to her head with clips that she expertly hid in Taryn's hair. Ellie's obvious excitement at Taryn's rise in station was marred by Cora's equally apparent disappointment. Her terseness each time she had to say *Highness* didn't go unnoticed. Not that Taryn cared if Cora liked her, but having a maid living with her, privy to her daily activities, warranted someone who at least respected her.

Ellie's enthusiasm slowly enveloped Taryn. Despite her

best efforts, she looked forward to the garden party. For Ellie, nothing could be better than becoming a princess. Whereas the crown and title burdened Taryn, Ellie saw it as more than simply being a princess. To her, it was a chance to better her life, and possibly those of Aelinae's subjects. Ellie saw beyond the card games and gossip to future world leaders. Her rambling gave Taryn something to think about.

When the girls finished their preparations, they left Taryn to rest and enjoy a quiet tea alone in her sitting room. She fingered the gems on Nadra's crown, noticing they were the same as the stone Brandt had given her for her birthday. Moonstone and stardust. That's what Nadra said made up the elaborate headpiece. Taryn held it up, letting it catch the light. The room filled with a dazzling array of colors, and Taryn gasped when she realized it was the night sky she saw reflected on her walls. *Keeper of the Stars.*

She put the crown and her sword in a cupboard near the giant bed in her sleeping chamber. In the chaos of the morning, she'd hidden the seal in a cloak pocket, willing it to be weightless and invisible. It was somewhere in the pile of things in the dressing room, but she would have to wait until the others left before she could look for it. In the meantime, she placed several wards over the cupboard. Then she set her looking glass in a place that allowed a view of most of the suite.

The day was hot and the air still, but a chill pricked the back of her neck and icy trembles ran through her. An unseen forced gripped her soul, at once seducing and suffocating.

Your time has come, Eirielle. Awaken.

Taryn spun around, looking for the voice, but she was alone. She left her rooms in a rush, the taunting dogging her every step. Only when she reached the garden did the terrifying voice stop.

Chapter 26

NOBLES wandered through the garden, remarking on the cleverness of the empress to hide a daughter while simultaneously questioning the timing of the girl's reappearance. To hear them speak of Lliandra in such candid tones amused Valterys, as if their words were private and not to be overheard by the Overlord of the West. He pulled the shadows closer around him while following a stumpy courtier and his attractive companion. The thinnest of fabrics covered her overripe body, making Valterys swell with desire. Later, he would find her. For the moment, he needed to focus.

Taryn had not yet made an appearance, and with each passing moment, his concern grew. She might skip the festivities, no doubt courting the wrath of Lliandra, but the girl was a mystery to him. That made him nervous.

Zakael and Marissa walked past, oblivious to his presence as he slouched beside the palace wall, hidden from view. Shadows could be manipulated much easier than sunlight, and he'd never been fond of the heat.

They stopped a short distance away, their voices low and taut. Valterys had to strain to hear and then only caught fragments of their conversation. Marissa stormed away from Zakael before Valterys gleaned anything of importance. The shadows drifted away slowly, making it appear he'd been standing there the entire time. Zakael approached, a smile on his face.

"What do you think?" Zakael asked. "Will you take her?"

Valterys watched Marissa bend low toward some noblemen, exposing most of her breasts. "Are you tired of her already? I thought your desire for the crown princess knew no bounds."

Zakael followed his gaze. "And you are immune to her charms?"

"Hardly, but she is of no use to me. I leave you to your amusements with her. Does Lliandra know?"

"Should I care if she did? It was she who tossed me from her bed, if you'll recall."

Valterys remembered well the reason for Zakael's banishment from the Crystal Court; his abuse of Lliandra had left her close to death. Her single crime had been miscarrying Zakael's child. The only reason Zakael still lived was that Valterys had pleaded with his former lover for his son's life. The venom Lliandra spewed that day, not just about Zakael but about Valterys, as well, bore deep into his core.

The memory hurt—far more than he cared to acknowledge, and therefore he ignored it, as usual. Lliandra had waited less than a season after their own child's death to take Zakael into her bed. He assumed it was to conceive the Eirielle with him, but once he learned of Taryn's existence—well, the woman could be cruel.

"I meant Lliandra's next born," Zakael cut into his thoughts. "From what Marissa tells me, she has very little power and never uses it. I don't see how she can be the Eirielle."

Valterys had heard the same thing. Never had he known someone with ShantiMari to withhold using it.

Lliandra stepped in front of them with a slight curtsey, as befit their station. Zakael and Valterys bowed in unison, sweeping their arms out to the side and then kissing her outstretched fingertips. When they rose, each still held the delicate fingers of the empress. Valterys tamped down a rush of jealousy. Although it had been ages since either he or Zakael had bedded Lliandra, the competitive need to best his son never ended. A fact he was certain she used against him.

Her smile was nearly brighter than the sun. "What are you two planning over here? Should I hide my jewels?"

"I don't think you left any in the treasury, Your Majesty," Valterys joked. Even in the heat of summer, Lliandra wore full gowns with gems dripping from her elaborately coiffed hair to the tips of her silk slippers. She wore the wealth of her position on her person as much as possible. It was a ploy to intimidate, and so he consciously dressed as minimally as possible, wearing only black. His austerity achieved the same results Lliandra sought.

Zakael razed Lliandra with a look that suggested he'd happily resume his place in her bed if she were to ask. "Empress Lliandra, you look more ravishing today than you have in many seasons. The return of your daughter certainly agrees with you."

Lliandra's eyes flashed a moment before the smile returned. "Won't you join me in a tour of the garden? There are so many people to receive. It would be a shame to greet them alone when you are here, and many of them long to speak with you." She held her arm out to Valterys, who took it with a look of triumph cast at his son.

She made idle talk while they strolled through the crowd of nobles, giving nothing away, but then he really hadn't expected her to brazenly confess her plans to him. When Taryn arrived, a buzz of excitement spread through the crowd and several nobles clapped at her entrance. Valterys paused in his greeting to an old acquaintance to admire his daughter. Lliandra gave a small gasp, her grip on him faltering. He tightened his fingers over hers, and she smiled gratefully.

Taryn stood in the doorway of the palace, surrounded by people, but apart from everyone. Wary. Alert. Prince Rhoane approached, and Taryn's face softened with the same look Lliandra used to have when he himself would enter a room. Whether Taryn knew she was in love, he wasn't certain. She looked shy and unsure of herself. But when Rhoane placed his hand on the small of her back to lead her through the crowd, she stood taller.

Verdaine's prophecy held little credence in the West, but Valterys wasn't so ignorant. Taryn's fate was tied to the Eleri prince. If he were to succeed in freeing Rykoto, he needed to break their bond.

"Valterys, are you listening?" Lliandra hissed.

"I'm sorry, my darling, what were you saying?" The words were out before he could stop them, and Lliandra regarded him with a bemused smile.

"Never mind." They moved on to other guests, greeting them or reminiscing about the old days. For a few bells, he was Lord of the Court once more, with Lliandra on his arm. The two greatest powers on Aelinae united as one.

When Lliandra shyly suggested they retire for a bit of rest, he followed her without complaint and spent a pleasant afternoon in her bed, reliving the delights of her body. Only afterward, when Lliandra scratched a finger down his back, did his senses return, and he remembered the emotional pain she'd caused. *Never again*, he'd sworn. Yet there he was, in her snare once more.

When she dismissed him to ready herself for dinner, he was grateful for her brusque manner for once. If it were a ploy of Lliandra's, he needed to be clearheaded and ready for her next move. She hadn't asked him to her bed out of any sense of love for him. That was folly. He meandered through the crowd, as inconspicuous as possible, half shadowed out of habit.

An argument between two of Lliandra's courtiers caught his attention. A fat little man with sausage fingers and spittle at the corner of his mouth was gesticulating wildly to an attractive woman Valterys remembered seeing with Marissa on several occasions. Interest piqued, he cloaked himself fully in darkness and hovered near enough to hear their words.

"You should've told me, you stupid cunt. You've jeopardized everything."

"Calm down, Herbret. So what if the Offlander cow has a tiara? It changes nothing. Stick to the plan." The woman placed her hand on the man's plentiful cheeks, smoothing the ruddy skin. "You'll have your Summerlands whore. Have you located Kaldaar's stones?"

The mention of Kaldaar set off alarms in his mind. The legends of the banished god were murky in his memories, but he knew one thing—Rykoto would not be pleased to learn his brother was involved in Aelinae's future.

The man, Herbret, shook his head. "We need access to the oracles, but Lliandra won't grant them to me. You must see if Marissa will help."

"And have her get involved? I don't think so. It's bad enough you keep begging her to intervene with the empress. Grow some balls, man. Fight for your petition to claim Sabina." The woman tapped her finger on Herbret's cheek. "Actually, I think I know a way to gain access to the archives." She removed her hand and wiped it on her gown, a look of disgust flitting across her face. "Do try to be a brave boy while I do all the work. Again."

She left before Herbret could reply. He muttered a slur and headed in the opposite direction, his stout little legs moving with surprising speed. Valterys followed the woman.

She stopped to chat with a couple, and Valterys learned a name to put with the pretty face, Lady Celia. She hummed beneath her breath as she danced through the rose garden, as if an unseen lover swayed with her. Still cloaked in shadow, Valterys moved in step with Celia, embracing her from behind. Her startled expression at the empty air pricked his desire. The weak minded were far too easy to fool.

He stroked his fingers down her soft arms then interlaced his hands with hers. She moaned and rested her head against his chest. "My lord, is that you?"

Her words, whispered in a breathy rush excited him. He knew she thought him another man, but the temptation to play along was too strong. "Yes, my darling. You've done well."

"Have I?" Her eyelashes fluttered up to where she thought his face would be, missing the mark by a hand's width. "I had hoped, but how it is you are here?"

Valterys ushered them to a secluded corner of the garden, where he could see much of the party, but they would be concealed. His fingertips pressed between her legs, and she jumped. "It is your devotion that allows my presence."

"I had hoped, dreamed of this day, my lord." She spun around to face him, groping in the air for Valterys's face. "I have done what you asked. The vessel will be secured, and your seed will flourish once more."

Kaldaar's seed. His mind spun with old wives' tales and forgotten myths. "Excellent, my darling." He bent and kissed her, a savage taking of her mouth that left her breathless.

"Kaldaar, my lord, my love," she murmured against his lips. "Kaldaar."

"Celia?" Marissa's sharp tone cut the air like the crack of a whip. Valterys stilled, pulling his shadows tighter. "Ohlin's cock, Celia! What are you doing? Have you lost your mind?"

Celia froze and then a calculated demeanor overcame her. Docile, compliant. She coyly turned around to face the princess. "I was practicing for a play Herbret and I are working on. It's a surprise for the empress and her daughters."

The young woman wasn't as daft as he'd originally thought.

"Then do it in the privacy of your room. You look a fool out here alone, groping the air."

Celia straightened her skirts and nodded. "You're absolutely right. What was I thinking?"

They moved off, and Valterys heard Marissa ask in that sweet tone that meant danger, "Did I hear you mention Kaldaar?"

"Kaldaar? Not at all. I was saying *kal daresh*. It's a loose translation from Ullan meaning *horse master*."

Before they disappeared completely, Celia cast a last glance to where he stood, fanatic desire in her eyes.

He wandered the maze, sloughing off his cloak of shadows, and mulled over what he'd learned. Celia was no doubt bright, but her ready belief he was Kaldaar concerned him. Someone was directing the girl toward an end Valterys couldn't allow. But who would want the banished god returned? Who would have the most to gain from spreading the seed of the Black Brotherhood? More questions simmered in his mind and he made mental notes on how best to thwart this new enemy's plans.

A snap of twig startled him, and he glanced at the orchard, not quite knowing how he had arrived there.

Taryn stood not more than three paces from him. When their eyes met, trepidation crossed her face, as if she debated turning from him. He held out his hand to stop her. "I was hoping for a chance to speak with you." He motioned to the courtiers milling around the garden. "It's difficult to hear one's thoughts with so many people. I thought I'd seek solace here. How fortuitous you did the same."

A moment of hesitation, then she curtsied. "My lord." Her glance flicked to where Baehlon stood a short space away.

"Don't worry, your man is nearby. I just wanted to talk—to get to know you." He sat on a bench, patting the seat beside him.

Taryn perched on the edge, her slippers set to run if need be. "There's not much to know. I was raised by Brandt. I thought he was my grandfather, and I had no idea who I was until the empress told me last night. End of story."

"Dearest Taryn, there is much more to your story than that. Where have you been this whole time?"

She kept her face pointed toward the garden, only glancing at him once. "Did your son tell you he murdered Brandt?"

Valterys shouldn't have been surprised, but her forthrightness caught him off guard. "I believe he sought to defend himself against Brandt's attack. He felt terrible for the loss of the high priest, you must believe me." She stiffened, and he quickly added, "This is not how I envisioned our first meeting. Just as you knew nothing about me until last night, I knew nothing of you until today. Now that I know I have a daughter, I would very much like to know this child of mine." He kept his voice sincere, his eyes soft and placating.

"Lliandra truly never told you?" Her eyes searched his. They were blue, like the depths of the sea. Like Lliandra's.

"Not until the throne room this morning. Nadra bade me come to Talaith for reasons she would not divulge. In all honesty, I thought Lliandra wished to lure me back to her bed." It wasn't a complete lie.

Taryn glanced over the crowd, settling on Marissa. "This is all new to me, but I'm learning there are those adept at presenting themselves to the world as one thing when in private they are quite another. Take the crown princess, for example." Her gaze shifted to him, and he did his best to look innocent. "The courtiers adore her. She is the life of the party. Yet what do we really know about her? What is it she does in the privacy of her own bedchamber?"

"I would think what most people do—sleep."

Taryn's eyes became hard bits of blue granite. "What about you? Are you really as charming as you'd like me to believe? You come here with your offer of friendship, but there is more to you, Lord Valterys, isn't there?"

"Why is it you bear me such ill will? I've done nothing to deserve your scorn."

There was strength in the girl; determination shone from her eyes. "Your son killed the one person who meant the most to me, and you hung a sword over my friend with every intention to kill him. Yet you say you've done nothing wrong."

"I like your honesty. It's refreshing. I've already explained that Brandt's death was a tragic accident. As for young Hayden, he was never in any real danger."

Taryn's jaw tightened. Her back went rigid. "I'm sure the poison you wrapped around the sword was harmless?"

Poison? That wasn't part of the plan, and it vexed him Marissa would do such a thing.

"My dear, one does what one must in times like these. That sword should be mine. Besides, I've heard you were there to rescue him, so it all worked out in the end, yes?"

In a strained voice, she said, "I feel it unnecessary to continue this conversation. I don't want to be your enemy, Valterys, but if you continue to seek what is rightfully mine, I will have no other choice. Good day." She swept away with the grace and dignity of a princess.

Taryn walked with her protector along the seawall until they reached the Eleri prince and others of her group. The air vibrated around her and Valterys watched her with keen interest. Beneath her anger, he could tell she fought to control vast amounts of ShantiMari—Light, Eleri, and Dark—which could only mean one thing.

He rose in a languid fashion, smoothing out his tunic before strolling away from the orchard. If Taryn wouldn't submit to him of her own accord, he would have to find another way to contain her.

Chapter 27

TARYN sat upright in bed, the nightmare chasing through her thoughts. She threw off the covers and padded around the huge apartment, willing the dream to dispel. The image of Zakael holding Rhoane's still-beating heart stayed fixed in her mind, the scent of his blood in her every breath. The rich food she'd eaten at the feast and the wine—too much wine— threatened to make a repeat appearance. Taryn poured herself a glass of water, taking small sips to keep the nausea at bay.

She'd been in Talaith just a few days, but it seemed like she'd lived a lifetime since Paderau. Too many changes, too much responsibility thrust on her in too short a time.

She stood in the darkness, inhaling the salty tang of ocean air, letting the last fragments of her nightmare dissolve. Even the sound of waves crashing on the cliffs and the cool morning air did little to ease the accelerated beating of her heart. She checked that the sword was safe and then retrieved the looking glass.

If ever she needed the comfort of her grandfather, it was now. She snuggled under her blankets, cupping the orb in her hand. Brandt's image flared inside the glass. Taryn's chest compressed with a silent sob, and she kissed the ball, whispering, "I love you, Baba."

On impulse, she asked it to show her who had entered

her rooms the previous day. The glass flared to life and several images of Cora and Ellie zipped past, along with a few other maids Taryn didn't recognize. They prepared her rooms and unpacked her belongings. Nothing nefarious. She asked to see anyone other than her maids.

The ball sparked once, and then showed Marissa creeping about the apartment before going to Taryn's dressing room. She methodically went through Taryn's armoires until she found the cloak where Taryn had hidden the seal. A cold sweat broke out on Taryn's forehead. No one else had been present when she'd placed the seal in the cloak pocket.

In the glass, Marissa pawed through Taryn's personal belongings. When she found the hiding place of her sword and crown, Marissa felt along the wall, trying to unhinge the cupboard door. Taryn hoped Marissa would use her ShantiMari and get a nasty shock, but to Taryn's disappointment, she didn't. Marissa fumbled with a curtain near the glass doors that led to the balcony. After a few moments, she left the room.

Taryn was about to put the looking glass down when the ball flickered to life again.

A figure stepped out from behind the curtain. Taryn stared in disbelief at the image of Zakael standing beside her bed, watching while she slept. He'd been inches from her. A chill swept over her clammy skin as she watched Zakael bend low to whisper in her ear.

His words drifted on the breeze, "Come to me, my Taryn. We are meant to be united. In power, in life, in all things."

With an intimacy they didn't share, he stroked her face with his fingertips. His lips rested on hers.

She shook with suppressed anger at his impertinence. That he'd treated her with such familiarity, and while she slept, enraged her. ShantiMari burned in her belly like an out of control wildfire, igniting crazed thoughts that involved causing Zakael a great deal of pain. She scrubbed her lips with the blanket, ridding herself of his touch.

Like Marissa before him, Zakael felt around the secret compartment. Unlike Marissa, he tried to use his power to open it. He jerked back, his fingers ablaze in a fury of blue and orange flames. When the fire subsided, the ink she'd woven into the ward stained Zakael's fingers.

Swearing under his breath, Zakael cast a look of contempt in her direction and then left by the secret doorway. A few moments later, Taryn awoke. She'd missed him by mere seconds.

Her heart thumped wildly in her chest. Even snug in her covers, she was vulnerable and exposed. She ached inside as if she'd been physically violated. Her fury escalated and sparks snapped at the ends of her tangled hair, snaking their way down her arms. She jumped from the bed, patting out the fire. When the flames wouldn't cease, she poured water over her arms, but the blaze remained.

There was no burning of her skin, no singeing of hair—only an uncomfortable heat. She held her arms out in front of her. "Ice." Immediately, the flames turned to chilly crystals. "Fire." Flames danced along her arms. "Ice." Again, crystals.

Sunlight streaked the balcony and movement in the palace signified the start of the day. There wasn't much time before her maids would arrive. She went outside and shook her arms over the balcony, clearing her skin of the frozen water. She'd play with her new discovery later; for the moment, she had to secure her rooms. First, she went to look for the seal in the pocket of the cloak Marissa had searched. Relief flooded through her when her fingers touched the soft pouch. After she locked it in the cupboard with the sword and crown, she moved quickly, placing wards over doorways and walls.

If Marissa thought she could enter her rooms anytime she pleased, Taryn would make certain to change her mind.

On the secret doorway that Zakael had used, Taryn infused her wards with the vilest suggestions she could think of. She couldn't bring herself to inflict violence, but the results would have a lasting effect. Boils and weeping pustules were only the start of what the visitor could expect. Later, she would set physical traps in the hidden corridor.

Fresh anger boiled inside her. She had to get away, from her rooms, from her thoughts. She had to *do* something. She dressed quickly and headed to the barracks with Ohlin's sword. A sleepy soldier informed her Sir Baehlon wasn't in his room. Undeterred, she continued to the training yard without him. A few soldiers meandered about, but each one she asked, declined to practice with her.

She attacked the stuffed sacks with an anger she fought to control. On a particularly vicious attack, her sword swung wide, meeting another blade with a jarring clang. Taryn staggered back, holding her hands over her ears. Rhoane, too, stumbled a few paces before righting himself and approaching with caution.

"What was that horrid sound?" Taryn asked.

"Godsteel. Our swords are both made of it and do not like to be struck in anger." He held his sword loosely in his hand, but Taryn saw his jaw tighten in anticipation. "What has you so vexed this morning?"

Not wanting to tell him about Zakael in a public place, she indicated the thirty or so men and women who had gathered around the ring. "Seems a tiara frightens them. No one will train with me, and Baehlon is nowhere to be found."

A smile tugged at Rhoane's lips. "I will train with Her Highness." His sword gleamed in the sunlight. "But I will not go easy on you."

Ohlin's sword sang in her mind, and she took a step back, focusing herself. "Then I will return the compliment."

Rhoane flourished his sword before swinging his leg out

in a formal bow. Then he raised the weapon in front of his face. "I would expect no less."

Before she could reply, he was at her, striking from the left and then right in rapid succession. A well-placed jab narrowly missed her ribs. She moved on instinct, defending against Rhoane's blows with parrying shots of her own. The crowd cheered, whether for her or Rhoane, she wasn't sure. Not that it mattered. Nothing mattered except keeping away from his deadly strikes.

As promised, he showed no mercy. Sweat dripped from her brow, blurring her vision. Rhoane looked fresh, without a trace of exertion or fatigue marring his features. Taryn's confidence faltered.

A nick of Rhoane's sword snapped her focus back to him. Blood seeped through her tunic, but Taryn kept her feet moving, dodging and then striking at Rhoane. Her paltry few weeks of training were nothing compared to his skill. Yet she fought as if they were of equal talent.

Rhoane crouched low, circling Taryn, his arm out to the side, leaving his body open to attack. Taryn moved opposite him, her sword held low before her. She was about to lunge when a voice called out, "Enough!"

Startled, Taryn and Rhoane paused in their advances, both heated by the combat. Empress Lliandra strode to the center of the ring, her slippers causing a rush of dust in the air. "What in Ohlin's name do you two think you're doing?"

Rhoane made a show of bowing to the empress. "Your Majesty. You look lovely this morning."

"Don't you dare try to flatter me, Prince Rhoane." Then, seeing the stain on Taryn's sleeve, she said, "You drew blood on a princess of the realm? I could have you flogged. Or worse."

To his credit, Rhoane didn't flinch. "You could. However, if Taryn is to lead an army someday, she must be ready.

Coddling will do her no good on the battlefield where her enemies will show her little mercy."

Taryn stared at him. "Don't be ridiculous. I'm not leading any army."

Lliandra held up her hand for silence. "If it comes to that, you will do as needed. Know this, Prince Rhoane of the Eleri, should your blade ever mar my daughter again, I will not be so forgiving. Is this understood?"

Rhoane's jaw hardened. "Yes, Your Majesty."

Lliandra fixed Taryn with a cold stare. "As for you, Princess Taryn, you may continue training. I will have my soldiers available to you for your hand-to-hand fighting. However, I want you to train only with the sword masters. You are lucky you didn't harm Prince Rhoane. I wouldn't want to have to tell his father that bit of good news."

Taryn inclined her head. "Thank you, Your Majesty. The other princesses…they've expressed a desire to train. If you would consider it, I would be most grateful."

Lliandra's mouth tightened to a thin stain. "You are bold, young Taryn. I hope you are not also foolish. I will take your request into consideration." She left them without another word, sweeping through the crowd in a swirl of rose and lavender chiffon.

To Taryn's surprise, Rhoane was smiling. "Baehlon has taught you well. I thought I might be bested by you today." He inspected the cut on her upper arm. "I was careless."

"It's not your fault. I was too slow." His Shanti wrapped around her like a warm blanket in the dead of winter. It caressed and soothed her, mending the wound he'd inflicted.

They left the training grounds amid excited babbling from the soldiers. After hearing the empress, they were more than willing to continue working with her. Rhoane led her away from the barracks toward the gardens, all the while talking about their sword fight and the ways she could improve.

When they reached the orchards, Rhoane took Taryn's hand.

Their runes glowed briefly, and Taryn asked, "What did Ohlin mean when he said that when I'm ready, he'll add his blessing to our bonds?"

Rhoane cleared his throat. "Strictly speaking, we are fully bonded, but to make them immutable, we need Ohlin's and Verdaine's blessings added to these. As it is now, we are bonded by the Light only, and if we are not careful, they can unravel."

"Nadra said they're permanent."

Rhoane kissed her fingertips. "They are, but when they were placed on us, you were unaware of the true meaning of the bonding. Therefore, they are not as strong as they could be."

"I see." She looked away, embarrassed by her lack of understanding of so many things a woman her age should know. "I don't have a lot of experience with this." She glanced up at him, searching for reassurance in his eyes. "With relationships, I mean. None, actually."

The little half-smile that made her pulse zigzag tugged at his lips. "Neither have I."

"But you're so old. Surely you've had women before?" The words were out before she could pull them back. "Oh God, I'm sorry."

His laugh surprised her. "For an Eleri, I am not that old. Besides, I have known since birth that my destiny was with you."

"What if you didn't like me once you met me?"

Rhoane stepped closer, brushing her hair back with his long fingers. "I loved you the moment I first saw you in the cavern. Before that, I loved the possibility of you. Now that you are here before me, I love the reality of you." He covered her mouth with his.

For the space of a heartbeat, she faltered, frightened but

also thrilled by the heat coursing through her. His clean, forest scent filled her nostrils, overwhelmed her senses. His strong arms held her close. Everything about him was comforting, as if the world could stop and as long as she had him, there would be life.

Rhoane pulled back, his eyes fogged with desire, questioning. She crushed him to her, not wanting to ever let go. They clung to each other beneath trees heavy with fruit. The smell of sargots warmed by the summer sun intoxicated her, adding to the deliciousness of the moment. Ideas that made her blush skittered through her mind as her hands roamed over his body. She wanted to feel every inch of him, to know him in ways only she could, but she hesitated. When they finally parted, Taryn could hardly grasp a single thought. Rhoane moved behind her to kiss her neck.

"You're sure you've never done this before?" Taryn asked in a voice steeped with a slurred huskiness she didn't recognize.

"Quite sure." He nuzzled her neck, and she swayed against him. "But I have often thought of doing exactly this with you. Only you."

Her ShantiMari rose, and she surrounded him with it, enveloping them in a cocoon. If only she could take them far from the palace and everything that might threaten their happiness. A surge of her power threatened to overtake her. Rhoane's body shook and his ShantiMari enclosed hers, subduing the force.

"We should stop," she forced herself to say. "I'm afraid of what might happen if we don't."

His arms circled her, pulling her close. When he spoke, his voice sounded much like hers, deep and full of unspent emotion. "As you wish, *Darennsai*."

Raw desire edged his words. All she wanted was to pull him down beside her and lie on the grass, letting his fingers trail over her body, finding ways to excite him as much as he excited her. Her heart no longer beat in her chest but settled between her legs and pulsed with a terrifying urgency. She turned back to face Rhoane, and all thought vanished. She lost herself in the mossy depths of his eyes.

Electric current ripped through her as their lips met again, this time with a heated fervor she embraced. Her nails scratched up his scalp, her fingers tugged at his curls. His tongue scraped along her teeth, and she savored the feel of him, the taste of him.

Him.

A tempest of power swarmed around them, drowning out sound and light.

Rhoane ended the kiss with airy touches of his lips to hers, lingering a moment before kissing the tip of her nose and then her eyelids. A fine misting of sweat dotted his forehead, and his breath came in shallow pulls. His ShantiMari cloaked hers, soothing, calming, protective.

Concern. Apprehension. Rhoane's worry slid over her.

The torment within terrified her almost as much as it excited her. She swallowed down the urge to release her power, to consume them in a vortex of ShantiMari. Rhoane shook as he stroked the sides of her arms, whispering to her in Eleri until her shuddering subsided, the tempest dissipated, and the light shone bright around them.

She could have killed them.

The thought crowded her mind. If she didn't learn to control her power, she would hurt Rhoane. Or someone else close to her.

"I, uh," she faltered, unsure what to say. "I don't know what happened. I'm sorry."

Rhoane tucked a strand of hair behind her ear. His runes flared in the sun's rays. "I, for one, am not sorry for anything." He flexed his hand a few times. "Look what you have done. And they were just starting to settle down." His lips met hers in a tender kiss.

Except she saw beyond the casual tone of his words. The anxiety he tried to hide was clear in his eyes. She'd frightened him. Of that she was certain.

He took her hand, and they walked beneath the sargot trees to the seawall. She kept her power in check, but in the depths of her consciousness, the darkness lurked.

Waiting.

Chapter 28

THE sun beat down on them, warming the sand beneath their damp bodies. Taryn stretched along the rough blanket they'd brought and blinked against the day's brightness. After the orchard, Rhoane had taken Taryn to her rooms, where Sabina had been waiting with the younger princesses and the promise of an afternoon lazing on the beach.

She plucked at the damp fabric of her swimming frock, making a mental note to have Tarro design something more fitting for the ocean. Having yards of fabric billowing against the tide wasn't ideal. Nor was the wool blanket that scratched her exposed limbs.

"Stop fidgeting," Sabina scolded, a hand over her eyes to block the sun. "Why are you restless?"

Oh, I don't know. I can't control my ShantiMari and almost killed my boyfriend this morning. My parents are power hungry freaks. My sister is plotting against me. Pick one.

"I'm not. It's just…these clothes are awful. How can you be expected to swim in something like this? It's torture. I'm surprised more people don't drown."

"In the Summerlands we wear our small clothes to swim. Or we go naked. We don't have the same prejudices as they do on the mainland."

"It sounds like you Summerlands people know how to

have a good time."

Sabina rolled to her side, her face suddenly serious. "Can I confide something in you?" She glanced to where Tessa and Eliahnna strolled along the shore, looking for seashells. "Whatever we say here must stay between the two of us."

"Absolutely. You have my word."

A ripple of relief washed over Sabina's features. "As you know, I have no loyalty to Marissa but must pretend otherwise. She is heir to the Light Throne. Once she is crowned, she will be the most important person on Aelinae. Even those in the West know that the true power in all the seven kingdoms resides in Talaith. That is why Valterys is anxious to have you side with him."

"I'm not siding with anyone."

Sabina gave a short chuckle. "Everyone has to take a side eventually and your father would love nothing more than to have you live at Caer Idris with him. All the other kingdoms would have to bow and scrape before him because he sired the great Eirielle, and look, she sits at his side, blah, blah, blah. But never mind that for now." She waved a dismissive hand, "Marissa is determined to marry me to Lord Aomori. I have no wish to marry him, and I'm sure he would prefer another life partner." Sabina's tone held a hint of amusement.

"You mean Tinsley?"

Sabina smiled, her pearlescent teeth bright against her dark skin. Her two front teeth had the slightest bend to them, giving her a charmingly crooked smile. "Ah, yes. Because of him. I, of course, have other reasons," she added with a hint of mystery.

"Hayden?"

Sabina's cheeks blossomed the color of cherry trees in springtime. Her shyness regarding the marquis delighted Taryn. "What can I do to help?"

A shadow fell over Sabina's supine form, and the girls

looked up to see Marissa standing a few paces away, Lady Celia by her side. Lords Tinsley and Aomori spoke with animated gestures a pace behind them. Hayden was nowhere in sight.

"Ladies, I thought perhaps you'd enjoy some company." Marissa said with exaggerated politeness.

Taryn gave Sabina a we-won't-let-her-win look and rolled to a sitting position. "Sure, the more the merrier. Do you guys know how to swim?"

The men dashed off, kicking sand at each other and diving into the waves. Marissa took a seat on the blanket beside Taryn, digging her toes into the sand. She wore a long skirt and loose-fitting chemise, neither of which was appropriate for the water. Celia hung back until Marissa glared at her. She plopped on the sand with an unhappy grunt.

"I guess that answers your question," Marissa joked, indicating the two figures who were now racing to the rocky island not far from shore.

"What about you?" Taryn asked.

"I've never been a fan of water." Marissa shielded her eyes. "Or the burn that occurs if left too long in the sun."

Taryn lifted her face to the light. "I love it. The sun, the sand, the salt water. It feels like home."

"I suppose you missed this place while you were gone," Marissa said cryptically.

"I didn't know about Talaith, or you, or any of this while I was gone, so there wasn't a chance to miss it. But I have to admit, I am glad to be here now. With all of you." Taryn forced a shy smile for her sister. "I like having a family."

Marissa leaned back and shook out her long mane of dark curls. They cascaded down, nearly touching the blanket. "It must be strange, though, to find yourself in this awkward position. To realize that you have blood relatives and have to learn about your life in a short time."

"I love a good challenge. Since you brought it up, what can you tell me about my half-brother?"

Marissa cut her a look from the corner of her eye. "Zakael? I don't know him that well. Why don't you speak to him and find out for yourself?"

"I will, but I was hoping you could give me some idea of what kind of man he is. The few times I've met him haven't exactly been positive experiences, and I'd like to change his impression of me."

"Sabina," Marissa intoned with an air of authority, "the boys are returning, why don't you take them a towel?"

Sabina gave her a worried glance, but Taryn nodded that it would be fine. Sabina grabbed two towels from the basket and sashayed to the shoreline where she spoke with Eliahnna until the men came splashing out of the water.

"They make a fetching couple, don't you think?" Marissa studied the way Sabina and Aomori greeted each other with polite cordiality.

"I suppose." If Marissa were baiting her, Taryn wasn't going to play into her hand. "What about you? Is there a special someone you're interested in?"

Lavender ShantiMari made lazy loops around Marissa's reclining form. "No one has caught my attention yet. But then, it isn't prudent for the heir of the throne to claim one suitor. It's tradition that the empress has many lovers to sire her children."

"Sweet gig."

"Are you saying you don't favor your bond with Rhoane? He is a much sought after bachelor. Any woman would be honored to have his hand."

Damn. "That's not what I'm saying at all. Rhoane is perfect. I am honored that Verdaine chose him for me, and I look forward to spending the rest of eternity with him." The words echoed in her mind, mocking her. "I mean, all you have to do is look at him. He's totally hot."

Marissa cast her a scathing glance. "Hot?"

"Trust me, that's a compliment. It means he's attractive. Very much so." Heat burned in her cheeks. The kiss she'd shared with him earlier replayed itself in her memory, igniting a spark of passion that she tamped down.

"Then yes, he is hot. I wish you happiness in your union." The blessing rang false.

"Thanks. And who knows, maybe you'll find your true love one day. It might even be Zakael. The two of you, both rulers, maybe you could unite Aelinae the way your mother once sought to do."

Celia's eyes bulged with suppressed laughter. Marissa glared at her, and Celia sniffed haughtily. "Truly, Offlanders will believe anything they hear. The empress never sought to co-rule. She mated with Valterys for one purpose and one purpose only."

"Celia." An undercurrent of anger vibrated that single word.

Celia looked to Marissa with exaggerated innocence. "You told me yourself the only reason your mother endured Valterys and then Zakael was to create this abomination."

With a start, Taryn realized Celia meant her.

A guard approached and gave Taryn a quick bow. "Princess, it is nearing sixteenth bell, you have an appointment to keep."

"Already?" But it couldn't be soon enough for her. Celia was one insult away from finding herself face first in the sand. Taryn might be new to this royalty thing, but she was fairly certain what Celia said was punishable. And Marissa had allowed it.

Taryn shouted her goodbyes to the others before she raced back to the palace and up the stairs that led to the gardens. To her horror, Celia followed.

"Your Highness, wait." She panted when they reached

the top step. Bent over and wheezing as if that was the most exertion she'd ever experienced, Celia held out a hand to keep Taryn from leaving. "I'm sorry. I know"—huff, puff, wheeze—"you don't like me very much, and I can't say that I blame you, but there's something you should know."

She straightened, and Taryn was taken aback by the color of her face. Red from lack of oxygen, but also faint blue lines marked her features. As her breathing returned to normal, they faded until Celia's face was again clear.

"What is it? I'm late for an appointment, and I don't have time for games." Taryn started to move away, but Celia grabbed her wrist.

Taryn glanced at her hand. "Let go of me."

Celia dropped her wrist and took a reflexive step back. "Hear me out, please." She took a deep breath and began. "Marissa asked me to be cruel to you. I don't know why, perhaps she was testing you. Or me. Or both. It doesn't matter. I can't do it any longer. I'm sure I'll be punished, perhaps even sent back to my family, but you're kind. Truly, I've never met anyone like you. Please accept my apology."

There was a muddiness to Celia's ShantiMari that intrigued Taryn. She might be playing her, pretending to offer an apology to gain access to Taryn and her friends, or the offer could be genuine. Either way, Taryn had nothing to lose.

"Of course, Celia. It must be difficult to be in your position."

Celia's features relaxed, and for the briefest moment, Taryn thought she saw the markings again. They appeared to be runes similar to her bonds. "I hope someday you can forgive me, and perhaps will call me friend."

Taryn gripped Celia's hand in her own, sending a thread of her ShantiMari up the woman's arm. The markings started at Celia's temples and disappeared beneath her gown. "That would be lovely. But I truly am late."

She left Celia standing alone at the top of the stairs and hurried to her rooms where Cora and Ellie waited with a bath already drawn.

Despite her rushing, Taryn arrived late to Lady Faelara's suite. She was ushered into a formal sitting room, which was decorated in various shades of green. The walls were a soft sage and the couches a deep forest that complimented Fae's pale skin and auburn hair. The open windows allowed in a nice breeze, and the scent of flowers freshened the air. Tiny threads of ShantiMari were woven throughout the rooms.

Rhoane rose to greet her, giving her cheek a simple pass with his lips. Even that brief touch sent a spiral of giddiness through her.

Once seated, Faelara got straight to the point. "Now, Taryn darling, since you've been practicing with ShantiMari, I'm going to assume my father's wards have all dissolved. From what Rhoane shared of the events in the orchard this morning, it is imperative we teach you to control your powers. The sooner the better."

Taryn glared at Rhoane, hurt evident in her voice. "You told her?"

"Not everything." That damn half-smile tugged at his lips, and her heart. "Just about the surge of your powers."

"Show me what you can do," Faelara ordered.

Nerves fluttered in Taryn's belly. The simple tricks she'd taught herself were probably far below what Fae expected. She never thought she'd have great power, therefore had never challenged herself to great things. "Well, I, um, can light a candle. I can…" Faelara held up a hand to stop her.

"I said *show* me." Faelara flicked her wrist, and a bolt of light flew at Taryn. She swatted it away. "Again, but use the power. If you try to deflect ShantiMari with your bare hands, you'll get burned." Another bolt zoomed at Taryn, and she did as instructed.

"Good. Now, what else can you do?"

Rhoane remained quiet while Faelara clucked or nodded as Taryn showed them everything she'd been practicing. She lit a fire on her palm, hid several small cakes, warded her teacup, and so on, until she'd shown them everything. Except the fire and ice she'd created that morning. Until she had a chance to recreate it, she wouldn't share that power with anyone.

At length, Faelara nodded an end to the demonstration. "It appears you've only attempted to use your power for sensible things, like guarding the sword. Rhoane and I are going to show you how to use ShantiMari to defend yourself, among other things. Rhoane will help with your Eleri strain of ShantiMari and I will concentrate on allowing your full powers of Light to come through."

"What about the Dark? Don't I need to know that, as well?" Her pulse quickened. "You aren't going to make me work with Valterys, are you?"

Fae's lips pursed together. "Of course not. You'll have need of Dark power—it's true—and when the time is right, I will have a proper instructor for you. But for now, let's work with what we have, shall we?"

Taryn sighed with relief. There were two sides to her father and each frightened her more than she was willing to admit. The polite gentleman she saw at Talaith was very different from the angry man she remembered from Ravenwood.

Faelara showed her how to pull ShantiMari from the light around them, making her skin tickle with the amount of power in the room. Taryn lost herself in the silken caress of ShantiMari. She could feel Faelara's strength in her threads and the subtle touch of caring she wove into her Mari. Rhoane's Shanti flowed over her, through her even. She sensed others, as if the Eleri shared a collective power as one. When she opened herself to the strength of the two sitting opposite her, the sheer force of their power overwhelmed her. Seductive, it called to her, embracing her. Like the void from the cavern but more intense, more immediate. For one moment of sheer bliss, she let it consume her.

The feeling shifted, and flecks of light popped against her closed lids. Her breath came in rasps as the power tore at her thoughts, ravaging her mind. A rush of ShantiMari flooded into her, thickening her blood in her veins, cutting off air. She choked and fought against it, forcing it out. The room tilted and she opened her eyes.

Faelara grabbed her wrist. "Taryn! Don't ever do that again." Amber sparks flew around her. "You could have killed us."

Confusion addled her thoughts. "It felt so good, intoxicating, but then I couldn't breathe. What did I do?"

"You drew our ShantiMari to you, *Darennsai*," Rhoane said quietly. "It is forbidden to take another's power without their consent."

"I didn't know—I'm so sorry. I have a lot to learn, don't I?"

"Yes, you do. At least you were able to pull away before any damage was done. Now, let us begin our training."

Failure clung to Taryn. Try though she might, she couldn't push it aside, making it difficult to focus on what Faelara and Rhoane were saying. They discussed the need for etiquette when using ShantiMari, the various laws that must be obeyed.

"With so many people gifted with the power, it is imperative everyone follow rules or there would be chaos of epic proportions. ShantiMari exists in everything, from the vast oceans to the smallest insect. The way to use your power most effectively is to pull from what is around you and command it to do your bidding," Rhoane explained, and

Faelara agreed.

"The word you use is as important as the idea you form in your head. If, for example, you say you want a piece of toast, but in your mind you are thinking crumpet, you'll get a toasted crumpet. There cannot be any wavering in your command. However, you must be able to focus completely on what you are doing while simultaneously understanding what is going on around you." Faelara paused for Taryn to absorb the concept.

"In a way, it isn't much different from sword fighting or martial arts," Taryn said.

Faelara lifted an eyebrow, and Rhoane explained. "Precisely. In both, you must focus all of your attention on your opponent but also keep your peripheral vision attuned to those around you. Excellent, Taryn."

It took her years to learn everything she knew about martial arts; she couldn't expect to master ShantiMari in one evening. "What else is there to know?"

"More than I fear we'll ever have time to teach you. If you'd been raised here, you would've learned all the basics by the time you were out of swaddling clothes. I want you to come here every day so we can drill you on not only the basics but the distinctions among the various strains as well. After you've mastered that, we'll move on to more difficult workings." Faelara looked at Rhoane. "I think it important that you be here each day. Do you have the time in your schedule?"

"I will make the time."

Taryn was surprised. "You have to make time? What do you do?"

Faelara laughed, but Rhoane just smiled. "He is the unofficial ambassador of the Eleri. Most days he sits in on Lliandra's Privy Council meeting, but there are other duties he must perform, as well. If anyone wishes to conduct business with the Eleri, they must speak to Rhoane first."

"While I am *sheanna*, I am not allowed to speak in the Privy Council, but Lliandra affords me a certain amount of autonomy in my dealings with merchants and other nobles."

Faelara gave a little snort. "She keeps you on a tight leash, all the same."

"So, you all have jobs here?" The idea had never occurred to her.

"Of course, and you will, too. Someday, when you are ready, you will sit in on meetings, too. As the head of House Galendrin, it is your right," Faelara explained.

It could take months, or even a season, before Taryn was ready for court politics. She was too trusting and Aelinaen politics too convoluted for her to attempt before she had acclimated to her new role.

"My darling," Faelara said, "we don't mean to upset you. Please know we have only your best interests in mind."

The truth burned in her belly, and the words that she'd been afraid of saying tumbled out. "Everyone thinks I have this great power, that I'm the most important person on Aelinae. What if I'm not who everyone thinks I am? What if the whole Light and Dark thing is wrong and I'm just an average woman?"

Tears dropped on her hand, illuminating her runes. The designs shifted and moved. A sword. A moon. A sun. The great tree of the Weirren. A bright star. Their meanings were clear now; the others would be in time.

Then her vision shifted beyond the runes to a crypt deep beneath the ground. A man with eyes of fire glared at her. His long dark hair hung limp around his face. His blunt nose was swollen, as if he'd been in a fight, and a deep scar ran from his right eye to his chin in a crescent shape. A moment later it was gone.

The man held something, a small circular disk with

engravings on it. A Seal of Ardyn. He laughed, a horrible cracking sound that hurt her ears. Her sword cried out in unison with her pendant and crown. Their song called for justice. They wanted the man's blood. The passionate anger of the song frightened Taryn but not as much as what the man was doing. He held the seal between his fingers, snapping it in two as if it were nothing but unfired clay.

His fiery eyes gleamed at her while he rasped, "Taryn Rose of House Galendrin, I call you forth. Child of Light and Dark, Destroyer of the Eleri, I call you forth."

"Rykoto," she whispered the name. The man let forth a deep laugh that shook her to the marrow in her bones. "I know you."

Memories flooded her of a time before time itself, when the gods and goddesses lived on Dal Tara. She saw the birth of Aelinae as Nadra and Ohlin nurtured the new planet. She witnessed Rykoto's love of Daknys, followed by his betrayal with their daughter; she saw Kaldaar's banishment and the Great War that almost destroyed the lands. Daknys held the Sword of Ohlin—Taryn's sword—and cast Rykoto into the Temple of Ardyn. The god screamed when all the others sealed him in his prison.

Rykoto's fury grew as he simmered and plotted, century after century.

He showed her the night of her birth when her brother, her twin brother, was born lifeless and set aside to allow for her entrance into the world. When Taryn's tiny hand touched the pommel of Ohlin's sword, Rykoto recoiled from the light, hissing against her brilliance.

The next day, when her father arrived at the palace looking for his son, Rykoto infected Valterys with the madness that drove him still.

Taryn had to stop him from destroying Aelinae. But Valterys was willing to grant Rykoto his freedom in exchange for immortality. To become a god. Somehow, some way, she had to stop them. If she failed, Rykoto won and all of Aelinae—and the people she cared about—would cease to exist.

"Now you understand." His smile was nothing more than a crimson line across his face. A forked tongue snaked out, smearing blood down his chin. Taryn stared at him, too afraid to look away. "You are mine, daughter. Only mine. I will consume you."

"No." Taryn shook her head, denying the visions, denying him. "Never."

"Your time has come, Eirielle. Awaken." He threw out his hands, and flames shot toward her. His laughter echoed into the darkness.

She covered her ears to stop the hideous sound. "Get out!"

"Taryn, we are here, you are safe."

She blinked at Rhoane several times, the slow realization that she wasn't with the madman anymore dawning on her. "It was so real."

Faelara's face was inches from hers. Lines of concern creased the woman's creamy skin. "What was real, darling?" She handed Taryn some tea. "You were screaming. What happened?"

Taryn took a long drink, trying to recall what she'd seen. "A man. Rykoto. He—" She stopped, eyes wide. "Oh my God. He broke the seal!" She grabbed Rhoane's hand. "He broke the seal, Rhoane."

He was shaking his head. "That is impossible, Taryn. It was only a vision. None of it was real. What did he say?"

"I… He…" She put her hand to her head. The flurry of visions continued unabated. "I saw the war. The one you told me about, with the gods. My sword sealed him away, and now he wants out. What they did to Julieta…" Fresh tears streamed down her cheeks. "It was horrific. Rhoane, he showed me the rape. Said he would consume me, that I was his." Her body trembled hard enough to clatter her teacup on the saucer.

Faelara removed the china from her hand and stroked her hair, making comforting sounds. Her Mari embraced Taryn, but it wasn't enough to keep out the chill in her heart.

"He's using Valterys to do his bidding. And he called me the Eirielle. He showed me things. Terrible things. He wants me to kill people." Taryn rose and paced around the room. She looked at Rhoane, eyes brimming with tears. "He said I'll destroy the Eleri." She fell to her knees. "Oh God. I don't want this. I don't want the power to kill people." She hugged herself, rocking back and forth.

Rhoane knelt beside her. "*Darennsai*, you will not destroy anyone. I promise. Not my people, not anyone. You were born for peace and balance. That is your destiny. Rykoto is trying to manipulate you." He held her close, his heart beating as fiercely as her own. "You know who you are now, but you must believe in what you can do. You are much stronger than you realize." He leaned back to look in her eyes. "I have always believed in you. So have Fae, Baehlon, Brandt, and many, many others. Our belief is nothing, though. *You* must believe it."

"What if I fail?"

"You're not alone in this, Taryn. We are all here to help." Faelara sat beside her on the floor. "Drink this." She handed Taryn a glass of wine. "My darling girl, we'd never let anything happen to you."

As much as she wanted to believe her friend, it wasn't true. In the end, it would be Taryn's responsibility to protect them, not the other way around. She drank the wine in one long swig, handing the glass back to her friend. "I hope I don't let you down."

The older woman pulled her into a protective hug. "You could never do that." She held Taryn until she relaxed into her embrace.

"I hope you're right." Taryn swooned a bit. "What was in that wine? I feel strange." She tried to focus on Fae's amber eyes, but they slid across her skin in a most unbecoming way. "You're all wobbly."

Faelara motioned for Rhoane to help her stand Taryn up. "I put a sleeping draught in your wine, darling. I thought you might need a good night's sleep after this evening."

"Oh, thass a good idea. No more bad guys."

With Rhoane's support, they made their way to the door where Faelara whispered to Rhoane, "I think you should stay with her tonight."

Taryn's head rolled back and she said, "I heard that. I don't need a babyssssitter." She started to tell Faelara she could take care of herself, but her thoughts were mired in muck inside her brain. Instead, she opened the door and staggered into the hallway.

Once they got her to her rooms, with no small effort on Rhoane's part, Taryn, fully dressed, collapsed on the bed.

Chapter 29

TARYN and Nadra sat on a star, far above Aelinae. Made of the same crystals found in the cavern on Mount Nadrene, fragile spikes branched out from the center of the star in a glittering display of radiating color. Taryn's heart was light and full of joy as she laughed with the innocence of a child. They gazed down at the oddly shaped planet of Aelinae. Not round as she'd expected, and where the oceans met the planet's edge, vast waterfalls fell into nothingness. Aelinae had mountains and forests, islands and the sea, deserts and grasslands, but nothing beneath the world. Nothing except dirt and molten lava, as if the underside of Aelinae was one huge volcano.

"Doesn't it need spherical adhesion? Won't it disintegrate?" Taryn worried for the inhabitants of the planet, worried for the world she'd only just come to know. Worried for her home.

"Aelinae is a young planet, only about fifteen thousand seasons or so. She is a prototype of sorts," Nadra explained. "She is as sound as any other planet, I assure you."

The feeling of lightness made her giggle. She spied Aelinae's moons, the smaller of the two shadowing the larger, always visible moon. "It doesn't disappear at all, just hides for a bit. Brilliant."

To the south, a small island drifted high above a larger island in the Southern Sea. A waterfall cascaded into a pool beneath it. "That must break over a hundred laws of physics."

"When you are a god, physics is a matter of semantics. I don't expect you to understand it now, dear one, but someday you'll have need of this knowledge." Nadra rested her head on Taryn's, and wrapped her arms around her waist.

"Why did you send me to Earth with Brandt? Why not let him raise me on Aelinae?"

"There are elements to Earth that are important for Aelinae's survival. Earth is a dead planet, without much ShantiMari to sustain her. She lives on machinery now. In a few centuries, she'll be unrecognizable from the world you know." Nadra smoothed Taryn's hair and kissed her temples. "Don't worry about these things, my beloved. When the time comes, you will know what Aelinae needs."

The happiness that embraced her was all-consuming. Nothing could darken her mood, and she laughed with unbridled gaiety when Nadra sprinkled stardust over her head. Then the goddess whispered through the early morning air. "Awaken, Eirielle, Child of Light and Dark."

Taryn sat upright in her bed, the feeling of tranquility still cloaking her. The sound of ocean waves crashing against the rocks drifted through her open window. The sky was dark and birds had yet to begin their morning song. Half expecting to find Nadra beside her, she was disappointed with the empty bed.

The last vestiges of the sleeping draught Faelara had given her lingered in her sluggish thoughts. She stretched and nestled deep beneath her covers, recalling by turns her dream and the events of the previous evening. If Rykoto was trying to frighten her, he might have succeeded once, but she would be damned if he ever did it again.

A low growl came from her stomach. She'd had little to

eat or drink since lunch the previous day. She stretched again and flicked her wrist, lighting several candles with a thought. When she rose from the bed, she stopped mid-stride, staring at the figure sprawled across the divan.

Still clothed in the silk tunic and leather breeches he had worn the previous night, Rhoane lay with his long legs hanging over the edge, nearly touching the floor. All throughout the room, she could see his ShantiMari woven into powerful wards to protect her.

Her life would never be simple. The path set before her would test her limits in ways she had yet to even conceive. She only hoped Rhoane could withstand the trials, because without him, she would fail. But it had to be his choice. Without an oath or royal command. He had to want to be with her.

She crept from the bed to kneel beside him. His breath came and went in an even flow. His eyelashes fluttered with his dreaming. She brushed a few errant curls off his face, tracing a finger over his slightly pointed ear. He moaned softly in his sleep. She ran her fingers through his hair, liking the way the candlelight caught his golden highlights. When she kissed the corner of his mouth, his lips parted with another moan.

He and Faelara said they believed in her, but what if she failed him? They were linked, bonded by powers beyond her understanding. If she failed, would he die?

She placed a featherlight kiss on his lips before padding to the sitting room, where she called for a page to send up breakfast. While she waited, she checked the sealed cupboard. Not satisfied with her previous wards, she added several more, with a nastier surprise for anyone who so much as touched the wall surrounding it. A plan was forming in her mind. She would not fail; it simply was not an option.

As she passed a mirror, she caught her reflection and gasped.

Thin strands of silver shone among her dull blonde hair. Stardust from her dream. Her hair was longer, too, reaching to her lower back, and silkier than she remembered. She ran her hands through her hair, uncomfortable with the ease with which Nadra had altered her looks. That the gods could manipulate her features, or enter her mind without her consent troubled her. She was accustomed to living with free will and wasn't about to give it up for the whims of a few capricious deities.

Just as she finished lacing her breeches, there was a soft knock on the door, and the page entered with their meal. Taryn took the tray from him and placed it on the balcony table. She was pouring their grhom when Rhoane appeared in the doorway.

"It is not even light yet. Are you always this motivated in the morning?"

The sight of him made every nerve in her body dance. "Yes. Especially when I have things to do. Now, sit down and have some breakfast. I've been thinking, and I need your help."

Rhoane took a seat beside her, stretching his legs. "What is so important it could not wait a few bells until at least the birds are awake?" He motioned to the still dark sky. "And why are we out here when you cannot see anything?"

Several songbirds began their morning greetings, filling the air with their trills and whistles.

"You were saying?" She teased and lit several candles she'd placed around the ivy-covered alcoves. "It's my favorite time of day. Everything is fresh. Anything is possible."

Rhoane yawned loud enough to wake the sea king, shaking his head. "Then by all means, share whatever it is that has you so motivated."

Even on the road, Taryn had not seen him so disheveled. He'd never complained of the early hour before, or spoke in grumpy tones. She took her seat and sipped some grhom, easing into her planned conversation, allowing him to wake up before showing him the looking glass.

"I was thinking maybe I'd visit the library and see if I can find more information about the prophecies. They might help direct me in my path." Rhoane nodded absently and she took that as a good sign. "Then I was thinking I might want to sit in on a few Privy Council meetings." At his look of alarm, she added, "Not right away, but sooner rather than later. I can't possibly understand everything that's going on, but I have to start somewhere."

Rhoane swallowed a bite of his eggs. "Just remember, there are those in power who will try to use you. They are clever, these courtiers. Do not be deceived by their false grace."

"Trust me, I know. Now that I have a crown, they're all going to want to be my best friend. That's why I want to observe at first. Get a feel for how they work. I'd also like to tour as much of Aelinae as I can to learn about the various races and cultures."

"Lliandra will never allow it. A tour like that will cost too much and right now she cannot spare the coin."

"Who said she was invited?" Taryn said around a sip of grhom. "I was thinking maybe an extended trip with just you and me. Baehlon and Faelara, too, if you think we need the protection."

Rhoane shook his head with a devious smile. "Your mother will not like the idea, I can guarantee it."

The sun was breaking over the horizon when Taryn took a deep breath and pulled the looking glass from her pocket. "Okay, fine. We'll table the trip for the moment. But there's something you need to see. You aren't going to like this." She eyed him skeptically. "Show me the intruders." The glass glowed to life, showing Marissa moving through Taryn's rooms.

Rhoane's gaze was tempered, but his jaw tightened, his nostrils flared.

"There's more." The ball flicked to Zakael entering her room through the secret doorway. When he stood over the sleeping Taryn, Rhoane's fists clenched. When Zakael brushed his lips over hers, Rhoane pushed away from the table.

"Enough." He paced along the balustrade. "What madness is this? To enter your rooms? To accost you so?" He spun around, looking at her, his glare accusatory. He kicked his chair closer to the table and sat back down. "Show me the rest." The ball sparked again, showing Zakael trying to break into the warded cupboard. Rhoane exhaled slowly. "Why wait until now to tell me?"

"I was going to tell you yesterday right after it happened, but then we were training and later, in the orchard, it slipped my mind."

"Slipped your mind? Something this important? So that is why he left in such a hurry."

"He's gone? Where?"

"Back to Caer Idris, for all I know. He and Valterys departed while you were at the beach." Rhoane gave her a sidelong glance. "I found out last night before we met at Fae's."

A pang of rejection sucked at her heart. Valterys, her father, had left without saying goodbye. She tamped down the feeling and said brightly, "I wonder how Zakael explained his hands."

"I am sure he will be wearing gloves for a while. That was very clever of you."

"Thank you." Her tone became serious, again. "Rhoane, Marissa knew exactly where to look for the seal. That means she's been spying on me the whole time. What should we do?"

He poured the last of the grhom into their cups and said, "We need to secure your rooms, and then I am afraid we must tell the empress. She will not like what she sees."

"Will you find out when Lliandra has time to see us?"

He stood and nodded, pulling her to him. His lips were on hers before she could stop him. She stiffened in his arms. "Is something wrong?"

"There's one more thing about Marissa I need to tell you. She's bedding Zakael."

Anger flashed in his eyes. "How do you know this?"

"Hayden and I found them." A shudder of disgust went through her at the memory. "The first night we arrived in Talaith, but Hayden didn't know it was Zakael."

He stepped away from her, and a chill invaded the space between them. "She would not dare."

Taryn didn't like the tone of his voice or the feeling of jealousy that pinged in her gut. "He was at Paderau, remember? With Marissa. Rhoane, is there something going on with you two that I should know about?"

"Of course not. My concern for Marissa is that of a brotherly sort. I do not have romantic feelings for her, if that is what you are asking. I just find it hard to believe she would be involved with Zakael in that way. You must be mistaken."

Taryn glared at him. "You know what, Rhoane? Fuck. You. You're just like everyone else around here. You think you know what's going on, and so everything I say must be a lie."

"I do not understand what you are saying."

"Of course you don't." She moved closer to him, lowering her voice. "You have no idea what I'm going through or how hard this is for me."

The emotions she'd fought hard to bury deep within her came bubbling out before she could stop them. "Do you have any idea what I left behind? It was amazing and terrible and uneventful in ways you'll never understand. I had a life. Sure, it was an average, insignificant life, but it was mine. No one told me how to dress, where to go, or who I was going to marry. Then I step into the cavern, and suddenly life as I know it is gone. Done. Over. There are all these expectations now." She thudded him on the chest. "You, for one."

She paced the balcony, the words tumbling out, "You've had your whole life to get used to the idea that you'll be stuck with the 'Eirielle.'" She made quotation marks in the air. "I've had *one day*. For what it's worth, I don't take much stock in prophecies and I prefer to make my own destiny, thank you very much." Forcing herself to take a deep breath and stop talking, she climbed onto the ledge and dangled her legs over the side.

Rhoane stood where she'd left him, and she hated him for his inaction. She wanted him to hold her, but at the same time, to leave her alone. Her anger wasn't for him but for the brutal way she'd been forced into her position.

In a quiet voice, she said, "I'm supposed to protect all these people, but I saw their faces the other day. In the throne room and again on the street during the parade. Some of them fear me, which I can handle, but others hate me." She looked at him through unshed tears. "I felt it in waves as powerful as your ShantiMari. I've never known such hatred—have you?"

She stared at the ocean, longing for the simplicity of her former life. "I don't know what they want from me, and I'm scared. Of my power, of my feelings for you, of the responsibility that's been thrust upon me.

"You tell me I've got friends who love me and won't let anything happen to me, but no one protected me the other night. Marissa or Zakael could've killed me, and no one would've known it was them. How many others out there want me dead? How soon will it be before one of them is successful?"

Saying it out loud did nothing to diminish its potency. Instead, it made her more vulnerable than she'd been before.

"Darennsai." He climbed onto the balcony ledge and faced her. "Sometimes I forget. In my mind, you have always been here, in some small way. We have spent so many seasons protecting the secret of your existence and now to have you returned—it is what we waited for, for so long." He touched her face with his fingertips, and warmth bloomed under her skin. "It is easy to forget that you knew nothing of this world. You are so strong and confident." He shook his head. "I suppose I did not want to admit that you might be frightened. That was ignorant of me."

He looked to the sea, his face a mystery to her. "We are all afraid, Taryn. The empress, Faelara, Myrddin, myself. Underneath the everyday life on Aelinae, there are cracks forming that, if left unchecked, will tear this world apart. Someday you will see for yourself and understand what I am talking about. Until then, it is our job to prepare you for what is to come." His shoulders sagged as he sighed. "I wish I could tell you what that will be, but I do not have the gift of foresight. I have accepted my path and never once have I thought that being by your side was akin to being 'stuck with you,' as you say."

"What do you want from me, Rhoane?"

His voice was a whisper when he spoke, emotion raw around the edges. "I want to be with you in all things, *Darennsai*. In love and battle, in the quiet moments of the evening." He took her hand and pressed their flesh together. Their runes melded into one design. "I want to be with you so completely that your thoughts are mine. I want to know your body better than my own, to know what pleases you and how to soothe your pains." He closed his eyes, and their bonds glowed bright with his ShantiMari. "I want a smile to light your eyes every time you see me. I want to know you, your dreams, your desires, and your fears."

He opened his eyes and stared into hers. "Prophecy says alone you fail. If you do not wish for this," he let go of her hand, leaving her feeling hollow, empty, "I will not force you."

"Rhoane," emotion choked her thoughts. "I want all of that, as well, more than anything. But first I have to find out who I am and what I'm capable of." She looked at him from beneath her lashes. "Everything hit me at once. I need time to make this all my new normal. Do you understand what I'm trying to say?"

"Not really, no."

"That's the problem. I don't, either. It's all mashed up in my head right now, and I can't sort one thing out from the other. I need to learn how to use my power. I need to make the empress happy. I need to figure out how to stop Valterys from taking over the world. I need to keep my sister from killing me. And if that wasn't enough, I need to take a crash course in court politics so I don't get used by anyone. Oh, and let's not forget I need to find a way to satisfy a boyfriend while also training to lead an army. It's a bit much, wouldn't you say?"

"Taryn, you do not have to do all of this on your own. We are here to help and advise you. Do not make all of this your responsibility."

A spark of anger lit through her. "Isn't that what being the Eirielle is all about? Please don't placate me, Rhoane. This burden has been put upon my shoulders, not yours or Faelara's or anyone else's. I know I have all of you to help me, but when it comes down to it, I'm the one who will be facing Rykoto in the end."

"You mean Valterys."

"That's what I said." Taryn shook her head to clear her thoughts. The morning had not gone the way she'd planned, and her emotions were spent. "We better get going. I want to meet with the sword master."

He kissed her lightly on the lips. "I will, as always, be by your side, but I will not pressure you for anything beyond what you can give."

She ran her hands through his hair, wishing things could be different. "What about Marissa?"

A shadow crossed over his eyes, and his jaw clenched. "We will take what we know to the empress and let her deal with her daughter."

"So, you don't really believe me? I know you took an oath, but I don't want you here because of a promise you made before I was born. And I certainly don't need you second-guessing me all the time. I want you to be with me because we're partners. Equals who trust each other. I don't lie, Rhoane. And I don't hurt people to make myself look good. If we're going to be together, you're going to have to trust me."

She left before he could deny her allegations. She'd already heard enough of his excuses.

THE summons came three days later. As she dressed to meet with the empress, Taryn fought her anxiety. She hoped Rhoane would be there, but because they'd not spoken since the morning she showed him the looking glass, she couldn't be sure.

He'd missed her training in the yard, but that wasn't unusual. However, when he failed to show up at Faelara's, Taryn worried that she'd upset him more than she'd thought she did. She sent several notes to his room but didn't receive a reply, which only heightened her concern. And made her doubt Rhoane's insistence that his feelings for Marissa ended at friendship. Since he wasn't speaking to her, she had nothing but her dark thoughts to keep her company.

She arrived at the empress's lavish rooms early and was ushered into the empty sitting room. Lliandra entered, holding her hands out to Taryn. "My darling daughter. I am terribly sorry I haven't made more time for you since the crowning." Her Mari stretched across her face in a smooth mask, hiding Lliandra's imperfections.

But Taryn saw them, just as she saw through her mother's calculated concern.

"I treasure any amount of time you can give me. I know you are busy."

"Still, I should be ashamed of myself. Here I've been pining for your presence for the past many seasons, and once you're finally home, I all but ignore you."

The same thought had nagged Taryn since her last visit with the empress. After her argument with Rhoane, she had plenty of time to sort out her situation, and one thing became clear—Lliandra was very good at public spectacles, but not at being a mother.

They made polite small talk while waiting for Rhoane, but after half a bell Taryn started to suspect he wouldn't be joining them. She toyed with the looking glass in her pocket, hesitant to broach the subject. After discussing her desire to visit the libraries, which Lliandra favored, even going so far as to insist Taryn have a tutor, Taryn took a deep breath and held the looking glass out to the empress.

"This happened the night of my crowning." Taryn started. The glass flared to life, showing Marissa and then Zakael moving around in Taryn's rooms. Lliandra watched in its entirety, not saying a word until Taryn put the ball away.

"I see. Do you have an explanation for this?" Lliandra's voice was neutral, as were her features.

"The only thing I can think of is that Marissa is spying

for Valterys. They were obviously after the sword because the cupboard Zakael was trying to open held it, along with the crown." She realized she'd not breathed since showing Lliandra the vision. Slowly, she let out her breath, taking a deep inhale.

"Your valuables should be locked in the treasury where they will be guarded night and day. See to it that they are moved immediately."

Taryn stammered a reply. "I didn't come here to discuss the safety of my items. I'm more concerned with Marissa's actions. Either you asked her to search my rooms, or she's spying for Valterys." The accusation was out before she had time to consider the consequences.

"Why would you think that?"

"Because she and Zakael are so, um, close." Taryn looked away, embarrassed.

"You mean they are lovers? Do you have proof?"

Taryn was more than a little tired of people doubting her word. "Nothing I can show you, but I heard them."

"Heard them? Explain." Her tone became cooler, more distant, with each demanding question.

Heat flushed up her neck to the roots of her hair as she told Lliandra about her tour of the palace with Hayden, culminating in coming upon the princess and Zakael in a hidden passageway.

"Are you certain they were rutting?"

"Yes."

"You say this was the very night we returned to the palace?" Lliandra's tone held harshness still but took on an edge of indifference, too.

"Yes, Your Majesty."

"Who else knows?"

"Hayden." Taryn almost told Lliandra that it was Marissa's Mari on the sword at Ravenwood, and how her sister had searched her rooms at Paderau, but held her tongue. Unless she had proof, Lliandra wouldn't believe her.

"Say nothing of this to anyone. I will deal with Marissa. Now, tell me what's been keeping you busy." Lliandra's voice oozed with false cheer. The immediate change of tone, and topic, took Taryn by surprise.

"I, well, I've been training with the sword master and soldiers." She fumbled for words. Her head was still swimming with the abrupt turn of conversation.

They spent the next bell chatting about everything *except* Marissa and Zakael. Eventually, Lliandra stood, indicating the visit had come to an end. "Thank you, daughter, for your company. I look forward to seeing you again soon." She gave Taryn a kiss on the cheek and a cold embrace. "Oh, and Taryn, whatever troubles you are having with the Eleri prince, resolve them."

She turned away, leaving Taryn to stare at her, open-mouthed. When the servant approached, only then did she remember herself and regain her composure.

In the hallway, Taryn let loose a stream of expletives that would make a soldier blush. At that moment, Rhoane made the unfortunate mistake of arriving at Lliandra's suite.

"Now you show up. I can't believe you left me to deal with her on my own."

Rhoane looked at her, perplexed. "I was told to meet with the empress at this time, and I assumed you would be here, as well."

"Well, I was told to meet her earlier." She glanced back at the door. "She is so fucking annoying." Taryn glared at each guard in turn. "If you so much as mention a word of this to her, I swear I'll arrange it so you never want to make babies again. Are we understood?"

The guards swallowed hard and nodded.

Taryn turned her fury back to Rhoane. "I'll thank you

not to tell Her Majesty every detail of our relationship."

"I have not told the empress anything about us."

"Then why did she just tell me to resolve our problems? You've been ignoring *me*, not the other way around. I sent several notes to you, but you never replied."

Rhoane looked positively flummoxed. "I thought I would give you time alone, nothing more. As for notes, I have not received any from you."

Taryn was about to challenge him when the door flew open and the empress stood before them. "What is all this shouting about?" She looked first at Taryn and then Rhoane. "Your Highnesses, I expect better behavior from both of you. Really, you do need to work on your communication skills. You always seem to be fighting. Whether it be with a sword in your hand or words on your lips."

She motioned for Rhoane to enter. "Prince Rhoane, I'm happy you could make it on such short notice." She addressed Taryn. "Princess, you may go now. Quietly." She waved her hand in dismissal before closing the door.

Taryn seethed in the hallway while trying to decide what she hated more—duplicitous politicians or game playing Eleri princes.

Chapter 30

THE woman sat at her dressing table, powdering her once-magnificent breasts. She hummed a pleasant tune and regarded herself in the mirror. When she saw Rhoane's reflection, she jumped, a slight squeak coming from her sultry mouth.

"Naughty boy! You scared poor Nena. Is it your wish to kill me?"

Rhoane chuckled good-naturedly at her melodrama. "Not at all, beautiful Mistress."

"No. How many times do I have to tell you this? You do not call me 'Mistress' unless you share my bed." Her eyes narrowed, and a sly grin cracked the heavy makeup she wore. "Is that why you have come today? Finally, you will give Nena what she longs for?"

"I am afraid not. I am only here to make certain the crown princess is well cared for."

"You know I cannot discuss my clients. I will only say that Armando is the best I have, and he gives the princess exactly what she requests."

"I should hope so. She comes here frequently enough." He knew for a fact she was two doors down at that very moment. If he focused his concentration, he could hear her. He did not so desire. "That is far more valuable than her coin, I would think."

"In this business, reputation is all you have." Nena fluffed a strand of her luxurious copper hair and winked toward the bed. "It's a shame to waste, no?"

"It is a shame, but you know I am promised to another."

"Nena knows about the mysterious golden beauty." Her tone became serious, and Rhoane sat forward in his chair. "You know Nena would never compromise her business relationships, but I have heard rumblings that some at court do not believe she is the empress's daughter. Sword or no, there are those who count her false."

"I would be surprised if there were not." He stood and took the madam's hand in his own. "I was at her birth. She is Lliandra's legitimate daughter. If she was not, do you think I would be able to deny your charms?"

Nena actually blushed crimson and giggled like a young maiden. "Flatterer."

Rhoane employed an Eleri trick of folding time and left her rooms, chuckling to himself at Nena's exasperated cry. To her, it appeared that he'd been standing before her one moment, and the next, he'd disappeared. In reality, he simply made the minutes slow for her and leapt from her open window. Only his people knew how to manipulate time, and even then, few could manage it without serious complications.

He rode Fayngaar through the streets of Talaith, delaying his return to the palace. Lliandra's meeting with him earlier that morning had not gone well, due in part to her refusal to hear his plea about Marissa, but more so because of the arrival of his father's messenger.

When he finally returned to the palace, his kinswoman Janeira tapped a booted foot against the packed dirt as he rode into the stables. As tall as most Aelan men, Janeira was King Stephan's fiercest warrior. "You are late."

"I had business to attend. Why are you not dressed for dinner?"

"I am without escort."

Propriety mattered to the Eleri, but since Janeira had arrived unannounced, and with his father's demand that he return to the Narthvier at once, Rhoane cared little about her discomfort. A fact, he was certain, would be shared with the king. "I am here now. Let us change and arrive at the feast together."

Half a bell later, Janeira gracefully curtseyed to the empress, her long leg extended in the Eleri tradition. Deep slits up the side of her floor-length skirt allowed ample views of her tanned limbs. Janeira's short top of green silk, embroidered on the edges with gold thread, did little to contain her breasts, and her arms and midsection were bare. She wore her dark hair in braids that hung to the dimples above her buttocks.

A few of the men closest to her stared appreciatively until their gazes met Rhoane's. A few brazenly took one last glance at Janeira before drifting off. Most of them had never seen an Eleri woman, and Janeira was among the most beautiful of his race.

Janeira rose, adjusting the gold chain she wore around her slim waist. To the Eleri, it signified she was unavailable, but for some reason that thin piece of jewelry sent spasms of desire through the Fadair, the non-Eleri. Sometimes, Rhoane just didn't understand the Fadair mind. She was promised to Rhoane's brother, Bressal, and even though she wore the gold chain, she had not yet accepted Bressal as her mate but was considering him.

After greeting the empress, Rhoane led Janeira through the crowded ballroom, scanning the area for Taryn. He'd not seen her since the altercation outside her mother's rooms, nor did he see her now.

Lliandra sat on her ornate chair, overseeing the proceedings with a satisfied smile. When they met earlier, she'd made it clear to him that nothing should go wrong that evening. She was livid at having an Eleri arrive unannounced and order her around for the Eleri king. At least they had that in common.

It wasn't like his father to dabble in Fadair politics. Rhoane had kept quiet to the empress, waiting until he had a chance to speak with Janeira about his father's plans, but Janeira, it seemed, was more loyal to their king than he. She would say nothing on the subject, save that he and Taryn had been summoned to the Weirren Court, the seat of the Eleri king, and his home.

"These Fadair are repulsive." Janeira seethed when another courtier passed, openly gawking at her near-nakedness. "They think not with their minds, but with their cocks, wanting only to satisfy the moment."

"That is an unfair assessment. Some of these men have shown restraint." Rhoane resented the way Eleri believed everyone to be beneath them. For some of his people, calling other races Fadair was the worst kind of contempt they could show.

Janeira scoffed as she glared down Lord Herbret's watery-eyed appraisal. "Do they not realize the power they waste in trifling endeavors? They know nothing of what it means to share one's body, to allow the exchange of ShantiMari to strengthen both parties. They are like children. Easily amused, easier still to lose interest once they have obtained what they chase."

"They worship in their own way. It is different, not necessarily worse." He surveyed the few riders who had come with Janeira. They stayed off to the side, speaking only to each other. The Eleri didn't understand the customs of people outside the Narthvier, nor did they wish to, which made it difficult for Rhoane.

"They use something sacred for personal gain. They are disgusting."

Rhoane let it drop. The visit was not off to a great start, and he couldn't risk offending Janeira. If she gave a negative report to his father, it was unlikely the Eleri would revoke his *sheanna* or accept Taryn as their *Darennsai*. Both of which needed to happen.

Sabina dipped a brusque curtsey, her glare uncharacteristically cold. Her greeting to Janeira was the opposite, warm and inviting. The women dressed in similar clothing, which was to say, not much at all. Sabina wore the traditional attire of the Summerlands, a filmy gown that covered her breasts and lower regions, but left her midsection and most of her legs bare.

Hayden barely contained his desire as he stood beside the princess, only looking away to speak with Rhoane and Janeira. To his credit, Hayden didn't gawk at Janeira's dress as others had, but Rhoane saw the telltale flush to his cheeks.

A familiar laugh brought Rhoane's attention away from his companions. He turned in time to see Taryn spin around the dance floor, a wide smile on her face. A pinch of jealousy stung his insides, but he kept his face calm. Since the morning she showed him the looking glass, he'd kept his distance to let her sort out her feelings, but seeing her laughing with another man brought forth unwelcome thoughts.

When Janeira asked after the couple, Sabina said, "Princess Taryn and Lord Aomori. You remember him, don't you, Rhoane? We met him in Paderau when Taryn made us dinner."

Rhoane did remember him. He came from the Danuri Province but was fostering with Lord Tinsley. His family was one of the wealthiest in Aelinae. Not only that, he was young and quite handsome.

"Why does she dance with another man if she is your betrothed?" Janeira asked.

Sabina looked at Rhoane with one eyebrow raised. "Yes, Prince Rhoane, why does she?"

The tone of her voice and slight shake of her head meant she knew Rhoane had been avoiding Taryn. By way of answer, he bowed to Sabina before leading Janeira to the dance floor, where he kept his kinswoman far from his betrothed.

This was not the meeting he'd envisioned for the two. It wasn't Taryn's fault he'd been scarce the past few days. In an attempt to find the truth of Taryn's allegations, he'd followed Marissa.

Aside from meeting with Armando, Marissa rarely left the palace. Once, she'd roamed the gardens for several bells, stopping to sit atop the seawall at the farthest edge of the orchard, and staring out to sea. Even Rhoane's surreptitious conversation with Hayden hadn't garnered anything useful. Marissa had been with someone in the servant's quarters the night they arrived in Talaith, but Hayden had no idea who.

Even with that piece of information, Rhoane hesitated to think it could be Zakael. He'd actually managed to convince himself it wasn't Zakael Taryn had seen at the ball in Paderau, that she had been mistaken. He'd known Marissa all her life; she was a devoted daughter, not just to Lliandra, but to the throne. She would never jeopardize Aelinae's future.

Of the notes Taryn had mentioned, neither he nor his valet had received them. A few quiet inquiries left him no closer to finding the mysterious papers, either. Somehow, from Taryn to Rhoane, they'd disappeared.

For most of the evening, Rhoane kept Janeira busy with introductions to powerful nobles who could benefit the Eleri. As much as she believed the Eleri didn't need the Fadair, Rhoane knew differently. Having lived with them, he understood how the races were intertwined in a way the Eleri could never imagine.

Although he appeared to pay her no mind, Rhoane kept watch over Taryn, grimacing each time she laughed or spun around the huge dance floor in another man's arms. She'd been drinking more than usual that night, and each time their eyes met, it was as if she challenged him to stop her. Suddenly his plan to give her some distance didn't seem like such a great idea.

"May I have this dance?" Marissa slipped beside him and placed her hand on his arm.

"The empress was worried about you," Rhoane said once they were away from Janeira. Marissa should've been to the feast bells earlier. The stench of her whore's sex lingered.

"I had another engagement, but I'm here now." She pressed herself into him, sliding her fingers down the front of his tunic to the top of his breeches. "I see your betrothed has found herself a new love." She flicked the front of his pants, and he grabbed her wrist.

"This is unseemly of you."

"You're right. I'm sorry, Rhoane." In a breath, her whole demeanor changed. She sagged into him, pouting beneath her fluttering lashes—the same little girl trick she'd used on him countless times over the seasons. It wasn't cute any longer.

"You are drunk." He noticed a bluish tinge around her neck, as if a bruise were just forming. A protective surge overcame him. "What has happened to you, Marissa? Did someone harm you?"

"Hardly." She scoffed and flicked her wrist with dramatic flair. "It's you, my darling, I'm worried about. I wasn't wrong when I said your betrothed has found someone new. I have it on good authority that Aomori has sampled the fruits of your love."

Rhoane glared at her. "You go too far."

Her breasts rose and fell in a shrug. Her low-cut gown of pale lavender matched her eyes. A challenge stirred in them, and something else. Remorse, perhaps? "Lady Celia saw them in the garden earlier. They thought they were being discreet but clearly not. I don't know how Sabina can bear it. She confided in Taryn that Aomori was going to petition the empress for her hand. To be betrayed by your friend like that, it must be awful."

They moved to the side of the dance floor where Rhoane slowed their movements, but could not temper the pounding of his heart or the rush of blood to his ears. "Celia is mistaken. She loves gossip more than power. I would not put my trust in anything she says."

"Dear Rhoane, you are bound by your Eleri ethics, but you forget Taryn is not. She didn't swear an oath when she was a child. Don't look so shocked. Only mother and I know about your oath, and I would never tell a soul. I've grown rather fond of my sister and hate to be the one to tell you this, but you have to know—Taryn is trying to break your bonds."

He caught Taryn watching them from the other side of the room. She looked frail and alone to him. Aomori laughed at something another lord had said, but Taryn ignored him. The sadness in her eyes touched Rhoane. He shook his head. "You are wrong, Marissa. Taryn has more honor than that."

"For your sake, I hope so. You don't want to be bound for all eternity with a woman who does not want you." The dance ended, and Marissa ran a finger along Rhoane's jaw. "You deserve better than her, Rhoane." The musky scent of her sex wafted after her as she moved through the crowd.

Although he'd been promised to Taryn since birth, he'd had less than two moonturns to get to know her. He didn't like the predicament Marissa and Taryn created. If they both told the truth, they betrayed not just him but the entire realm. The problem was that he had no reason to doubt either woman. Yet he couldn't forget the image he saw in Taryn's looking glass of Zakael touching Taryn as if they were lovers. Rhoane's ShantiMari boiled through his veins.

From across the room, Janeira shot him a look of warning. He didn't need her to remind him what could happen if Eleri ShantiMari was unconfined. The image of his mother consumed in flames of power was forever embedded on his heart.

Taryn's laughter cut through the ballroom, too loud, too forced. She grabbed a goblet from a passing servant before Marissa caught her in a dancer's pose and spun them both onto the dance floor. Aomori held Sabina in his arms, a league between them while Hayden watched the pair with jealous hunger in his eyes. Rhoane hated the games nobles played. Hated the way they used lives for their own entertainment. Hated the fact he'd been lured into their schemes.

At the helm of it all, Lliandra sat on her throne observing the guests with a calculated coolness that unnerved Rhoane. Nothing happened in her kingdom without her knowledge. If Marissa was bedding Zakael, Lliandra would know. If Taryn had bedded Aomori, the same. For a heartbeat, Rhoane wondered if Lliandra had orchestrated the tryst between Taryn and Aomori. It would serve her well to break Rhoane's bonds with Taryn. Without his influence, Lliandra would be free to manipulate her daughter.

He roamed the room, scanning the area periodically while Janeira danced with an aging nobleman and Taryn lounged on overstuffed couches with the other princesses, wine goblets filled, and plates of faerie cakes overflowing before them. They talked and laughed and drank. Except little Tessa, who neither spoke, nor ate. Something was wrong. He sensed it. Could almost feel the darkness creeping in. Ready to take hold, to strangle the light.

"I've seen happier faces on pigs ready for slaughter. What's got you so down?" Baehlon leaned against the open window, sucking in the scant breeze. "Gods, but it's hot tonight."

Rhoane glanced at his friend, noting the sweat on his brow, the stains beneath his arms, "Are you ill?"

Baehlon shook his head, and the golden bells chimed. "It's Faelara. The blasted woman insisted I dance with her." He patted his belly, "I've been lax in my training."

Rhoane nodded absently, his attention on Janeira's approach. He turned back to Baehlon and motioned toward Taryn. "She has had enough for one night. Can you escort her to her rooms?"

Baehlon didn't question his friend but went to quietly speak with Taryn. She gave him little fight and left without a glance in Rhoane's direction. Janeira watched Taryn's exit with a look of disgust on her face. He could just imagine her report to his father—that Taryn was nothing more than a silly girl who couldn't control her drink. The Eleri would never accept her as *Darennsai*.

The band struck up a hopeful melody, and Rhoane took Janeira into his arms, turning them both onto the dance floor. "Tell me, are my brothers well?"

They spoke of the Weirren and Rhoane's family through two songs until Janeira said finally, "I have had enough dancing for one evening. If you do not mind, I would like to get some rest." She curtseyed to him before making her way to the empress, where she stayed a few minutes. The last Rhoane saw of Janeira, she was trailing after Aomori as he left the ballroom.

Whatever her intentions, it wouldn't be good for him or Taryn.

"Interesting kinswoman you've got there."

Rhoane glanced at Baehlon, suddenly feeling his many seasons. "Where is Taryn?"

"In bed, I hope. I left her with her maids. She'll not enjoy the morning sun, that's for certes. Drunk as an Artagh on Smelting Day."

Rhoane nodded absently.

"Is there something I should be made aware of? You two have been acting odd since her crowning."

Rhoane debated only a moment before confessing to his friend. "Taryn believes Marissa is bedding Zakael, and tonight Marissa told me Taryn is bedding Aomori. Neither can give me proof other than her word."

"I see." Baehlon crossed his arms over his chest. "So, your dilemma is, if I am correct, whether you should believe a girl who has no reason to lie to you or someone who's been in love with you all her life and would do anything to have you for her own."

Marissa's laughter drew his attention. She and several ladies were walking through the ballroom. Lords bowed out of their way, many of whom followed the crown princess with looks of longing. "Marissa and I are friends, Baehlon. Nothing more."

"No, you are friends with her, but she's in love with you. You're just too blind or foolish to see it."

If not for the hypocrisy of that statement coming from Baehlon, Rhoane would've been insulted. Baehlon had been in love with Faelara, and she with him, for going on ten seasons, yet neither one would admit to it.

"You've got a choice to make, my friend. Where do your loyalties lie? With Marissa or with Taryn? You can't play both sides of this war or you'll be the one left for dead on the battlefield."

Damn the man and his honesty.

Chapter 31

LLIANDRA raged at Taryn for the better part of two bells. She paced around the room, shouting at times or whispering in a deadly voice at others. Taryn's replies varied from, *Yes, Your Majesty. I'm sorry, Your Majesty*, to *Yes, Mother. I'm so sorry, Mother*. Lliandra had demanded Taryn use the moniker, and her tongue tripped around the unfamiliar word. Nothing placated the angry empress. At one point, Taryn was certain the woman would throw her out the window into the sea below.

Finally, Lliandra calmed down enough to glare at Taryn. "Well? What do you have to say for yourself?"

Dizzy from hunger and her head swimming with the ill effects of her hangover, Taryn replied a bit too sullenly. "I don't know."

"You don't know? How lovely! I wish I could use that as an excuse. Let me see…Empress Lliandra, why has your daughter made a mockery of my son and messenger in front of the entire court? I'm sorry, King Stephan, but I don't know." Lliandra moved her face a hair's width from Taryn's. "You damn well better know. I thought I made it very clear to you yesterday that whatever problem you have with Prince Rhoane, you were to resolve it."

"Yes, ma'am, you did."

"And you thought the best way to do that would be to dance with everyone else in the room but him?"

"I didn't think about that."

"I'm afraid to ask what it was you did think about."

Taryn met her angry stare and said in a clear voice, "I thought about myself, which I see now was wrong. I wanted to have some fun." Her anger fumed within, making it difficult to control her power. "I'm sure you remember what it's like to be a young woman and have men fawn over you. I liked it. I felt beautiful for once in my life."

Lliandra scoffed. "What's that supposed to mean? Of course you're beautiful. You're my daughter, for Ohlin's sake. You don't need a bunch of libidinous boys to tell you that! Look in a mirror, you fool!"

Taryn took a deep, calming breath. "Yes, Mother, I'll do that."

Lliandra's hand cracked across Taryn's cheek with enough force to rattle her teeth. "Never speak to me in that tone." Lliandra's ShantiMari streaked around her body.

No one had ever struck Taryn before, and she trembled where she sat, frightened to her core. She put a hand to her cheek, feeling the stinging warmth, tasting blood in her mouth.

"I don't know what you want me to say. I'm sorry. I won't do it again. Please, just tell me how I can make it better, and I will," Taryn pleaded.

Lliandra's Mari subsided, and it alarmed Taryn even more how quickly the empress could summon and dismiss that much power. "What's done is done. I've been commanded by King Stephan to bring you to the Narthvier and Janeira will be traveling with us. I expect you to be cordial to her and, if at all possible, win her over with your charms." Lliandra's tone made it clear she doubted Taryn had any.

Taryn stood to go. "Thank you, Mother. I will do my

best."

"Sit down. That boy you were with last night—Lord Aomori. Did you fuck him?"

Shocked by the crass question, Taryn stammered, "No, of course not! Why would you ask such a thing?"

Lliandra studied her a moment too long. "I have it on good authority that you did. You were in the gardens for quite some time."

"Nothing happened, I swear."

Lliandra's face relaxed a fraction. "I have ways of finding the truth, so do not lie to me."

"I promise you," Taryn said with a slight break in her voice, "I did not have sex with Lord Aomori or any other man last night or any other time in my life. I am still a virgin." Her body trembled with anger and disgust. With forced deep breaths, she held her ShantiMari in check, just barely.

"It would be best if you didn't make it a habit to go wandering through the grounds late at night with a boy you hardly know. And you should really learn to control your wine. I also heard that Sir Baehlon had to escort you to your rooms last night. I expect more from you, Princess Taryn."

"I'll remember that, thank you." She bowed her head in defeat. "There are so many rules to this princess thing. Is there a guidebook or something to make sure I don't mess up again?"

To her astonishment, Lliandra laughed, a full-bellied laugh that made Taryn nervous. "Oh, you are a prize. Of course, you wouldn't know not to traipse around with strange men. Sometimes I forget you were raised as an Offlander. I only wish Brandt had better prepared you for this life."

"You and me both." Taryn couldn't feel any more miserable. The slight against Brandt left her battered and drained. She wanted nothing more than to crawl back to her room and sleep for the rest of her life.

Lliandra rose, indicating Taryn do the same. "I'll send someone to instruct you on court etiquette. You've much to learn before we reach the Narthvier. King Stephan is not as forgiving as I." She kissed Taryn on each cheek before waving her off.

Taryn mumbled a goodbye, thanking her again—for what, she wasn't sure. Not killing her, perhaps? Then just before Taryn reached the door, Lliandra said in a nonchalant tone, "Duke Anje will be returning to Paderau today. He'll be taking Hayden and the other young lords with him."

A fissure in the dam that kept her anger in check threatened to buckle, to release all of her rage. She pressed her nails into her palms, focused on the pain, eased her anger. "You're sending Hayden away? Why?"

"We'll be traveling through Paderau on our way north. There are preparations to be made. Besides, I can't have any distractions around while Janeira is here. We need King Stephan's support, Taryn."

"But I don't understand. Hayden did nothing wrong." Lliandra gave Taryn a look that said to leave it rest, but Taryn pushed. "Who told you that I was with Aomori?"

Lliandra made a show of straightening her gown, a frown creasing the Mari she carefully kept in place. "It pains me to tell you this, my dove. I know you and Sabina have grown close over the last few weeks."

"Sabina?" Taryn barely whispered the name. No. She wouldn't, couldn't have said anything. Sabina was with Taryn most of the night; she knew nothing had happened. And then it clicked. Marissa. That scheming, duplicitous bitch had lied to Lliandra. "But why?" Taryn faked a hurt tone.

"Darling, isn't it obvious? She's in love with him." Lliandra took Taryn's hands in her own. "I know this will be difficult, but you mustn't blame your friend. In fact, it would be best if you didn't say anything to her about all of this.

As far as I'm concerned, it never happened. Aomori would make an excellent match for a girl like Sabina. We should do everything in our power to help her."

"Yes, of course." Taryn curtseyed low to her mother and left the opulent rooms in a haze.

Later that morning, as she said her farewells to Duke Anje and Hayden, she couldn't hide her disappointment. Hayden assured her it wasn't her fault; he even went so far as to take some of the blame. If he'd known Lliandra's response would be so hurtful, he would've stepped in the previous night. Taryn didn't have the nerve to tell him what Lliandra had accused her of with Aomori, although she suspected he'd already heard from the court gossip mill.

Tinsley gave her a warm hug in parting. Aomori's was a bit restrained.

"I'm sorry," she whispered to his ear alone. "I'll do what I can to make it up to you."

He gave her arm a slight squeeze. "I don't blame you." The meaning behind his words relieved her guilt somewhat, but there was a lot of work to be done on her part to clear his name. If his family heard he'd sullied a princess, they might insist he marry her. That was a complication neither of them needed.

Taryn stood with Sabina, waving until the carriages were through the gate. Her friend was stoic, but underneath her calm demeanor, Sabina was devastated to have Hayden leave so soon after arriving in Talaith. Knowing she was to blame compounded Taryn's guilt.

When the last of the carriages disappeared, Taryn steered Sabina toward her rooms. "We need to talk."

Lliandra's rant that morning made it clear where her mother stood as far as loyalty. It was time Taryn figured out who *she* could trust. If the empress thought she could control her second-born, she was dead wrong. The tricky part would be convincing her she was right. With Sabina's help, she just might pull it off.

THE fortnight before they traveled north was a haze of activity for Taryn. Lliandra made sure her schedule was full each day. Training with Sword Master Tudyk, followed by another bell of practice with the soldiers in martial arts. In the afternoon, Sabina and Eliahnna gave Taryn etiquette lessons. If she thought Hayden harsh in his instruction on the road to Paderau, he was a kitten compared to the young women. They took their role seriously and made Taryn walk, talk, bend, and eat like a princess. Muscles she didn't know she had ached from holding a fork at just the right angle.

When they finished with her, Taryn was turned over to Master Gameson, the head scholar in Talaith. His job was to school Taryn on everything from ruling Houses in the seven kingdoms to trade routes across the sea. Her mind swam with the information he crammed into her brain each day. Myrddin often joined them in the library, helping translate archaic texts or lending support to Gameson's lesson. Wary that he might be spying for Lliandra, Taryn kept her interactions with him brief until it became evident he was there out of a genuine interest in her education. It was Celia's presence that truly confounded Taryn.

Several times, she arrived with a tray of tea and cakes. After seeing to Taryn's comfort, she would either sit quietly while Master Gameson instructed Taryn or she would peruse the stacks of books. Rarely did she interrupt the lesson or try to ingratiate herself with Taryn aside from the refreshments. Taryn tolerated her but made no offer of anything that could be construed as trust.

When her schedule permitted, Taryn spent time at the

beach with her younger sisters and Sabina. Thankfully, after that one time, neither Marissa nor Celia joined them. It was at the private cove they spoke of their plans.

Sabina had been rightfully incensed when Taryn confided that Lliandra had blamed her for the Aomori Incident, as they began calling it. She knew as well as Taryn did the affair was a fabricated lie to tarnish Taryn's reputation, quite possibly to destroy the bond she shared with Rhoane.

Lliandra and Marissa continued with their plans to match Sabina with Aomori, but on those afternoons at the beach, Taryn and Sabina carefully constructed ways to thwart the empress. At first, they were careful not to say too much in front of the younger princesses, but Tessa insinuated herself into their scheme. Eliahnna listened to their argument with equanimity, eventually offering her support.

A major complication they found hard to resolve was Herbret's insistence Sabina would be his bride. He constantly hounded her, making promises of a life lived in luxury, of being spoiled by a man who adored her. He professed his love at every occasion, making certain Lliandra saw everything. To Taryn's and Sabina's horror, after the Aomori Incident, the empress had made concessions to Herbret, offering to reconsider his petition for Sabina's hand.

Taryn used Celia's closeness to Marissa as an opportunity to learn. Not just about her sister but Herbret. It was no secret at court that Celia and Herbret shared a rather unique interest in each other, with some courtiers going so far as to suggest they were both Marissa's lovers. Of course, the last was always whispered behind a concealing hand, with a knowing nod or wink to accompany the rumor.

In those two weeks, Taryn became adept at playing the game. It wasn't about just her anymore but Sabina, as well. For her friend, she would wallow in the filth of politics and court intrigue.

Taryn sent several messages to Rhoane, which were once again left unanswered. The few times their paths had crossed in the palace, he'd pretended not to see her, and after a while, she quit looking for him. Only at night, when she was alone in her rooms, did she allow the heartache. Only there did she cry bitter tears of hurt and disappointment. She'd already failed him in so many ways. She didn't blame him for his distance, but as long as her bonds sparkled in the light, she held onto hope.

On the morning they were set to travel to the Narthvier, Cora brought Taryn a dainty silver circlet with tiny fleur-de-lis, each petal studded with sapphires.

"The empress sent this for you to wear on the road."

Taryn admired the little crown in the mirror. "It seems a bit impractical for travel, don't you think?"

"It's what Her Majesty wishes."

Taryn knew better than to argue with what Lliandra wished. Her cheek stung at the memory of the slap she'd given her.

The others were gathered in the courtyard, talking excitedly to one another when Taryn arrived. Sabina wore a deep green riding gown with her luxurious hair piled on her head. Her coppery skin glowed in the early morning sun, and Taryn smiled at her friend.

"Are you excited to see Hayden?"

Sabina blushed prettily. "Do you think he's looking forward to seeing me?"

"I'm certain of it. What are you going to do for eight whole days?"

"Don't tease. I've grown rather fond of the marquis," she whispered to Taryn. "I've written to Mother about him. She wants to meet him, of course, but I think she approves."

"That's wonderful news." The bold move was a calculated risk. Lliandra outranked Sabina's mother, Queen Prateeni, but not even the great empress would court the wrath of the Summerlands. At least they hoped.

Sabina put a finger to her lips. "I don't want to hex it. Tessa and Eliahnna don't know yet, and I'd like to keep this between Lord Hayden and me for as long as I can."

"My lips are sealed." Taryn pretended to lock her lips, turning a key. "She'll find out anyway, you know. That woman has eyes in the back of her head and ears everywhere."

"I know. That's why I've only told you. I know I can trust you."

"That means the world to me." It did. More than Sabina would ever know.

Rhoane approached with the Eleri woman by his side. He wore a circlet very similar to hers, with emeralds dancing in the sunlight.

"Your Highness." Taryn curtseyed low to Rhoane. She made a smaller curtsey to Janeira. "It's nice to make your acquaintance." Then in Eleri, she said, "*Cyr doyensa. Me palaith tu daer oyensais gardainen.*" She'd begged one of the riders who had come with Janeira to teach her the traditional greeting.

Janeira regarded her with curiosity. "I was unaware you spoke Eleri," she said in stilted Elennish. "I am happy to meet you, as well. But your apology is unnecessary. Prince Rhoane has explained everything to me."

Taryn bowed her head. "Thank you, fair Mistress. I am humbled by your forgiveness."

"I said it was unnecessary; I did not say you were forgiven." She slapped Rhoane on the back and walked away.

Taryn stared after her. "How rude."

"Interesting, that is what she said about you the night of the ball," he said flatly.

Ouch. "About that. There's really nothing I can say that would adequately convey my apology. I was foolish, and

I'm truly sorry." By the look on his face, Taryn could tell he thought it was more than her dancing with a few men and drinking too much. "You don't believe the rumor, do you? Rhoane, I didn't sleep with Aomori."

His glance flicked to Sabina and back to her. "The empress had it on good authority that something happened in the garden."

"Rhoane, I was with Taryn the entire night. Even in the garden. Hayden and Tinsley were there, as well."

Confusion, hurt, anger, disbelief—all crossed his features. His lips pursed into a tight line, and his jaw flexed several times. "Why would someone lie to the empress?"

Sabina opened her mouth to speak, but Taryn cut her off. "Seriously? You can't think of anyone who would love nothing more than to have you and me fighting? Think about it, Rhoane. Who has the most to gain? I sent you, I don't know, half a dozen notes asking to meet with you to explain, but you ignored them. Again."

Aware of the stares around them, she lowered her voice. "Now, you come down here all higher than thou and tell me that you believe Marissa's lies. Again. Do you honestly think Sabina, my best friend, would lie to the empress?"

"I have received no notes from you. Not previously, nor now. As for the other issue, there is no proof Marissa had anything to do with this."

"I guess back in Paderau when you asked me to never doubt you, that was a one-way promise."

Taryn didn't wait for a response. She turned away from him and stalked to Sabina's carriage. Let him have Marissa; if he didn't have complete faith in Taryn, then he didn't deserve her.

When they reached the carriage, Sabina put a soothing hand on Taryn's arm. A prickling beneath her touch, like ShantiMari but twisted and crimped into a painful knot, singed Taryn's skin.

"He will come around, Taryn. Do not lose faith." At Taryn's rolled eyes, Sabina continued, "Am I truly your dearest friend?"

Despite herself, Taryn chuckled. "Yes, you ninny. Now get inside so we can be off."

After leaving Sabina with her younger sisters at the carriage, she meandered through the crowd to where a groom waited with Ashanni. As she approached, she saw a familiar figure pawing through the leather bag Rhoane had given her that first day in the cavern. She kept her most treasured items in there. The silver hairbrush he'd produced for her, the ornate dagger from Tessa, the book of Aelinean fairy tales Eliahnna had given her for her birthday, a journal, and the Seal of Ardyn.

"Did you need something, Herbret?"

His squat little body swiveled around, the color draining from his face. "I was making sure you had everything you'd need for our trip north."

"Right. Because you're my steward now?"

He splayed his hands wide. "One can never be too prepared."

Taryn retrieved the bag from the pommel of her saddle and slung it over her shoulder, adjusting the fit across her body. She rested a hand on the hilt of her sword. "And am I prepared?" She tapped her fingers along the flared dragon's wings. "Or am I missing anything?"

His pasty cheeks blossomed like roses as he stammered out a reply. "I-I-I m-m-meant no disrespect, Your Highness. The empress asked that I ensure you're taken care of for the journey."

"The empress? And why would she do that?"

"Well, I would think that is obvious, Princess. The Eleri prince is otherwise occupied, and your mother wanted me to satisfy any needs you might have."

Taryn threw up a little in her mouth. She would definitely have a talk with Lliandra about who should be satisfying what. "As you can see, I'm fine." He started to shuffle away when Taryn said, "And Herbret? Don't ever touch my things again. The next time, I won't be as lenient. Imperial command or no."

When he'd disappeared between the horses, she slipped a hand into the bag, feeling for the hidden seal. When her fingertips brushed against the soft velvet pouch, she let out a sigh of relief. It was going to be a long ride to meet King Stephan.

Chapter 32

RHOANE crouched behind the royal tents, his legs cramping with the effort. Each night they camped, he roamed the darkness, looking for answers. Taryn's final words before they left Talaith had stung. Sabina had found him their first night on the road, and swore upon Julieta's honor she said nothing to the empress, reiterating she was with Taryn the entire night.

Until Taryn's arrival, he'd managed to avoid court gossip, but each day brought forth new challenges and rumors.

He stretched up, catching the scent of body odor masked with floral oils. A few paces from where he hid, a lithe figure moved quietly past the tents. Intrigued, he followed.

The figure reached a wooded area behind their camp and disappeared into the foliage. No good ever came of surprising someone in tight, densely packed quarters, so Rhoane stayed hidden under a tree, resting his foot upon the trunk, his back pressed into the wood.

After three-quarters of a bell, the figure emerged from the trees. A branch snagged her hood, revealing Celia's pale face.

His blood sped through his veins with his quickened pulse. When the figure approached, he straightened from where he'd slouched and said quietly, "Out for a midnight stroll, Lady Celia?"

At the sound of his voice, she squeaked and pulled her cloak tight around her neck. "Your Highness! You frightened me." The cloak slipped off her face and she glared at him. "Are you following me?"

"No, but I do find it curious that you are roaming the campsite without an escort, dressed in a heavy cloak in the midst of summer."

She tossed her hair and looked haughtily at him. "There is no law against it. I can do what I wish. Now, if you'll excuse me, I must see to my mistress's comfort before she retires."

"Yes, of course. Would you like me to accompany you?"

"I can find my way." Another toss of hair followed by a wicked smile. "But if you're asking for my company, then I would be honored." An undercurrent of meaning rested in her words.

She started for the camp, and he moved in step beside her. Faint blue markings marred her otherwise pretty skin. "Taryn tells me the two of you have become close." It was a bold lie, but something was not right with Celia.

"Quite. She is dependent upon me for so many things. I help with her research, you know."

"Indeed. You are an asset to her work."

"Not just that, but in all facets of her life. I know every intimate detail."

Warning flares lit in his mind. "You must be honored. To gain her trust is not easy."

"You should know." Celia snorted.

"Celia," Rhoane held her arm and stopped, "is there something you are not telling me? Something I should know?"

"Isn't it obvious? She doesn't love you. Why, just this evening I saw her with one of the soldiers behind the tents. Her appetite for pleasure is immense, like her mother's." Fully caught up in her story, Celia continued in a rush, her face shining with excitement. "There are times I've had to sneak courtiers into her rooms through the secret passageways. The cries I hear from her bedchamber, you'd not believe. Forget about her, Your Highness. Find someone worthy of you." She patted his cheek with false sympathy.

"I thank you for the warning." They continued on as Rhoane sorted through her lies. If Taryn had met a soldier that evening, he would've known. When they reached Marissa's tent, Rhoane thanked Celia for her information. "You have spared me much heartache this night."

"I just want what's right for you."

"Your concern touches me. Do you still have the notes Taryn sent to me, or have you destroyed them?"

A flicker of guilt cut across her face before she pulled a look of offense over her features. "I'm sure I don't know what you're talking about. Thank you for escorting me. Good night, Prince Rhoane."

She slipped into Marissa's tent, and he heard her rustling around for several minutes before she grew quiet. He checked on Taryn's tent and listened to her gentle breathing through the rough fabric for a long time before returning to his own cot for a fitful night's sleep.

The next few nights he watched for any sign that Celia might again sneak away, but each evening after dinner, she and Marissa would remain in their quarters. Taryn kept close to Sabina and the younger princesses, riding by their carriage during the day or sometimes hanging back to ride with the soldiers. He doubted Celia's word but asked Baehlon to ride with the guard all the same. If anything inappropriate was going on between Taryn and a soldier, he'd hear about it.

A few days before they were to arrive in Paderau, Rhoane sat with Baehlon and Janeira, apart from the others, a small fire crackling against the night. A few bold men stared at her with an open invitation in their eyes, but she ignored them.

She had exchanged her court attire for leather trousers and a tight-fitting vest, which did as much, if not more, to inflame the Fadair.

"I tell you, there is no merit to Celia's accusation. I've spoken with dozens of men and women, most of whom respect Taryn and want no harm caused to her or you." The bells in Baehlon's braids chimed softly with his movements.

"There is something not right about that girl, though." Janeira stated. "I sense in her much disarray and darkness." Janeira didn't mean Taryn.

"I as well." Rhoane poked a stick into the fire, churning embers. "I should speak with Taryn. Sort out the lies Celia has told."

Janeira placed a hand on his arm, surprising him. "Leave her for the moment. I am near certain nothing happened in Talaith, but I will not know for sure until we reach Paderau. Let her stay unbalanced where you are concerned. Either she will do something to prove the rumors true, or she will do nothing and prove them false. Her anger can be mollified later. If someone is casting suspicion upon the *Darennsai*, it is better to learn who than to protect her feelings."

Rhoane looked across the camp to where Taryn sat with her sisters. The furtive glances she gave him were getting fewer. Anger and hurt simmered beneath the calm exterior she showed the world, and he was the cause of those emotions.

"That is a dangerous game you are playing, Janeira," Baehlon said. "Taryn is not like you or these other women. She deserves an apology, and to hear it from Rhoane."

"Why does he need to apologize? He has done nothing wrong." A flush spread from Janeira's exposed cleavage to her neck.

Baehlon shook his head, his eyes resting on her face, far above her breasts.

It was Rhoane who answered. "That is where you are

wrong, my kinswoman. I have wronged Taryn in a grievous manner. When she presented information to me, I demanded proof, but when information was brought to me about her, I asked for none. I am as guilty as the rest of these courtiers." He rose, tossing the stick in the fire. "I cannot let her suffer my silence a moment longer."

"You must, Rhoane." Janeira stood to face him. "Say nothing to her until we reach Paderau. Whatever is happening here is beyond you and the *Darennsai*."

Rhoane studied her features, looked beyond the glint of anger in her eyes. "Until Paderau, then. But not a moment longer."

Baehlon cleared his throat, "I'll talk to Fae, have her keep an eye on Taryn and give her a word or two of encouragement where Rhoane is concerned. You keep skulking around and terrifying everyone." He grinned at Janeira. "And I'll keep my ears open to anything that might be useful. I don't agree with Janeira that you should avoid Taryn, Rhoane, but I've not been lucky in romance, so what do I know?"

Rhoane and Janeira resumed their seats, she with arms crossed over her chest, he with serious doubts.

"For the record, my informants have found nothing to incriminate your betrothed," Janeira offered after the conversation stalled. "If my instincts are proved correct in Paderau, I will tell King Stephan Taryn is worthy of you."

Shocked by her admission, Rhoane hid a smile. "Thank you, Janeira. That is high praise, indeed."

"She is not Fadair." Janeira reached into her vest and pulled out a cream envelope. Taryn's elaborate scrawl spelled out his name. "You, on the other hand, are an ass."

Rhoane took the envelope from her, anger burning in his belly. "You stole the notes?"

"Not me," Janeira said, offended. "That twit the crown princess favors. I found them in her belongings. I only took one to not cause alarm."

He tucked the note in his tunic for later reading. "When did you find them?"

"This afternoon. You do not want to know what other treasures she keeps in her locked box."

Rhoane glared across the camp to where Celia lounged with Marissa, her laughter tinkling above the din. He owed Taryn much more than an apology.

Chapter 33

THE trip to Paderau was uneventful in a welcome way. She and Rhoane kept a respectful distance, each wary of the other but neither meeting a glance or speaking to the other. It made for a difficult journey emotionally, and by the time they approached the city gates, Taryn was ready to be out of the saddle and away from Janeira's constant scrutiny.

The large group moved through the city and finally made their way to the palace proper, where Hayden and the duke were waiting for them. Before Taryn could greet either one, Sabina almost ran her over. Hayden smiled at Taryn over Sabina's head, mouthing the words, *I'll find you later.* Taryn nodded and moved on to give a warm greeting to the duke.

After the hellos were said, Taryn was shown to a different set of rooms than those she'd been given on her previous visit. She heard giggling from the bedchamber, and Taryn went in to find Mayla and Lorilee unpacking her bags. When they saw her, both girls squealed as they raced to give her a low curtsey before hugging her.

"Girls, please, you're going to crush me," she said, wrapping her arms around them. "I've missed you."

"We're just so excited, miss. I mean, Your Highness. Why didn't you tell us?" Mayla asked.

"Honestly, I didn't know. I was taken from court when I

was only a baby, and Brandt raised me without any knowledge of who I was." They had a dozen more questions, and Taryn did her best to answer. Finally, she held up a hand for silence. "I could really use one of your special baths. You know, with the scented water and oils."

They were, as ever, her chatty maids, telling her the gossip and news about Paderau.

Lorilee was combing out her hair and asked, "Miss, have you colored your hair?"

"It was a gift from Nadra." It was the only way she could explain that stardust had given her silver highlights.

"I like it. Your hair is longer, as well."

"You have a good memory. Is there any way I could take you two with me to Talaith?" Taryn asked in all sincerity. It was refreshing to have people around who enjoyed her company. Especially when they knew her before her title and accepted her without a thought of recompense.

Once dressed, Taryn left the maids and headed to the kitchens. As she expected, Carga was in the center of the room, shouting orders while simultaneously whisking a bowl of egg whites and tasting from a pot. Taryn stood in the shadows for several minutes watching the woman work. When there was a lull in activity, Taryn stepped from her hiding place to greet her friend.

"I've missed you, Carga."

"I can see they are not feeding you at Talaith. You are skin and bones, girl." She made up a plate of cheese and bread for Taryn. "Eat this while we talk." She poured two cups of grhom before sitting beside her. Like Mayla and Lorilee, she took Taryn's rise in station with equanimity, as if she'd never thought of her as anything but a friend.

"I've been dying for a cup of grhom. Thank you." Taryn took a sip of the steaming liquid, eyeing Carga over the rim. "I suppose you've heard about what happened in Talaith.

About my supposed evil deeds with an unnamed man?"

"News travels fast, especially scandal."

"Did you also hear that Rhoane's kinswoman was there that night and probably thinks I'm a total slut or something. As if." Taryn snorted.

Carga's lip quirked up in a grin, "Who is she?"

"A gorgeous creature named Janeira." Taryn waited for Carga's expression to confirm her suspicions about the cook. When a flicker of alarm crossed her face, Taryn said, "You're Eleri, aren't you?" If she weren't Eleri, she'd have no idea who Janeira was. Her short hair meant she was *sheanna* within her race. In addition to her research about the prophecies, Taryn had been learning all she could about the elusive people.

Carga glanced around the kitchen, making certain she couldn't be overheard. "No one here knows this."

"Does the duke know?"

"Yes, but none other. You will keep my secret, yes?" Taryn nodded. "Thank you. About your dilemma—Janeira is one of King Stephan's greatest warriors. If you embarrassed Rhoane, she will take it personally and not forgive the slight easily."

"I got that impression. She and Rhoane have barely spoken to me since that night. I need your help. How can I get in her good graces, and more important, how can I impress King Stephan?"

Carga absently shredded a piece of bread. "King Stephan will simply look into your heart to know the measure of you. Janeira—now, that is going to be more difficult. But she is a soldier. If she sees you training like you mean it and that you have the respect of the other soldiers, that might help soften her feelings toward you. One thing is certain, though, Taryn of House Galendrin, you need her support. If what the trees are whispering is true, you will need as many allies as you can get."

"The trees talk to you?"

"Of course. If you listen, they will tell you some amazing things."

"Can I come here again tomorrow to get Eleri lessons from you? Anything at all you can give me that might help." Taryn stood, taking a last sip of her drink. "I could drink your grhom all day, every day."

"You honor me, Princess. Come by tomorrow morning. I will tell you what I can."

"You're the best. Thanks."

She left the kitchens more confident than she'd been in several weeks and headed outside for some fresh air. She strolled along the river's edge, her mind drifting far from Paderau.

"I'd be willing to wager what your thoughts are right about now."

Taryn spun around to find Hayden standing a few feet away. She almost suffocated him in a great bear hug. "I've missed you so much. You've no idea how boring the palace is without you."

"Is that so? I've been hearing tales of your wicked deeds."

She groaned. "What did I do now?"

He waggled his eyebrows at her, making her laugh. "You mean people are still harping on that one night? Can we please move on?"

"They will once there is an even bigger scandal to gossip about. Right now, you're it."

She took his arm, directing them toward the river. "I'm sure I'm going to get into trouble for this, too. It seems I'm not allowed to be alone with a man."

Hayden nudged her with his shoulder. "Yes, but I'm a perfect gentleman, so it's fine."

"Like that matters to *Mother*. God, I hate calling her that. She has Rhoane convinced that Aomori and I had sex."

"Rhoane's loyalties run deep. Give him time, Taryn.

Besides, Aomori and Tinsley have become more vocal about their affection for each other. He sent Lliandra a formal letter declining any intention of courting Sabina."

"You don't think that will hurt Sabina, do you? Lliandra is singularly focused on her marrying Aomori to further her cause."

"Sabina will handle this with as much grace as she's handled what your mother's put her through thus far. The woman is made of silken steel."

Taryn rested her head on his shoulder. "I really have missed you. Since you've been preoccupied with Sabina, I've hardly gotten to see you."

"There will be a place in my life for you. Always." He kissed the top of her head. "There. That should give the empress something to talk about."

Taryn slapped his arm. "You are bloody wicked, you know that? Do you have any idea what a temper she has? I'm terrified of her." She resumed her place on his shoulder and said dreamily, "So, now that Aomori is out, will you petition Lliandra for Sabina's hand?"

"It's still her wish that I make a profitable union for her. One not limited to coin." There was subtext beneath his words that he tried to hide, but Taryn caught it.

"Why do I get the feeling there's more to this?"

The scandal of Sabina's family was that she was born without any ShantiMari. Some at court only saw her as a suitable wife for a high noble but not a male descended from both Houses of Light and Dark. In their opinion, Sabina's beauty or intelligence didn't outweigh her powerlessness.

"I've heard a rumor that Lliandra is going to support Herbret's claim," Hayden said.

"*No!* She wouldn't. He's a disgusting toad."

"Yes, but his family is the wealthiest in the region, aside from the empress, that is. She needs his money more than I need a powerless wife, it would appear."

"Don't you dare give up on her, Hayden. You two are perfect together. Power or no."

"Well, as you're unavailable, I suppose I'll have to accept her as a pale substitute."

"Ha! Didn't you see that dress she wore to the feast? There is nothing pale about her."

"Yes, I did see. And so did half of Talaith. By the gods, that girl is amazing." From the pure love in his voice, the smallest bit of jealousy tugged her heart.

"It's obvious you have deep feelings for her." She looked across the river to the north. "We'll find a way to make this work. I know you two will be happy together. Always. You just have to name your first daughter after me. I am, after all, the one who got you together."

"Hold on. I never said anything about marriage. We've only just met. These things take time. It's not like you can just meet someone and spend the rest of your life together."

"For you, maybe."

Hayden turned her to face him. "I'm sorry, Taryn. That was insensitive of me."

"I'm getting used to the idea."

He looked surprised. "You don't love Rhoane?"

"That's just the thing. I do." Her pendant burst into song, startling her. This was the first time she'd admitted it to herself or anyone else. She hushed her *cynfar* and continued. "But I wouldn't blame him if he wants to undo our bonds and find someone worthy of him. Like Janeira."

"There's only one woman worthy of a man like Prince Rhoane. She's the same girl who kicked that sword away from me. Have you talked to him since the feast?" They turned back toward the palace. The setting sun gleamed against the windows, turning the walls into shining plates of gold.

"Not really. He's always with Janeira."

"Maybe all he needs is an apology."

"I already tried that." A dark sadness was descending over her thoughts. "How about if you give me one of your special tours to take my mind off these unpleasant things?"

"Now?"

"Dinner is ages away, and we've got some time to kill. Besides, I've never seen the whole palace."

Hayden showed her a dozen rooms in the time they had. They ran, laughing, through secret passageways and slid across the marble floors of the audience chamber. Their last stop was a suite of rooms near the duke's. "My mother's," Hayden said, opening the door for Taryn. "She loved it here. We keep the apartment exactly as it was when she was living, as a reminder of her beauty and love of life."

Taryn saw touches of Gwyneira in every detail of the rooms—a rose laid on a table, or a painting of Hayden and his brother placed just above her dressing vanity. Reminders of her family were everywhere. She was a woman devoted to her husband and children.

Taryn took Hayden's hand in hers. "Thank you for sharing this with me. I feel as if I know your mother just from being near her things."

"Only a few servants are allowed in here. It's heavily warded against intruders, but of course, you are welcome to visit anytime." He gave her hand a squeeze. "I think Mother would enjoy your company."

Tears stung her eyes. "I would like that." Her stomach gave a loud grumble, and Hayden laughed.

"Perhaps now we can eat?"

"If you don't mind. I'm starved. Let's go find your princess and then have dinner together."

THE next morning, before meeting with Baehlon for their training, Taryn made a stop at Gwyneira's rooms. As soon as she stepped through the doorway, a calm that eluded her lately embraced her. She wanted to sit in one of Gwyneira's comfortable chairs to simply be in her presence, but Taryn had come for a single purpose.

After a few minutes of searching, she found a suitable place to hide the seal in a small cupboard behind a decorative chest. Once she had it tucked safely away and warded with as many alarms as she could think of, she stood in the center of the room.

If you are here, I want to ask that you keep this item safe. Someday I'll have need of it, but until then, I thank you for protecting it. Taryn lowered herself in a formal curtsey. *I wish I could have known you in life, Aunt Gwyneira.*

A gentle breeze rustled Taryn's hair, and the faint scent of roses filled the room. With the knowledge Gwyneira would take care of the seal, she left the apartment with a promise to visit often, as well as to keep her husband and son safe.

Taryn walked with purpose through the hallways of the palace. Once outside her mother's rooms, she entered without knocking, surprising several maids who fussed around Lliandra.

Her mother gave her a cool glance. "Good morning, Taryn. To what do I owe this visit?"

"If you make Sabina marry Herbret, or anyone other than Hayden, I will take that as a personal affront and do everything in my power to block their union."

"By what authority do you come in here and order me around?"

Taryn glanced at the maids who stood like statues around the empress, silent, impotent. "Seriously? You want to go there, Mother?" Scorn dripped on the last word. "I have a sword and a crown that give me the right to tell you not to mess with me or my friends. Sabina chooses who she'll marry. Not you. Are we understood?"

Lliandra stared at her, mouth agape. A tiny squeak was her only reply.

"Good. I'm glad that's settled. Now get off your high horse and start acting like my mother. We shouldn't be on opposite sides of the playing field. We need to work together."

She swept from the room, adrenaline pumping through her veins, making everything crisper, more refined. When she reached the end of the hall and turned a corner, she gave a whoop and danced around. There would be repercussions, but for the moment, it felt good to stand up to Lliandra. Damn good.

She had just a few days in Paderau to prepare to be presented to the Eleri, and she wasn't going to spend it making apologies. She was done with everyone making suppositions about her life. If the court wanted to gossip, so be it. If Janeira wouldn't forgive her, that was the woman's prerogative.

Taryn was tired of trying to be what everyone wanted her to be. Including Rhoane. It was his future at stake, as well, and if he wanted to place his trust in a lying, conniving bitch, then she wouldn't stop him. What she could do was train hard and meet with Carga every day.

Without meaning to, she kept her distance from Rhoane and his kinswoman. Anje didn't have any formal dinners, so she dined alone in her room, or with her younger sisters and Sabina. Her focus wasn't on gaining Rhoane's trust, but on her meeting with King Stephan.

She'd read Verdaine's prophecy. Without the Eleri, she would fail.

Chapter 34

THE attack came on the fourth day of their journey north. The endless landscape of rolling hills coupled with a stultifying heat from the late summer sun made the travelers indifferent to their surroundings. When men on horseback raced down a ravine toward the caravan, screaming and brandishing swords, it took a few moments for the entourage to act.

The invaders' hairy chests were nearly indistinguishable from the fur vests they wore. Feathers and bones dangled from strips of cord tied to leather pants. Their horses were small but fast.

As they charged the group, the captain of the guard yelled at his soldiers to form a line. Faelara and Duke Anje pulled in front of the two royal carriages, where Myrddin joined them. Sabina popped her head outside the door, saw the men, and shut the door tightly behind her.

Rhoane rode up to Taryn, shouting, "Get to the carriages," while Baehlon galloped toward her and the Eleri warrior woman away from her. Taryn sat motionless on Ashanni, trying to make sense of the confusion.

Time slowed as the invading men engaged in battle with the soldiers. Horrific, huge, lizard-like horned creatures ambled down the ravine toward them. Larger than horses, they were covered in red scales with frilled gills that circled long, wide heads. Huge fangs protruded from their muzzles with spittle dripping from their gaping maws.

"Baehlon, look," she called out to her protector.

He swung around, shouting to the others, "Vorlocks!" To Taryn, he commanded, "Get to cover."

It took her only an instant to make up her mind. She grabbed her sword from its scabbard, directing Ashanni toward the fighting. Baehlon swore and rushed after her. She swung her sword wide at the first man she came upon, splitting his skin with a deep, red gash. Bone crunched beneath her blade, and she reeled with the impact. Her sword sang a battle cry, fueling her bloodlust with its intensity.

She raced past the man she'd attacked, veering left to cut down another of the hairy invaders, this time taking his head clean off. A jolt of revulsion ripped through her. She called on the focused calm she used in martial arts to keep her mind tuned to each man she fought. She ignored the blood and gore, focusing on protecting those she held dear.

A giant of a man rode past and then wheeled around, slicing at her with his curved sword. When she blocked his attack, a great clang rang out.

His eyes widened, a grimy smile cutting across his face. He let out a trilling call before swinging at her head. More men rushed to them as she blocked his attack again and again.

Baehlon reached her, screaming, "Get out of here!" But Taryn ignored him. The big knight swore at her and then turned to fight men who rode up from the rear.

She studied the man before her, his scraggly beard and pointed teeth making her want to retch. He was circling her, chanting. He pulled power from around them, his threads forming a web. Without hesitating, she charged, slicing his power and plunging her sword toward him. His horse leapt aside, and she missed her mark. His blade did not. The dark metal slashed through her leather pants, making a clean incision on her leg.

Taryn cried out and swung Ashanni around. For an instant, she met his stare, seeing into his mind. Rabid with hate, his sole focus was to kill her. She kicked Ashanni hard and kept her sword close to her leg. At the last moment, when he raised his sword to attack, she thrust her blade into his side, connecting with his ribs.

He roared in pain. She kicked Ashanni again, steadying for another attack, but Lliandra's captain of the guard rushed in, blocking her. "Leave him to me. See to the others."

"Like hell I will."

Two more soldiers joined the captain, edging her out.

"Bullocks!" She raced off to find a new victim. About two hundred paces away, one of the fanged creatures bore down on Rhoane. It stretched out a claw, knocking Rhoane's sword from his hand before rearing up on its back legs, ready to strike.

She raced straight at the creature, pulling her feet up onto her saddle, balancing precariously. When they neared Rhoane, she let out a fierce cry and jumped from the saddle toward the creature's fanged jaws.

She plunged her sword deep into its throat, and jerked viciously upward. The beast's head split in two with spittle and foam coating her arms. A horrifying scream rent the air as the thing fell backward, shuddering in its death. Plumes of black smoke came from its mouth and spiraled into the air.

She gagged against the fetid stink.

Rhoane recovered his sword and approached her, his face a raging storm. "What in Ohlin's name was that? Blood's truth, Taryn, you could have been killed! What were you thinking?"

She glared at him with open-mouthed incredulity. "What was I thinking? I don't know, maybe I wanted to kill that thing before it ate you!"

She stormed off to find Ashanni, trembling at the pain that ripped through her. A gash ran from under her left arm to above her ribs, oozing blood down her midsection. "Shit," she muttered. It must've come from the vorlock. When she tried to mount Ashanni, the wound robbed her of strength.

Knowing Rhoane watched, Taryn bit down and pulled herself into the saddle. She rode back into the battle, engaging the first shirtless man she found. He raised a spear, which she knocked aside before cutting him down. Adrenaline and battle rage eased her pain, but only just. Baehlon rode at her side, and together they fought any man that came near. The enemies' trills and cries went unheard. All that mattered was her sword and their deaths.

Her mind raced as she surveyed the carnage. The battle was nearly finished, with only a few of the hairy men still fighting the empress's guard. Myrddin sent a fireball at one of the vorlocks, killing it instantly. Faelara held a protective barrier over the carriages, and the younger princesses were outside, using their ShantiMari to calm the frightened horses. But Marissa and Lliandra were nowhere to be seen. Taryn grunted in disgust at their cowardice.

Baehlon wheeled around to face her. "I told you to get to the carriage."

Anger swelled inside. "And do what? Hide and cower? Why the hell am I training every day if you won't let me use it? For show?"

"You could've been killed."

"Better to be killed defending myself than hiding away in a carriage. What good is that? Why have all that power and do nothing?" She stared at him, willing him to defy her.

"Bah!" He wheeled his horse around, letting loose a string of curses. Janeira rode past, inclining her head to Taryn before spurring her horse toward an invader. Ignoring the wound in her side, she did the same.

Once all the attackers had been captured or killed, the captain sent men riding west to scout for any stragglers. Many of his men had been injured, but only a few were dead. Taryn wanted to turn away from them but forced herself to look at every face.

She slid off Ashanni and offered her help to the wounded. Someone handed her a cloth and bucket filled with water. She moved among the solders cleaning, healing, and giving what comfort she could, her own wound forgotten. Sometime later—she couldn't say if it was minutes or hours—Baehlon found her and took the bucket away. The water was as clear as when she'd first taken it, the cloth unstained.

"Rykoto's balls, Taryn, what have you done?"

"They fought bravely today." She looked over her shoulder at the soldiers, most of whom stared at her in awe. "It was the least I could do."

"Aye, help you did, lass." He clapped her on the shoulder, and she winced. "Saved a few good men and women, I'd wager."

She gave him a weak smile. "Killed a few bad ones, too. Does it ever get easier?"

"Never. Not even when they are nasty bits of business like these today."

"What were they?"

"Vorlocks. They come down from the north, beyond the vier. Those hairy beasts are their handlers. For every man, there is a vorlock tied to him. We've not seen their kind in many a season. More than passing strange they would choose to attack on this day."

"What do you mean?" Taryn walked with him toward the carriages, her legs threatening to give out at any moment, but she kept up with his long strides.

"We're smack in the middle of nowhere. Four days out from Paderau and a good ten more to the edge of the

Narthvier, with not a lot of villages or cities in between. Perfect spot for an ambush, if you were to ask me."

"You think someone set this up?"

He cocked his head, his lips twitching. "Sure looks like a pile of dung to me."

Lliandra strode toward them with a look of venom in her eyes. Taryn shrank back, expecting an onslaught of abuse. Instead, Lliandra grabbed her in a fierce hug, pulling her to her bosom. Taryn bit her lip to keep from crying out.

"Don't you ever do something so rash and undisciplined again. You could've been killed, you stupid girl." Despite her words, there was no harshness in her voice. "That was a brave and foolish thing you did."

Taryn debated telling her to make up her mind. Was she brave or stupid? Instead, she pulled away. Without warning, Taryn's stomach roiled. She ran to the bushes where she emptied the remains of her lunch. For several minutes she stayed hunched over, until she was certain nothing remained.

Mortified the others had watched her get sick, she rejoined the group and with a little shrug said, "Sorry." She looked at Lliandra, expecting some retort, but all the woman did was touch her cheek before moving away.

The princesses surrounded her, but she pushed through them to the carriage, flinging open the door to flop on the soft seat within. The world spun with vicious intensity. Never again would she wonder what it felt like to be in battle, or to experience the thrill of striking an opponent. She liked the feeling she'd had when she plunged her sword into the creature, of hearing the crack of his jawbone, of knowing she'd defeated the beast. It felt good to win.

She must have dozed. When she woke, camp had been set up, with lights glowing softly in orbs around the fire. When she stepped from the carriage, Baehlon offered her his hand, and she jumped in surprise.

"Forgive me, Princess. I thought you knew I was here."

She stretched her aching body, working out a cramp in her leg, wincing at the wound in her side. "Just for the record, those carriages aren't all that comfortable. And why would I think you'd be here?" They walked together around the tents, following the sound of voices.

"As your protector, it is my duty to keep you safe. Asleep or awake."

"I keep forgetting you're my babysitter."

His jaw tightened. "Protector. There's a difference, but," his voice was low, "I'm not above giving you a good cuff if that's what's needed."

"You wouldn't dare." She tried to punch him, but a jolt of pain shot up her body. "Damn."

Baehlon held out her left arm, whistling at the gash he saw. "Why didn't you mend this?"

"In all the excitement, I forgot." He turned them away from the fire toward her tent. "Baehlon, when I killed that creature, it was," she searched for the right word, "satisfying. Does that make me a bad person?"

"Nay, lass, it doesn't. If you'd killed a man and enjoyed it, then I'd say we have a problem."

"Today, I just put myself on autopilot and did what had to be done. It was a kill-or-be-killed mentality."

Baehlon nodded slowly. "That's the way it should be on a battlefield. There's no place for emotions. If you hesitate, you die."

She lay on her cot, staring up at the tent ceiling. "I was afraid to use ShantiMari."

Surprise lit across his face. "You killed that beast with only the strength of your sword?"

"Remember that day on the road to Paderau with all those feiches? I couldn't risk something like that happening. Not until I learn to control my ShantiMari. All of it."

Faelara entered the tent, glancing first at Baehlon and then Taryn. "Where is she injured?" Of course, Baehlon would call Faelara to help. Taryn tugged her tunic up to show them. "This is from no blade." Faelara touched her skin, pulling her hand back immediately. "Vorlock venom."

"As in poison?" Taryn groaned. "Just my luck."

"Why didn't you call for me sooner? We need Rhoane," Faelara told Baehlon.

"No. You can't tell Rhoane," Taryn begged.

Faelara gave her a long look. "I need his help to heal you."

Taryn dragged her sword from its sheath. "We can do it without him. This is different from the poison on the sword, I can feel it." She placed the blade against her skin and bit back a scream. Instead of healing her, the sword burned through her skin, leaving a dark red blister over her festering wound.

Faelara ran from the tent, returning with bandages and water. After she cleaned the dried blood and pus, she poured an inky liquid into the wound that made Taryn squirm. Searing pain ripped across her midsection every time Faelara touched her. She gave Taryn a cup of wine, and she drank it in one long gulp, willing the alcohol to take immediate effect. When Faelara pulled out a needle and thread, Taryn bit her lip to keep from crying.

It took seventy-four stitches and three cups of strong wine to close the gash, each stitch burning more than the last. After another dousing of the black liquid, Faelara rubbed a paste onto the wound while saying a few healing words. Her Mari embraced Taryn, sinking into her skin. After she wrapped Taryn's middle in clean bandages, she put another ward over the cloth and kissed Taryn's cheek.

"Do try to be more careful. At least this seems to be from an adolescent vorlock whose venom is not yet at full potency." Faelara's voice was gentle. "A little like you." She tweaked Taryn's nose.

"Thank you, Fae." The wine was working on the pain, but a deep throbbing continued. "Why do you think the sword didn't work?"

"I don't know. Perhaps there was still vorlock venom on it, but that's just a guess. I do know this—you were lucky you only suffered a burn."

They joined the others by the firelight. Several soldiers stood to salute her while others regarded her with curiosity. She nodded shyly to them, not wanting any added attention.

Marissa approached first, taking Taryn's hands in her own. "Sister, we owe you our deepest gratitude for what you did today."

"Thank you." Giddiness and a bit of lightheadedness from the wine, compounded with her shock from the battle and the venom that still coursed through her blood, made her sway on her feet.

"Are you well?" A genuine concern for Taryn shone in her sister's lavender eyes.

"Well enough. I'm just exhausted." It was with no small amount of difficulty that she took her seat beside Sabina.

"I was afraid I would lose my best friend today," Sabina whispered.

Taryn glanced at Rhoane. "Me, too."

THE rest of the trip was tense for the travelers. Conversations were hushed and stops brief. When they camped for the night, myriad threads stretched overhead, warding the group against any nighttime invasions. Each day, Faelara checked Taryn's wound, applying a fresh paste and bandage. The pain diminished, but every pit in the road threatened to tear her flesh anew.

Each night she slept fitfully. Her anxiety grew the closer

they got to the Narthvier. A dark presence dogged Taryn's vision, much as it had her first days on Aelinae when she'd traveled with Rhoane to Ravenwood. Whoever or whatever it was that followed them, she hoped it couldn't pass through the fabled veils of the forest.

When at last they approached the huge expanse of trees, her breathing became more labored, her pulse quickened to dizzying levels. What lay behind them was only slightly less terrifying than what lie before her.

Rhoane and Janeira rode ahead of the group, parting the mystical veil that kept the Narthvier protected from enemy invasion. Lliandra stiffened as the veil lifted, looking around quickly to make certain there were no ambushes waiting for them. Since that one brief show of emotion after the battle, Lliandra had once again withdrawn her feelings. The disappointment slid off Taryn like an oiled cloak.

The trees, as old as Aelinae itself, towered over their heads. Their white trunks stretched up, their branches making an archway for them to ride beneath. Rays of sunlight drifted through the natural latticework to caress the ferns and flowers that grew alongside the road. The forest smelled fresh, like after a recent rainfall. Like Rhoane.

They left the bulk of Lliandra's entourage at a clearing just beyond the first veil. The Eleri were protective of their land, not often letting visitors through. All of Lliandra's guard, save for the captain, and most of her ladies and maids would stay at the camp until the group departed the Weirren. Marissa pouted that her favorite, Lady Celia, couldn't accompany them. No amount of begging changed the outcome, and so it was a smaller group continued, leaving a disgruntled Celia and Herbret behind.

The procession traveled through the woods, stopping often to raise another veil or to close the one behind them. By the time they reached Lan Gyllarelle, the great lake of the

Narthvier, Taryn had counted eight veils. Janeira greeted the two Eleri riders who met them at the lake with a hand over her fist and a low bow. Rhoane nodded to one of the men before giving a quick bow to the other. Lliandra emerged from her carriage, followed closely by Marissa and Myrddin. The empress curtseyed prettily to a young Eleri man and laughed at something he said.

Janeira stood beside the man, the same one Rhoane had bowed to, a protective look on her face. He had to be Rhoane's brother. Carga had told her of the warrior's commitment to the prince. Similar in features to Rhoane, Bressal's hair shone like sunlight on water, a shimmering expanse of white and gold that flowed down his back. He wore a handsome circlet on his head that caught the light when he turned his horse to lead them on.

When Rhoane walked toward Taryn, she saw the misery in his eyes. Her hand moved to him instinctively. "Rhoane." Her voice caught as she said his name. The simple acknowledgment was the first time since the battle that she'd spoken to him.

He glanced her way, shaking his head while he kept walking. Her gaze followed him and then she turned, only to meet Janeira's unblinking stare. She lifted her chin and met the woman's gaze. Janeira inclined her head to Taryn before moving off.

Chapter 35

THEY passed through two more veils before reaching the heart of the Narthvier, the Weirren. It was not a single structure but a series of graceful buildings connected by arched walkways high above the ground. In the center of the Weirren sat an enormous tree that reached far into the sky—its trunk half as wide as Paderau Palace. Taryn followed Baehlon through a set of doors that dwarfed even the large knight. They stood in an immense entrance hall carved from the trunk of the tree, with passages leading off in every direction.

The interior was as ornately decorated as the Crystal Palace in Talaith, if not more lavish. Paintings and chandeliers hung from internal branches, and a grand staircase wound its way up the trunk, to dizzying heights. A page led her to a set of rooms even more spacious and opulent than the hall below.

She'd imagined the room would look like a hollowed-out burrow, but once inside, she couldn't tell the difference between the rooms at the Weirren and Paderau. Only the bed gave any hint she was in a tree. A four-poster, it was made from living branches that arched above the mattress. A cascade of leaves and flower blossoms created an enchanted canopy.

A cry escaped her lips at the sight.

The page nodded appreciatively. "It is one of the wonders

of the Weirren. These are Queen Aislinn's rooms."

Taryn looked at him, surprised. "Are you sure it's okay that I stay here? I wouldn't want to upset His Majesty."

"It was he who bade me bring you here." The man bowed to her. "I am King Stephan's third son, Eoghan."

He looked to be Eliahnna's age, a young teenager. His eyes sparkled as he spoke, mesmerizing Taryn with their three shades of blue, dark to pale, with gold flecks around the irises. Their depths intrigued her.

Taryn curtseyed low to him. "I am Empress Lliandra's second daughter, Taryn. Thank you, Eoghan, for escorting me to my rooms."

"I was impatient to meet you, and now that I have, I am well pleased. You are even lovelier than the trees led me to believe."

Two girls no taller than Tessa arrived, and Eoghan gracefully bowed in farewell, saying he would see her at dinner. The maids helped with her bath, applying a thick paste to her wound, followed by a soft wrap tucked around her midsection. Between her little Eleri and their broken Elennish, Taryn discerned they were sisters, Illanr and Carld. When she introduced herself, they gently corrected her.

"Nen, vu tendl Darennsai." They kissed their thumbs before placing them to their foreheads and then over their hearts. Their greeting and Eoghan's compliment left her hopeful about her meeting with the Eleri king.

The gown they laid out for her was, by far, more beautiful than anything she owned, save her coronation gown. When she touched the fabric, it moved beneath her fingertips like a living, breathing thing, seeming to react to her body heat. She ran a finger down one of the folds, gasping when the fabric drew in on itself like a sea anemone.

By the time they were done styling her hair, it hung straight down her back, nearly to her hips. The silver strands

Nadra had given her were several inches thick, with only a hint of her golden hair shining through. The girls grinned and nodded to her, saying in their broken Elennish, "Princess pretty. So pretty."

"Thank you." She searched her scant knowledge of Eleri for anything that might convey her gratitude. *"Celaina."*

They nodded again. "Yes, *celaina*. Thank you."

She slipped into a pair of silk slippers, welcoming the softness against her callused feet. Eoghan arrived just as she finished dressing.

His eyes widened when he saw her. "Princess Taryn, you are a vision to be sure. Like a forest nymph emerging from a budding flower to greet the sweetness of the day."

She blushed furiously and curtseyed a thank you before taking his arm. They passed several Eleri, who greeted them with polite interest. "You look a lot like your brothers. Do you resemble your mother or your father?"

"It is difficult to tell. All Eleri look alike."

Taryn shook her head. "Not my maids. They don't look like any of you."

"That is because they are not Eleri. Carld and Illanr are Faerie folk."

"Aren't they supposed to have wings?"

"Carld and Illanr are woodland faeries. They do not have wings, as such. Only air faeries do."

"I didn't know there was a distinction." She sighed. "Just when I think I've got it figured out, something new pops up."

Eoghan looked down at her. "You are a very curious creature, Taryn ap Galendrin."

"I get that a lot."

They stood outside two enormous doors carved with detailed pictures of the Narthvier. Taryn studied the images to keep her mind occupied and nerves settled. If her mother feared the Eleri king—Taryn shuddered—what must he be like? The chamberlain announced Eoghan first and then simply, the *Darennsai*. She was so accustomed to hearing her name and titles that when the doors opened, Taryn stood awkwardly, waiting for the rest of an introduction that never came.

Eoghan nudged her, and they entered the Great Hall. The Eleri elite wore gowns in every color, but no ornamentation in their long hair, or around wrists or necks. Slim gold chains hung from a few hips, but that was the only decoration Taryn saw. The only jewels that sparkled in the room came from her dress and what her family wore.

Eoghan led her to the high table, taking the seat to her right. Beside him sat Bressal and next to him, Rhoane. At another table sat her mother, Marissa, Eliahnna, and Tessa. The rest of her friends sat directly in front of them. An empty, ornate chair occupied the space between her and her family.

The chamberlain banged his staff three times, and everyone in the hall rose. "His Majesty, King Stephan of the Narthvier, Ruler of the Eleri, and trusted son of Verdaine." The doors opened, and King Stephan entered. Tall, with hair the color of freshly fallen snow, he held himself with such authority that even without the chamberlain's announcement she would've known he was the Eleri king. His people made an elegant bow to him, sweeping their right legs and arms out to the side. Taryn stood with the others at the high table, keeping an eye on Eoghan for any clues as to what she should do.

King Stephan made his way through the crowd, stopping to greet a few of the nobles. When he reached Myrddin, he patted the man on the back. They shared a few words, and then Stephan moved on to greet Duke Anje. He made his way past Taryn's sisters, giving Lliandra a warm embrace before standing in front of his great chair to address the gathered crowd.

"Friends," he said in Elennish, "we have gathered here this evening to mark an auspicious event in our lives." He turned to his left, gesturing toward Rhoane. "My son, the *sheanna* of Verdaine's prophecy, has returned." The crowd mumbled under their breath. A few of them made a figure eight in the air. "With him, he brings Empress Lliandra, Lady of Light." Lliandra gracefully bowed to the nobles. "With her, come her daughters. They are my guests in the Weirren and therefore should be shown every courtesy." His voice was tense.

The Eleri's distrust of the newcomers thrummed throughout the room. Stephan raised a hand for silence. "With them also travels the *gyota* of Verdaine's prophecy." Their stares traveled to Taryn. She kept her eyes trained on the king. "Who presents her to our court?"

Taryn expected Rhoane to speak, but he remained silent. Her face flamed with indignation at his slight. Myrddin stepped forward, as did Eoghan, the duke, and Lliandra, but it was a clear voice from the crowd that made Taryn's heart stop.

"I do, Your Majesty." Janeira, ethereal in white silk, her dark hair framing her tanned face, strode to the high table.

The king gestured to her. "Janeira, tell us why you believe we should accept this girl as our *Darennsai*."

Rhoane glared so hard at his kinswoman, Taryn worried his eyes might pop out of their sockets.

"I have had the opportunity to observe this girl. Although she may be impetuous at times, she has shown herself to be among the bravest of fighters I have ever known." The crowd twittered, and a few nobles looked at Taryn with newfound respect.

"That is quite a claim, warrior Janeira. What is your proof?"

Rhoane's fists clenched and released as Janeira continued. "Without so much as a season of training under her belt, this girl destroyed a vorlock with her sword. Nothing more. She bears the mark of the vorlock's venom even now." Janeira paused, taking in those gathered in the hall. "It was not for her own safety that she risked this injury." Finally, Janeira looked at Rhoane. "It was to protect the Eleri prince, who was under attack."

Rhoane continued to glare at Janeira. Obviously, they had spoken about this, and he disagreed with her telling the story in front of the Eleri Court.

King Stephan held up a hand for silence. "Is this true, Prince Rhoane?"

"It is as Janeira says. Princess Taryn risked her life to slay the beast that attacked me."

"Were there other witnesses to this event?" The king asked the group.

Baehlon stepped up from the crowd. "Aye, Your Majesty. About a hundred of Duke Anje's and Empress Lliandra's best soldiers, as well as myself." He bowed low. "Your Majesty."

Tessa spoke up, as well. "I saw everything. She jumped from her horse and stuck that creature right in the gob!"

"Tessa!" Lliandra scolded, but her youngest sister grinned cheekily at Taryn before stepping back.

Myrddin spoke in a voice even those in the back could hear. "The event happened as has been told. Princess Taryn showed remarkable courage that day in battle." He held out his hand to show a small glass orb and replayed the scene for the court. Somehow, he managed to project the event above their heads, as if on a screen. Everyone in the room watched in silent fascination as Taryn leapt from her horse to stab the vorlock.

Taryn's mouth watered with impending sickness as she relived her actions. To see it displayed was far more ghastly than the actual doing.

Myrddin tucked the glass ball into a pocket. "She showed

great courage, yes, but what she also showed, Your Majesty, is her devotion to your first son, Prince Rhoane of the Eleri, *sheanna* of Verdaine's prophecy."

The crowd grew silent. That was what the night was truly about. King Stephan wanted to get the measure of her as far as his son was concerned. Whether she was the Child of Light and Dark was only secondary.

Stephan leaned on his fingertips, looking out at Myrddin. His face gave nothing away until finally he turned to Rhoane, saying in a near whisper, "Do you accept this girl, the *gyota* of Verdaine's prophecy, as the *Darennsai* of the Eleri?"

"Yes."

Stephan's eyes glistened as he stood before his first son. "So be it." He beckoned to Taryn. "Girl, come here."

Heart pounding in her ears, legs quivering as if they would give out, Taryn stood beside Rhoane. The king took their hands in his, looking into her eyes, through her to the very depths of her being. His thoughts brushed against hers. She let him in to wander through her mind. Good, bad—she let him see it all. Where she came from to what brought her to his Great Hall that night.

When he finished, he looked tired and drawn. His eyes were filled with immense sadness, and she wondered what he'd found in her memories to hurt him so.

"I do not envy either of you your paths. If you join together, your trials will be lessened. Do you, Taryn ap Galendrin, wish to have Rhoane at your side always as a friend, a lover, a companion, and Verdaine willing, as a shepherd to your final resting place?"

A moment of panic seized Taryn as she realized he was going to bond them, taking her one step closer to finalizing her union with Rhoane. "Yes." Her *cynfar* buzzed in her mind, but she shut it out.

Stephan turned to Rhoane. "Do you, Rhoane, First Son

of the Eleri, wish to be joined to Taryn ap Galendrin in battle, as well as peace, to look to her for comfort and diminish her pain, to keep her safe always, and to live your life knowing none other but her?"

"I will honor my vow as before. Yes."

Stephan wound a thread of green ShantiMari around their wrists. Taryn heard the trees sighing around them, as if they, too, held their breath in anticipation. When Stephan finished, new runes glowed brightly against their skin. He bent to kiss her forehead. "Welcome, Taryn ap Galendrin, *Darennsai* of the Eleri."

She curtseyed as she'd seen the Eleri do when he entered the hall. "Thank you, King Stephan of the Eleri, most favored son of Verdaine."

He seemed pleased with her reply and gestured for his sons to move down, allowing Taryn to sit beside Rhoane. To the gathered crowd, he said, "Tonight, we drink to the *Darennsai*."

Doors opened and servants rushed in to place steaming plates of food before the guests. Taryn sat beside Rhoane, toasting her cup each time a noble or courtier raised their glass to her. She sipped her spiced grhom while nibbling at her food. In the eyes of the Eleri, she was married to Rhoane, but he sat silent beside her. She tried to engage Bressal in conversation, but his frown dissuaded any comment from her.

So Taryn sat between two brooding Eleri, trying to look content in the Great Hall of the Weirren. Once the plates had been removed, tables were pushed back and a group of musicians entered the hall to great applause.

"My lady, would you honor me with a dance?" Taryn looked up at Rhoane in surprise. They were the first words he had spoken to her all evening. Since that terrible day with the vorlocks, even. She put her hand in his, and they made their way to the floor. Already a few Eleri were arm in arm in a complicated dance.

She faltered in her step. "I don't know this one," she whispered to Rhoane.

"Just follow my lead."

Her body matched his, her feet deftly touching the ground before finding air again and again. They moved as one, the music flowing through them. Rhoane's jaw no longer held the tension she'd become used to, and a small smile played at the corners of his lips. When the dance ended, he held her tightly against him, unmoving. In his eyes, her chaotic emotions reflected back to her. She raised her body a few inches until her lips met his. Their kiss was hesitant at first. Then weeks of frustration and unspent emotions coiled and snapped, manifesting in an all-consuming kiss that blocked out all sight or sound. The court no longer existed. The great tree dissipated. The world came down to only them.

When finally they parted, the room was silent. Taryn looked at the astonished faces, feeling her own grow hot with embarrassment.

King Stephan stood at the high table with his glass raised. *"Cynfarran teldielle!"*

The Eleri cheered. *"Cynfarran teldielle!"*

Taryn curtseyed, having no idea what he'd said. Rhoane bowed to his father and then the court. Taryn glanced at her mother. Tears glistened in her beautiful blue eyes. Eliahnna and Tessa also had wet cheeks. Rhoane led her out of the Great Hall, up several stairways, before she finally found her voice.

"Where are you taking me?"

"Somewhere private." He smiled down at her. "Unless you would rather go back to the hall?"

"Not really."

"Good," he said. "Because there is something I want

to show you." He led her up and up, until she thought she couldn't take another step.

At the top of the tree, he opened a hidden door, leading her on to a pathway of branches covered in leaves. The only thing above them was the clear night sky and twinkling stars. She clutched at his arm. "How high are we? Could we fall?"

Rhoane laughed, and it sounded like rainfall after a drought. "You are afraid of heights? A great warrior like you is afraid of something as insignificant as falling?"

"Don't tease. Yes, I'm afraid of heights, if you really must know." They made their way along the branch to a cluster of leaves that created a bower of sorts. "Will it hold us?"

"We are perfectly safe. Come here," he commanded, pulling her to him. "No one will disturb us." His lips sought hers with a hunger she returned. Their ShantiMari tangled around them, uniting as one strength—hers new and untried, his as ancient as the tree they stood upon.

When their heat became too much, she pulled away, afraid of the powerful emotions that swept over her with a speed she fought to control. Afraid of the dark tempest that swirled just under the surface, ready to break free.

Rhoane stretched out on the leaves, beckoning her to follow.

"Why didn't you speak up for me tonight?" She carefully lay down beside him, hampered by her wound.

"I am *sheanna*; my word is not recognized at court." The sadness in his voice cut Taryn in two.

"I should have known. I'm sorry."

"I have grown used to my status." He rolled to his side and brushed aside a strand of her hair. "Tonight, I want to stay here, with you."

"Rhoane, I…" Irrational fear seized her. She wanted him, the gods only knew how much, but it was too soon. Their trust had been shaken. Sharing her body with him would commit them to an eternity together. She couldn't take that step until she was certain beyond any doubt Rhoane trusted her and was committed to their future. "I can't. Not yet. Not until you're sure."

His hand cupped her cheek, warm, with a slight tremble. "I owe you an apology, Taryn. Not just for my behavior. When you needed my loyalty, I faltered. That will never happen again."

A fierceness she didn't recognize lurked in the depths of his eyes. "I let a long-standing friendship cloud my judgment when, in truth, I never had reason to doubt you. Your actions were not worthy of the scorn I showed. I am ashamed of my behavior but was too proud to admit it. I am afraid when it comes to love, I am ignorant of that which is clear to others. I only hope you can forgive me."

The sincerity in his voice and pain behind his words cracked the hardened shell she'd erected around her heart. A month of his silence had made her leery of their future, but she desperately wanted to believe in him. In them.

"I want to remember this night as being full of nothing but you, this tree, and the stars. Whatever happened before is forgiven." She reached to kiss him, grimacing with the effort.

He gently laid her back, his eyes full of concern. "You are in pain." His glance searched her body. "Where is this wound you suffered from the vorlock?"

Taryn put a protective hand around her midsection. "It's fine, really. Every day it gets better. I just have to remember not to move too quickly."

"You should have been brought to me. The Eleri are skilled at healing."

"Faelara is taking good care of me, I promise." She gave him a gentle push. "Can we go back to enjoying the stars?"

"I would like to see for myself." He placed a hand on her abdomen, his Shanti flowing over her. Taryn held still while he prodded her through her gown and bandages. Finally, he said, "There is still some infection. Tomorrow we will find the salve you need."

"If I say yes, can we relax for the night?"

He placed his lips on hers in answer.

Chapter 36

BRESSAL was in a mood. Rhoane sat at his desk, half-listening as his brother ticked off the reasons Rhoane should never have accepted Taryn as the Darennsai. Each of them was incredibly shortsighted and self-serving, but Rhoane had no intention of telling this to his younger brother. When Bressal finished, Rhoane put his feet on the desk, crossing his hands behind his head.

"Thank you, dear brother, for your informal education on my many mistakes. The first of which would seem to be my birth. Now, if you will excuse me, I have work to do before we leave."

"What do you mean *leave*? Father thinks you have returned permanently. And now that you have brought the abomination with you, he thinks you mean to make good on your oath."

Rhoane took a deep breath before walking around his desk to face his brother. "I will only say this once. If you continue to insult Taryn, I will personally dole out your punishment. She has shown her merit, and Father accepted her in front of the court. What is more, Nadra and Ohlin have given her their blessing. What I do not need from you is a compendium of what ifs and why nots. I need your support."

"That I cannot give, no matter what Father thinks. He was a fool to let the empress and her lot through the veils. He is a fool to think this *gyota* is anything but an ignorant girl. She stinks of Fadair and offends me."

Rhoane slammed his brother against the wall, his Shanti tight around Bressal's body. "I said I would not tolerate any more slurs against the Darennsai. What you have said here is tantamount to treason, and I could have you hanged for it."

Bressal's face paled a fraction. "Father knows my opinion on this matter."

"Yes. And now so do I. Again, I thank you for elucidating your thoughts." Rhoane released his brother from his power.

"It is not too late. You can still undo the bonds, as long as you have not united your bodies as one." Bressal looked at Rhoane and groaned. "Do not tell me. When? Last night? Is that where you disappeared to?" He slapped his head in frustration. "I knew I should have followed you. I could have prevented this disaster."

Rhoane clenched his fists to keep from striking his brother. "Your assumption is inaccurate. As you will not heed my advice to stop this maligning of the Darennsai, I will thank you to leave my chamber." His body shook with barely contained anger.

"Then you can still undo the bonds."

"I will undo nothing. Taryn was chosen for me by Verdaine. I will not go against the wishes of our goddess. I will, however, ask that you make an effort to accept Taryn for what she is—the Darennsai of our people and my betrothed."

"I have nothing against the girl. It is what she will do to the Eleri that concerns me. If you cannot see that she will be the destruction of our people, then you are blind."

"The prophecy is unclear, as you well know." Rhoane ran a hand through his short hair, a constant reminder of his sheanna status. "Perhaps if you tried harder to find a way for her to succeed, you would see that she could be exactly what the Eleri need right now."

"We need nothing," he spat, disdain laced through every syllable. "We have been here for as long as the first seed of this great tree."

"It is that thinking that will be the downfall of the Eleri, not the doings of an innocent girl."

"We will see in the end, will we not?" He half turned to leave. "You had better inform Father you will not be staying. I think I saw him polishing your crown this morning."

"Is that what all of this is about, Bressal? You think I want to take the throne away from you? I thought you knew me better than that, my brother. It has been too long since we shared our secrets. Too much fear has crept into your heart. I am the chosen one of the Darennsai. I can no more sit on this throne than I can the Crystal or Obsidian Thrones."

Drained by their conversation, Rhoane sank into his chair. "I am a prince without a palace. My place is at the side of a girl whose fate is undetermined. I might have one season or a thousand on this terrarae. Nothing in my life is certain right now, so if you want to be concerned only with what crown you will be wearing, then let me assure you, I will not fight you for something as trivial as that."

The sadness in Bressal's eyes bespoke a fear his words would not convey. "You have changed, brother. Your time with the Fadair has corrupted your thinking. I can remember when there was no greater purpose than protecting the Weirren Throne."

"Indeed, your words are true." Rhoane rose and placed a hand on his brother's arm. "The Weirren Throne is never far from my thoughts. Do not ever doubt that I hold its safety close in my heart. It seems Verdaine had something else in mind for me, however, and I must go where she wills."

"Then there is nothing more for us to discuss. May the

next time we meet be in sweetness and not sorrow." Bressal touched his thumb to his heart.

Rhoane echoed his gesture. "When next we meet." They put their foreheads together in the ancient custom.

How many Eleri shared his brother's feelings? They would accept Taryn as the Darennsai out of respect to his father, but would they support her when the time came?

He paced his room a few times, checking hiding places he'd used as a small boy and re-familiarizing himself with his childhood home. He'd been gone nearly sixty Aelan years. To an Eleri, it was but a moment in time, but spent away from the Weirren, it seemed an eternity to him.

He breathed in the musty scent of the tree and was lost in memories of his youth. Many bells had been spent at that very desk still sitting near the window overlooking the courtyard. How many times had he hidden beneath it, waiting for his brothers to find him? If he hid there now, would they even bother to look?

A distressing melancholy hung over him. Bressal was right; he needed to talk with his father and explain why he must leave the Narthvier. Rhoane left his room and hastened up the steps leading to his father's study. When he stood at the door, he took a deep breath and gave a quick knock before entering.

His father sat at his desk with papers strewn all about. Rhoane picked up a sheet of parchment and studied the writing with a frown. "It never changes, does it?"

"Unfortunately, no." He walked around the desk to greet Rhoane. "It is good to have you home." He sat in a chair, indicating Rhoane do the same. "You are not going to stay, are you?"

Rhoane was surprised by his directness. "No, Your Majesty, I will be leaving with the others."

His father ran a hand over his face. "I thought as much.

Verdaine works in mysterious ways. When she took your mother, I thought my life would end, but then when you told me you had to leave the Weirren for an Aelan girl, I thought she was playing a cruel joke on me. Your mother used to tell me you were special. If only I had listened to her, I would have understood what she meant." He studied Rhoane. "You have sacrificed everything for this girl, and she does not even know what she is. You should have told her."

"She is young and frightened. Telling her will only make it worse." He held out his right hand to his father. "You see what these symbols mean, you know what is coming. Would you have me tell her what she will have to do one day just to satisfy your desire for her to fail? What if she succeeds? Have you thought of that?"

His father scoffed. "An Aelan surpassing Eleri, to sit at the side of Verdaine herself? No, I will not believe it. Your Mother," he paused to clear his throat, "could not even conceive of that."

Rhoane swallowed his hurt. "Then why did you claim her Darennsai last night?"

"Because, my son, I need the other Eleri to believe it possible." He stood, as did Rhoane, and embraced Rhoane with surprising force. "Tonight, at table, I will declare you no longer sheanna." He touched Rhoane's short waves. "Grow your hair and let the world know you are Eleri."

Tears stung Rhoane's eyes. "Thank you, Father." He held his father close, wishing things could be different. "You saw last night what is in her heart. She will not fail you."

"For the sake of the Eleri and Aelinae, I hope you are right." A clash of metal drew their attention to the courtyard outside his window. "One cannot say she takes her obligations lightly," he said as he watched Taryn jump aside, narrowly missing a slice of Baehlon's sword. "Does she always exhibit such abandon?"

"In everything she does."

"Is this what you wish for yourself?"

For a long moment, Rhoane didn't answer. The previous night he, too, saw into her heart. Saw her innocence and her anguish. Saw the entirety of the life she'd lived with Brandt, saw her conflicted love for him. Over the long seasons of waiting for her, he'd asked himself many times if honoring Verdaine's prophecy was what he truly wanted. He at last had an answer. "If ever I had the choice, this is what I would choose."

His father nodded slowly. "So be it." He indicated his desk. "I should get back to this."

"Then I shall leave you to your work." He moved a few steps and faltered. "Father, Carga...?" He could not bring himself to finish the question.

Stephan shook his head. "Your sister knows when her punishment is complete. Only then can she part the veils."

"I know the man, and it was not her fault. Zakael is clever and manipulative. He was using her to find Taryn."

"Stop. Is it not bad enough that one of my children is destined to share his body with a Fadair? Once your sister is purified, I will forgive her. Now, go."

When Rhoane approached the door his father called to him. "I do not completely trust the empress. There is something unsettling about her. A force I cannot name that has permeated her ShantiMari. Tread with care. Because you are no longer sheanna, when you are at her court, you are beholden only to Eleri law and not her whims. And Rhoane, as Darennsai, neither is her daughter. I will explain this to her when I meet with her later today."

"I do not envy you that."

Lliandra liked her control over Taryn a little too much. His father's declaration would anger the empress, but Rhoane vowed to not let her take that anger out on his beloved. He'd been livid at her treatment of Taryn after the Aomori scandal, going so far as to question Lliandra over her actions. Not only did she deny abusing Taryn but she warned him it was not his place to debate her actions regarding her daughters, which included Marissa.

Her thinly veiled threat to leave the crown princess's affairs well alone confirmed his suspicion Lliandra knew Marissa was involved with Zakael. More than likely, Lliandra was using her daughter as a spy, but Rhoane couldn't be certain. If he so much as mentioned Zakael's name to Marissa, she immediately changed the subject.

Rhoane took the winding staircase to the back entrance where he could find peace in the dense forest. He walked through the woods, touching buds that yearned to ripen, and coaxing saplings to grow straight and tall. It had been too long since he'd been home. Too long since he'd been one with nature.

He returned to the Weirren as the sun was setting, casting shadows through the leafy canopy. He had just enough time before dinner to check on Taryn, make certain the paste he'd made for her wound was intact, and then change for the evening. On the way to her rooms, Rhoane caught sight of Marissa at the end of the hallway. Dressed in her dinner attire, she stood a hand's width from an Eleri youth Rhoane didn't recognize. From the way he leaned in toward the princess, it looked like the conversation was more than casual.

Changing course, he headed for them, whistling his approach. Marissa feigned a giggle and slapped the boy's hand before taking it in her own, lacing her fingers with his.

When the lad saw Rhoane, he straightened, a furious blush staining his cheeks. "Your Highness," he stammered. "I, we, uh, the crown princess was lost."

"Yes," Marissa purred. "And this lovely young man was helping me find my way."

The boy's thoughts hammered against Rhoane's. Confusion. Embarrassment. Fear. Arousal. Escape.

"You may leave us," Rhoane said to the Eleri. "I can direct the princess where she needs to go."

The boy apologized several times before fleeing in the direction Rhoane had come.

"What a charming race the Eleri are. So helpful, too." Marissa tilted her head, giving him a coquettish smile.

"Do you know the Eleri share a collective bond? That is not to say every Eleri knows what the other is doing or thinking at any given moment, but in times of severe duress, it is possible for one Eleri to feel another's emotions."

"Oh? That must be rather tiresome."

"Indeed. Especially when someone I have trusted her entire life tries to bribe one of my brethren." He towered over her, using his size to intimidate her. She didn't cower, but straightened to her full height, her chin jutting out defiantly. "Do what you will with your own courtesans, but leave my people out of your schemes. Am I understood?"

"I don't know what you're talking about, Rhoane. We were just having a friendly chat."

"Then why does he have Talaithian gold in his pocket and the scent of you in his mouth? Your actions could have cost him his home. The Eleri do not use their bodies as Fadair do. I will kindly ask you to remember this."

He stormed away before he did something he might regret. Later, he would find the lad and return Marissa's gold. The taint of her ShantiMari lingered in his senses until he reached Taryn's rooms. He paused, letting the realization sink in. He could sense another's power in much the same way Taryn could see it.

Chapter 37

THAT night King Stephan announced Rhoane was no longer *sheanna*. To mark such an auspicious occasion, the king produced two silver crowns, setting them upon Taryn's and Rhoane's heads. Rhoane's was a simple coronet of leaves that resembled Taryn's *cynfar*, but hers was elaborate, more a headdress than a crown. It circled her head in a complex arrangement of twisted silver. Long swags of jewels interlinked around the sides and back, catching the light every time she moved.

The Eleri celebrated Rhoane's return to the Weirren with dancing and drinking into the wee hours. Instead of retreating to the bower when they'd had enough celebrating, Rhoane left Taryn at the door to her rooms with a promise he would collect her three bells later to show her the forest.

Dreams of a darkness without a name disturbed her rest. The shadowy figure who tracked her travels loomed over her sleep, taunting her with fragmented oaths spoken in a voice cracked with death. When Rhoane knocked on her door at the first sign of daybreak, she greeted him with false enthusiasm.

The beauty of the forest distracted her from the sense of dread that burned beneath her skin. They rode along paths lined with trees so tall she couldn't see their tops. Their trunks and lower limbs were covered with ivy or moss, some with flowers dangling almost to the ground.

"Look, over there." Rhoane pointed through the trees.

"I don't see anything."

"Come, but be silent." He edged Fayngaar forward, with Taryn following. Suddenly, she saw two great wolves loping toward them; each held a tiny pup in its muzzle.

"They're magnificent. I've never seen wolves this close."

"Not wolves—grierbas. They are rare and very territorial. We must keep our distance."

"Where are they taking their babies?"

"I do not know. To move them so young must mean their den was disturbed." The grierbas ran by, close enough Taryn could see the pups still had their eyes shut. The smaller of the great animals marked Taryn as they passed. Her golden eyes were filled with fear. "We must see what spooked them." Rhoane turned his horse, leading them away from the clearing.

When Taryn glanced back, the grierbas were gone. She kicked her horse to catch up with Rhoane, scanning the trees around them. A flicker of ShantiMari tickled the edge of her vision, but every time she turned to see where it came from, it would disappear. Her anxiety grew the farther they moved into the vier. When she looked to her left, nausea overwhelmed her.

"Rhoane, there's something over here, but I can't tell what it is." She pulled Ashanni off the path and wandered through the low brush until it became too thick for her mare to traverse. "Stay here," she told Ashanni after sliding from the saddle.

Rhoane dismounted Fayngaar to search in the opposite direction. She pulled her sword from its scabbard, holding it by her side, her grip loose but wary. The pull of power became stronger, the unease more pronounced. She ducked under branches and through brambles until she came to a wall of ShantiMari so strong it nearly knocked her backward.

She reached out to touch the threads when a voice said, "Now is not the time."

Taryn spun around, her sword glowing with her ShantiMari. A woman stood before her, dressed in a white gown that pooled in a wide circle. Her dark, waist length hair was held back by a silver crown similar to the one King Stephan gave Taryn the previous night. The woman smiled at Taryn, but there was sadness in her eyes.

"Who are you?"

"I think you know the answer to that, Taryn of House Galendrin, Child of Light and Dark, Eirielle, and *Darennsai* to the Eleri."

"I didn't ask who I am—I asked who are you?" She held her sword level with the woman's chest. "If you are who I think you are, then you must be a ghost because Queen Aislinn is dead."

The woman gently moved Taryn's sword aside. "You do not need this, my daughter." She took a step toward Taryn, holding out her hands. "I am unarmed and wish you no ill will."

She sensed no power coming from the woman, but her presence unnerved her. Aislinn had died in a horrific fire, but the woman standing before her looked very much alive. And unmarked. The wall of ShantiMari tugged at Taryn with a viciousness that burned to her marrow.

"I am neither ghost nor dead, and at one time I was the Eleri Queen." Aislinn made a motion toward the wall, and the discomfort stopped. "Put the sword away, Taryn."

She sheathed the sword and looked warily at the wall. "What is this?"

"That is not for you to know yet." Aislinn approached, and Taryn flinched from her touch. "Much has happened to you in a short time. I do not blame you for fearing a phantom. I have longed to meet you and now that you are here. I am well pleased."

"Are you a figment of my imagination?"

The Queen laughed, and it sounded like the singing of birds in the evening sky. Soft but resigned. "I most certainly am not. It is too much to explain now, but know this—there will come a time when I will need your help. It is then all will be revealed. For now, you must tell no one of this meeting." She brushed aside a strand of Taryn's hair. "Not even Rhoane."

"I don't like secrets."

"Neither do I, *mi carae*, but to be a great ruler, you must learn when it is prudent to keep information to yourself and when to share only what is needed." Her eyes held such great sorrow Taryn had to look away. "If the Eleri knew of my existence, it would change the course of what is to come."

"And what is to come?"

"No one fully knows. We have glimpses, but nothing more."

Frustration boiled inside her. "Forgive me, Your Majesty, but I'm getting tired of only having part of the story. If I'm to accomplish whatever is expected of me, don't you think I should know what that is?"

"If I were to tell you about this," Aislinn waved her hand at the wall, "I might upset the balance of events. There is a progression to your knowledge. This is further along your journey. You will have to trust me."

"That's easier said than done. I've not had much luck trusting people lately. It doesn't help when everyone is telling me something different. They can't all be right."

"I see your quandary. You are very young and inexperienced. In time, you will learn to trust yourself. Only then will you know to whom to give your trust in return." She held Taryn's face between her hands. "I believe in you, my daughter, my love, *mi carae*." She placed her lips on Taryn's and kissed her. Cool air passed between them.

When Aislinn pulled back, Taryn was strangely calm. "What did you do to me?" A chill lingered in her lungs, as if she'd taken a deep breath of frigid air.

"When the time comes, this will allow you to step through the wall. For now be content, knowing I am with you, always." She touched Taryn's cheek with icy fingertips. "You are quite exceptional, yet you do not believe this to be true. Trust in yourself, my love. We will meet again. Until then, tell no one." She waved in farewell before disappearing through the threads of ShantiMari.

Taryn stood unmoving, her fingertips on her lips. By the time Rhoane cried out for her, the exchange with Aislinn was no more than a hazy dream, easily forgotten. Rhoane called her name once more, urgency in his voice, and she shook herself. Each time she glanced toward the wall, her stomach pinched and nausea roiled in her esophagus. Not quite knowing what she was doing there, she shrugged off her unease and set out to find Ashanni, answering Rhoane as she did.

The brush was thick in this part of the forest, wild and untamed. As she was ducking under a low-hanging branch, she caught sight of a small bundle of fur lying near the opening of a burrow. On her hands and knees, she crept to the animal, alert to what might be lurking in the shadows. The pup was no bigger than the span of her hand and cool with impending death. She breathed into its face while rubbing its fur until the little thing whimpered, kicking its legs against her. A wave of relief washed over her.

"Rhoane! Come quickly. I've found a pup. It's still alive." She heard thrashing of bushes and suddenly Rhoane was beside her, breathing heavily.

"We should try to find the others," she suggested. "It's

only a few days old, I'd guess."

"They are long gone and will not take this one. I would wager it is the runt, not meant to live anyway. Leave it here."

"To die? I don't think so." She put the pup in her tunic, nestled between her breasts. "I'll take it with me."

"Taryn, that is a wild animal, not to be domesticated."

"I'll only keep it until it's big enough to go off and live on its own. If I leave it here, it will surely die."

He started to argue with her, but she marched off to find their horses. When she approached Ashanni, the mare snorted and backed away. "It's okay, girl. It's just a little puppy, nothing to harm you. Just a tiny little thing." The horse sidestepped when Taryn lifted herself into the saddle, nearly making her fall. She held the reins tight. "Stop that. It's just a puppy."

"What will she think when that beast is full-grown? I tell you, Taryn, leave the thing here and let the vier decide its fate."

The pup nuzzled against her skin, looking for milk. A fierce protectiveness overcame her, and she glared at Rhoane. "I'm taking the grierbas. If you don't like it, that's your problem." She kicked her horse, setting off for the Weirren. Rhoane caught up to her, and they rode in silence. When they arrived at the clearing, they circled it several times searching for tracks but found nothing.

"It's as if they were never here," Taryn mused.

Rhoane looked at her, a curious expression on his face. "If I am not mistaken, I believe you were meant to find that animal." He shook his head, laughing. "Verdaine, what folly is this?" Glancing up to the sky, he laughed harder. "Oh, you cruel Mistress." Taryn stared at him, afraid he'd lost his mind. "There is nothing for it. You will have to raise the whelp."

"The sky told you that?" The puppy scratched her chest and she winced. "I think we need to get some milk, and soon."

They galloped back to the Weirren, going straight to the kennels. As luck would have it, they had a choice of three bitches. The first two snarled at the pup, but the third gave Taryn a tired look while lying on her side. The pup ate hungrily for several minutes before rolling over and falling fast asleep. The dog licked the grierbas clean before nosing it to the pile of other sleeping pups.

"We can leave her with Sheela for tonight, but do not get your hopes up. Grierbas are not like other dogs."

Taryn knelt next to Sheela, stroking her fur. "Thank you, sweet girl."

After a brief, yet heated, discussion with the kennel master, Taryn and Rhoane made their way to the Weirren. The man wasn't happy about the grierbas but would allow her to stay as long as Sheela and the other pups accepted her.

Taryn kept the grierbas a secret from everyone, including her friends. It wasn't easy, but she managed to visit the kennels every day, bringing treats for Sheela. By the time their departure date arrived a week later, she'd decided to keep the pup, not wanting to risk her fate if she left her to the vier. She asked the kennel master's advice on everything from what kind of milk to feed her to when she should teach her to hunt on her own.

His knowledge of the animal was vast, and he made extensive notes that he gave to Taryn on the morning she was to leave. Along with the papers, he handed her a sling of sorts. "To carry the wee one," he explained. "Keep her close to ye, so she gets the scent of ye on her. She'll be wonderin' what's friend or foe, but if ye treat her with respect, she'll know what's right and what's not."

"Thank you. For everything." Taryn gave him a warm hug, even going so far as to brush his cheek with her lips. His scraggly beard scratched her skin much the same way

Brandt's had.

He helped her fit the grierbas into the sling. Then Taryn carefully strapped the pup under her leather tunic.

"I would wish ye luck, but you'll be needin' more than that when she gets older. Have ye got a name for the lass?"

"Kaida. It means *little dragon*."

His laughter trailed her all the way to the stables where Eoghan waited for her, half hidden behind a stall. At her approach, he waved her to him and put a finger to his lips.

"What's wrong, Eoghan?" Taryn glanced around, making certain she couldn't be heard.

Eoghan's glance took in the bulge of her tunic and he smiled. "I was told you would one day nurture the forest." At Taryn's look of alarm, he said, "Your secret is safe with me." He pulled a small package from a pocket and held it out to her, "As long as my secret is safe with you."

"Your secret?" She took the parcel and turned it over in her hand. It looked innocent enough.

"Please, when you are far from the Narthvier, will you give this to Princess Eliahnna?"

Taryn groaned, "Are you kidding me? No. No way. Your father would kill me." She pushed the gift into his hands.

"I beg of you. The princess and I shared many conversations and this is nothing more than my way of saying thank you." He placed the packet in her leather bag with a smirk. "Some day, I will return the favor." Before she could object, he kissed her cheek and raced from the stables.

Taryn spat several curses at his retreating back. If the king ever found out, she'd be more than dead. Patting her satchel, she went to find Ashanni, a secret smile on her lips.

King Stephan and his sons rode at the front of the caravan, acting as escorts to the empress. When they reached the last of the veils, they paused long enough to gather Lliandra's guards and others who had stayed behind. Their parting with the

Eleri was brief, as they'd already exchanged lengthy farewells at the Weirren.

A lone grierbas watched them pass through the final veil, and Taryn inclined her head to the mother of Kaida. The animal sat perfectly still, but Taryn could have sworn she saw the creature give the slightest of nods. Taryn blinked, and the grierbas was gone.

The caravan moved from the cool of the forest into the scorching heat of midday. Within a few minutes, her chemise clung to her skin. The added heat of Kaida's small body under her leather tunic only made her day more uncomfortable.

When the sky began to darken, several scouts rode in from opposite directions indicating an end to the day's ride. The captain of Lliandra's guard set posts around the campsite while nets of ShantiMari crisscrossed overhead like invisible sentries.

Taryn was removing the sling with a sleeping Kaida inside when Sabina entered their tent, hands on her hips, a pout on her mouth. "I know you're keeping something from me. I demand to know what it is." Her gaze drifted to the sling. "What in Julieta's name is that?"

"Really, Sabina, taking your goddess's name in vain?" Taryn teased. Kaida's low whimper filled the space between them. "You have to promise to keep this a secret." Even though Sabina swore to keep silent, hiding the puppy from Tessa and Eliahnna would be impossible. When they entered the tent a few minutes later and saw Kaida, their expected squeals of delight amused Taryn. After several minutes of them fussing over the pup, Taryn reiterated the need for secrecy. Tessa immediately agreed on the condition Taryn let Kaida ride with them in the carriage.

Eliahnna, in typical fashion, kept calm about the ordeal, looking at it from a pragmatic viewpoint. "It makes sense that you would have this animal as your own. You are much like a grierbas, when you think about it."

Taryn cocked her head. "I don't follow."

"You are both rare and misunderstood. Aelinaens fear them, as they fear you, and even the Eleri are cautious of the animal."

Taryn couldn't help but laugh. "I guess you're right. She is perfect for me."

Chapter 38

EXHAUSTED and road weary, the caravan entered Paderau near dusk less than two weeks after leaving the Narthvier. Ashanni trailed the other horses to the stables, and Taryn slid off, barely able to walk. Her long nights of caring for Kaida, followed by even longer days of trying to keep her a secret, cost a heavy toll. She hid the puppy in her leather bag before she and the princesses dragged themselves to their rooms.

Mayla and Lorilee waited for her, a steaming bath at the ready. When they saw the grierbas pup, they smothered Kaida with kisses while she mouthed their hands. Taryn cautioned them that Kaida would have teeth soon enough and their fingers would make a tasty snack. She shook her head in disbelief when they let the puppy bite the tips of their hair instead. It seemed a puppy, no matter how ferocious she would grow to be, was still adorable.

Once bathed and dressed, Taryn left Kaida with her maids to get milk for the growing pup. Carga already knew about the grierbas and had a fresh jar of milk waiting. She gave it to her with a warning that Kaida would need raw meat in less than a week's time, explaining that grierbas grew much faster than regular dogs.

Before Taryn left, she took Carga's hand in hers. "I know you're Rhoane's sister." She'd heard the name whispered during their time in the Narthvier.

Instead of the anger Taryn expected, a look of resignation crossed Carga's face. "I did not think I could keep it from you once you went to the Weirren." Carga squeezed her hand. "I am happy you know, but please, keep it to yourself. It is difficult to be a cook when everyone knows you are a princess."

"As long as you tell me what *mi carae* means."

Carga gave her an odd look. "Where did you hear that?"

The memory was foggy, uneasy to recall. "I think I heard King Stephan say it when mentioning Queen Aislinn."

Carga's eyes grew soft and misty. "It is an ancient saying of the Eleri. It means *my heart* or *my love*. It is not said lightly, as the words themselves are an oath. My father loved my mother very much. Their love was sacred."

"That's beautiful." She took her supplies and left the kitchens, wiping at her wet cheeks, slightly appalled at how easy it was for her to tear up. Before Aelinae, she'd rarely cried. Since stepping into the cavern, she was a bloody waterworks.

When she arrived at her rooms, the other princesses were on the floor with her maids, laughing and playing tug-of-war with Kaida and a piece of rope. The little furball was snarling and snapping at them with all the ferocity she could muster.

"Has she been out lately? I don't want any accidents in here."

"We were waiting for you. Have you told Mother yet? She's meeting with the duke in his rooms, which would make the perfect time to break the news." Eliahnna offered.

Tessa sat up. "You might want to take Kaida with you. How can she get angry with such a sweet face?"

"I'm sure she'd find a way." Taryn scooped up Kaida, saying farewell in her best melodramatic voice. "If you never see me again, you'll know it didn't go well."

She stood at the duke's door for a long time, her hand

wavering over the handle, unsure if she was making a mistake. She was about to turn away when the door opened, and Myrddin loomed before her.

"Ah, Taryn, we were just going to send for you. Come in, child." He peered down at the ball of fur nestled in her arm. "What have you there?"

Taryn put a hand over Kaida. "I need to speak with my mother. I was told she's here."

Lliandra didn't glance up or stop her conversation with Rhoane when Taryn entered, so she took a seat opposite them and waited, making small talk with Myrddin. A few minutes later, the duke and Hayden entered and took their seats. Lliandra glanced at Taryn, seeing her for the first time.

"What in Ohlin's name is that?"

Taryn cleared her throat. "It's a grierbas pup. She was abandoned in the vier. I'm taking care of her."

Lliandra's eyes popped briefly. "Get that abomination out of here this minute. I'll not have a wild animal running loose around the palace."

Duke Anje spoke with a quiet authority that was not to be challenged. "Pardon me, Your Majesty, but this is my home. If Taryn would like to keep a pet, I have no objections."

Lliandra glared at the duke as if to argue but calmed herself. "You might allow that beast here, but I'll not have it in Talaith. Is that understood?"

"I understand your concern, but this animal was put in my path by something greater than myself. It is not for me to deny what the gods wish for me. If you won't allow Kaida in Talaith, then I will gladly stay here, as long as His Grace will welcome me." Anje inclined his head to Taryn in consent. "Thank you, Duke Anje, for your kind hospitality."

Myrddin laughed, making them all jump. "Let the girl have her dog, Lliandra. I'm sure Taryn will train her and keep her penned up at night so she won't eat the horses. Isn't that right, Taryn?"

She gave Myrddin a sideways glance and smiled. "I'm sure Kaida will be no trouble at all."

Lliandra twisted a ring around her finger, her angry stare focused on Myrddin. An unspoken argument crossed between them while the others waited for the outcome. Finally, Lliandra tossed her hair with a sniff. "I don't want that beast near me or my court. You may keep her in the kennels, but away from the horses. If I hear of one accident involving your pet, I'll kill her myself. Is this understood?"

Taryn swallowed hard. "Yes, Mother. Completely. Except—" Lliandra stared at her, and she mustered her courage. "She will sleep in my rooms with me. If we leave her in the kennels, who's to say she won't take to the scent of horses or men as prey? But if she stays with me, then Aelan smells will be imprinted on her as friends." She stroked Kaida's soft fur. "Would you like to hold her?" For the briefest moment, Lliandra's eyes widened; her face softened.

"I think not. She might be cute, but never forget what she is." She turned away from Kaida, straightening her skirts. "Now, if we can get to the business at hand. Taryn, as my daughter and head of House Galendrin, you are due a monthly stipend as well as property. I've been informed you have yet to receive either, a fact that will be remedied when we return to Talaith."

By the smug look on Anje's face, Taryn suspected her uncle had intervened on her behalf.

"And, as my niece, I would like to offer you land north of Ravenwood, Downington Grange. The soil is rich and there is plenty of grazing land for sheep."

Lliandra's lips pursed into a tight little knot. "That's very kind of you, Your Grace, but Taryn won't be needing your land. She will have the choice of three properties to choose from, I am certain she'll find one suitable for her position."

The monthly stipend alone made her a woman of means, but the added property made her quite wealthy.

"Thank you. Both of you. Really, it's more than I ever expected." Taryn gushed, overwhelmed by their generosity.

"Yes, well, you need to keep up appearances now. As for Hayden," Lliandra looked away from Taryn's leather breeches and loose-fitting blouse, "he will travel with us to Talaith and take his father's place on the Privy Council."

Again, Taryn suspected her uncle of manipulating the situation so that Hayden could be close to Sabina.

As if reading her mind, Lliandra continued, "In addition, we have learned that Queen Prateeni has granted your request to court her daughter. After much consideration, I have decided to allow this union."

Hayden barely suppressed his excitement. "Thank you, Your Majesty."

She turned next to Rhoane. "Because your father has lifted your exile, you are permitted once again to speak in chambers and be an active part of the council."

Rhoane inclined his head. "I am honored to serve, Your Majesty."

Lliandra stood, smoothing her skirts. "These changes will, of course, be presented publicly once we return to Talaith. I think our business here has concluded. If there are no questions? Very well. It has been a long day, and I am quite tired from our travels. I think I'll dine in my rooms this evening. Myrddin, won't you join me?" She held out her arm, not waiting for his reply.

"Rykoto's balls, it's about time," Hayden said once the door clicked shut.

"Hayden." The duke's tone had an edge to it Taryn had never heard.

"Father, you know as well as I that the only reason she relented is that she's terrified Taryn's rank is higher than hers.

If you hadn't badgered her, then I'd be stuck here and Sabina would be married off to that oaf Herbret. All to benefit the empress."

"His family is very powerful," the duke warned. "You do not want to make an enemy of him."

"I have no intention of making enemies this day. If you'll excuse me, I plan to celebrate this good fortune with a very special lady." Hayden bowed to his father and then to Taryn and Rhoane.

Taryn relished in the small victory. Lliandra's change of mind wasn't solely due to her, but she'd been a part of Hayden and Sabina's happiness. That alone filled her with a warm contentedness.

Anje handed her a heavy pouch, placing both his hands over hers. "Take this. A girl needs a little pocket change." She started to protest, but he shushed her. "If I know your mother, it will be some time before she sorts out your allowance. Just consider this an advance."

"I promise I'll find a way to repay you."

"You are so very like my late lady wife. You have her impulsiveness and generosity of spirit." He gave a melancholy chuckle. "Not to mention her beauty and dazzling blue eyes. She was there at your birth, you know. Lliandra entrusted her secret to only a few people. When Brandt took you away, I think it broke Gwyn's heart nearly as much as your mother's."

"I remember her. She had the sweetest voice. She told me there is always light in the dark and darkness in the light."

Rhoane and Anje passed a look between them. "I was there when the duchess said this to you. You were naught but moments old. It is remarkable you remember," Rhoane said.

A chill raised the hair on her neck. "It isn't a conscious thing. Memories just come to me at odd moments."

"You always surprise me, *Darennsai*."

"That's a good thing, right?" Then, in a serious tone, she

said to her uncle, "I thank you for what you've done today. There is so much more I need to understand and not enough bells in the day."

"Don't be hard on yourself, Taryn. You've had much to learn in a short time. You will be busy in Talaith for the next while, but I want you to know you are welcome here anytime. And your ferocious pet."

She laughed and thanked him as Rhoane led her and Kaida out to the gardens where the grierbas rolled over and chased bees. "Yeah, she's a real killer."

"Have no doubt, *Darennsai*, your mother's fears are not without merit. Kaida might not look like much now, but in time she will be, as you say, a real killer."

"Then we'll just have to convince her we're not the enemy."

Chapter 39

MARISSA watched from her window as Taryn and Rhoane walked through the gardens, holding hands and laughing at the antics of the beast Taryn had brought from the Narthvier. That Taryn was able to hide the pup was vexing. Either Taryn was getting better at warding, or Marissa's spies were lax in their duties.

She had underestimated Taryn. If not for those damned vorlocks, Taryn and Rhoane would've met King Stephan with their relationship steeped in doubt. Marissa had worked too hard to make that happen, and whoever was responsible for sending the vorlocks would be punished as soon as Marissa had a name. Until then, she had to rethink her strategy where her sister was concerned.

"Are you even listening?" Herbret's nasally voice whined. "She gave Sabina to Hayden. You promised me." His sniveling took on a dangerous edge. "I demand you speak with your mother and change her mind."

Marissa turned from the window and watched with curious detachment as Herbret's Adam's apple bounced up and down with anxious regularity. Once, when he was a minor noble and she inexperienced with men, she'd let him seduce her. It was a night filled with monosyllabic bleats that echoed through her mind. He was, at the very least, a limp lover, and Marissa had tired of him after that first night. Herbret, convinced otherwise, had pursued her with singular purpose until, in a fit of desperation, she'd thrown Celia his way.

Her favorite lady had used Herbret admirably. Not just in the bedchamber but to raise her own status with the court. Celia's uncanny ability to look beyond Herbret's physical inadequacies allowed her to form a bond with a rising force in Talaithian politics.

A fact that now haunted Marissa. It was Celia's subtle manipulations that helped raise Herbret up, and his status threatened Marissa's plans. A quick death would solve her problem, but Herbret was not dispensable. She took a deep breath and softened her features.

"My darling Herbret, you know I can't do that. Mother has already written to the Queen and given her permission. Why is Sabina so important to you? She has no ShantiMari. Her family is wealthy, but that's not something you covet. I can't help but wonder what it is about the Summerlands princess that has you in such a tizzy."

Herbret cleared his throat, making his Adam's apple jump once more. "The princess would raise my status at court, as you know. I have land, yes, but not a title anyone cares about. Your mother has promised me an earldom several times, but has yet to make good on her troth."

"A title? Is that really what this is about? I thought you told me it was for shipping routes?"

The flush to his cheeks and the constant tugging at his waistcoat told Marissa there was more to this than he let on. Much more. Celia had to know the true nature of Herbret's obsession with Sabina, but the girl played innocent remarkably well.

Marissa stepped forward until she was close enough to touch Herbret but kept herself apart from him. Their body heat filled the empty space, warming her in places left wanting for far too long. If she wasn't already planning her trip south, she would've considered letting Herbret pleasure her. She imagined his plump buttocks turning red beneath her lash and moaned so softly he cocked his head, a look of warning crossing his face, followed by a look of expectation.

She raked her fingernails through his hair, loosening the leather thong that held his tresses in a long tail that flowed down his back. Once released, he had marvelous hair. It was the only thing about him that was beautiful. She licked her lips, imagining the tips of silken strands brushing against her nipples.

Herbret's cock jumped in response, straining against his trousers to press her thigh. A fat tongue protruded from his rosy lips, a drop of saliva formed at the corner of his mouth.

Marissa swallowed a snort of disgust and pressed her breasts upward until his chin nearly rested on them. "Surely there is more to it. One powerless girl cannot be worth a title."

His too-small eyes darted around the room, anxiety dancing in their depths. "I tell you true." He took a step back, hurriedly retying the thong around his hair. "If you won't speak to the empress, I'll see her myself."

Marissa flicked a dismissive hand at him. "Be my guest, but it'll do you no good. The Eirielle wants Sabina and Hayden married. I'm afraid the empress isn't concerned with your feelings on the matter."

Herbret stopped in his movements, mouth agape. "Your sister? But I thought Lliandra had her under control?"

"Apparently not." Marissa beckoned to the sofa. "Why don't you have a seat and tell me exactly what it is about Sabina that you covet. I'm sure we can come to some sort of arrangement to help you achieve your goals."

"So long as my goals don't interfere with yours, is that

it? Sabina has captured my heart, and although it isn't a love match on her part, I would hope in time she would love me, as I adore her. That's all. I want a virginal wife to be my life companion. If there is nothing more, I would like to see to your mother."

Marissa excused him with a pitying wave. He might fancy himself in love with the Summerlands girl, but he'd given her much more than a sob story. He needed Sabina unspoiled. When she returned, she'd seek out Celia and uncover the truth of Herbret's motives.

A quick glance at the sky hurried her pace. It had been too risky to chance a visit during their travels, but now that the court was in Paderau, Marissa would waste no more time. If the two maids the duke had assigned her were as proficient at lying as they professed, she could be gone a full day, possibly two. If nothing else, the feel of Talaithian gold in their pockets would keep their mouths shut.

Marissa walked as swiftly as she could without drawing suspicion to the secluded place she used for her transformation. The change was effortless; she focused on the bird's black feathers, beak, and claws until she became a sleek levon. Nothing, except Zakael's lovemaking, equaled the feel of flying. She beat her wings hard to take to the sky, spiraling up as quickly as possible, delighting in the feel of wind on her feathers.

It would take until the moon was far overhead before she reached Gaarendahl Castle, and Zakael. Soon she would feel his skin next to hers, his delicious ShantiMari flowing around her. As she flew, she fought off the bird's natural instincts to hunt.

Shape shifting was easy to do but difficult to maintain. The key was to not let the animal's mind interfere with one's own. Otherwise, she might permanently become what she changed into. She'd once turned an idiot servant into a field mouse. His tiny brain melded with the animal so completely Marissa was unable to separate them. She'd kept him as a pet for a few moonturns, until he bored her and she let a palace cat have him.

The castle loomed against the sky, far in the distance. She descended, coasting on a warm current, giving her wings a rest before landing. Salty air tickled beneath her feathers, and the temptation to become one with the animal and fly for the rest of her life tugged on her sensibilities. Her talons touched the hard rock of the castle, and she shook herself, ruffling her feathers before tucking in her wings. The flight took less time than she'd anticipated. With a slice of regret, she transformed back into a woman and stepped into Zakael's study.

He was reclining in a chair, feet on his desk. Two dogs, great shaggy beasts the color of warm chocolate, perked their ears. Seeing her, their tails *thwump*ed on the floor, but they did not rise to greet her.

Zakael looked up with some surprise but did not frown. "I thought you might be joining me soon." He set aside the paper he'd been reading. "It's been a while."

"We just arrived in Paderau. Aren't you going to give me a proper greeting?" She slid out of her dress, revealing her naked body. "As you said, it's been a while."

He took her hard and fast. No tender kiss to warm her, no fondling of her breasts to ease them into the moment. That would come later, in his bed, when he would coax her to the throes of ecstasy and leave her there, dangling perilously over the edge of sanity, his Dark Shanti shutting out life. As much as she wanted to languidly enjoy his body, right then she needed the release only he could give her. The violence only he knew she craved.

Her tender skin scraped against the rough wool rug with a satisfying intensity. Fiery shadows played across his face, contorting his features, exciting her even more. Her Mari snaked around them, entwining with his Shanti, plucking at her nerves. His lips sought hers, hungrily sucking, his tongue thrusting its way into the dark recess of her mouth. She raked her nails down his back, drawing blood, and he arched into her touch, his face twisted in delirious passion as he slammed against her with his release. She thrust her pelvis upward, shuddering with her own climax, tightening her power, cutting into his flesh.

Panting, heart racing, with sweat dripping from his forehead, Zakael rolled onto his back, his hands flung out to the side like ships bereft at sea. Empty, alone. They did not seek her for comfort as she hoped they would. She lay next to him, lazily running a finger down his torso.

His body flexed with his exhale. "How is the Eirielle? Has she mastered her powers yet?"

Marissa's Mari snapped against the air. "Don't speak to me of her at a time like this."

"When would you like to then?" His voice was cold, distant.

"We can discuss her when we're clothed." She stroked his limp cock, but he pushed her hand aside.

"There's time for that later. We must discuss our next move."

She yanked her dress over her still tingling skin. "I thought we were to wait for your father's instructions." Her hands shook as she poured herself some of his fine Summerlands red. "Will everything be ready by frost end?"

He stared at the ceiling, oblivious to her hurt and anger. "Father thinks so, but I'm not sure. Taryn's defeat of the vorlock has spread through the West. Her favor is growing."

"She's pathetic and never uses her power." Marissa spat. "Except to lay traps for me, which I can easily detect. Her wards, however, are quite good, but you already know that. How long did it take you to rid yourself of that ink?" She took a sip of wine to keep from laughing.

He shook out his hand but didn't answer the question. "If she hasn't learned to control her powers yet, it could work to our advantage." With a catlike stretch he stood, his lean body shining in the firelight.

Mesmerized by the magnificence of his physique, Marissa drank in his muscular frame, his dark hair a contrast to his pale skin. Drank in the lean legs that reclined against the chair, drank in his beauty until she was drunk.

Her body tightened, and wetness spread between her legs. She cursed her response to Zakael, cursed the power he had over her.

In an even tone, she said, "I don't see how. From what I hear, she's never touched her Dark Shanti. We need the trinity to be complete."

"Exactly. And who better to help her?"

"You?" Marissa snorted into her cup. "I'm afraid, my darling, she doesn't trust you, and I can't say that I blame her. What with you killing her beloved Brandt and all."

Zakael's lips thinned to a dangerous white line. "Then you must convince her otherwise. We need Taryn to come to us of her own free will." He looked pointedly at her. "She has to want to be here."

Marissa's mind raced with possibilities. Getting Taryn to leave Rhoane would be best, but Marissa doubted Taryn would venture to Gaarendahl alone. "Give me time to think about how to go about it." Marissa fluttered her lashes at Zakael and asked in a little girl's voice, "Do you really want to discuss this right now? It's been ever so long since we've had a chance to play." She ran her fingertips along the collar of her gown and tapped the little divot at the base of her throat.

Zakael descended on her, his mouth sucking at her neck, his tongue scraping over her collarbone. She swooned against him, a current of power racing through her.

With one swift movement, Zakael spun her around and held her hands behind her back. "No Mari. Is that understood?"

She nodded her acceptance of his terms, thrilled at the prospect of what came next.

They marched to his bedchamber, she in front, he behind with a firm grip on her wrists. It was awkward to walk in such a manner, but Marissa made certain her bare feet made no sound on the wood floors. Zakael's beasts raced down the corridor, their barks echoing off the stone walls.

"Out," Zakael ordered, and the dogs retreated to another part of the castle. Marissa was relieved. The animals always watched with a sense of judgment.

Zakael released her hands and pulled her gown roughly over her shoulders, tossing the garment aside without a thought. "Kneel."

Marissa obeyed, her eyes focused on the floor in front of her. She loved this game of his. Loved the commanding tone in his voice, the way he could make her wild with pleasure, the way he made her feel cherished.

He stepped out of her sight, and her skin tingled with excited expectation. She heard him rummaging through a drawer, and then he left the room completely. The wait for his return wasn't long, but in the space of those few minutes, she became frantic with need. When finally he stood before her, he was naked, his cock hard. A drip of his pleasure teased her from the tip of his shaft.

He gave a slight nod, and she flicked her tongue, catching the drop of salty sweetness. Zakael stroked her long curls, pressing her face against his thigh.

"I have a surprise for you, but you must promise to be a good girl." He pulled her hair until she looked up at him. "No Mari, is that understood?" Her heart tripped in her chest. She'd consented to not using her power before; it was an easy enough promise to make. She nodded her acceptance again. He beckoned with his other hand, and a lovely young man stepped from the shadows.

A sliver of fear cut through her. "Zakael?" Her voice was barely a whisper.

"Shhh, don't fret. Eiric and I are going to take very good care of you."

Eiric's smooth, lanky body gave him the look of a youth, perhaps no more than seventeen seasons. He moved beside Zakael and snaked a hand over his cock, stroking it while covering Zakael's mouth with his own. The intimacy Eiric showed enraged Marissa. She'd never fooled herself into believing Zakael only bedded her, but they had an agreement that no lovers would be discussed. Or shared.

She knelt between the two men, gazing up at them as they devoured each other in a soul scorching kiss that, despite her best intent, excited her. Zakael by turns stroked and tugged her hair. Her nipples tightened into little nubs, eager for attention. Eiric's cock bumped against Zakael's, and the older man gave a shuddering moan. Her jealousy spiked, and she lashed out with her power.

"Enough!" Zakael glared down at her. At once, her Mari was cut off. She reached for it, desperately searched for it, but it was gone. A wall shut her out from her power.

"How are you doing this?" Fear, real fear, coursed through her. To block another's power was forbidden beyond all else.

Zakael's face relaxed, and her ShantiMari crept through her, embracing her like an errant lover. "Promise me, no power," he demanded once more.

"But, how?"

Zakael shook his head and yanked on a strand of her hair. Shaken by Eiric's presence and Zakael's revelation that he could render her powerless, she nodded. "I promise."

"You must trust me," he cupped her chin gently with his fingertips, "in all things."

"I do." She looked up at him, meeting his hardened gaze with adulation. His hand cracked across her cheek, snapping her head back. She tasted blood, licked her lips for more.

"Say it again."

"I trust you, Zakael." This time a lash of leather whipped across her naked buttocks. Eiric stood behind her, waiting for Zakael's command. Marissa's insides clenched into a tight ball of hopeful expectation. Her blood thrummed through her, buzzing in her ears. Her vision swam, and she swayed back the slightest bit. Another crack of the lash and she pulled herself up to kneel before Zakael. "I trust you. In all things."

Please, one more lash.

But it didn't come. Instead, Zakael pushed himself into her mouth, tearing the delicate skin at the corner of her lips. She opened herself to him, taking him deep. He rocked against her, his eyes never leaving hers. Her hands cupped his balls, massaging them in time to his thrusts. She teased him with her tongue, scratched the soft skin with her teeth, all the while watching his face.

The lash snapped hard against her back, making her cry out and gag on his thickness.

Zakael gripped the back of her head. "Deeper."

Another lash and she began trembling. Her fingers faltered, pinching his scrotum. Another, harder crack across the tops of her thighs. That fragile area just beneath her arse where the skin was sensitive. Tears streamed down her face, and she choked on Zakael's cock. She was suffocating, but his hand pressed harder. Panic overtook her, and she tried to pull back, flailed her arms to make contact with something, anything.

"Breathe, Marissa," Zakael cooed. "Trust me." He stroked her hair, resumed his gentle thrusts. She relaxed into the movements, finding a rhythm. Eiric knelt behind her, and she stiffened, not knowing what to expect. "Easy now." Zakael tapped her head, and she opened her jaw wider, pulled her lips over her teeth.

With a shock, Marissa felt Eiric's hands on her, rubbing the little nub between her legs. Pleasure jolted through her, and she twitched against his touch. Her breathing quickened, her heartbeat throbbed in that small space. Zakael grew thicker in her mouth with his mounting release, and Marissa moaned into him, opening herself to take him deeper.

Eiric's fingers quickened their pace, slick with her wetness. Zakael pounded into her, harder, faster, until he groaned and thrust deep, spilling his seed. Marissa greedily sucked it in, milking his cock with her tongue and lips, hungry for more.

Zakael slipped from her and motioned to Eiric, who stopped his wonderful ministrations. She whimpered her displeasure. The very hair on her skin stood on end, but they left her on the brink of being shattered.

Careful not to touch her, Zakael and Eiric placed leather cuffs around her ankles and wrists. At Marissa's worried glance, Zakael smiled with genuine pleasure and assured her she was safe. They pulled her arms and legs wide and secured her to the wall with cleverly disguised restraints.

Unable to move, to touch herself for release—or to shield herself from their probing eyes—Marissa stared blankly at Zakael as he took Eiric to his bed. She watched them make love in ways she never could. The ecstasy on Zakael's face tore at her soul. They moved like lovers well accustomed to each other's likes and dislikes. Tears shimmered in her eyes as Eiric took Zakael's cock in his mouth, loving it the way she had only a short time ago.

Zakael left the bed and knelt before her, looking up at her with as much adoration as she'd surely looked at him. He slipped his tongue between her legs, instantly igniting the flames that burned brightest for him. Only him. His hands slid around to her buttocks, pinching tiny bits of skin between fingertips. Eiric rose too, and her breath caught with anticipation.

He took her breast in his mouth, the warmth soothing her, his tongue grazing over her nipple, exciting her. They worked in tandem, bringing her to the edge of delirium. At the first shudder of her release, Zakael pulled back, leaving her wanting, pulsing, waiting. She needed one more touch to send her over the precipice, but he left her and returned to the bed where Eiric joined him.

Marissa sobbed against her shoulder. Frustrated, confused, impotent. With heartbreaking clarity she realized Zakael was not hers, had never been, would never be completely hers. And there, bound to the wall where she was forced to watch her lover with another, she concluded that she had never really been his, either. And yet, watching him with Eiric, unable to use her ShantiMari, completely under Zakael's control, she had never been more connected to him.

Zakael turned from Eiric's embrace and met her even stare. What passed between them in that instant was deeper, more binding, than any oath.

Chapter 40

TARYN emptied the pouch on the bed, touching the multihued coins and gems. Hayden separated them, explaining the region and worth of each: gold crowns from Talaith, silver feathers from the Danuri Province, gems in several colors from Haversham, and more. Every kingdom or province made its own currency, which meant every piece had a different sum attached to it. A few of the coins were made from a black metal she'd never seen. Aergan, Hayden had called it. Its value was more precious than gold.

Trying to remember it all gave Taryn a headache. She scooped up the lot, saying, "I think the best way for me to learn is to put this into practice. I'm going to the market. Would you like to join me?"

"We must let Rhoane know you're leaving the palace."

"It's no big deal. I just want to get some gifts for my maids. If I could, I'd steal them away from here."

"A thief, eh? I should have you locked away in the dungeons." Hayden brandished his sword, and they mock fought around his suite. When he swatted her behind, she called a truce, rubbing her backside.

"You win! I won't steal my maids."

Hayden set off to find Sabina while Taryn checked on Kaida. On impulse, she went to the kitchens to see whether

Carga needed anything.

After making an extensive list, Carga decided to join them, instead. The youth Taryn had met once, but often saw in the kitchen when she breakfasted with Carga, trailed them to the courtyard.

"We have a stowaway." Taryn glanced back to where Gris leaned against a tree, inspecting the hem of his shirt.

"You may come along, Gris," Carga finally agreed. "This will be good practice for when I send you on your own." His face lit up, and he jogged to stand close to Carga.

Hayden called out to them from where he waited in the courtyard. "The sun will be high above our heads soon enough. Let's be on our way while there is still the sweetness of morning."

Baehlon stood with the other princesses, his arms crossed over his chest. He directed his ire at Taryn. "I should put you over my knee and paddle your arse until you can't walk."

"What did I do?"

"You would have left the palace grounds without alerting me. If I hadn't run into young Hayden here, I might not have known you'd gone."

"I don't need a babysitter to go shopping."

"Princess, you are too innocent for your own good."

Sabina took her arm. "Don't worry, Taryn. You'll get used to having guards accompany you. Back home, I was assigned four guards at all times. Imagine trying to have a private conversation with a quartet of soldiers standing only a pace away."

"You aren't guarded here," Taryn pointed out. "Won't your father be upset?"

"He doesn't know. I have guards, don't be mistaken about that, but they are staying with the other soldiers. I've paid them to send reports to my father saying exactly what he wants to hear."

"Who would've thought? Princess Sabina, a rebel."

The streets teemed with people trying to get their shopping done before the heat made the day miserable. Taryn cringed with each elbow that struck her wound. It seemed every basket or wayward hand they passed hit the mark. It had finally healed enough she'd stopped putting salve on it, but beneath the scar, it was still tender. She dodged the crowd as much as she could, keeping close to Baehlon, all the while worrying the wound might split open. She wrapped a hand protectively around her midsection.

"Are you well?" Baehlon bent low to ask.

"I didn't know it would be so crowded."

The bells in his braids made a tinny sound when he shook his head. "We should turn back. I don't think this is a good idea."

Taryn agreed, but the happiness on the other princess's faces stayed her words. It was rare they ventured from the palace; she didn't want to take away their joy.

"Gris and I need to meet with a merchant a few streets away. We will find you later, yes?" Carga and the boy slipped into the stream of people, disappearing before Taryn had a chance to reply.

They wandered from stall to stall, looking at ribbons and trinkets. Taryn purchased several brightly colored ribbons for her maids in Paderau and some others for Cora and Ellie. The spice merchant Tabul treated them to tea, using his finest silver and tripping over himself in gratitude. Sabina spoke with the man at length about her homeland and then arranged for half a dozen spices to be delivered to the palace.

After tea, they strolled through the streets, stopping at various merchants before wandering to the bookseller's stall. Eliahnna and Taryn spent a good amount of time rummaging through the old texts. When the others became restless, they left the stall under protest, but with several volumes tucked into their baskets.

Once in the open center of the square, the sun beat on them relentlessly. Several children ran past, and as Taryn stepped out of their way, she caught a brief glimpse of Rhoane in the distance. When she looked closer, he was gone.

"Is something amiss?" Baehlon asked quietly.

"Just the light playing tricks on my eyes."

Sabina led them to a produce stall with fruits and vegetables in every shape, color, and size. Tiny flies swarmed over the produce, drunk from the scents that lingered in the air. Melon, citrus, berry—it was intoxicating. Taryn delighted in everything she sampled.

Flavors of sour and sweet tickled her tongue, sending shivers through her. It had been far too long since she'd had fruit this fresh. The palace cooks tended toward a heavy hand with sauces and spices that overtook the simple goodness of the food.

Sabina squealed and picked up a round spiky apple. "Treplars!" She held the fruit to her nose, inhaling the heady scent. "Oh, how I adore them."

At her request, the merchant put several of the odd-looking things in her basket. Not stopping with just the treplars, Sabina pointed to other items until her basket was overflowing. When there was no room left in hers, she loaded up Taryn's, as well.

"I was not aware our goods were sold so far from the coast," Sabina said by way of explanation for her indulgence.

On their way to the next merchant, Taryn bit into what looked like a pear and was surprised that it tasted more like a watermelon. On impulse, she turned back to buy more, coming face-to-face with the shadow man from the tavern all those weeks ago.

He stood not more than three paces from her, his hand on a dagger. Too stunned to move, Taryn stared at him. Black

ShantiMari crisscrossed his body, swirling in a haze of motion when he moved.

In one fluid step, he threw a dagger straight at her. Instinctively, she hid behind her basket. The blade impaled a treplar with an efficient *squish*. She lowered the basket and saw Gris race toward the man, fists raised. The stranger dodged a strike and grabbed Gris by the front of his tunic, tossing him aside as if he were a rag doll. His body hit a stone column with a deafening *crack* and slid to the ground, unmoving.

Before she had time to react, Baehlon and Hayden had their swords drawn, facing the stranger. Behind him, Rhoane and a half-dozen soldiers stood with their swords held aloft. Myriad threads of ShantiMari wrapped around the stranger, binding him.

"Your weapons." Baehlon's quiet voice held a deadly edge. He motioned to the ground. "Easy now and no one gets hurt." His sword was inches from the man's heart.

The shadow man sneered at them before he looked Taryn full in the face. Nothing but hatred emanated from his ice blue eyes. His hood slipped, revealing golden hair that shone in the sun, and something stirred within her. In a breath, it vanished. She took a step toward him, her hand outstretched. With a flash of light, he was gone, without a trace of ShantiMari for her to follow.

"Ferran's bells." One look at Rhoane's rage-filled face and the crowd slunk away into the background. He turned to Taryn, taking her by the shoulders. "Are you injured?"

"I don't think so."

Rhoane spun her around and started walking quickly toward the palace. Two guards ushered Eliahnna, Tessa, and Sabina a step behind. "Is that the same man you saw before, when you were with Carga?"

Taryn turned back. "Where is Carga? She's still here. We

can't leave without her. And we need to see to Gris."

"They will be looked after. We need to get you back to the palace." He pulled her along beside him. She held her basket of goods protectively to her chest.

"But that man—he might find her."

"Never mind her. We must hurry."

The others raced with them through the palace gates. Hayden stayed behind to warn the guards of what happened. A barrier of ShantiMari rose over the palace walls, and her knees weakened.

"Rhoane, what's happening? Why are you rushing me?"

He said nothing until they were safely inside. "Baehlon, find Faelara and Myrddin. Meet in my rooms. Hayden, find your father." He turned to one of the guards. "I need you to inform Her Majesty of today's events, but do not alarm her. Ask her to join us in my rooms. Take the princesses to their rooms, as well. Station guards at their doors."

Her sisters remained calm, but Tessa's anxious glances and Eliahnna's constant tugging of her dress gave them away. Three guards left, with Tessa and Eliahnna hurrying ahead of them. Rhoane motioned to another guard before rounding on Sabina. "Princess, please go to your rooms."

She nodded and then stopped herself. "No, I will stay with Taryn."

"Very well, but you must say nothing of what transpires."

"You have my word." She kissed her thumb and put it to her heart. Sabina's hand shook when she held Taryn's hand in hers.

Rhoane gave one last command to the remaining soldiers to search the market for Carga and bring Gris back to the palace. With that, the three of them hurried to Rhoane's rooms. Several times, they had to slow to appear natural when courtiers or servants crossed their path. When they finally reached his suite, Taryn put her basket on a table and confronted Rhoane.

"Why did that man attack me?"

Rhoane paused in his warding. The look of fear in his eyes made her stumble backward.

Sabina led her to a couch and said, "Because you are the Eirielle. That is why, Princess."

Rhoane finished his wards before kneeling in front of her, taking her hands in his with great care, as if she were a doll that might break. "We will find him, Taryn. I promise you."

A knock at the door made her jump. When Duke Anje and Hayden entered the room, her anxiety heightened. Faelara arrived, and a few minutes later Myrddin joined them.

"Lliandra cannot get away from her meeting. She has bidden me to inform her what is decided here," Myrddin told the group.

Baehlon slipped in and carefully closed the door behind him. "The palace is secure. The captain of His Grace's guard has his men and women on alert." Baehlon stood behind Taryn, his arms crossed.

The rest of the group took their seats, and Rhoane addressed them. "An attempt was made on Taryn's life today in the marketplace. I believe it is the same assassin I learned of when we were here previously."

"Assassin?" Taryn's voice was raw.

They all spoke at once, or so it seemed to Taryn. Hayden wanted to storm the city to find the man, while Myrddin cautioned for patience. Baehlon thought they should delay their travel, but Faelara was certain the empress would do no such thing. On and on it went. They connected the first sighting of the assassin in Paderau and spoke only of those two events, but it dawned on Taryn that he'd been following her far longer than any of them realized.

He was the shadow that teased her sight all those times.

Yet she had no proof. Nothing she could give them except a feeling. Later, when she had more to go on than just an intuition, she'd tell Rhoane.

"Why attack now, in the middle of the day in a crowded city?" Myrddin asked, stroking his beard as if he might milk an answer from it.

"He's taunting us. He wants us to know he isn't afraid. That he can get close to Taryn even while she's being guarded." Baehlon stood with his back to the window, arms crossed, eyes fixed on Taryn as if challenging her to say more. He didn't know. Couldn't know. And yet his look told her he at least suspected she was hiding something.

Rhoane slammed his fist on a table, making everyone in the room jump. "We were never more than ten paces from her. Where did he come from?"

"A Shadow Assassin," Hayden offered.

"What did you say?" Rhoane stared at him.

"Shadow Assassins existed long ago. They were Kaldaar's elite force and served only Dark Masters. All of them were thought to be wiped out in the Great War, but they are neither dead nor alive. He must be a Shadow Assassin. And only a very powerful sorcerer could conjure one."

Faelara reminded everyone of the need for discretion. "Everything said here must stay between us or more attempts will be made on Taryn's life. Is this understood?"

They agreed, swearing to Faelara. Sabina's body trembled as numbness cloaked Taryn. Whether from shock, anger, or fear, she wasn't sure.

While they argued, Taryn carefully removed the assassin's blade from the treplar, studying it. More a throwing knife than a dagger, with intricate designs etched into the handle and blade, similar to the scrollwork on the seal. The total length of the knife was no more than a few inches. Strangely, it felt light in her palm. She handed the weapon to Rhoane.

"Maybe this can give us some clue to his identity."

Myrddin moved quickly to retrieve the blade. "I should take that. It might be poisoned or bespelled with Black ShantiMari."

Rhoane hesitated and then handed the knife to Myrddin. "Let us know what you discover, but be discreet."

"Of course." Myrddin snorted, offended. He folded the dagger in a scrap of fabric and then tucked it in his robe. A thread of his ShantiMari glowed in his pocket and then dissipated. Patting his robe, he said, "We'll find this assassin, don't you worry, my dear."

Taryn didn't share his optimism. "Not anytime soon, I fear. I think we need to be vigilant but not change a thing."

Hayden put his hand on the hilt of his sword. "And risk another attack? I saw his face—so did you, Baehlon. I say we go now and find this bastard."

"If you saw his face, then you know he's not all there, Hayden," Sabina argued. "His eyes were soulless. He wants Taryn, but he won't hesitate if you get in the way."

Hayden started to argue with her, but Taryn interrupted. "Stop!" She looked directly at Baehlon. "You accused me of being too innocent; I understand now what you meant. I'll not cower behind a wall of good men and women, waiting for him to strike. You're both right—he wants me, but he'll kill whoever gets in his way. We'll find a solution but not while we're this emotional. So if you'll excuse me, I've got a puppy that needs tending. Sabina, would you care to join me? Now?"

Sabina looked to Hayden, who nodded, and then curtseyed to the group. "Lady Faelara, gentlemen."

Taryn all but ran with Sabina to her apartments, making it to the chamber pot just in time. Sabina held her hair back, saying soft words of comfort while Taryn threw up. When she finished, Sabina wiped her face with a wet cloth. When

Mayla and Lorilee offered their assistance, Sabina sent them to the kitchens for some herbal tea and toast, blaming Taryn's illness on something she ate at the market and saying it was nothing to worry about.

Taryn gave Sabina a grateful look. "Thank you. Please don't tell anyone about this."

Sabina shushed her while embracing her friend. "I was so frightened today. I don't ever want to feel that helpless again."

"Neither do I." Taryn had no tears to shed, only a hollow feeling that gnawed at her confidence.

She stretched out on the floor of her sitting room, and they played with Kaida. Hayden arrived a short time later with her basket of fruit and several books that would help Taryn understand the Shadow Assassin.

After he and Sabina left, Taryn went to the kitchens to find Carga. The woman was standing at a table chopping onions when Taryn pulled her into a hug. "Thank God you're safe. Where is Gris?"

Carga gave a quick shake of her head and then gestured to a seat before getting them grhom. "I was too late to help Gris."

Anger welled inside her, suffocating. She hadn't known Gris, but the way the assassin had tossed him aside as if he were nothing enraged her. The boy had died defending her. He would be avenged. "I failed him today. Failed everyone."

"You did no such thing."

Taryn grabbed Carga's hand. "I froze. All my training was gone. I could've done something, anything, but instead I stood there like an idiot. And now Gris is dead because of me."

"Stop, Taryn. Gris's death was not your fault. He acted on his own conscience."

"Why would he do something so foolish?"

"Gris bravely defended you. It was not foolish." Carga

lifted Taryn's chin to look at her. "Gris believed in you, Taryn. That is why he attacked the man."

"But, why? He didn't know me."

"What? Because he did not sit at table with you? Or he never played one of your football games? Perhaps he was not a part of your daily life, but he knew enough about you to know you stood for something good. Something worth fighting for."

Taryn shook her head. They didn't understand. She wasn't who they thought she was. She had failed. Didn't they see that? "How can I be this great protector if I can't even defend myself?"

"Taryn, are you not the same person who killed a vorlock single-handed and saved my brother's life?" Carga's words were soft but fierce.

"That was different. Rhoane would've been killed if I didn't do something."

"So, you think his life is of more value than your own?"

"No. Well, maybe. I don't know. Okay, yes, I do. His life is worth far more than my own."

Carga released a long-held breath and smiled. "At last."

"What?"

"Look."

The runes on her hand shifted and then glowed with a soft iridescence. "What's happening?"

"It is time you stopped being a child, Taryn, and become what you are meant to be. Your path will not be easy. People will die, yes. There is no way you can avoid this. They will die for you or possibly because of you. It is a hard truth you must ingest and allow to become a part of your very marrow. Embrace this truth, but do not hide from it. If you do, it is you we will be mourning. And you are no good to my brother dead." The chill in her voice sent a shudder through Taryn.

"I'm frightened, Carga."

"It is good to be afraid, but do not let fear keep you from living. Put that feeling aside, but never forget it is there. You must learn to use your fear for great things."

"That's easy for you to say, hiding here in the kitchens, afraid to be in the world." Her words cut harsher than she'd meant, but she was tired of people telling her what to believe. She knew what had happened earlier that day. Knew she'd have to live with the consequences of her cowardice. Knew that Gris had died in vain because of her.

"That is not fair, and you know it. I choose to work here for my own reasons."

"Rhoane was *sheanna*, you didn't see him cowering behind an apron."

Carga stood and motioned to the door. "I think it time you leave."

Taryn stood to her full height, matching Carga's glare with her own. "And I think it's time you're honest with me. What made you *sheanna*?"

Tension snapped at the air with the viciousness of an angry cobra. A kitchen cat hissed and darted off, his tail a bushel brush.

Carga glanced around the kitchen with wariness in her eyes. "Since the first day you arrived here, I knew there would come a time when I would have to share this tale with you. You will not like the telling of it, though." She took her seat, and Taryn followed.

"Does it involve Rhoane?"

"No and yes." Carga took a deep breath and began. "There was a man, an Aelan, who used me to get information. I was besotted with him. He was incredibly beautiful. Tall and dark, with eyes the color of a wintertide's sky."

"Zakael?" A flick of anger surged through Taryn. The air vibrated around them.

"Yes, the heir to the Obsidian Throne," Carga continued. "I was beyond the veils, on the moors. He said he was traveling the world, to gain experience in the ways of the East so when he took over the throne he could maintain the peace his father had worked for. He was very young." Carga looked away in misty remembrance. "It has been nigh on twenty summers since he seduced me and since I have been to the Weirren."

"He knew you were Eleri. He must've known you'd be exiled."

"He knew all of that and more. I suppose he thought I had information that would lead him to you. His father believed you were with the Eleri during your absence."

Everything kept coming back to Zakael. Marissa was a distraction; it was Zakael and Valterys who controlled the events happening around her. Possibly even the Shadow Assassin. If Zakael had seduced Carga twenty summers earlier, that meant he—and Valterys—knew about Taryn, probably since her birth.

"I'm sorry he did that to you. I'll make him pay."

Carga placed a hand on Taryn's wrist, her touch cool. "No. I will deal with Zakael once I am purified. Until then, you must stop reacting and face your fears. Before someone you love gets killed."

Of all her fears, losing another loved one ranked highest. Taryn left the kitchens more despondent than she'd been before seeking out Carga. She'd not been prepared for any of this. Perhaps if she'd been raised with the Eleri, she would know what to do, but as it was, she was fumbling in the dark without any hope of finding the light.

Chapter 41

TWO men moved through the backstreets and alleyways of the city's poorest district with silent determination. Swords hung at their sides, fists clenched as they traveled swiftly toward the oldest building in Paderau. Its weathered walls leaned in on themselves, supported by a shingled roof that looked one storm away from collapse. At the back door, Rhoane held up a hand. He pressed himself to the wall, and Baehlon did the same. A lone figure stumbled out from the tavern into the alley, slurring a profane greeting.

Rhoane stepped around the drunk into the cool darkness, and the rank smell of stale cider, piss, and vomit assaulted his heightened Eleri senses. The men and women seated around the room were an assortment of thieves, prostitutes, and mercenaries. Just the kind of crowd a Shadow Assassin could get lost in, but he wasn't looking for the assassin. After a quick scan of the customers, he pulled a chair to one of the tables, indicating Baehlon sit across from him.

A serving maid brought them tankards filled with sour-smelling ale. When she left, a slight figure slid into the empty chair beside Rhoane.

"I believe the one you seek can be found at the Golden Feiche." The little man looked longingly at Rhoane's drink. When Rhoane pushed it toward him, he gulped the ale in several noisy slurps and then set the tankard down with a satisfying belch.

Rhoane grimaced at his vulgarity. "What makes you so certain?"

"I followed him from the square today." The man's dark eyes darted around the room.

Without moving, Rhoane tightened his ShantiMari around his neck. "Why would you do something like that, Ebus? If you followed him, how are we to know he did not follow you?"

Ebus sputtered and gasped, his hands gesticulating wildly as his face turned an ominous shade of red. Rhoane released his power, and Ebus massaged his throat, coughing dramatically. "Your Highness, I am offended. I was only trying to help." He moved as if to stand. "When you remember to act in a civil manner, then we can proceed."

"Sit down, Ebus." Baehlon's quiet voice came from the shadows of his hood. "You're making a scene." He pushed the fabric back a fraction. "I believe the prince asked you a question."

Ebus paled to the color of spoiled milk. "What are *you* doing here?"

Baehlon's stare didn't flicker. "Killing you, if you don't answer the question. Did the assassin see you or not?"

"Of course not. I'm the most skilled thief in all of Paderau. No one follows Ebus."

"Your ego is too large for your head, I think," Rhoane whispered to the man. "Why were you following him today?"

Ebus shrugged. "When I saw him trailing Princess Taryn, I thought perhaps he meant to rob her. Let him do the dirty work, I figured, and then I'd just take from him what he'd stolen from her. He looked like a safer bet than the princess with all her friends around."

"I was not aware of him until he attacked Taryn. How is

it you saw him?" Rhoane asked.

Ebus smiled, spreading his hands expansively. "It is my job to notice the unseen. Now," he eyed Baehlon once more, "are we going to gossip all day, or would you like to catch your man?" He held out a grubby hand to Rhoane. "Fifty trins."

"You will get nothing until I see this demon for myself. If he is where you say he is, you will get a gold piece for your trouble."

Ebus's eyes bulged, and he swallowed hard. The amount was triple what the thief had requested. "We must make haste before he departs."

They walked several blocks in the shadows of the glaring sun. The Golden Feiche was in a part of Paderau that faced south, overlooking the river, in a small port district that dealt mainly in goods coming and going to the various houses of ill repute.

Rhoane stopped the group a half block away from the shabby inn. He glanced up and down the street, getting the lay of the surrounding area. Four windows on the second story and two on the floor above that faced the street. "What room is his?" Rhoane asked Ebus.

He scratched at his dingy black hair, looking up at the windows, counting on his fingers. "I'd say the third from the left."

"There are only four windows, you dolt. Why didn't you just say the second from the right?" Baehlon smacked Ebus on the back of his head.

Ebus shrank away from the knight. "Because he didn't come in from the front, now did he? Used the back door, so I'm figuring he went up the backstairs."

"Did you see him enter the room? How can you be sure it is the second from the right?" Rhoane asked in a strained voice.

"I hid over there." Ebus pointed to a recessed part of the wall. "When he got to his room, he closed the shutters. Are we just going to stand around all day?"

"You stay here," Rhoane commanded.

He and Baehlon jogged across the street and went into the inn. The Golden Feiche wasn't busy at that time of day, but Rhoane had to dodge several women who offered to keep him and his friend company. They silently made their way up the stairs, going to the second door and unsheathing their swords. He sent a thread of ShantiMari into the room. Sensing nothing untoward, he slowly opened the door and went inside.

The room was tidy with no personal belongings on the bed or floor. Little light filtered through the closed shutters, but a slight breeze managed to squeeze between the slats. As he turned back toward the door, a dark figure leapt out at him, sword drawn. Rhoane swung his own sword up to counter the attack. The assassin assaulted him with a blade black as pitch. A hard kick to Rhoane's sternum sent him sprawling against the wall. The black sword shot out to impale him, but he threw a wave of power, knocking the demon against Baehlon, who took the opportunity to conk him on the head with the hilt of his sword.

Dazed from the blow, the assassin staggered as he circled Rhoane in the small confines of the room. Raw Shanti slithered over his skin, and he hid his surprise. The assassin either had no ShantiMari of his own or was ill trained in the power.

"My friend," Rhoane started, "there is no escape from this room. Put down your sword and come with us."

The assassin's light eyes never flinched. He swung his sword, grinning when Rhoane missed a step and was almost cut by the gleaming black blade. Rhoane parried his thrust and then slammed the assassin against the wall. Blood seeped from a large gash on his shoulder. Fear finally sparked in the assassin's eyes, and he pushed past Rhoane, crashing through the window to the street below. Rhoane leapt after the man, landing gracefully on the empty street. A trail of blood led toward the docks, and he set off after the assassin.

At the street crossing, the trail split in opposite directions. He walked in a circle, trying to differentiate which to follow when Baehlon caught up with him. "You take that way, I will go this."

Rhoane strode down the street without waiting for a reply, keeping his eyes trained on the ground, his power stretching around him. Near the docks, the trail suddenly ended. A flash of light warned him a moment before the attack.

He swung around, facing the assassin. They held their swords out before them, Rhoane's godsteel gleaming in the sun, the assassin's blade fading into shadow. The man wore a long black tunic with a wide belt around his waist. Several knives and dagger hilts protruded from the belt. One spot was empty.

They circled each other, Rhoane intent on the man, all other sights and sounds peripheral. A sick grin spread across the assassin's face. He leapt, his sword held a little too high. Rhoane bent low, elbowing the assassin in the ribs. He grunted and spun around, slicing his blade toward Rhoane. He countered a thrust at the man, keeping enough distance between them to avoid the deadly blade.

By then, a crowd had gathered to watch the spectacle. The last thing he wanted was a public brawl, but there was nothing for it. He caught sight of Baehlon heading off the duke's guard, and Rhoane let the assassin stay on the attack, hoping to expend all of his energy before going on the defensive. Each time the assassin missed his mark, Rhoane, quick as a carlix, would knock him with a kick or punch. But instead of tiring, the assassin gained strength with every passing minute. He attacked without any finesse, his cuts random, his form incomplete. Antiquated, like Kaldaar's soldiers of old.

Rhoane smacked his open wound, and the assassin let out a laugh that startled the crowd. Sunlight caught his golden hair, giving him a shimmering radiance that did not extend to his lifeless eyes. Hayden had said the assassin was neither alive nor dead, and yet his wound bled. Demon that he was, the assassin could kill Rhoane as certainly as he'd dispatched the boy in the market.

Rhoane redoubled his focus, pulling his ShantiMari close in a protective shield. They crouched toward each other like animals about to pounce. Rhoane tightened his muscles in anticipation of a lunge when the assassin vaulted not toward him but away, running a few steps before jumping from a cart to a nearby rooftop. His golden locks bounced and then disappeared.

Rhoane clenched his jaw. "Damn it, man, how does he do that?"

"He is truly a shadow." Baehlon cursed in the direction the assassin fled.

Ebus ran up to them, panting. "I followed him as far as I could, but then he was gone. Not a trace—just disappeared."

"Thank you, Ebus." Rhoane handed him a gold coin. "If you see him again, send word to me immediately." To the guard, he said, "Tell only the duke what transpired here today. I do not want the princess or empress to know of it." When they moved off to clear the crowd, he wiped his forehead with his sleeve. "Blood and ashes, but it is hot today."

Baehlon was watching him closely. "Are you well, my friend?"

He flexed his hand, noting the new rune that appeared. "Well enough. We must return to the palace—something has happened. I must see to Taryn." He spoke to Ebus. "We will be leaving Paderau soon. Have you any desire to travel to Talaith?"

"The capital city? What thief doesn't dream of such a place?" "Am I to assume the prince has a job for me?"

"I do, but I must warn you, if your fingers are caught on anyone's purse strings, I will cut them off."

Ebus snort laughed, shaking his head. "If you can catch me. What is the job?"

"Come to the east gate of the palace tomorrow morning. All will be revealed to you then. Ebus, this should go without saying, but do not speak of this to anyone."

The little man's dark eyes glittered like polished obsidian. "As you wish, my liege." He bowed gracefully to Rhoane before disappearing into the thinning crowd.

"What the hell are you thinking, man?" Baehlon grumbled as they made their way back to the palace.

"He is the only one who can trace this Shadow Spawn. His eyes are sharper than mine are, and he is quick enough to follow the demon. We will put him in the duke's livery, calling him your page or something, and then we will let him travel with us to Talaith. If the Shadow Assassin tries anything while we are on the road, Ebus can alert us."

"And help himself to the empress's jewels while he's at it. I don't like this plan, my friend."

"I am afraid it is the best one we have right now." The runes on his wrist swirled and shifted. "We must hurry."

TARYN was sitting near the river, curled on a bench reading a book. Kaida asleep in her lap. Rhoane paused before approaching, waiting for the wave of relief to pass. For the surge of desire to lessen. The need to be near her was overwhelming.

She looked up, her eyes lighting when she saw him. That small gesture tugged at his gut. Made his bones feel like jelly. It was no good, this power she had over him. He carefully put his emotions to the back of his thoughts. If their enemies ever knew what she meant to him, they would exploit that knowledge with deadly precision, he was sure of it.

"Hey." She scooted aside to allow him room. "Want to join me?"

He sat next to her, petting Kaida absently. The grierbas pup yawned and stretched under his touch. "She is getting big."

"Carga says she should start on solid food soon." Taryn patted Kaida's pudgy belly. "I think she likes milk a little too much."

A boat made its way down river. Across the water was the dock where he'd fought the Shadow Assassin. Too far for an Aelan to see the fight but not for an Eleri.

"You left my rooms in quite a rush."

"I was overwhelmed all of a sudden."

He studied her profile, committing to memory every freckle on her straight nose and the way the sun glinted off her cheekbones. Her skin shimmered slightly with her first signs of Glamour. She was becoming more Eleri with every passing day. Soon her ears would end in delicate points. That is when he'd know she was full Eleri. That is when she would no longer be his alone.

"This is all very real, isn't it?" She met his even look. "Carga says I need to stop being a child and embrace who I must become."

"Carga speaks out of passion when a level head might be more kind."

"No, she's right. I've been acting as if this is just an elaborate game of dress-up. I've come to like all the tiaras and gowns and having maids who pamper me." She scratched

Kaida under her chin and then linked her fingers with Rhoane's. "Thinking like that will only get me—or worse, someone I love—killed." Her eyes clouded, like a sudden summer storm. "I failed today, and that can't happen again."

"You were taken by surprise by an assassin. He is trained to be untraceable."

She held up her book. "According to this, there is a master for every Shadow Assassin. We need to find out who is controlling him."

"That will not be easy. Black ShantiMari is difficult to trace. Those who practice it do not want to be known." He skimmed the pages. "Where did you get this?"

"Hayden found it in the library. It has information about all the great mages and sorcerers. There are only a handful who could raise a Shadow Soul. Before I search for them, I need to control my powers—all of them."

Rhoane didn't like where the conversation was headed. She was right; she did need training in her Dark powers. But he dreaded it all the same. Dark ShantiMari meant Valterys, and he couldn't let her near him until she was strong enough to defend herself. That could take more seasons than they had.

He placed her hand against his, palm to palm. Their runes glittered in the sunlight, and his desire increased. "Something happened, Taryn. I felt a shift in our bonds."

"It was my conversation with Carga, I think. We were talking, and then there was a new rune. I didn't know that could happen."

"They will shift and change as does your path, *Darennsai*." Rhoane said, less concerned with the bonds than he was the curve of her lips.

Her power enveloped their hands, melding them into one. Her Mari caressed his skin while her Shanti plucked at his nerves, sending sparks of heat through his body. He should separate their bonds, should pull away, but it was too good. He opened his mind to hers, craving more than she was willing to give.

He watched her face, saw the smile on her lips, heard the whispers of fear that lingered in her thoughts. The same whispers tormented him. She desperately wanted to be brave. For him.

Underneath all her doubts and desires was a single thought.

Rhoane.

He fought to control his emotions, but they spilled over, finding their way into her mind. His power melded with her ShantiMari—the trinity of power that marked her as the destroyer of his people.

When she opened her eyes, they were filled with raw desire. "What was that?" Her voice low, husky. Seductive.

"That is what happens when Eleri share their bodies."

She looked over her shoulder at the guards, who stood watching the surrounding area. A sweet blush spread across her cheeks. "That was incredible." Reluctantly, she pulled her hand away. Her ShantiMari subsided, leaving him empty and wanting.

"When you are full Eleri, it will be better."

She laughed, and he treasured the sound. "I can't imagine it being one tiny bit better than that."

Silver strands of her long hair floated around her suddenly serious face. "Rhoane, I can't live like this. I won't live like this. Not with guards following my every move. Always looking over my shoulder. I must learn to control my power. All three strains of it."

"You will. You have already grasped much of what I have been teaching you. In time, Faelara will send a tutor to instruct you in the ways of the Dark."

"I'm afraid that won't be enough. I need someone more

powerful than a dithering old priest of Ohlin. I need to train with either Zakael or Valterys." A look of apprehension rested in her eyes.

The air left him as surely as if she'd punched him in the sternum. "Have you forgotten about Brandt, or what Valterys did to Hayden? It is your power they covet, Taryn. It would be suicide for you to go anywhere near them."

"I haven't forgotten, and I won't forget how it felt to be inches from an assassin's knife."

"Let us not make any decisions just yet. You are too raw and untrained. If you went to Valterys or even your brother now, they could easily gain control over your powers."

A thousand more arguments came to his mind, but she pressed her lips to him, trembling slightly. If he could, he'd take her to the Narthvier and they'd never leave. There, he would give her a future of peace and laughter. As much as she resented being the Eirielle, he hated having to share her with the world. He let his mouth travel over hers, holding her hand in his.

They sat quietly in each other's company, neither speaking as they watched ships sail down river. Kaida toddled and pounced on unsuspecting insects. It was a serene moment, one that wouldn't last. He committed every detail to memory. It was enough. It had to be.

"Carga wants us to accompany her to the Narthvier for her purification." Taryn broke the silence with a sideways glance at him. "In three moonturns."

"Then we shall." He kissed her fingertips and chuckled at the antics of her grierbas. Kaida was stalking a lizard, keeping low to the ground, her puppy tail whipping behind her. "Look how she has started to hunt."

Taryn frowned at the animal. "Do you think Lliandra's right? That when Kaida gets bigger she'll attack the livestock?"

Kaida plunged a claw into the reptile, pinning it against

the pebbled shore. "It is in her nature. I cannot say for certain that she will not be a threat to us all."

"I've seen him before, you know," Taryn said almost as an aside.

Rhoane faced her, confusion clouding his thoughts. "Who?"

"The assassin. He's been tracking our movements. Remember in the mountains, before we met up with the others? Then on the road, I'd see a shadow in the corner of my eye. Always just beyond my vision. I'm sure it was him. He was probably the one who set the vorlocks on us."

Rhoane's chest tightened, and he clenched his hands into fists, air coming in shallow drags to his lungs. "Why are you telling me this only now? Why not sooner?"

"I didn't realize who or what it was before. This world is kind of topsy-turvy to me, and to be honest, I didn't know if I was really seeing something or if I was imagining it." Her eyes bore into his. "Let it go, Rhoane. We can't change the past, and I already have enough guilt to deal with. I just thought you should know. I promise, from now on, if anything strange happens, I'll tell you right away."

Rhoane pushed his hands down his thighs, settling his palms on his knees. His fingertips tapped out his annoyance. He was as much to blame for the day's attack as Taryn was. She'd tried to tell him about the shadow in the mountains, but he'd brushed off her concerns. *Never again.* Too many times, he'd questioned her concerns and each time her words had been proved true.

He hated that she was right about her Dark powers. Only her father or brother were strong enough to coax them from where they dwelled. Rhoane didn't doubt they wanted to use her, but he'd be damned if he'd let her go to them alone and vulnerable. If they controlled the Shadow Assassin, she had more to fear from them than their command of her power.

"Hey." Taryn's soft voice cut into his thoughts. Her warm hand squeezed his. "You okay?"

He blinked at the creeping darkness. "We should be getting dressed for dinner. Allow me to escort you to your rooms."

"I'd really like to get some more studying done tonight. I have a whole stack of books in my room to conquer."

"I am sure word has spread of the attack. It would be best if you arrived at dinner looking very much alive and unhurt."

"I thought you might say that." She melded her body to his, wrapping her hands in his hair, which hung in waves below his shoulders. "I like the new look."

He folded his arms around her slim waist. "You should always wear your sword."

She pulled back a few inches to withdraw two daggers, one from her blouse and another from her waistband. "I've got it covered."

"Are there more?"

"Maybe, maybe not. You'll just have to find out." She danced away from him. "But we'll be late for dinner if you keep distracting me."

He scooped up Kaida and took Taryn's hand. Together, they walked to the palace with her guards following close behind. When they reached the glass doors, Rhoane cast a last look across the river where he knew the Shadow Assassin waited. Next time they would not be surprised.

A whisper of heat singed his ear, taunting him as if to say, *We shall see.*

Chapter 42

MARISSA purred with contentment as she made her way to Zakael's study. He sat at the desk, a piece of parchment in one hand, a mug of ale in the other. A plate with scraps of bread and bits of cheese hung off the edge of the desk.

"I see you're eating well." She strutted into the room, her robe trailing behind her. "What business keeps you from my side?" When she leaned over to read the paper, he moved it away before grabbing her by the waist.

"I thought after last night you could use the rest." Zakael's grey eyes razed her half-naked body. "You've dressed for company."

He tasted of ale and something else, dark and rich, the source of which eluded her. His hands explored freely, touching her secret places, sending waves of desire through her. In a husky voice, she said, "I won't deny I was disappointed to wake alone in your bed." The robe fell to her waist with only a twitch of her shoulders. She glanced around, hoping Eiric would be seated at one of the couches. The room was empty save for them and Zakael's faithful dogs.

He kissed her breasts, squeezing them between his hands. "Alas, we'll have no entertainments today. We must discuss your sister before you return to Paderau."

Marissa stepped away from him, tugging the robe

over her shoulders. The air vibrated with her anger, and thunderclouds gathered outside the open window, sparking bolts of light. His mug of ale shimmied on the desk, and the discarded plate fell, shattering on the floor.

Zakael glanced out the window and then back to her. A scowl crossed his handsome features, and his Shanti wrapped around her with a viciousness she rarely experienced. Although she was nearly as powerful as Lliandra, Zakael and his Dark Shanti were more powerful still. Remembering how easily he'd blocked her power the previous night, she pulled her Mari under control. The skies calmed with her breathing.

"Put aside your petty jealousy and see the Eirielle for what she can be to us." His Dark Shanti slithered up her body; she shivered against her will. Zakael grabbed her roughly to him, his eyes a smoky haze. "Once we control her power, we control all of Aelinae."

A goblet of wine appeared, and she took it, drinking from the murky red depths. A slight metallic taste lingered on her tongue. "I think your wine's gone bad." She placed the goblet on the table, but Zakael pressed it into her hands, raising it to her lips.

"Drink more. The taste grows on you."

She tipped the goblet to her mouth and drank. The first sip slid over her tongue with the same metallic flavor, but the next was sweeter, mellower. Another followed by one more and the goblet was empty. She licked her lips, catching every drop.

"Better?" Zakael asked, taking the goblet from her.

"Much." He pressed his mouth to hers, invading her as if he wanted to reclaim what she'd drunk. When he lifted his head from her, his eyes were glossy with desire.

"I'm glad you enjoyed my Eiric."

Marissa's heart stilled. He didn't mean the wine. Couldn't have meant that. "Last night? Immensely."

"Mmm, last night, the wine. He makes an excellent breakfast sausage. Are you hungry?"

Marissa stepped back, her eyes tracking down to the spilled food. Zakael's beasts panted not far from their master's feet. A scrap of meat a hand's width from their muzzles. The sickening white of a bone stuck out from under a massive paw.

"You killed him?"

"He served his purpose. Now," he grabbed her by the shoulders and gave her a shake, "are you ready to stop fucking around and do what needs to be done? This isn't a game, Marissa. If we're to rule Aelinae, we need to be ruthless. We cannot show compassion to our enemies or each other."

She braced against the desk, noticing for the first time that his study was devoid of any artwork. No paintings hung on the walls; no decorative sculptures adorned the tabletops. The furniture was comfortable but not fashionable. A few tapestries hung from the ceiling to keep out drafts, but otherwise the room lacked any personal touches. Save for the wall of books on the far side of the room. The castle, like Zakael, was elegant in structure, but within was cold, efficient, and unrepentant.

She picked up her goblet, filled once more, and sniffed the vintage as she'd been taught to do. "This is a very fine reserve." Her tongue licked the rim before she took a healthy sip.

Zakael grasped the edge of her gown and pulled her to him. "As I was saying, I have a plan for the Eirielle."

MARISSA flew through the darkness, her thoughts a tempest. Their plan was dangerous. Dangerous and thrilling. His little game with Eiric taught her much more than he could've imagined, and she vowed to never let her feelings for Zakael jeopardize her own plans. Plans he could never know about. She'd given him her complete trust last night, but he'd given her something even more precious. Now she knew, even just a little compassion might kill her.

She buzzed with drunken excitement and careened to the left. After righting herself, she beat her wings to catch an updraft, concentrating on the spot of light before her. Paderau Palace was too well lit for that time of night. She cursed her luck that the duke would have a feast while she was gone.

She swept down from the sky, transforming before landing lightly in her hiding place. When she arrived at her rooms, the maids were in a panic.

"Your mother has come by three times this evening looking for you," one of them said.

"I'm here now. Just fix my hair and be quick about it. And please, no chattering. I need silence."

Within half a bell, Marissa was heading down the stairs to the Great Hall. When she saw Rhoane standing by himself, her stomach tightened and heat swept up her body.

"Your Highness." She curtseyed her greeting, "It's a lovely night. Would you accompany me in the garden?" She looked up at him, her eyes full of unspoken emotions, a smile on her lips.

"Marissa." He bowed at the waist. "We were beginning to wonder what had become of you. Your maids said you were ill all day. But it seems you have recovered."

"I thank you for your concern." She held out her arm. "Shall we?"

"Not tonight." His eyes were shrouded from her; she couldn't read his emotions. She sent a small thread of Mari to his mind but found his thoughts blocked.

Swallowing her hurt, she forced a dazzling smile. "Of

course, you must want to spend the evening with your betrothed." She scanned the area. "Where is she, anyway?"

Rhoane nodded to his left. "She is there, with Sabina and her sisters." His eyes lingered on Taryn with a look she longed to see reflected back at her.

"Why is it you are here and not with them? It seems to me that your beloved spends too much time with her friends." She put her hand on his sleeve. "But then, they are young. I'm sure you don't have much in common with them, what with their follies in the ocean and such. Children can be so tedious, don't you think?"

A chill invaded the space between them. "Good evening, Princess." He joined the others, taking Taryn's hand in his, kissing her fingers before wandering off to speak with a few nobles.

Marissa watched him for several minutes, seething with anger. Lightning sparks lit up the clear night sky.

"Be careful of your emotions, Princess. They are evident in your beautiful eyes."

"I'm certain I don't know what you mean, Myrddin." She cleared all thoughts of Rhoane from her mind. "I was simply taking in the night air." She inhaled a deep breath. "I do so love the warm evenings this time of year, don't you?"

He touched her raven curls. "They do make for wonderful flying weather. If you can avoid the lightning storms." His fingers skimmed down her arm, lingering against her breast.

Her body ignited at the familiar touch. "Is that so?"

"I know you've been to see him. What news have you?"

"I've been abed all day. I only just started to feel better, so please don't upset me." She put a hand to her forehead. "I'm still quite delicate, you see?"

"Indeed. And while you were recuperating, someone tried to kill your sister."

Marissa kept her features set, her face bland.

"Your absence has been noted. You should pay your respect to your mother and let her know you're feeling better."

"In a moment. The fresh air is doing me so much good." Nadra's tit, who would have the audacity to try to kill her sister? "Do you have a suspect for the attack?"

Myrddin's gaze traveled the length of her.

He thought she was behind it? He was a bigger idiot than she'd guessed.

"None. Whoever it was, they were clumsy in their attempt, and fortunately, your sister is unharmed." Myrddin nodded to the garden where Taryn sat with the other princesses. Celia was among them, speaking animatedly, hands flailing in the air to punctuate her words. "You might want to let her know you're relieved she lives."

"I will. Thank you for your sage advice."

"Don't linger long. The empress is waiting." He shuffled off, touching her mind with an offer to visit her rooms later.

Unlike most men, Myrddin enjoyed the fact she had other lovers, often asking her to tell him of her encounters. The only reason she shared her bed with him was for those few moments when she could slip into his mind. Those were the times she could pluck out information her mother withheld.

Marissa strolled to the ladies and bade Taryn well, apologizing for the illness that kept her away for much of the day. Taryn's concern for her health chafed Marissa. It was she who should've been worried about Taryn, but instead it was Taryn who worried about her. She inclined her head and graciously accepted her well wishes.

Celia followed Marissa when she left the others, muttering in a rush, "My lady, thank the stars you have returned. I had a terrible time explaining your absence. What do you think of the attack?"

"I don't know what to think of it. Were you there?"

"No, but the entire palace was secured for the remainder

of the day. I'm surprised the duke had dinner tonight."

"He's showing his enemies Taryn cannot be broken."

Celia told her the details of the day's events, trying Marissa's patience with her long-winded account. When she had everything she needed, she tucked her lady's hand in her own, silencing the gossip. "Stay with me a while."

"As you wish, Your Highness."

Marissa entered the garden room and curtseyed low to Lliandra, nodding to the women surrounding her. "Mother, I was told you've been concerned for my welfare. I thank you. As you can see, I've nearly recovered."

"Please, Marissa, join us. You too, Lady Celia. We were just discussing the upcoming Harvest. Tell me, what are your thoughts on the matter?"

Marissa sipped her wine with an inward groan. She didn't give a fig about Harvest or the ridiculous festival they had each year, but it was one of her sisters' favorites. Each season Lliandra tried to outdo the previous festival with booths and games and nonsense that irritated the crown princess. She did, however, find it curious her mother didn't mention the assassin.

Much later, after several glasses of wine and not enough food, Marissa slouched against a wall in Lliandra's rooms, being berated for her foolhardy trip to the West. Despite the fact she was old enough to make decisions for herself, Lliandra demanded she be alerted if Marissa left the palace, especially if she were going to see Zakael. That her trip coincided with an attempt on Taryn's life cast doubt on the crown princess, something Lliandra had spent much of the day subverting.

When it looked like Lliandra's rant wouldn't abate for some time, Marissa slumped into a chair. "Please, I'm exhausted. You and those crones rattled on for bells about nonsense. My head hurts, and I need sleep. Can't we continue this in the morning?"

Lliandra grabbed a handful of Marissa's hair, pulling her head back. "We will discuss it now. Need I remind you that I am still the empress and you do as I command?" She released her, but not before giving another tug. "What happened at Gaarendahl? What did you discuss?"

Marissa's Mari flowed through her, easing the pain, giving her clarity to answer. Not for the first time, she imagined the thrill of killing her mother and taking the throne for herself. But it wasn't time yet; she had to be patient.

She told Lliandra the lies she wanted to hear: Valterys was preparing an army of trolls and men from the West. He believed Lliandra wanted to use the Eirielle against him to seize his throne. It was the same each time they spoke. Valterys might very well be gathering an army, but Marissa didn't care about war. Her plans only involved Taryn.

Lliandra tapped her fingers on the table. "You told Zakael I have no wish for the Obsidian Throne?" Marissa nodded. "What is that fool thinking? He is playing a dangerous game, one I don't have time for. What more, Marissa? Did you discuss our plan for Taryn?"

For once, Marissa could tell her mother the truth. "We did. Zakael is most eager to have his sister visit Gaarendahl. He agrees that we need to control her Dark Shanti." Sparks of her Mari played across her fingertips.

"Stop that. You know it upsets me to see you abusing your power," Lliandra scolded. "Faelara tells me Taryn is progressing with her Light skills and Rhoane is pleased with her Eleri abilities. Are you certain Zakael will work with us to constrain the girl? If we are to destroy Valterys, we must have his complicity in this."

"You have his full cooperation, Mother."

"Excellent. Now go and bathe. You stink of Zakael, and it offends me."

"Do you miss it?" Marissa said before she had time to

think of the consequences. "The feel of his Dark Shanti wrapped around your body like the finest velvet? The silky sweetness of his power pulling you under until you feel like you can't breathe and all you want to do is linger in the Dark until there is no more Light? Tell me, Mother, do you regret whoring me out to him?"

Lliandra's face contorted with anger for a split second before she covered it with a mask of calm. "You go too far, daughter." She stared into Marissa's eyes. "If I'm not mistaken, you took up the charge without much provocation."

Marissa met her mother's glare. "I won't deny I enjoy it. He is young and virile, like me."

Lliandra's hand cracked across her face and the blow knocked her back. Marissa lashed out at her mother with a force contained for far too long. The empress slammed against the wall, her arms and legs held with bonds of Mari.

She moved close to her mother's face. "Never strike me again. Lest you forget, I am the crown princess and heir to the Light Throne. All you hope to accomplish is but a wish away from me." She swept from the room, releasing her power on her way out.

When she reached her rooms she stood at the open window, sucking at fresh air, her palms pressed against the sill. Her body ached from Zakael's abuse, and she wanted nothing more than to soak in a hot tub until the morning light.

Her maids scrambled to run a bath and arrange for her comfort while she calmed her racing mind. Things were moving too fast and yet not quickly enough. It would be too risky to kill Lliandra now, and yet she was tired of having to answer to her mother's shortsighted whims. Lliandra thought only of her petty revenge on Valterys. She wanted control of both thrones but was willing to let Zakael be a puppet overlord if it meant Valterys was out of the picture.

Marissa laughed at the folly. Lliandra never dreamed very big. Her limited vision was only the first step in Zakael's plan, one that was necessary if Marissa were to attain her own goals.

Lady Celia rushed into the room, her hair unbound, her dress askew. "My lady." She lowered herself near to the floor.

"What are you doing here?" The girl's arrival was impertinent. Marissa was far too sore to entertain any thoughts of a dalliance with Celia. She needed to rest.

When Celia looked up, it was with wild-eyed confusion. The blacks of her pupils filled her eye, leaving only a sliver of blue around the edges. "You called for me."

Marissa started to deny the claim but stopped. Something was not right about the girl. "Of course. I was just about to bathe. Join me." Watching Celia's erratic movements, the ping of dread she often had when things were not as they ought to be plucked at her nerves. There was too much at stake for anything to alter her course.

"Harvest." Celia looked up from her undressing, calm clarity in her eyes. "It must be done at Harvest."

Marissa took Celia's hands in her own, soothing her. "What is troubling you? Please, unburden yourself to me."

Celia shook her head with an imbecilic giggle. "It's Herbret. He's in a fit because of Sabina." She shrugged out of her gown and stood naked. Her skin glowed with the faintest dusting of glitter, like black stars on a field of snow, and then it was gone.

"Herbret? I already told him there is nothing to be done. Mother's mind is made up."

"No. He must have Sabina first. Must be unbroken."

Tired of the charade, Marissa went to the bathing room where her maids helped her with her gown. Once rid of the garment, she slipped into the steaming water, wincing when it invaded her tender regions. She was exhausted. In the morning, she'd worry about what that rutting pig Herbret was doing. She closed her eyes and laid her head on the cool porcelain of the tub. The water sloshed with Celia's entry, spilling onto the floor.

The heat did Marissa's aching muscles good. Knots of tension worked themselves out, and when Celia moved behind her to massage her neck, she relaxed into the girl's nimble touch. Celia's deep breathing and the feel of her breasts against Marissa's back sent warm tingles through her body. The girl's Mari encircled her, delightfully strong and tinged with a darkness Marissa craved. It burned through her, easing her anxiety, quieting her concerns.

When Celia's hands slid over Marissa's breasts to rest between her legs, a blackness overtook her. Sweet, lulling, seductive. She opened herself to the sensations, lost to the pleasure Celia brought.

Chapter 43

TARRO dressed Taryn in a gown of deep blue that matched her eyes. The luxurious silk bodice hugged her cleavage with a scandalous lack of fabric and draped to the floor in a shimmering pool. She fidgeted before the mirror, anxious to be done with dinner and returned to her rooms. A light knock at the door stilled her movements. Kaida, roused from her nap by the sound, yipped at the intruder.

Eliahnna swept in wearing a sheath of jade that made her strawberries and cream skin look ethereal. With her grace and lightness, Eliahnna's father had to have been a Faerie. Taryn tucked away the thought and greeted her sister.

She sat on the sofa, stroking Kaida's soft fur as they chatted about the day's events until Tarro finished his preparations and excused himself. When they were alone, Taryn retrieved the small packet from her bureau and sat beside her sister. Taryn turned the parcel over again and again, debating her decision. At length, she handed the bundle to Eliahnna.

"This is a gift from Eoghan. He asked me to give it to you once we were away from the Narthvier." Taryn held Eliahnna's hands in her own and met her sister's gaze. "Normally, I would've cautioned you against this, but after what happened yesterday, I've realized life is too precious to waste doing what others think is best for you."

Her sister opened the packet and held up a snippet of wood hanging from a leather cord. Eleri script was meticulously carved into the sanded piece. "Can you read it?"

"I'm afraid not. And please don't ask me to have Rhoane translate it. If he or his father knew I gave this to you, they'd eat me for breakfast."

Eliahnna placed the pendant around her neck and, with a bit of Mari, hid it beneath her gown. "Thank you." She kissed her sister's cheek, lingering there for a moment. "I'm ever so glad you've returned to us and that you're unharmed. But please," Eliahnna leaned back, her eyes reflecting the shimmer of jade from her dress, "do be more careful. Vorlocks and assassins? I've just found you. I couldn't bear to lose you."

"I love you, too." Taryn choked back more than a few tears.

After Eliahnna left, Taryn called out, "You can come out now, Tarro."

The tailor entered her room looking chagrined. "I didn't mean to eavesdrop. I left my basket of supplies." He retrieved the bundle from the floor and bowed low to her. "I will speak of this to no one."

"I would appreciate that. If they continue this folly, it will come out sooner or later, but I would like to stall that day as long as possible." She gave him a wan smile, "Love is a tricky business, is it not?"

A lovely stain spread across his cheeks. "Indeed it is, my lady."

"Do you have a special someone in your life? A handsome rogue, perhaps?"

The stain darkened to a furious red. "His name is Armando. He is a whore in Talaith, gods help me, but I love him."

A whore? She couldn't imagine the logistics of loving someone in that profession. It would certainly have its drawbacks, but the benefits might be worth it. "Does he return this affection?"

"He does. We live in a comfortable house in the Arlo district. Seven seasons we've been together."

Taryn was impressed. "You must be a remarkable couple. I would love to meet him someday." At Tarro's look of shock, she hastily added, "Not in a professional manner, just as friends."

"I would like that."

At dinner, Taryn feigned interest during much of the conversation. The nobles still chattered about the attack, even a day later, each having their own idea of who was behind it and why they would target Taryn on a busy summer morning at the market.

Herbret hovered nearby, asking after her comfort, bringing her wine if her glass was empty. His false concern for her well-being intrigued her. Since their return to Paderau, his cavalier attitude had been replaced with one of modest servitude. At every opportunity, he tripped over himself to get in Taryn's good graces.

The charade droned on until dessert when Taryn excused herself and joined her sisters in the garden. They sat beneath clear skies with a gentle breeze cooling the late summer night.

The princesses kept the conversation light, not wanting to dwell on the attack, instead they gossiped about courtiers and boys—their two favorite subjects. Marissa and Celia joined them, reclining on a sofa together. Several times throughout the evening, Celia would stop mid-sentence and glance off, never returning to what she was saying. When they pulled her attention back to the conversation, Celia would giggle and give a nonsensical excuse for her behavior. Too much wine, not enough dinner. Too many sweets, not enough sleep.

Taryn exchanged a look with Sabina that said, *Something*

is not right with that girl.

"Sabina!" Celia said, a giggle beneath her tone. "Congratulations on your betrothal to Lord Valen. I couldn't be happier for you. Truly."

"We're not betrothed. We've only just had permission to court. It might be several seasons before we take that step." Sabina told the group.

"Oh, poo. We all know you'll marry in the end, why not just skip to the fun part now, while you're still young and beautiful?"

Eliahnna looked sharply at Celia. "I doubt Sabina will ever be anything but beautiful. Why are you suddenly so in favor of the match? I thought just last wintertide you asked my mother if your father could petition Duke Anje for Hayden's favor."

A collective gasp made the round of ladies who reclined on the sofas, sipping wine and eating delicate pastries.

"Eliahnna," Marissa said, her voice low, "this is most unsettling. I thought gossip beneath you."

Taryn's sisters glared at each other, a rare display of emotion from her younger sibling. But Celia ignored them both.

"Surely you don't think I'm in love with the marquis? I fancied him for a spell, as every girl at court is bound to do, but I've found someone else." She giggled again and fanned her face. "I'm in love."

All eyes stared at Celia. Romance was the number one court intrigue, and none of the ladies had any knowledge of a lover.

"With whom?"

"Why haven't I been told of this?"

"When can we meet this suitor of yours?"

It was a volley of questions lobbed at the poor girl.

Celia did a little shimmy with her shoulders and giggled

some more. Taryn and Sabina shared another look. Something was definitely not right.

Marissa stood to leave, but Celia stayed seated. "Oh, I don't know. Harvest, perhaps. There are so many plans to be made. You'll be the first to know, I promise you," Celia said to no one in particular, her gaze off in the distance.

Marissa yanked Celia's arm until the girl stood, wobbling against the princess. "Ladies, I'm afraid Celia's caught whatever malady I suffered from yesterday. If you'll excuse me, I should get her to her room."

They stumbled through the garden, Marissa's hissed recriminations echoing above the flowers.

"Too much wine," one woman said.

"Far too much," another concurred.

The conversation lulled for several minutes until Sabina asked, "Do you think Hayden wants to get married?" Her tone suggested she wasn't sure if she liked the idea or not.

"If you're just going to talk about boys, I'm going to bed." Tessa stretched out her lithe body and yawned. "Boys are stupid."

"I'll go with you." Taryn took her little sister's hand in her own. "And we'll talk about something other than boys, okay?"

They discussed toads and poisons and swords on the way to their rooms. Tessa was fascinated with anything creepy-crawly or deadly. Almost as much as she was with weaponry. Having to endure the older princess's obsession with courtship was akin to torture for the young girl.

When they reached Tessa's rooms, Taryn knelt in front of her sister. "Would you like to have a sleepover?"

"A what?"

"You get your jammies and sleep in my room tonight. We'll stay up late talking about whatever you want. And maybe, if you're very good and you promise not to tell anyone, we can have a sword fight."

Tessa's entire face blossomed. Despite Taryn's begging, Lliandra had yet to let the other girls train with her. Taryn knew Tessa had a wooden sword hidden in her belongings and told her to grab it, along with anything else she might need overnight. They made a quick trip to the kitchen gardens with Kaida, then to the kitchen itself, making sure no one saw them, before returning to Taryn's rooms with an armful of pilfered food from the pantry.

They ate, talked, and laughed for much of the night. Taryn had never spent much time with someone Tessa's age, but the girl was acutely aware of what happened around her. More so than anyone gave her credit for. Being the fourth in line to the throne and too young for marriage prospects, most courtiers discounted her, but the girl had potential. Tessa was a fighter who had learned how to navigate the murky waters of court life without a safety net and made an island for herself where she could anchor when storms got rough.

Kaida slept with them in Taryn's giant bed, curled into Tessa's midsection, her paws over her muzzle. Taryn woke early and watched the two of them sleep. Their chests rose with each breath in and snuffle out. Tessa's clear skin and fair curls shone with streaks of sunlight that filtered through the windows, and Taryn's heart hiccuped with the amount of love she had for her sister. She ran her fingers through Kaida's impossibly soft fur. Her failure in the market could never happen again. If that had been Tessa or Eliahnna instead of Gris... She squeezed her eyes shut against the thought. Tears fought for release, and Taryn leaned close to Tessa, kissing her forehead.

"I promise I'll do everything I can to keep you safe."

When she looked down, Kaida watched her with a cognizance not expected of a puppy.

"What are you looking at, furball?" Taryn scratched

beneath Kaida's chin. "I love you, too, if that's what you're worried about."

Kaida stretched and yawned, her milky sweet puppy breath filling the space.

"Is it fair that I took you from your home? Would you have rather stayed there to fend for yourself?" Kaida licked Taryn's fingertips and then groomed her fur. "I'll take that as a sign that you like me, but remember, no eating the palace cats. Or anyone's dog. If you get hungry, eat the rats. Not the horses. Or the people."

"Well, some people." Tessa's sleepy voice cut through the morning air. "There are a few I can think of, but they might not taste all that good."

"That's not very nice." Taryn tickled her sister until they were both laughing so hard their sides hurt.

Once dressed, Taryn took them to the kitchens for breakfast. Carga gave Taryn a curious look but said nothing about her guest. At the sight of Kaida, the Eleri princess lost a touch of her usual reserve and held the bundle of fur with something close to glee.

After they ate, Taryn led them to the training ring where she set up a pen for Kaida and gave Tessa one of the wooden swords to practice with. Tessa's eyes grew large, questioning, but Taryn assured her it would be fine.

Her youngest sister wore one of her shifts, which limited her range of motion considerably, but the girl had spirit and moved through the lesson with admirable speed and dexterity. Half a bell into their training Baehlon arrived, grumping about the early hour and the brightness of the sun. When he saw Kaida, he frowned, but when he saw Tessa he outright bellowed.

"Does your mother know she's here?"

Taryn signaled for him to keep his voice down. "I'll deal with her when I have to. Get in here and help or go back to bed."

He chose to stay, much to Taryn's astonishment, and relief. Lliandra would be pissed when she found out, but then, when wasn't she upset with Taryn for one thing or another?

For the remainder of their stay, Taryn's secret didn't reach the empress. Or if it did, the empress chose to ignore it. Each morning, Tessa would join Taryn in the training ring, and in the afternoon, she would run alongside the servants and nobles in their impromptu football games. Sabina chose to sit beneath a skirm tree and watch the game rather than playing. Eliahnna joined them on one occasion, and even Marissa gave the game a go, begging off after only a few minutes.

The games were more of a time killer than anything, and they often played with more than the requisite number of players on the field. Taryn had Tarro make Tessa a pair of shorts and a loose blouse for her to wear for their training, but the girl had taken to wearing the garments around the palace at all times, except for dinner. Even Tessa knew not to court the wrath of their mother that much.

The evening before they were to leave Paderau, Duke Anje held a grand feast. They dined outdoors where tables had been set up on their playing field. Candles drifted overhead, suspended on tufts of ShantiMari. Servants brought them dishes on silver platters, and they ate until their waistbands expanded a little too much.

After the meal, a band set up in the garden, and they all danced between rose bushes and ornamental hedges. Taryn's pendant hummed along to a somber song as she waltzed with Rhoane. The lyrics teased her memory, but she couldn't quite grasp them.

"Do you know the words to this tune?" she asked.

Rhoane thought for a moment, keeping step with the music. "I do not believe there are lyrics, only melody."

"I could swear there are words."

Duke Anje tapped Rhoane on the shoulder. "Mind if I cut in?"

Rhoane released Taryn into Anje's waiting hand and stood to the side where she knew he would watch over her. Since the assassin's attack, Rhoane made certain Taryn was guarded at all times. Each morning she would wake to find at least one soldier positioned outside her rooms. Whoever had drawn the short straw had her sympathy. Certainly, no one was going to volunteer for that job.

"Do you know the lyrics to this song?" Taryn asked Anje, pulling her mind back to the moment.

"Not that I can recall. It's rather a sad tune, don't you think?" He hummed a bit, shaking his head.

"It's a song of the Dark," Taryn said, uncertain how she knew. "Hey, you can teach me to use my Dark ShantiMari. Why didn't I think of that earlier?"

"Ah, my sweet lass, I've lived too long in the Light. ShantiMari needs to be stretched and let free to gallop, like a fine horse. I'm afraid I've let my skills fade. Hayden though," he cast a quick glance at Lliandra, "will know a trick or two. Nothing as powerful as your brother, he could get you started. It's just a matter of unlocking the secrets."

Taryn groaned. "I really hate secrets. And riddles. Why can't this be easy?"

Anje's good-natured laugh jiggled his midsection, tickling her. "If it was simple, then what's the point?"

The music changed to a reel, and he moved her away from the other dancers to a part of the garden where jasmine trailed over arches, mingling with wisteria to perfume the air. Two guards strolled not far behind.

"When you get to Talaith, there are some arrangements I'd like you to make."

"Like what?" Taryn asked, curious what her uncle was

planning.

"Setting up your household for one. Seek out Master Beary, he'll help you with servants and the like. Take Hayden with you. I've informed him of everything you'll need."

"But why? I didn't have any of that before."

"Do you enjoy being a ward of your mother?" Taryn didn't need to answer. He knew she didn't. "This will give you autonomy. Yes, you'll be living in your mother's palace, but you'll have your own maids, your own servants, all loyal to *you*." Anje placed a pouch in her hands. "I understand you're having difficulties with one of your maids in Talaith. A little coin goes a long way with some folks."

Taryn shouldn't have been surprised he knew, but she was. "She doesn't like me. It's no big deal."

"It is a big deal, as you say, if she's in the pocket of your sister. You can either bid higher for her loyalty or fire her and find someone you can trust."

"Like that'll be easy. It's not as if I have a truth meter I can just whip out and see who's loyal and who isn't."

Anje shook his head. "You say the most curious things, my favorite niece."

"Favorite, eh? My sisters will be so jealous."

"You are my only niece by blood, which is why it is so important to me that you find servants at the Crystal Palace who you can trust with your life. Not so much maids as bodyguards. That giant of a knight of yours helped me choose six of my best soldiers to accompany you to Talaith. They'll be a part of your personal guard. Trust them to find a few more. You'll not get much help from your mother. Gods bless her, but she thinks only of her crown."

"I'm not sure I want her choosing my personal guards *or* my maids. I wish you were coming with us to Talaith."

"I have work to occupy my time here, but I'll see you before too long."

"Am I interrupting anything?" Lliandra strolled through the narrow space between the hedges, her jewels catching the candlelight, casting prisms over them. She noticed the pouch in Taryn's hand and cast a petulant look at Anje. "Spoiling Taryn won't bring her back, you know."

Anje's face paled, his cheeks turned crimson. "It's my right to give my niece whatever I like. Be it coin or advice. Neither of which she gets from her mother." He gave a curt bow and strode away, his footfalls heavy on the pebbled path.

Taryn glared at her mother. "That was cold."

"Perhaps. I don't like the influence he has over you. Anje is cousin to Valterys, never forget that." Lliandra smoothed back an errant curl off Taryn's forehead. "You do resemble her, you know." Taryn didn't need Lliandra to tell her she meant Gwyneira. Taryn had heard it often enough from the courtiers and saw it reflected back at her in the many portraits hanging throughout the palace.

"He misses her."

"He needs to find a new wife. Someone young enough to give him heirs. But I didn't come here to talk about Anje or my sister. I wanted to thank you for what you're doing for Tessa. She's positively in awe of you."

"You don't mind? I know I should've asked your permission first, but she seemed so happy that I didn't want to spoil it."

"Yes, you should have asked, but what's done is done. I'm glad that you've taken her under your wing, so to speak. She needs someone to look up to."

"Tessa's great. Eliahnna, too. You should spend more time with them, or at the very least let them have some space to run free. Cooping them up in the palace can't be any fun. Give them a chance to explore the world, get to know people besides courtiers and servants."

"So, you would tell me how to parent?" A dangerous

light shone from the depths of her dusky blue eyes. "Would you also tell me how to run my kingdom?"

Lliandra's stare could cut ice with precision and Taryn chose her words with care, her voice light and carefree. "Hell to the no. Kids, I understand, having been one myself not long ago, but politics? I'll leave that to the experts, like you."

She pressed her lips against Lliandra's cheek, feeling the aridness of the woman's skin, breathing in the scent of jasmine and death. Perfumed decay. Taryn stepped back to look her mother full in the face. Her Mari was intact, giving the illusion of robust health and beauty.

"Are you well, Mother?"

"Of course, why do you ask?" Lliandra tossed a long curl over her shoulder and sniffed the night air. "I don't enjoy being so far from the coast at this time of year, but I feel fine."

"And you look amazing."

"Flattery? And you said you don't have a head for politics. Should I hide the scepter now or wait until there's a coup?"

"You don't have to hide it from me. I was serious. I have no desire to take your throne. Should anything happen to Marissa, Eliahnna is the next in line, not me. Make a declaration, put it in writing, I don't care, but believe this with all your heart."

A chill surrounded them suddenly. Dark clouds moved overhead, and the air itself vibrated. "Would you aspire to the Obsidian Throne, then? Has Valterys wormed his way into your heart?"

"What? No!" Taryn glanced at the threatening clouds and back to her mother. "Is that you? You can control the weather?"

Lliandra sniffed and snapped a wave at the air. The clouds dispersed, moving over the river to the northeast. "Of course. It is my right as the Lady of Light. So you aren't in league with Valterys? You have no wish to sit either throne? Or the

Weirren?"

"None at all. I wasn't bred to be a queen or an empress. My purpose is balance. For all of Aelinae."

Mollified for the moment, Lliandra patted Taryn's hands. "Good. We shouldn't be enemies."

Taryn watched her mother's retreat with a heaviness in her heart. For Lliandra, there were enemies and allies. No middle ground. At least for the time being Taryn was considered an ally, but how long would that last? Surely, there would come a time when Taryn stepped over an invisible line and offended not just Lliandra but her father and who knew whom else?

There was much more to being the Eirielle than learning to control her powers. As the last vestiges of Lliandra's Mari drifted behind the hedge, Taryn knew exactly where to begin her search—with the Eiriellean Prophecies.

The library in Talaith was the largest in all the seven kingdoms. Somewhere in the scrolls, journals, and scraps of diaries she'd find clues to her path. She held her hand to the moonlight and examined the runes circling her wrist. If there was one thing she knew how to do, it was research.

She hurried to her rooms and retrieved her journal. Curled up in her favorite chair by the window with Kaida snuggled in her lap, Taryn set quill to paper and scratched out notes, making two columns: one for friends, one for enemies. Thankfully, the *Friends* column was longer than that for her enemies, but even that list was far too long to bring her any comfort.

It wasn't until she'd filled six pages that she realized with a shock she'd written everything in English. Seeing the familiar words and phrases brought a searing pain of homesickness that, instead of trying to shove deep into the recesses of her mind like she always had, she let wash over her. Reveling in the simple joys she'd once shared with Brandt, reminiscing about the life they'd lived, the adventures they had. Smells from her childhood floated to her—a seaside cottage in California, the sharp tang of olives from tapas in Spain, and the earthy loam of Scotland where they'd stayed for several years. Another scent joined the others, that of cigar tobacco.

Taryn jerked up and stared into the ghostly image of her grandfather. "You were teaching me all along, weren't you? Guiding me, really. Toward all of this. You clever, clever man."

Brandt chuckled and tapped his pipe against his bottom lip. "I knew you'd sort it out sooner or later." Kaida perked her ears at his voice, her eyes fixed on the place where Brant hovered. "Who's your friend?"

"You don't know?"

"Contrary to popular belief, we don't spend our days following your antics. We're busy up there. Besides, Nadra and Ohlin block most of what's happening down here. They have the misbegotten belief that you are better off left alone."

"Then how did you know to come here tonight?"

"I didn't. Nadra said it was time for a visit, and here I am."

His form took on the transparency she'd come to dread. "Do you know what I'm supposed to do next?"

He shook his head, already little more than mist. "But you're on the right track, I'd say." A wispy finger pointed to the journal.

"Kaida," Taryn called out to him. "Her name is Kaida," she said to the now empty room.

A soft chuckle drifted on the breeze, whispering, "Be well, little dragon."

Chapter 44

THE day they were to leave Paderau, Taryn met Carga in the kitchen for their usual meal. Afterward, they walked the short distance to where Gris had been buried a few days earlier. A simple plaque marked the grave, citing his name and date of death.

Taryn knelt over the grave and pushed her fingers into the soil as if to touch the lad one last time. To thank him for his bravery. His sacrifice. When she rose, words scrawled along the plaque. *In death may he find the peace that eluded him in life. He will forever hold a place in our hearts. May there be no Light without Dark, and no darkness without light.*

Carga took her hand as they made their way back to the palace. Neither spoke of what Taryn had done, but the Eleri princess approved. The murmuring of Carga's people sighed in her mind.

The carriages waited in the courtyard when they returned and Taryn rushed through the palace giving last minute gifts to the staff and saying her goodbyes. In her search for Ashanni, she dodged the chaotic loading of trunks and boxes. Lorilee waited by a cart, bouncing on the balls of her feet in anticipation of the trip ahead.

Anje had given her maids the choice to serve Taryn in Talaith. Mayla would stay at Paderau, because she had a "fella," as Lorilee put it, and Lorilee would permanently be a part of Taryn's staff. It was her first step in setting up her household, and she held herself a bit taller with the knowledge, her shoulders back a fraction more.

She said her farewells, with Taryn giving the duke an extended hug, thanking him for Lorilee and everything he'd done. He'd become like a second father to her, and it was with profound sadness she rode away from the palace. Despite his assurances they would see each other soon, there would be times in the interim she would need his guidance, crave his gentle reassurance she was on the right path. To know everything would work out in the end. She desperately needed to believe it would.

The caravan traveled from the palace through the streets, passing the market square where only days earlier the Shadow Assassin had attacked Taryn. Tension laced their movements, and the very air snapped with unspent ShantiMari. By the end of the first day, everyone's nerves were frayed, and dinner that night was a quiet affair. Even the soldiers, who normally caroused and sang, were subdued.

It was impossible to escape—the responsibility and the guilt. It sat heavy around Taryn's shoulders like a worn yoke cracked and rusted with age. Unable to endure the solemnity another minute, Taryn excused herself. As she entered her tent, a small man scurried to hide beneath her cot. Taryn set Kaida down on Sabina's bed and drew her sword from its scabbard.

She dipped it low enough he could see she was armed. "Come out from under there. Don't make any sudden movements and you won't get hurt."

He inched his way to the side of the canvas, his shoes scrabbling against the ground. Taryn sent a thread of ShantiMari toward him, entangling his legs. When he didn't move from under the bed, Taryn snapped a bit of heat at him.

She heard several curses followed by a plea. "I'm coming out. Don't harm me." He pulled himself from under her cot and stood, brushing the dirt from his pants.

At least a foot shorter than she and dressed in the livery of Duke Anje, he was no servant Taryn recognized. His greasy hair hung in dark clumps to his shoulders, framing a face with eyes that looked like little bits of coal stuck too close together.

She held Ohlin's sword at his chest. "Who are you and why are you in my tent?" Kaida tumbled from Sabina's bed to sit beside Taryn, a low growl coming from her throat.

The little man put up his hands in surrender, amusement clear in his voice. "Please, Your Highness, I was just making sure everything was arranged for your comfort."

"You're lying."

"Normally I would say yes, but in this case I'm not."

"If you're telling the truth, then touch my sword and swear." She flicked the sword closer to his face.

His eyes grew large and sweat ran down his cheeks. The mirth disappeared from his voice. "Your Highness, none but you can touch the blade."

"If you are true of heart, you may touch it with my permission."

He watched her closely, his nose twitching erratically like a rat on the scent of his favorite cheese. "Now who's lying? I'll do you one better. Ask Prince Rhoane. He'll vouch for Ebus."

"Prince Rhoane sent you?" Silently, she called Rhoane to join them.

Within moments, she heard his footfalls coming closer. He entered her tent, swearing at the intruder. "Ebus, you fool."

Taryn barely suppressed her shock. "You know this man?" Ebus moved an inch to his left, and she put the sword back to his chest. "Stay." He froze, a look of irritation in his eyes.

"Unfortunately, yes. Taryn, this is Ebus. He is working for me, undercover, to help flush out the Shadow Assassin."

"Why didn't you tell me?" A bitter hurt stung her words.

"He is supposed to be *invisible*. You were never meant to know he was anywhere near you." Rhoane looked pointedly at Ebus.

"You said she'd be dining with the others. She surprised me."

"Why is he in my tent?"

Kaida growled and snapped at the man. A foot high ball of fur couldn't protect her as well as the steel of her blade, but she loved that Kaida thought she could.

"He was checking to make certain your quarters were secure before you retired for the night. I sent him here," Rhoane explained.

Taryn lowered the sword, and Ebus took a deep breath. "It's about time." At Rhoane's scowl, he said without much enthusiasm, "Thank you, Your Highness. If I may?" He gestured to the doorway.

"Not yet. If you are going to be my spy, there are a few things we need to get clear. You are to never, ever enter my private sleeping quarters again without my consent." She reached out to touch his forehead, and he flinched. "Come here." She put a fingertip to his temple, feeling the thrum of Shanti, but it was off. Like Sabina's, twisted somehow. "You can speak to me in your thoughts." She allowed a slight opening in her mind for him. "Act as if we've never met."

"As you wish, Great Lady," Ebus said. His little pointed nose twitched, and he added, "If you'd like a little privacy, I could duck out and make certain no one entered."

"Leave, Ebus." When the man left, Rhoane apologized for the intrusion.

She threw her sword on her cot. "Why keep it from me?"

"I did not want you to worry. Ebus is able to see this assassin when others cannot, and right now, that puts us at an advantage."

"As long as he doesn't try to sneak in here without telling me, I guess it's okay." She yawned and sat on the edge of her bed. "I'm exhausted."

Rhoane sat next to her, rubbing her back. "Try to get some sleep. Tomorrow we will be one day closer to the Crystal Palace." He kissed her forehead and then scooped up Kaida, setting the pup in Taryn's lap. "I do not mind saying, I envy that beast." After another light kiss for her and a pat for Kaida, he left the tent with a promise to send in Sabina.

The grierbas pup snuggled next to her, warming her, but instead of her anxiety decreasing, it amped up. Seven more days on the road until they reached Talaith meant seven sleepless nights filled with stress and apprehension. Even with Ebus around, the assassin could find his way in if he wanted. Darkness was his cloak.

She sat up, heart pumping against her chest. The assassin had pulled shadows over himself the same way Valterys had at Ravenwood. That's how he was able to disappear seemingly without a trace. She paced her room, testing her memory to recall exactly how Valterys had done it. She'd been in another room, fevered and delirious; if she'd been near him, maybe she could recreate the effect, but without knowing exactly how he'd used his Dark Shanti it would be dangerous to try.

Sabina flung the tent flap aside and strode into the room. "If I never have to travel in a carriage again, it will be too soon. You have no idea how uncomfortable it is."

"You could always ride with me. I'm sure there's a spare horse to be found."

Sabina scrunched her nose. "Not until I'm better at riding. The few times Hayden's tried to teach me haven't ended well." She rubbed her backside. "I'll just take more pillows for tomorrow." Sabina flopped on Taryn's cot, a hand over her eyes. "Gods, but I'm exhausted." She propped herself on her elbow, and a frown made delicate creases in her burnished skin. "Do you know, I saw Celia just now. That fool girl is going swimming. In the lake. At night. Gah!"

"Well, the girl is odd." Taryn agreed, mind racing. Why the hell would Celia sneak off at night?

Sabina lay down again, covering her eyes once more, and mumbled about the idiocy of some people. Despite her prowess in the ocean, Sabina had a mortal fear of swimming in a standing body of water.

Taryn placed Kaida on Sabina's abdomen. "Look after her." She grabbed her sword and looked back at her friend, cutting Sabina off before she was able to respond. "I'll be back soon, but please stay here. And don't tell anyone I've gone."

And then she was out of the tent and making her way through the camp with as much speed and care as she could afford. Light from the many fires gave an ethereal glow to the area, making the surrounding woods look even more ominous. Her ShantiMari spread around her, probing for Celia's presence. When she felt a prick against her power, she pulled back, shrouding it from anyone who might be near. Low voices came from her right, and she turned in their direction.

Celia stood on the edge of the lake, her cloak billowing in the breeze. It was too hot for a heavy cloak, or even a hood, for that matter, but Celia wore hers low over her face. She spoke rapidly in that manic tone she'd had the other night. Half giggle, half hysteria. The hairs on the back of Taryn's neck rose, gooseflesh covering her arms.

Alone on the shore, Celia spoke as if to another. Taryn strained to hear the words, but they were a mumbled mass that tumbled over itself, incoherent. Then Celia stood on tiptoe and bent her head as if being kissed. The moan that came from her was of passion, shared with a lover.

Taryn stared hard at the air in front of Celia. She could make out no ShantiMari, no telltale threads to give away the mysterious invisible visitor.

The girl's cloak slipped to the ground, revealing her nakedness. Deep blue marks covered her body, shifting and settling with her movements. They flared as if being seared into her skin, and the smell of rotting flesh caught on the wind. Taryn gagged, but Celia paid the burns no mind. She writhed and undulated in the air, her body several feet above the ground. Whatever the creature was, it possessed Celia completely.

A twig snapped to her left, and Taryn froze, her heart pounding in her throat. She looked over her shoulder and saw Ebus crouched low, his eyes intent on her, a bit of broken branch in his hand. She motioned to the shoreline, and he nodded, indicating he too saw what was happening.

She slowly unsheathed her sword, but Ebus made a cutting motion with his hands. Then put his fingers to his lips. She replaced her sword and sat, hunched in the thicket, sweat coursing down her temples to her neck until Celia and her invisible lover were finished.

Long after Celia left, they sat there. Finally, Ebus tapped her shoulder. She'd not heard the man move. He jerked his head in the direction of camp, and she followed, careful to not make a racket. His moves were stealthy, his feet touching the ground only long enough to spring him forward, as if he used the breath of air to cushion the sound. When the firelight brightened their path, Ebus whispered in her mind. A tremor laced his words.

Go to bed, Great Lady. Say nothing of this to your beloved.

She wavered a moment, unwilling to trust him.

There is evil at work here. If you tell the prince what you witnessed, he'll seek justice, and then we'll never know who is behind that girl's possession.

He was right. Rhoane would insist on interrogating Celia, and they'd be no closer to understanding who or what that thing had been. Their only hope of catching it was to use Celia as bait.

We have to tell Rhoane something. I can't see what it is. We'll need his help, his strength.

I need time to sort this out. His little black eyes danced in the dim light, his nose twitching. *Trust me.*

Those two words… How often had she heard them? How many times were they spoken in deceit or in honesty? This time she had no choice. She withdrew her sword, and the dragon wings flared.

Swear on my sword that you mean me no harm. That your motives are true.

A panicked, frenzied look crossed his face. *I can't.*

You can, and you will. Do it or I tell Rhoane this minute.

Ebus reached a tentative hand toward her sword. It hovered above the glittering dragons for a long moment before he sighed and placed his palm against the pommel. When nothing happened he looked up at her with surprised relief.

Swear, Taryn reminded him.

I, Ebus, swear fealty to you, Great Lady. May my words and actions always be true to your purpose. May you trust I will never endeavor to cause you harm.

The dragon wings flared again, fluttering against the night before settling back to their immobile stations. A thread of her ShantiMari snaked up his arm, and he snatched his hand back, rubbing it against his waistcoat.

That wasn't so bad, was it? Her hands shook as she replaced the sword. It had gone much better than she'd hoped. They were both living, for one. *Whatever Rhoane is paying you, I'll match it. Keep an eye out for the assassin, but follow Celia, as well. I want to know everything she does.*

Ebus nodded and trotted off, making no sound. Taryn returned to her tent and collapsed on her cot. She couldn't shake the feeling she'd seen the devil tonight, and somehow, he'd seen her, too.

Chapter 45

MARISSA stood over the sleeping Sabina, a pinch of regret tugging at her abdomen. The mongrel pup watched her with solemnity but didn't growl or yip to give away her presence. She held Taryn's journal in her hand. An elaborate scrawl written in a language Marissa wasn't familiar with covered several pages. She tapped the book against her thigh, debating. No, she couldn't take it. That would alarm Taryn. It was probably nothing more than love sonnets written to Rhoane, and Marissa had no need of reading those.

She carefully replaced the book where she'd found it and returned to Sabina. She ran a hand lightly over the princess's sleeping form. This time, Kaida growled a warning that sounded much stronger than her size. Not wanting to try Kaida's patience, Marissa placed a light kiss on Sabina's lips and left the tent.

She kept to the shadows to avoid any unwanted attention. As she rounded the corner to her tent, a hand clamped over her mouth, and she was whisked into absolute blackness. Her scream fell in silent air. A moment later, she was standing on the far side of the lake, staring up at the steely gaze of Valterys. She twisted from his grip and looked around wildly.

"Blood and ashes, what are you doing here?"

"Protecting our future. Something you should be doing

but, since you are too preoccupied with satisfying your lustful cravings, have woefully overlooked."

Marissa could see the tents from where they stood, could see soldiers patrolling the perimeter. If she could see them, they could see her. "We should move this discussion to the trees."

Valterys barked a laugh. "They can neither hear nor see us, my darling." He stroked a finger from her temple to her chin. "While you were visiting my son, I've been spending time with your lady-in-waiting."

"Celia? Why?"

"Are you aware of her plans to use the Summerlands girl to bring Kaldaar out of exile?"

Marissa was agog. Celia? Her Celia? "Impossible. He was banished to the world of nonexistence. There is no return."

"False. She's somehow learned how to do it and is very close to carrying out her plans." He wrapped an errant curl around his fingertip. "Our lord is most vexed to hear his brother might gain his freedom while he simmers in his prison."

A tremble started in her heart and made its way to the tips of her toes. "She wouldn't. Couldn't."

"Oh, but she would and she has. She's working with a pathetic twit, but someone else is helping her. I can't tell who, but they are skilled in the Black Arts. A Master would be my guess."

"But why her? Why now?" Marissa glanced back to the encampment. "Is this because of Taryn?"

"She plays into this somehow, but I'm not sure exactly. From what I've learned, Celia's Master has been grooming her for some time. Several seasons is my guess. The timing of the Eirielle's return can't be a coincidence."

"For several seasons? I would've known."

"That's the tricky thing with the Black Arts. You never

know until it's too late. Celia was lured by the promise of everlasting love."

Marissa scoffed. "You're jesting. Love? She's jeopardizing everything for something as trivial as love?"

Valterys's eyes softened, his breathing deepened. "For some, love is the only thing that matters. For Celia, it's worth destroying Aelinae."

"What do you need me to do?" Marissa fumed. She'd given Celia plenty of love, but it wasn't enough, apparently.

"Stop her. Prevent her from carrying out the ceremony. If the vessel is filled, Kaldaar will return and all our plans will be for naught."

"What's this vessel?"

"That, my darling, is for you to discover. Even Celia doesn't know for sure." He looked to where several lights bobbed by the shoreline. "You should be in your tent or they might sound the alarm." He wrapped her in his embrace, and once again the darkness folded around them.

Sound returned, and she stood in the center of her tent, alone.

Celia wasn't in her cot, a fact that irritated her. The girl was out of control.

The tent flap opened, and Celia rushed in, out of breath, her hair in disarray. Upon seeing Marissa she knelt before her mistress, kissing her fingertips.

"Where have you been?"

"I went for a swim in the lake."

Marissa eyed her dry hair, the slight blush to her skin. "You are lying to me, my dove."

A frenzied madness lurked in Celia's eyes. Her cloak slipped to the ground, revealing her trembling, naked body.

"You were with him, weren't you? Your mysterious lover?" Marissa ran her hand along Celia's full breasts.

"I can't help it, my lady. When he calls, I feel compelled

to join him. I've tried to stay away, but I can't. I'm weak."

Marissa knew all too well the pull of Dark Shanti, its intoxication. "What does he tell you when you are together?"

"He tells me I'm beautiful."

Marissa let her fingers trail down the curve of Celia's belly to the apex of her legs. "And what do you tell him when you are alone?"

A shudder passed through the girl. Pleasure? Panic?

"I tell him what he means to me. How he makes me feel."

"Is that all?"

Celia's gaze darted around the room; an uneasy dance that ended with her eyes rolling up until only the whites could be seen. She collapsed in a heap.

Marissa leapt back, glancing from left to right for the source of Celia's ailment. She spread her arms wide, fingers outstretched. *"Morn dracthmas kuldirath benyous, soulvalkas teramir."*

A hiss issued from the unconscious girl, and a moment later the tent filled with blackened smoke. Marissa stared down the face that billowed in the haze. Its unrecognizable features shifted and expanded, its gaping mouth elongating, moving quickly over her until it consumed her and everything went black.

Chapter 46

A CHEER went up from the travelers when the Crystal Palace appeared on the horizon, with Taryn adding her voice to the others. The trip had been uneventful, but the amount of apprehension surrounding her was claustrophobic. Ebus kept watch on Celia but had witnessed no other visits. In confidence, he told Taryn about the conversation he'd overheard in Marissa's tent after Celia's visit with her phantom lover.

Ebus didn't see anyone else enter the tent, but when he heard Celia collapse and Marissa's hastily whispered spell, he'd known something terrible had happened. Not wanting to expose himself, he'd screamed, high pitched like a woman, calling the attention of a nearby guard. They'd found Marissa unconscious, a dark stain covering her hands.

It had taken the healers until morning, but Celia and Marissa had recovered, neither remembering anything. After that night, neither woman mentioned the lover again.

For the remainder of the trip, Taryn had divided her time between riding alongside the younger princesses' carriage and that of her oldest sister. Despite their claims of amnesia, Taryn suspected Marissa and Celia recalled everything. They'd danced and drank as normal, but a haunted expression hid in the depths of their eyes.

The entourage crested a ridge and outriders raced to greet them, once again escorting them through the streets of Talaith. Kaida rode in Taryn's pouch, face and paws hanging out to better see. She barked at the same time a chill ran down Taryn's spine.

Baehlon wheeled his horse, scanning the area, as did Rhoane, but they saw nothing. The icy clutch of dread did not leave Taryn as the group continued up the short hill to the palace; only once they were through the gates did Taryn truly let out her breath. She kissed the grierbas on her head, whispering, "Welcome to your new home, Kaida."

My home is with you, mi carae.

"Was that you?"

Of course. Who did you expect? Kaida's high-pitched voice sounded much like a small child's.

I didn't know you could speak to me.

Kaida's little mouth opened as if she were grinning. *It is you who finally learned to speak to me.*

Are we speaking the language of grierbas?

Of course. What do I know of the language of man?

Taryn laughed out loud, eliciting strange looks from Hayden and several other riders. She fluffed Kaida's fur, kissing her again. *I love you, my little furball.*

Kaida growled, but with her little muzzle and tiny voice, it came out more like a giggle and not at all threatening.

Taryn didn't know who was welcomed less at the palace—Lorilee or Kaida. Ellie reserved her opinion, but Cora made it clear neither was appreciated. When she refused to speak to Lorilee or acknowledge Kaida, Taryn had no recourse but to release her from service. Incensed, Cora stormed from her rooms, vowing the empress would hear of Taryn's actions.

"You've not made a friend with that one," Lorilee said with no small amount of relief.

"I think I'll get over it." As a precaution, she warded all

her rooms to keep Cora out.

Although little had changed at the palace, her return to Talaith was much different from the first time she'd arrived. She had a household to set up, and with Hayden's help, within the first week she'd added several members to her staff, including a new maid named Saeko. She blended well with Lorilee and Ellie, but there was something mysterious about the girl that intrigued Taryn. Margaret Tan supervised Taryn's choice for her House colors and insignia, settling on a silver sun and star pierced by a sword on a midnight blue background.

Settling into her new role as head of House Galendrin was only part of the challenge Taryn faced on their return. Kaida grew at an alarming rate, her soft puppy fur giving way to a smooth overcoat covering her gangly adolescent body. Despite her insistence that she knew nothing of man's languages, Taryn spoke to her mostly in Elennish, only using the language of grierbas for private matters.

Since Taryn refused to leave her penned up in her rooms, she brought her everywhere she went, except formal dinners and feasts, where Lliandra forbade her presence. Her mother's fear of Kaida becoming a wild beast was unfounded; in truth, Kaida was better behaved than most of the courtiers.

Taryn spent most of her free time in the library poring over ancient texts, trying to unravel the mystery of what happened between Rykoto and Daknys. Believing that in their story lay the crux of what was happening on Aelinae. She was determined to discover all she could about the prophecies and the Shadow Assassin.

She was rushing through the halls one afternoon, late to meet Sabina and the others, when she almost collided with Herbret outside the library.

"I'm in a bit of a hurry. If you'll excuse me." She said, motioning him aside.

Herbret stood in front of the heavy doors, and Taryn had to step around him to enter the library, but he blocked her with his bulk. "I've been meaning to find you to discuss Harvest festivities."

Taryn gave him a blank look. "What? Yeah, okay, make an appointment with my seneschal person. I really am in a rush." She nudged past him, but he was like a statue. "Herbret, what's wrong with you? Move." He harrumphed and planted his feet into the marble floor. "Seriously? If you don't move your ass this instant, I'll hang you from the top of the flagpole in your small clothes." She could probably do it.

Herbret scooted a fraction to the side, fat droplets of sweat dotting his upper lip.

"If I didn't know better, I'd say you're trying to hide something. Are you, Herbret?"

A slight squeaky tremor to his voice gave him away. "Of course not, Your Highness. You've been locked in here for too long, and I simply must discuss some important matters with you."

"As much as I'd love to stay here and discuss whatever it is you think is important, I'm late to something *I* think is important. I won't ask you again. Move."

He sidled a step to his left, and she pushed past him to open the door, breathing in the musty aroma of the library. A lightness settled around her as it always did when she entered the cavernous space.

The library took up five floors of the north wing. Merchants and courtiers moved through the stacks, silent in their quests. She sped past them to the secluded corner she'd staked out as her own. Dozens of threads of ShantiMari protected the space from anyone not permitted to enter. Not her ShantiMari, but the librarian's. Scrolls and parchment were scattered across the top of a huge table where she'd left them the previous day. She rummaged through a stack of papers, looking for the letter she'd received from her uncle. It had a message for Hayden she needed to share. Tucked under her teacup was a sealed envelope. The front was blank and Taryn knew the letter inside would be unsigned. She'd received several similar notes since arriving in Talaith. Always anonymous, always with a clue to help with her research. She had no idea who sent them, or even if they were an ally, but she read each and annotated her findings based on the clues.

A movement to her right distracted her from her search, and she looked up to find Celia pawing through a shelf of rolled scrolls. Taryn knew the section well. It housed ancient prophecies and utterances from oracles the world over.

"Celia? What are you doing?"

She spun around, a manic look in her eyes. Her hand whipped behind her back. "Nothing. I mean, the crown princess asked me to recover an old register." She waved the scroll in the air. "Found it." Before Taryn could ask to see the paper, Celia ran off, her slippers shushing on the thick carpet.

"Okay, then," Taryn muttered and debated following her. But she was already late, and Celia often borrowed scrolls from the library. She shrugged it off and resumed her search for the letter. Once found, she hurried to the beach.

Kaida ran along the shore, barking and snapping at the waves as they tumbled against the sand. Taryn paused in her steps to relax, to savor the moment. The people she loved most were at the cove, waiting for her. She looked down at the gathered group and counted her blessings, which, she was happily surprised to find, were many.

She jogged the rest of the distance and flopped on a blanket beside Sabina before handing the letter to Hayden. He scanned his father's words and carefully folded the parchment, placing it in his tunic pocket. Instead of the stiff breeches and heavy frocks they'd previously worn, Taryn had Tarro make them shorts, and for the girls, midriff-baring tank tops made from soft cotton. It was the scandal of the court, but with the next tide there would be a new scandal.

"I worry about you." Sabina sat next to Taryn, watching her face. "Since we've returned you spend your days fighting or studying. You need more of this." She waved her hand expansively around the cove.

"It's true, darling. You work yourself much too hard." Faelara sat under a skirm tree, its broad leaves providing shade, but still she wore a huge straw hat to keep the sun from her skin. That she'd even come to the beach surprised Taryn.

"No rest for the wicked, eh?" Taryn joked. But they were right. Since returning to Talaith she'd left little time for anything fun.

"Race me." Sabina took off before Taryn had a chance to recover.

She sprinted past Tessa and Eliahnna, who were introducing Kaida to the depths of the ocean, and dove into the waves. The cool water flowed over her, and she swam with even strokes to the rocky island where Sabina waited. Hayden splashed beside her, pulling himself up first before reaching out a hand to help Taryn. They lay on their backs, shielding their eyes from the sun. The days were getting shorter, the water colder, as they headed into harvest. Summer's last breath was sighing into the past.

"Where were you when I was growing up?" Hayden asked his cousin. "Those girls never liked to come down here until you arrived."

"I am quite curious to know where you were raised," Sabina admitted.

Taryn pointed vaguely at the mountains. "Over there or maybe there," she said, nodding toward Haversham.

"You're such a bloody tease." Hayden said, mimicking her speech. He pushed on her shoulder. "Why's it such a big secret?"

"If I told you, you wouldn't believe me for a start, and if you did, well, then, I'd have to kill you."

"I tell you my secrets; it's only fair you tell me yours." Sabina pouted.

Taryn leaned forward, beckoning them closer. "I come from beyond the stars." They both slapped her leg, and she laughed at their stricken faces. She rolled to her side, facing them. "Hayden, can you come to my rooms tonight? I want to try again."

His lips pursed in displeasure. They'd met several times since returning to Talaith, but Hayden hadn't been able to teach her any of his Dark skills. It was as if there was a void where her Dark Shanti should be. She could sense it, almost pull from it, but could never quite grasp it.

"Are you certain? Last time you nearly set yourself aflame."

That wasn't entirely true. She'd been recreating the ice and fire effect she'd discovered after her coronation and lost control for a split second. She'd doused the flames and no one was the wiser. Except Hayden, who'd witnessed the whole thing.

"I'll be more careful. Just one more time, please?"

"When have I ever been able to deny you?" He tugged on a strand of her silvery hair. "You'll be the death of me."

"Don't say that." Her tone held an ominous edge. "Never say such a thing."

"It looks as though your beloved has decided to join us." Sabina squinted toward shore, where Rhoane and Baehlon were setting down two large baskets. "And he's brought tea. I'm famished." She dove into the water and swam away with elegant strokes.

"She can sense the future, you know. It sometimes upsets her to the point of melancholy."

Taryn didn't know. Apparently Sabina *did* keep secrets.

Her friend emerged from the waves, shaking her long hair free of water.

"You were telling the truth, weren't you?"

"Yes and no." She didn't want to lie. Not to him. Not anymore. "Someday I'll tell you where I was all those seasons, but not yet."

"I think I've known since that day at Ravenwood when you kicked the sword off me. We were already connected mentally, but the sword strengthened the bond. It wasn't until the Narthvier that I realized all the strange images and memories I was having were actually from you."

Taryn stared at him, not knowing whether to be relieved or horrified. "You never said anything."

"I just did, didn't I? You can trust me, Taryn. I may not have Zakael's strength in ShantiMari, but I know enough to keep my mind locked. Let me help with your burden."

She wrapped her arms around him and muttered words of thanks and gratitude, of relief and fear that if he got himself killed the duke would never forgive her. Hayden chuckled, his strong chest heaving against hers. Having him know the truth was right somehow. She wasn't sure why, but Hayden needed to know.

"I wonder if the sword is blocking you from your Dark Shanti," he murmured.

"Why would you say that?"

He rubbed his chest where Marissa's ShantiMari nearly killed him. "Well, it sings to you, right? So maybe those songs are important. At Ravenwood, I'm certain it told me to ask for your help."

"It's possible. I'm always being told there's a progression to my learning. Maybe it thinks I'm not ready yet." Taryn recalled something else from Ravenwood—a beautiful woman with dark skin and flowing black hair. *Learn the words*, she'd said.

Hayden's stomach gave a thunderous rumble. "I know what I'm ready for. Shall we?" He held out his hand, and they dove into the water together, racing to the shore.

Chapter 47

A CRACK of thunder rattled the thick plates of glass in the old library, temporarily pulling Taryn from the fuzzy depths of thought. She was surprised at how dark it had become, the hours that passed without her noticing. Kaida lay on a pillow not far from her chair, paws twitching in sleep. Dreaming of chasing hares, most likely.

Taryn rubbed her eyes and knotted her hair into a sloppy bun atop her head. The beautiful cascade of curls and braids Lorilee had given her that morning had long since been destroyed. The papers she was studying served no purpose in answering her questions. If anything, they created more questions, and then more to answer those. She hated riddles, but it seemed the prophets of old were keen on twisting words.

She pushed the papers aside and banged her head on the thick wood. A loud *thunk* echoed through the empty rooms. She was alone. Vulnerable. She glanced at the place where her guard usually kept watch, a chill passing through her when she saw it empty. Her gaze traveled behind her, and up the tall stacks of shelves to the top of the palace. Books and scrolls were crammed into every conceivable nook and cranny. Thick beams crossed overhead, looking imposing where only a few bells earlier she'd greeted them with genial familiarity.

A skittering in one corner made her flex her hand toward her sword, but she wasn't wearing it. She'd left it in her rooms because it was ridiculous to wear it in the library.

Stupid, stupid, stupid, she chided herself.

A palace cat stretched across the entry to her little enclosure, reaching out with first one calico speckled paw, then the other, before extending its back legs. The cat sat on its haunches and groomed itself, ignoring her and Kaida.

Taryn sagged into the chair, apprehension sloughing off like a thick coating of mud.

Carina, one of the six guards Anje had chosen for her, popped her head through the entryway. "You have a visitor."

Tessa sidled past Carina to enter the space. She balanced a tray with a steaming pot of grhom and two plates piled high with food. "You missed dinner," she said in a disapproving tone. "Again."

Apparently, Taryn's hermit-like obsession wasn't approved of by her youngest sister. She'd slept in the library the previous night and—she sniffed beneath her tunic—apparently missed a bath or two.

"Thank you." She took the tray from Tessa and placed it on the table. "Are you joining me?"

Tessa shook her head. "I thought Carina might be hungry."

A slice of guilt cut through Taryn. She hadn't even considered the woman's needs. How unbelievably selfish of her.

"That was very nice of you." She cleared a place for Carina amid all the papers and bade her join them. Her guard looked suspiciously at the dark library and then pulled a chair to the table.

They talked about Taryn's work for much of the meal, with Taryn trying to explain the scroll she'd been reading. It had to do with a prophecy about Kaldaar, the firstborn son of Nadra and Ohlin. It documented his creation of the Black Arts, his manipulation of Rykoto, his rape of Julieta, and his fall from grace. All things she knew from Rhoane's telling those first few days on Aelinae.

What caught her attention was the repeated mention of a vessel. Without this vessel—and this was where the wording got tricky—to hold or contain their power, the Black Arts would not continue. Taryn was trying to unravel the meaning of the prophecy when the storm had interrupted her.

She shuffled through the scrolls on her desk. "There must be a second page, but I can't find it."

"Have you tried looking where you found the parchment in the first place?" Carina asked. "Perhaps it was placed on another shelf."

"I thought of that, but it's not there. Besides, the librarians are too meticulous to make a mistake like that."

"Maybe someone else took it." Tessa tapped a little finger to her lips. "Is there a reason anyone else would need to study the prophecy?"

"I suppose anyone who wanted to know the history of the Black Arts." Taryn got up and went to the section where the scroll should've been. She poked around again, moving aside scraps of paper and scanning several parchments before turning back to the others. "It should be right here." She smacked the shelf, and a light puff of dust rose in the air.

A quick stinging sensation from her pendant set her nerves on edge. Her skin prickled and she rubbed her arms, irritated at her pendant. Then she recalled the previous week when she'd searched for Anje's letter.

"I think I know who has it." Taryn rejoined the others and took her seat. She lifted her grhom to her lips, contemplating her next move. "We need to retrieve it, but I'm sure it's locked in her rooms."

"Who?" Carina and Tessa said in unison.

"Lady Celia."

Tessa chewed a piece of Taryn's bread, her fingers tapping out her thoughts on the crust. "I could do it. I know Celia's rooms like my own."

"We couldn't risk it. This is dangerous, Tessa. If you got hurt, Mother would kill me."

Tessa straightened in her seat, making herself as tall as she could. "I'm not afraid. Besides, I'm perfect. I know Celia, so my being in her rooms wouldn't look suspicious. I'm a princess. No one would dare question me if I want to visit her. And, I know all the secret passageways that lead to her rooms, as well as most of the hiding places she might use. If there is a spot of trouble with her Mari, I can always have you use your sword."

"It doesn't work like that, but you might be our best bet."

Taryn set the scraps of her meal on the floor for Kaida, who had awoken from her nap. The palace cat sat nearby and finished its meticulous grooming before blinking its amber eyes lazily and sauntering over to eat off the plate, too. Kaida regarded the interloper with a cautious glance but then resumed her meal.

The small group left the library and followed Tessa to a small alcove hidden behind a thick tapestry. Two orbs— one multihued and the other cornflower blue—led their way through a maze of corridors until finally Tessa stopped. She opened a slender door a crack and listened. A moment later she slipped through the door and out of sight.

Taryn and Carina waited in the cramped space for Tessa to return from Celia's rooms. She shifted against the cool wall and brushed a web from her face. "So," she kept her voice low, "what's a nice girl like you doing in a place like this?"

From the scant light of the floating orb Taryn had made, she saw Carina's brows pinch, her lips twist to the side in thought. "We're here to wait for Tessa."

Taryn chuckled, then checked herself. "It was a joke. Where I came from, that's how guys tried to pick up girls."

"Did it work?"

"I doubt it." A rat scurried past them, racing over Taryn's boot to get past Kaida. The grierbas watched it run off with detached interest. "What's taking her so long?" Tessa had been in Celia's suite at least a quarter of a bell. Taryn paced in a small circle, using all the space she had. "We should see if she needs help."

Carina put a hand out to stop Taryn. "She knows how to reach you if there is trouble. Calm. Breathe."

"You sound like Rhoane."

"I'll take that as a compliment."

The door creaked open the width of a hand, and Tessa slithered through clutching several papers to her chest. She made sure the door clicked and then looked up at them with a broad smile. "She had half the library in there. I took what I thought was most important." She gave a cautious glance at the opposite wall. "Let's not linger here."

Once in Taryn's rooms, they spread out the sheets and scanned them. Some were lineage histories, others mundane housekeeping records. Three of the pages made Taryn's chest tighten, her breathing quickened. One was the missing second page of Kaldaar's prophecy; another was a prophecy that dealt with her, specifically; and the third was a family tree.

Taryn gathered up all the sheets except those three. "We should return these to Celia's rooms. She might miss them and become suspicious."

"She won't. Trust me. There were books and papers everywhere. You would've hated it. No organization, no proper care, or handling—that's what took me so long."

Taryn chewed the inside of her cheek. In the morning,

she'd share what she found with Rhoane, but it was late and she needed rest. "You've been a great help tonight. Carina, can you take Tessa to her rooms, then give Kaida a break outside before retiring?"

Tessa started to argue, but Taryn cut her off. "We'll meet tomorrow and sort out what Celia is up to. I promise."

Before she left, Tessa handed Taryn several cream colored envelopes, each opened. They were the notes she'd sent to Rhoane. "I found these beside her bed."

Taryn tucked the pages into her tunic. "Thank you, Tessa." She kissed her sister's forehead, lingering to inhale the sweet scent of citrus and mint.

When the girls were gone, Taryn sat at her desk and read more thoroughly through the documents, becoming increasingly agitated. She hardly noticed Carina's return or the sky lightening in the west. Only when Saeko tapped her on the shoulder did she realize she'd spent the entire night making notes.

She cancelled her training that morning and sent messages to those she trusted most to meet in her rooms at ninth bell. When they started arriving, Taryn paced with the heightened anxiety of someone who hadn't slept but was fueled with determination and caffeine.

Carina and Timor, another of Taryn's guards, stood beside her door while the rest of the group gathered in her sitting room. She looked at their faces—expectant, curious, questioning—and began.

She indicated the anonymous notes she'd received, handing a few to Faelara to pass around. "Someone has been helping with my research. I don't know who, but these clues have led me to this." She held up the papers Tessa had retrieved from Celia's rooms. "I think it's best if I just read it, then we can figure out what it all means."

She read through the entire prophecy, stopping when she

came to the end of the second page. "I can't make out this last part. It's written in thick ink and a bit smeared, but I think it says, 'Bring night into day when the blood of the unbroken, daughter of deceit, will sow their seeds.'" She passed the pages to Faelara and Hayden. "Read them again. Oh, and this." She gave Sabina the sheet with the family tree meticulously drawn.

They took their time reading and rereading the pages. Eliahnna jotted down notes in a journal while Baehlon sharpened his sword. Taryn paced the room, wearing the carpet thin in a semicircle. She chewed on her cuticle, stopped herself, and then nibbled a bit more.

Ebus was helping her spy on Celia, but had been adamant his role remain anonymous. If the others knew about him, he claimed, they might inadvertently signal to him or otherwise call him out when they spotted him around the palace. With only Taryn knowing his purpose, he'd be able to follow Celia without drawing attention. He was, at that very moment, in the far reaches of the orchard, perched high in a tree observing Celia and her invisible lover. They'd met many times since their return to Talaith, but this was the first time the mysterious stranger had come on palace grounds.

His proximity corroborated Taryn's suspicions that their confidence grew with each encounter. Ebus had been right— if she'd told Rhoane, he would've severed Celia's ties with the phantom, who then would've been free to find a new victim. They were close to learning his identity.

And now, telling Rhoane and the others she'd been hiding something from them was not going to be pleasant.

Sabina's nose wrinkled in thought, a lock of hair stuck between her teeth as she absently chewed. "This is of my family tree, I believe."

The others turned their attention to her.

"The names are spelled in the archaic language, but I

recognize many of them. And see here, on the lowest branch are my mother and father, with my siblings and me listed just below."

Hayden craned his neck to get a better look. "Sabinth Aarendhi." He looked off, thinking. "I've read that name before, but I can't recall where."

"Did it have to do with Kaldaar?" Rhoane asked, taking the paper from Sabina.

"I'm not sure. I'll search my books. I know it was just in the last fortnight, so it must be here with me."

Faelara tapped the second page of the prophecy. "This part at the bottom looks like it was added later. The script doesn't match the rest."

"That's what I thought, as well," Taryn agreed. She took a deep breath. It was now or never. "Last night, Tessa found these papers in Celia's rooms." All eyes focused on her, and she continued without elaborating. "For some time now Celia's been acting odd. Talking to herself, having bouts of mania followed by spells of discontent. Something's not right." She pointed to the sheets in their hands. "I have no idea what all of this means, but I'm certain it's not good. That's why I asked you here, to see if we can collectively figure this out and how Celia is involved."

At length, it was Rhoane who spoke. "Hayden, see what you can uncover about Kaldaar and the Black Arts. Since Sabina believes this is her family tree, she should look further into that, and Taryn, continue your research into the prophecies that revolve around you. As for Baehlon and myself, we will keep watch for anything untoward in the palace. As well as keep a guard on Sabina."

"What should we do?" Tessa's eyes were alight with the possibility of adventure.

"You, my young friend, need to watch Lady Celia. Be discreet, see where she goes, whom she speaks with, but never go alone. Do you understand? You must never be by yourself if you are to help us. We need to be certain you are safe. Always." He chucked her on the chin, and Tessa beamed at him.

"I will," she said in a breathless sigh.

"I'll keep watch over Herbert as well," Hayden offered. "His interest in Sabina isn't healthy, nor his relationship with Celia. I'm betting he's involved somehow."

"Excellent point, Hayden." Faelara said. "I've never trusted that young man."

Sabina shuddered and Hayden placed his arm protectively around her.

"I'll help Taryn in the library. I'm sure there is order to all of this," Eliahnna added.

"Are you insinuating I'm not tidy?" A hint of bemusement lifted Taryn's words.

Eliahnna gave her a suffering look. "Of course not. I'm merely suggesting that a fresh set of eyes might find what you've overlooked."

Faelara stretched in such a way that Taryn recalled the calico cat from the library. Their eyes met, and Faelara gave a sly smile. "I'll see what I can discover from the empress's spies. I doubt if Lliandra would openly share anything she knows with me."

"Have you fallen from favor?" Baehlon's voice rumbled through the room.

"Perhaps a little. I have been remiss in sharing everything I know about the Eirielle, and this vexes her to no end." The sly smile deepened.

"You did that for me?" Gratitude didn't come close to what Taryn was feeling. Faelara could've been hanged if Lliandra so wished it.

"Of course, my darling."

The meeting disbanded, and they began to file out. Taryn

stopped Rhoane before he joined Baehlon. "Tessa found these in Celia's rooms." She handed him the notes she'd sent that he'd never received. "If she's up to something, there's no way Marissa doesn't know about it."

He turned the envelopes in his hands, a frown pulling his lips dangerously low. "I will make certain to put a watch on her, as well. But it is wise to keep these suspicions to yourself. If they prove false, you will not have to explain your treason to the empress."

The bitter taste of acid lingered with his words. Despite what he'd told her at the Weirren, he still wished to believe in Marissa's innocence. Even if that meant not believing Taryn.

Chapter 48

THE air in her rooms thickened with the all too familiar mist that accompanied the phantom. Marissa recoiled, even as she knew it was impossible to avoid. It never spoke, never touched her beyond wrapping a single tendril around her pale wrist. That one wisp conveyed its latest instructions. She struggled to fight the demon, but her body obeyed his every command. Every request, no matter how small, was fulfilled. She could deny it nothing.

Tears coursed down her cheeks when the thing finally released her and dissipated. A gentle breeze cleared the room of its stench, like the rot of a thousand decaying bodies. Since that first night on the road from Paderau, the phantom had visited only twice, each time more insistent than the last.

Marissa must let Celia complete the ceremony.

A ruffle of feathers brought her attention to the balcony, and she squinted to see Valterys transforming. He glanced quickly around him and stepped into her bedchamber.

"Is it gone?"

"I don't like the control it has over me. We must find a way to break the bond or Celia will be successful."

Valterys placed his hands alongside her temples and pressed gently. Buzzing sounded in her mind, a hive of voices clamoring to be heard above the din. The shouts of the dead.

His Shanti spun around the din, silencing it. The powerful wards he placed on her mind helped to keep the phantom from taking over completely. Valterys thought she could protect herself on her own, but she craved his healing after each visit from the mist creature.

"You're not wrong," Valterys said. "This phantom, he is not Kaldaar but an agent of his. Someone who wishes to bring the god back from exile. He is powerful, yes, but not omnipotent."

"Then he lives and breathes?"

Valterys gave a low chuckle. "I believe he does. He's been visiting our Celia regularly, giving her immense amounts of pleasure, I'm afraid."

"It doesn't touch me except to give instructions."

"Are you jealous?"

She was. Very much so. "Not at all. Are you?" She suspected Valterys, on occasion, pretended to be the phantom.

"How close is Taryn to discovering Celia's plan?"

Marissa snorted. "Not nearly as far along as she should be. Without my clues helping her, I'm afraid she'd still be down at the cove, swimming with her idiot friends." Marissa herself wasn't certain what Celia planned, but each night she would slip into her room and rummage through the scrolls and notes Celia had made. She hated to admit she needed Taryn's help to stop Celia. She needed Taryn to stop the phantom from taking over her soul.

A small, impatient sigh slipped through his lips. He still held her head between his hands, and a shock went through her mind. "You give her too little credit. Taryn is a bright young woman. She'll get to the core of Celia's plans. You need to make sure she lives through the ordeal. Rykoto would be quite vexed to learn of her death. I've managed to keep this from our god, but he suspects something and is questioning our loyalty."

That was a complication she couldn't afford. Unless she had something better to offer Rykoto. "I'll go to Celia. She must know who the Master is but is being compelled to forget. If I can distract her, perhaps she'll unwittingly tell me."

Valterys released her head. "I've tried that. On several occasions. I truly don't think she knows. If she did, then she would certainly tell the difference between my presence and his."

True. There was nothing similar in their touch. But then, she'd known Valterys her whole life. Celia had never met him before Taryn's coronation.

"How fares Zakael? It has been too long since I've seen him."

"He is well, my darling. While I've been here dealing with this, he has been at Caer Idris."

"I hope we can both see him soon." She brushed her lips across his cheek. "My offer stands, you know."

He ran a fingernail down her cheek, scratching the tender skin. She moaned into his touch. "I will try to find this mysterious phantom. You see to Celia."

"Keep in contact." She tapped his forehead, and he nodded.

With a final kiss to her temple, he stepped onto the balcony and transformed into a levon. She watched until he was a speck in the sky before turning back to her room. Valterys didn't understand the pain she suffered when she tried to disobey the phantom's commands. More than physical, the horrors that went through her mind were enough to cripple someone of lesser power.

She could only imagine the hell Celia was living.

Kaldaar's agent offered her nothing and demanded complete obedience. Not unlike Zakael the night she'd spent with him and Eiric. Except she'd received plenty that night and the following morning. This agent of Kaldaar's was selfish, and Marissa never gave without getting something in return.

She rubbed her wrist, thinking, plotting. She could allow Celia to succeed, but then what? Was he, in fact, acting on Kaldaar's behalf, or his own? And if Celia succeeded in bringing Kaldaar back, how would her own plans alter?

The answers could only mean devastation to her, personally. Celia must fail. For that to happen, Taryn must succeed. With Taryn's limited abilities with ShantiMari, there was no way she'd survive the phantom.

Marissa smiled to herself, chuckling at the deviousness of her mind. Luring Taryn to her death would be as easy as coaxing a kitten to milk.

Chapter 49

OVER the course of the next several days, they searched Celia's rooms often, finding more prophecies and references to Kaldaar but getting no closer to a resolution. Their break came on the eve of Harvest when Hayden read an obscure passage in a book on the Black Arts.

They met again in Taryn's rooms with several strands of ShantiMari enclosing them in a web of privacy. Hayden held the book but recited from memory a paraphrased account. Before Kaldaar's fall, he'd settled in the Eastern Province, a short ride from modern-day Talaith. He'd built a temple to himself and gathered followers. The ceremonies held within the great standing stones were secret, with no written account intact. But a few who had witnessed the festivities recounted acts of brutality, mostly to young virgins.

He stopped then and looked at Taryn, "Perhaps this is what is meant by 'blood unbroken.' They needed virgins to rape and plant their seed."

Taryn's stomach roiled at his words. If Celia was working with a Master of the Black Arts, he might be using her as their vessel. But Celia wasn't a virgin, not by half. "What if it means a bloodline? Does Celia come from an important House?"

Hayden shook his head. "She is minor nobility, at best.

She's only tolerated at court because she is Marissa's favorite. I've searched her family history and found nothing to indicate that she is strong in the power or has ties to the Black Arts."

"What else does the book say about Kaldaar?" Rhoane asked.

"Only that these rituals were performed every few hundred seasons."

"What about the link to Sabina's family? Have you found more about that?" Baehlon sat forward, his hands pressed on his knees, as if he was ready to spring forward at the slightest provocation.

"None."

"Where did you say Kaldaar's temple was located?" Eliahnna checked her notes, frowning.

"The Stones of Kaldaar," Hayden supplied. "The ruins are southeast of Talaith, about a two- possibly three-bell ride."

She flipped to a page near the end of her journal. "That's on Herbret's property. His family purchased the land forty seasons ago. Before that, they were lesser merchants living in Anklam, on the coast. No ties to the Black Arts that I could find."

It made no sense, and yet it had to make sense. What would Herbret's family want with property tied to the granddaddy of the Black Arts?

"What did Herbret's family deal in?" Taryn picked up Kaida and scratched her under the chin. The pup was restless, but playtime would have to wait.

Eliahnna tossed her strawberry blonde hair with a shake. "I couldn't find any mention of what they traded."

"Books," Faelara supplied. "I remember my father bought plenty of books from them before they moved here. Most of those scrolls you've been reading came from Herbret's parents. They would search the world for rare scrolls for Talaith's library."

That Herbret's parents had supplied the books couldn't be a coincidence. There was more to it, but Taryn was missing something. Something important. If Herbret's parents were trying to hide something, they wouldn't have brought it to the palace.

"What if they found a scroll and kept it? What if it had information that on a certain day, if you did a certain thing, you would earn something amazing?"

"Like if you took a virgin to the Stones of Kaldaar?" Hayden provided the context to Taryn's simplified hypothesis.

A heavy silence fell over the group as they came to the same conclusion.

Sabina.

Herbret had wanted her hand for more reasons than supposedly loving her.

"Then I must be the vessel written about in the prophecy," Sabina said, her expression sober but tears brimming in her eyes.

Eliahnna scooted closer to the Summerlands princess, and Faelara took her hand.

"Now that we know what they're planning," Taryn said softly. "We just need to know when."

"Harvest." Tessa looked at Taryn. "Celia kept saying something about meeting her mystery man at Harvest. When we were at Paderau, remember?"

The pieces were clicking into place.

"Harvest is tomorrow. We must keep Sabina under guard until then," Rhoane said, pacing the room, his hand hovering above his sword.

"I have to miss the festival?" If it weren't for Sabina's genuine pout, Taryn would've thought she was kidding.

"It is for the best. We cannot risk you leaving the palace tomorrow. If we are correct in assuming Celia and Herbret have planned this all along, then you will be safest here, with guards at your door." Rhoane's voice was gentle, but there was steel beneath his words.

Great Lady, Ebus's voice echoed in her mind. *The phantom is in the palace. He is with Lady Celia. I believe they are going—*

The connection ended abruptly, and Taryn shook her head as if to regain his thoughts. She tapped her temples and hopped on one foot until she glanced up to see her friends regarding her with worried looks. Kaida growled her displeasure at being shaken.

"Right. So, um, Celia's boyfriend? He's here."

The next few minutes were a chaotic mash of voices, ideas, and weapons being drawn.

Finally, Taryn held up a hand to silence the others. "This *thing* can't be seen. I spied Celia with it once, but there was nothing tangible for me to actually *see*." She hoped Rhoane understood her meaning without having to tell the others she could see ShantiMari. "What I propose is someone follows Celia." At Tessa's excited gesture, Taryn added, "Not you. I'm sorry darling, you're too inexperienced."

"Actually, she's perfect," Eliahnna argued. "She's little, so no one pays her much mind. She's fast, she's nimble, and she knows this palace better than any of us. She can get around without being noticed."

"I don't like it." Baehlon crossed his arms over his chest. "I'll find Celia and this phantom."

More arguing ensued. Rhoane cast Taryn a questioning glance.

Ebus and I saw Celia on the road to Talaith. We didn't say anything because we had to be certain she was plotting something. Where is Ebus now?

Taryn blanched at the question. *I don't know. He was following Celia, and then I lost contact.*

"No," Rhoane said and everyone stopped talking. "Baehlon and Timon will stay here and guard the others.

Carina and Taryn will come with me." He took a few steps before adding to Sabina, "If something is afoot, the best place for you is here, in Taryn's apartment. Do not, under any circumstances, leave. Faelara, Eliahnna, and Tessa, scout the public areas, but do not engage with Celia or the phantom."

"I'll go with the women," Hayden took Kaida from Taryn and placed her on Sabina's lap.

Rhoane nodded his approval and they left, each turning in opposite directions. Their best option was to separate and canvas as much of the palace as they could, making discreet inquiries to Celia's whereabouts without garnering unwanted attention.

Taryn walked as fast as she could without actually running and headed to Celia's quarters. A maid told her Celia was out but offered to let Taryn wait for her in the sitting room. She made a quick check of the suite, sensing nothing untoward. On her way out, she left a message for Celia that she'd like to meet for tea later—something innocuous that wouldn't arouse suspicions.

From there, Taryn went to the place she'd last met with Ebus. She searched the room that led to the formal gardens but found no evidence he'd even been there. Several times, she heard from Carina or Rhoane about their progress. Or lack thereof.

Taryn checked the library before heading to the throne room. At the huge double doors, a slick coating of ShantiMari clung to her skin. *Black Shanti.* The phantom had passed that way.

She called Rhoane and waited until he and Carina were standing beside her before pushing open the doors.

The darkened room was empty from what she could tell. Carina lit several candles with a flick of her wrist. The action was so quick Taryn didn't have a chance to follow her Mari. The added light did little to dispel the vacant feeling in the

room, though. A thickness settled on her then, as if all the air
had been sucked from the space. Like the void.

Can you feel it too? Taryn asked Rhoane.

What?

The weight of nothingness.

*There seems nothing out of place here. It feels the same as
always.*

Sword held out before her, Taryn swept the area. Tiny
pinpricks crept up her arms the further she moved into the
shadows. When she approached the elaborate throne with a
moon carved into the wood, she swooned. The room spun
once then settled into a discordant replica of what it had
been. Rhoane and Carina were there, searching, as she was,
but they looked distant, as if a filmy wall separated them.
As if a mist had descended around her, blocking light and
sound.

She touched her pendant. Silence. She listened for the
familiar hum of her sword, but no songs played in her mind.
No melodies to mark her passing. Only a disturbingly lonely
silence.

Taryn reached out to touch the seat but hesitated. Her
fingertips wavered above the wood.

Taryn.

Rhoane's voice startled her, and she pulled her hand
back, releasing the haze. He motioned that the room was
clear, they were moving on.

Without giving the throne another glance, she left the
room, but the sensation she was being watched stayed with
her.

They searched the entire palace, finding neither Celia nor
her lover. Aside from the throne room, Taryn sensed nothing
and there was no sign of Ebus.

The hour grew late and, frustrated at their lack of
progress, they halted the search. That night Lliandra held an

informal feast. The following night there would be a grand ball, but Harvest Eve she liked to celebrate with just her closest courtiers and family. Taryn sat at the table, her foot tapping impatiently until Rhoane placed his hand over her knee.

Celia was there, as were Marissa and Herbret, all looking relaxed and enjoying the evening's festivities. Near midnight, exhausted and unable to keep her eyes open, Taryn said goodnight to her mother and sisters. She wanted Sabina stay with her that night, but the Summerlands princess insisted she was well protected with so many people around. Besides, she'd argued, Celia was there and no harm had come to her.

As a caveat, Baehlon promised to set four guards on Sabina's doors—two in the hallway and two on the balcony. In addition, her maids would sleep in her rooms and not let the princess out of their sight. Carina volunteered to stay with Sabina, as well. Taryn didn't like it. But Sabina was adamant. Hayden volunteered to patrol the grounds with Baehlon and Rhoane.

Outvoted and too tired to argue, Taryn shuffled to her rooms, curled Kaida into her arms, and fell into a fitful sleep. She woke before sunrise and took Kaida outside. While the grierbas snuffled around the bushes, ferreting out rodents, Taryn puzzled over all they'd learned. She still couldn't understand how Celia became involved, or how Marissa figured into the scheme. Or if somehow Zakael was behind the plot. She had too many questions and still no answers.

Time was running out. Today was Harvest. The one day of the year when Aelinae had no moons.

Bring night into day. It made no sense. If Harvest had no moons, then how was it possible to bring night into day?

She and Kaida walked back to the palace, taking the side entrance near the stables. A figure clad in a black cloak rode straight at her. Across his saddle, wrapped in crimson fabric, was an unmoving body. The wind whipped up a corner and she saw the delicate gold anklet Sabina always wore. He bore down on her, and she leapt aside to avoid getting trampled.

"Herbret!" She raced after him, demanding he stop, but he was too fast. She threw a net of her ShantiMari over him, but an unseen force blocked it. She raced to the stables, reaching for her sword.

It wasn't there.

"Motherfucker!" She screamed to the sky.

She spun around, grabbed Kaida by the scruff, and raced to her room. Along the way, she called to everyone's minds, waking them, telling them what she'd witnessed. When she burst through the door to her quarters, Lorilee jumped in fright, knocking over a pot of tea. Her apologies went unheard as Taryn sped to her dressing room, grabbing clothes at random and throwing them on. She ordered Kaida to stay in her rooms, to keep her maids safe, and then she ran, full-out, to Sabina's apartment. There, she found the two guards slumped against the wall, their foreheads bleeding.

Sabina's maids were unconscious, as well, with no noticeable wounds. Carina was groggy but able to stand. A fine trickle of blood oozed from her ear. Taryn sent her Mari to the girl, searching her for broken bones, mending surface wounds.

By the time they reached the stables, Hayden was waiting for them, horses saddled. "They aren't far ahead of us. We can catch them if we hurry."

Taryn took Ashanni's reins and climbed into the saddle.

Hayden kicked his gelding and took off toward the northern gate. After a worried glance to the palace, she followed with Carina beside her.

Rhoane, please hurry.

Chapter 50

THEY rode hard for close to two bells. None of them spoke, except to give directions. Hayden led them to where he believed Herbret had taken Sabina, to the Stones of Kaldaar. Taryn kept Rhoane abreast of where they were going. He and the empress were less than a quarter bell behind, and every so often Taryn would search the landscape, hoping to see them. Whatever Herbret was planning, she feared it was stronger than her and Hayden.

They crested a ridge and saw their first glimpse of the standing stones. Two rings—one of polished marble, the other deepest granite—gleamed in the rising sunlight. The way they overlapped was beautiful in its simplicity and proportions. In the space between the two circles, Taryn saw movement. She squinted against the increasing brightness, looking for anything to suggest Sabina was there.

Four horses grazed beneath nearby trees, and Taryn scanned the area. A man in a black cloak, and a woman, hovered around an altar in the center of the circle. Taryn's blood stilled when she saw three bodies lying immobile on the marble slate. She kicked Ashanni, spurring the horse to race faster than she ever had.

Close enough now to see their faces clearly, Taryn watched in horror as they prepared for the ceremony. Celia wore a white gown that showed her pale body beneath the filmy fabric. Blue marks covered her skin, clear to her temple. Her glossy chestnut hair hung loose around her shoulders with flowers woven throughout. She looked innocent, virginal. In her hand, she held an urn and sprinkled liquid from it onto the three bodies lying unconscious on the altar.

Herbret stood beside Celia, his fat cock enlarged and ready to impale one of the sacrifices.

"Stop!" Taryn screamed. She choked back a gag, ready to shout again, but he plunged forward, pumping his hips wildly while Celia chanted and tossed the liquid over his head. He moved swiftly, defiling the first girl and moving to the next.

She pulled Ashanni up short, stopping as close to the stones as she dared. She jumped down and ran to the inner circle. A vague uneasiness swept over her, pushing against her. Hayden darted past, as did Carina, both with swords drawn. Taryn jerked her sword from its scabbard and sliced at the unseen force blocking her.

Hayden tackled the man mid-ejaculation. His sperm sprayed on the legs of the helpless girl who lay beside Sabina. Taryn cast a quick glance at the women, each dressed in their nightclothes, her gown pushed up to reveal her sex.

"Carina, cover them and check to see if they are alive," Taryn commanded as she rounded on the still chanting Celia.

Herbret had regained his footing and circled Hayden, a sword in his hand, naked beneath his cloak. A shadow flickered at the corner of her vision, but when she looked it vanished.

"Celia, put the urn down. It's over," Taryn said in a soothing voice.

Celia's cackle was that of an old crone. "So you have come, Betrayer. It was foretold you would try to stop us, but we are far more powerful than you'll ever be." Her face began to crumble as she spoke, the lush ripeness of youth turning to age-spotted wrinkles in a matter of moments. Her nose extended into a crook that nearly touched the top of her lips. Her hair, still adorned with flowers, flowed to her buttocks in a dull sheet of grey.

A cloud passed over them, blotting out the sun.

The crone whimpered and flailed her hands, sending a blaze of power at Carina, who was thrown backward by the force. Another blow tossed Hayden into a stone. He shook his head as if dazed.

"It is time! It must be done now!" Celia pushed past Taryn with the strength of Baehlon, knocking her over, and grabbed Herbret by the cuff of his cloak. Hayden stared at the woman in angry shock.

"Do it now. Give the vessel your seed." She resumed her chanting and sprinkling of the liquid, ignoring Taryn and Hayden. Herbret moved in front of Sabina, his cock a grotesque appendage that reached for Sabina, as if alive.

The crone screamed her chant, and Herbret gripped Sabina's legs, pulling her toward him as he thrust forward.

Taryn regained her footing and lunged for the crone at the same time Hayden threw himself at Herbret, grabbing his neck and hurling him away from the altar. They tumbled and Hayden sprang up, his sword at Herbret's neck.

Taryn threw a right hook at the crone, catching her square on the temple. She wailed an insult and crumpled to the ground, her chanting ceased.

"Carina, watch her." Taryn commanded before seeing to Sabina. She pulled the girl into her arms, sending ShantiMari through her, searching for signs of trauma, healing what she could. Sabina remained unbroken. Herbret hadn't violated her. She choked back a sob of relief and held her friend tighter.

The other girls didn't fare as well. The rape left them

bleeding and bruised, and each had a gash near their temples. Taryn carefully covered them as much as she could. Her ShantiMari traveled the length of their bodies, healing what Herbret had defiled.

The sound of hoofbeats brought their attention to the rise, and Taryn glimpsed Rhoane riding toward them with about thirty others.

"Carina, check the surrounding area. Use your senses. The phantom cannot be seen, but you can feel him."

Carina moved to the outer circles, her ShantiMari flowing out from her, probing the shadows. The sun had disappeared completely, and Taryn looked up to see a bright ring around a dark circle. An eclipse.

Sabina moaned and Taryn searched her eyes. They were clouded and a bit dazed, but Sabina's courage fought through the haze.

"She is still pure. There is time yet to complete the Getting. The others are filled," the crone rasped, as she cowered against the ground. "There is still time! It must be done. Must fulfill the prophecy. Our lord beckons!"

"Shut up." Hayden pulled the crone to a sitting position, and with one swing of his sword took her head clean off.

"Hayden!" Taryn stared at him, incensed. "That's not the way it's done. We needed her."

Hayden shrugged Taryn off. "She wouldn't have told us anything. But this one," Hayden turned back toward Herbret, who stared up at him, eyes huge with fear, "will squeal the loudest." Before Taryn could stop him, Hayden plunged his sword into Herbret.

The cry that came from him sounded eerily like the death throes of a pig. Herbret clutched his chest and fell backward, his face ashen, his cock lifeless. His breath came in gasps, and Taryn sent just enough of her power to keep him alive but not a thread more. They needed answers from him, but he needed to suffer, as well.

The crone's words tumbled through her thoughts. Sabina held the power to produce Black heirs. It was in her blood.

Taryn held her blade out to Sabina. "Place your hand on my sword, Sabina."

Her friend looked at her, terror streaking her face. "I can't. None can touch your sword without the promise of death."

The riders were getting closer. She needed to hurry before they tried to stop her. "Touch the damn sword!"

Sabina gripped the blade, cutting her flesh on the sharp edge. She cried out but kept her hold, her eyes focused on Taryn, a silent plea in them.

Hayden pulled at Taryn, but she snapped at him to stand back. "Sabina's blood must be purified." She concentrated all of her thoughts on Sabina. Blocking out the cries she heard from the riders, Hayden's objections, Herbret's whimpers. *Sabina. Purity. Cleanse. Innocence.* Her love for her friend poured into her sword, into Sabina.

A shriek came from the mouth of the decapitated crone, followed by a dark plume of smoke that rose into the air, coalescing into the phantom. Sabina cried out again, her grip faltering. Blood oozed from the cut on her palm and out of her nostrils, dripping onto the ground.

"You're killing her, Taryn. Stop!" Hayden tried to wrestle the blade from Taryn's grip.

The girls who lay unconscious next to Sabina thrashed violently against the marble, their skulls cracking on the hard surface again and again. Hayden stared at them, then at Taryn, and finally at Sabina. Taryn forced more of her power into the sword, her hands shaking as she fought to keep control.

A streak of fire lit forth from the blade, turning it the color of blood. The demon's screams echoed over the land. Like Sabina, blood coursed from Taryn's nostrils, and for a moment, they were connected. She saw the girl's history, her power, suppressed beneath the taint of Black ShantiMari. Her lineage had always been one connected with the gods. *Sabinth Aarendhi.* Seventeenth Vessel.

Through his rape of Julieta, Kaldaar had sired a daughter. Hidden among the people of the Summerlands, she carried in her the future of the Black Arts. Sabina was the seventeenth of her kind.

Taryn's sword burst forth in song. Words flowed around them, through them, to the far reaches of the stones, to the sky, and deep beneath the ground. It sang of rebirth.

Light from the song filled the phantom. It expanded to blot out the sky, and then collapsed in on itself before exploding into a trillion fragments of dark dust.

A wind whipped up, scattering the ashes in every direction.

Taryn looked up to see Lliandra standing several paces from them, her hands outstretched, her Mari a blaze of blue fire springing from her fingertips, swirling through the stones like a cyclone.

The light from Taryn's sword paled and winked out. The song quieted. Sabina released her grip on the blade and collapsed. Hayden bent to catch her, cradling her against his chest.

Taryn, sticky with blood and sweat, staggered against the altar. The lifeless bodies of the two women stared blankly. A black ooze dripped down the side of the marble.

She turned away from the sight and met Rhoane's steely gaze. "You should have waited for us."

"If we had, we would've been too late. As it is, we couldn't save them." She jerked her chin at the women.

Carina returned with a small bundle in her arms. "I found him behind the far stone." She gently placed Ebus on the ground.

Several cuts ran the length of his arms, as if someone had tried to bleed him, but he was breathing. Taryn knelt beside the thief and placed her hand on his heart. Rhoane knelt opposite, his hand covering hers.

"Don't let him die, Rhoane. There has been too much death already today."

A bright shaft of light shone down on them as the moon moved away from the sun. The eclipse was complete. The threat of darkness gone. For the moment.

At the sound of a single rider, they both glanced up to see Marissa reigning her horse to a stop. "Celia!" She ran past Taryn and Rhoane to kneel beside her friend. "What have you done?" She sobbed, rocking the headless corpse against her bosom.

"She rode in with you?" Taryn asked Rhoane. He wasn't watching the crown princess, but looking past the stones.

His gaze shifted to settle on her. "No. She was not in the palace when we received your call." A thin thread of his ShantiMari flowed into Ebus, and Taryn returned her focus to healing the little thief.

"Rhoane," Taryn ventured, "do you still think Marissa knew nothing of this?"

His jaw tightened and a slight tic pulled at the corner of his eye. "Far from it. I think she planned today's events."

Taryn stared at him, dumbfounded. "What changed your mind?"

He indicated Marissa's mare, "Her coat is dry. The other horses are lathered from the run, but not Marissa's."

Taryn glanced at Lliandra, who was saying a prayer over the dead girls, and then to Herbret, who lay shuddering on the grass. A dry horse wouldn't be enough to convince the empress her daughter was involved, of that Taryn was certain. Lliandra swept down to comfort the crown princess and the look on her face chilled Taryn. Lliandra already knew. And

Taryn suspected nothing would come of that knowledge.

She glanced back to Rhoane and he, too, watched the empress.

She won't believe us, will she? Taryn asked in his mind.

I am afraid not.

There was something in the soft whisper of his thought that tore through Taryn's heart. As if, with those four words, he lost all hope that Marissa wasn't deceiving him.

Chapter 51

MARISSA'S sobs disturbed the late afternoon tranquility. Golden leaves fell from the trees, catching in the draft from the blaze that swept around Celia's body. A traitor's burial. Herbret lay beside her, his face devoid of color, his garments those of a pauper. The flames had yet to reach him.

Marissa reached for Taryn's hand, squeezing it slightly. "I don't blame you. You did what was necessary."

Despite Herbret's full confession and Carina's account of what had happened at the stones, Marissa believed Taryn's sword had ended Celia's life. Taryn was too tired to deny the allegations any longer and simply nodded her acceptance.

"But this," Marissa continued, "goes too far. Mother at least could've afforded Celia a plot in the crypt."

Eliahnna's astonished stare didn't affect their older sister. "She's a traitor, Marissa. Whether you want to admit that or not. She got what she deserved."

Marissa's grip tightened on Taryn's hand, but she held her tongue.

"I'm sorry, Marissa. Truly I am." Taryn spoke the truth. Losing Celia was difficult for Marissa, but she had sacrificed her favorite as surely as Celia had brought her fate upon herself. "I wish there was more I could've done." Again, the truth. Like, uncover the plot before it went as far as it did.

A crack from the fire sent a shiver down her spine. The flames reached several yards above the bodies, leaving nothing but ash on the marble slab.

The subdued group made their way to the palace, but Marissa held Taryn back. Rhoane cast her a concerned look, but she motioned him to continue with the others.

"Taryn, I'm worried about you."

That was a first.

"What happened at the stones, the danger you put yourself in for Sabina, you could've been killed. First the vorlock, then the assassin, and now this. You aren't prepared to deal with these attacks like you should be."

Taryn suspected Marissa cared about her own safety most, but she was right. "What do you propose?"

"I think you should go to your brother. Train with him as you do Faelara and Rhoane. Unlock your Dark Shanti."

"You want me to go to Zakael? Quite possibly the only person on this world besides my father who could do me the most harm?" Taryn baited her.

"He's your best hope for completing the trinity. I saw you in the stones. Your power almost overwhelmed you."

Taryn had hoped no one had seen the weakening of her knees, the way she'd braced against the altar for strength. Pulling that much power had taken its toll. If Sabina had held on for a few minutes more, Taryn might've lost consciousness.

"But it didn't."

"There is a price for using ShantiMari, Taryn. Even for you." Marissa patted her hand, giving another squeeze before steering her toward the palace. Behind them, the fire snapped and cracked with the last shuddering of the high priest's ShantiMari. "Write to him, Taryn. Write to Zakael and beg him, if you must, but please, for all our sakes, complete the trinity."

They had almost reached the palace doors when Taryn

remembered Marissa had arrived late to the stones. There was no way she saw Taryn's actions unless she was actually inside the circle, near the altar. A slither of Marissa's Mari crept up her arm and Taryn pinched it with a thread of her own, strangling it.

Marissa looked at Taryn in surprise, and then, to Taryn's amazement, she winked.

MUCH later, after the feast and empty toasts to honor her and Hayden's bravery, she found solace high atop the battlements, her back to the palace, her face turned resolutely toward the west. The lights of Talaith blinked in the distance, but she saw beyond them to a dark castle looming over the sea.

Kaida scampered away, and Taryn glanced over her shoulder to see Rhoane emerging from the heavy door that led to the barracks. He stood beside her and took her hand.

"Ebus has woken from his long sleep."

She nodded into the moonless night.

"He is asking for you. I wish you had told me about Celia, about your concerns."

"If I had, what would be different?"

His sigh sounded like the creak of trees in the forest. Heavy, burdened by things she couldn't see. "I cannot say. Perhaps Celia would be alive."

She studied his profile silhouetted against the flickering torchlight. "I need to go there. You and I both know it."

"No. I will not—cannot—allow it."

"They are the only ones who can show me how to tap my Dark Shanti. Hayden can't, Myrddin won't. I need all three strands of my power. I'm weak without the trinity."

"Not weak. Just not as strong as you could be."

"Semantics."

"Zakael, then."

She gripped his fingers tighter. "You'll come with me? But not until we return from Carga's purification."

They could delay as much as they wanted, but sooner rather than later, she had to seek her brother or her father out. It was the only way. Still, she wouldn't leave until her friends were fully recovered.

Sabina's ShantiMari had come in all at once, overwhelming her. Faelara was working with the princess to control the power and understand what had happened to cause Herbret to sacrifice her as he did. The amount of cruelty it took to do what he and Celia had done shocked the gentle woman. But Taryn understood.

Evil lived alongside kindness. There could be no Light without Dark and no darkness without light. Within each power were those filled with goodness and others equally as coldhearted. Except for the Black Arts—those practitioners sold their souls to the fires of Dal Ferran. No compassion dwelled in them. She'd sensed it in the phantom. The absolute void of anything human, and yet when it shattered, she thought she sensed the slightest hint of pain.

Rhoane turned Taryn toward him and ran his hands up her neck. He wrapped her silken hair around his fingertips and smoothed the tresses straight. In his mossy eyes lingered the same fear, the same doubt. His Shanti embraced her, searching for unseen injuries, soothing her fractured nerves.

"We are as one, *Darennsai*. Together, we are stronger than all of them. We must be united."

She swallowed down her excuses. He was right. She should've trusted him enough to tell him about Celia. Her ShantiMari flowed over his, entwining with his power until the strands became one.

"We are. Always."

His lips pressed down on hers, and she opened herself to him. Fully. Unconditionally. Without him, she would fail. All the prophecies said as much.

Kaida scratched at their legs, and they looked up to see the sun stretching above the sea far to the west. There would be time later to plan for what was to come. Taryn melded herself against Rhoane, curled her fingers in his hair. The sun warmed them as it rose, but it did little to dispel the cold that lingered since defeating the phantom. It was always there, the darkness. Waiting. Watching. Planning.

She tipped her face toward the light, welcoming the sun's rays. For now, she'd embrace every bit of warmth she could find.

THE sounds of the city rumbled past his window, deafening his fragile senses. The Shadow Assassin bathed his trembling body with warm blood, pressing the cloth against his white skin, bringing color back.

The Eirielle was stronger than he'd assumed. Her connection to the sword manifesting a strength he'd not calculated into his plans. At least before she'd expelled him, he was able to thread a link of Black Shanti to her core.

The vanquishing almost destroyed him.

Creating a phantom was not difficult for a seasoned Master, especially one as powerful as he, but there were few who could actualize physicality. He was the greatest the Black Brotherhood would ever know.

And he'd failed their lord.

Kaldaar remained exiled.

He would have to find another way to release him.

"Rest," the ragged voice of his son, his creation, whispered.

"Yes, rest." He placed a hand on the Shadow Spawn's

shoulder where the Eleri prince's sword had drawn blood. "We both need our rest. There is yet time."

A lopsided smile pulled the demon's lips tight. It did not reach his dead eyes.

There was still time.

Aelinae had waited thousands of seasons for the Eirielle.

The Brotherhood even longer.

Glossary of Terms

Aelan (Ay-lan) ~ Any person born of Aelinaen descent. These are usually men and women descended from the Elder Gods: Nadra, Ohlin, Daknys, Rykoto, and Kaldaar. In modern times, Aelan refers to those not of another race.

Aelinae (Ay-lynn-ay) ~ A world created by Nadra and Ohlin. It is disk-shaped with waterfalls at the edge of the world, and volcanoes beneath it.

Aelinaen(s) (Ay-lynn-ee-an) ~ Of or having to do with Aelan culture.

Aergan (Air-gahn) ~ An ancient, valuable ore found in only a few places on Aelinae.

Air Faerie ~ Winged Faeries who call on the elements of air for power. Usually diminutive beings no more than six inches tall.

Anklam (Ahnk-lahm) ~ A city on the coast, south of Talaith.

Artagh (R-tah-g) ~ Related to the Eleri, Artaghs lack the Eleri Glamour, as well as the sophistication of the ancient race. They are rumored to be the best at making weapons and working with metals, especially the fabled Godsteel found only in the Haversham Mountains. Outsiders are often distrusted and it's rare to find Artaghs far from their caves.

Black Arts ~ A twisted version of ShantiMari that binds one's soul forever to the banished god, Kaldaar. Practitioners can be either male or female, but females become barren once they invoke the Oath of Fealty. Because of this, they are viewed as Brothers alongside the men.

Black Brotherhood ~ The oldest, most secret religion in

Aelinae's history. Much of the Brotherhood is unknown to any except those who are counted among the members. Once a practitioner is invited to join the Brotherhood, they are challenged to a series of tests, many of which require virginal sacrifices. See also Vessel. Membership is often passed from one family member to another, but the terms must be satisfied before being accepted. Those who do not satisfy the requirements, or are not deemed worthy are destroyed.

Black Shanti and **Black ShantiMari** ~ See also Black Arts. This form of ShantiMari uses chaos to fuel its power. External and internal sources give practitioners their strength. They pull their power from the world around them, or the inner conflict people try to conceal. The use of Black ShantiMari is shunned by the Light and Dark, but there are those who have found a way to manipulate the strands of light and shadow into a woven tapestry of devastation that cannot be traced. These are Masters that even the Black Brotherhood fear.

Caer Idris (Care Ee-dris) ~ The ancestral home of The Overlord of the West. Currently, Valterys, Lord of Darkness sits on the Obsidian Throne.

Carlix ~ A sleek, winged feline who makes her home in the mountains known as the Spine of Ohlin. One of the first creatures to inhabit the planet of Aelinae. Often referred to for their flexibility and quick responses, the number of people who have actually seen a carlix is few.

Cockleberry ~ A yellowish fruit that grows in glens and meadows throughout Aelinae. With a taste similar to blackberries, cockleberries are often used in pies and tasty treats.

Crystal Court ~ The accepted nickname for the court of the Empress of Talaith.

Crystal Palace ~ The accepted nickname for the palace in Talaith where the Empress rules. It's fabled walls are made from a thin layer of rock clear enough to see through, yet unable to be penetrated by weapons or ShantiMari. No one knows who built the great palace, or where the stone came from.

Cynfar (Sin-far) ~ The Eleri name for a talisman given to someone. Usually a pendant, it can also be a bracelet, earrings, or even a small stone. It must be kept close to the recipient for maximum benefit, hence the use of jewelry.

Dal Ferran (Dahl Fair-en) ~ The fiery pits of hell beneath Aelinae's surface.

Dal Tara (Dahl Tar-a) ~ A celestial resting place for the Gods and those they deem worthy. It is located in the second quadrant of the Meirdia Nebula.

Danuri ~ A Province located in the West. The second largest city to Caer Idris, Danuri is widely known for their wine and ale making skills.

Danurian ~ Anyone of Danuri descent.

Darennsai (Dar-en-sigh) ~ An ancient title given to Taryn by the Eleri. Most don't know the true meaning of the word, thinking of it as nothing more than an honorific bestowed upon her by the Goddess Verdaine. Only a few know the word means, Daughter of the Sky. Less an oath than a promise that one day Taryn will sit at the side of Verdaine, as a goddess in her own right. The Eleri reject this idea.

Dark ~ The part of ShantiMari that is derived from the sun. Only men are skilled in the ways of the Dark, except for the anomaly. To have Dark powers does not automatically make one bad, or evil. There are many men who use their Dark Shanti for good.

Dark Master ~ A highly skilled practitioner of Dark ShantiMari.

Dark Shanti ~ The male side of ShantiMari.

Darathi Vorsi (Dah-rahth-ee Vor-see) ~ Aside from the carlix, *darathi vorsi* are the oldest creatures on Aelinae. Several thousand seasons ago they disappeared from the planet, but the Eleri hold the belief that one day they will return.

Delante (Day-lan-t) ~ A dance performed with a group of people.

Dreem ~ A whisky-like drink that ladies don't usually partake of.

Drerfox ~ Cousin to the fox, a drerfox is bigger, with fangs coated with poison. Their coats shimmer in the sunlight, blending them into the background, making them difficult to see during the day.

The East ~ A geographical location on the map indicating all lands, properties, kingdoms, etc east of the Spine of Ohlin. Includes the Narthvier, Ulla, Talaith, and the marshes near Kaldaar's Stones.

Eirielle (Air-ee-elle) ~ The one of prophecy. Said to be the destroyer or the savior of Aelinae, depending on which prophecy you read. Only one Eirielle is ever said to be created, but that doesn't stop those of the Light and Dark from trying to make one. The Eirielle is rumored to possess all the strands of ShantiMari: Light, Dark, Eleri, and Black. Although, the last is only known to the Brotherhood.

Eiriellean Prophecy ~ A collection of prophecies that record various oracles' visions and ramblings about the Eirielle. Throughout history, there have been those that decried the prophecies, and those that touted them as truth. Nearly everyone fears either version coming to pass.

Elennish (Elle-enn-ish) ~ The oldest language on Aelinae still spoken in the East and West.

Eleri (Ee-ler-ee) ~ A mysterious clan of elf-like men and women who live in the Narthvier. They stay within the borders of their forest and don't like outsiders coming on their land. The Eleri share a collective conscious, in that they can call on the wisdom of past and future Eleri in times of duress. The oldest race on Aelinae, they and the *darathi vorsi* share a common bond. Thought to be caretakers of the beasts, when the *darathi vorsi* disappeared, it was a time of great mourning for the Eleri.

Fadair (Fah-d-air) ~ The name Eleri have given to anyone not Eleri. It is meant to be used as a way to signify someone not of Eleri descent, but often it is used as a disparaging slur against non-Eleri.

Faerie Cakes ~ Small cakes light in texture, but filling. Made with sponge cake and jam, these are Taryn's favorite. Don't ever leave a plate sitting around or she'll eat them all.

Feiche (Fee-ch) ~ A large black bird similar to a raven, but faster and a bit bigger. They hunt in packs and are capable of taking down a small horse if so inclined.

Gaarendahl (Gare-en-doll) ~ An older castle located between the Spine of Ohlin and the Summer Sea. It belongs to Valterys's family, but Zakael uses it most often.

Geigan (Guy-gan) ~ A warrior race of people. Dark in coloring, they are rumored to be the source of mating with the Sitari.

Glamour ~ A slight shimmering beneath the skin. Found only on Eleri.

Godsteel ~ A metal forged by the Artagh of Haversham. Stronger than any other metal, godsteel is unbreakable. Long ago, only the gods could wield weapons made of godsteel (hence, the name), but at least two swords have made their way into mortal's hands. Rhoane's and Taryn's. But there are rumors that a few other swords have been tainted by Black ShantiMari. Their owners are unknown at this time.

Grierbas (Greer-bah) ~ A large, wolf-like animal that makes its home in the Narthvier. Wild and territorial, grierbas keep away from civilizations, even avoiding the Eleri.

Grhom (Gr-om) ~ A spiced drink made by the Eleri. It has healing properties and gives strength through the many ingredients used to make it. Taryn likens the taste to a thick chocolate mixed with chai. Occasionally, the Eleri will add alcohol to the drink.

Gyota (Gee-o-tah) ~ In Eleri, *gyota* means 'destroyer'.

Harvest ~ The months during the season between Summer and Wintertide. On Earth, this time is referred to as Fall.

Haversham ~ A mountainous region where Artagh mine for gems, minerals, and the necessary metals to make weapons. Highly guarded, outsiders are not welcome in Haversham

Hildgelt (Hill-d-gel-t) ~ A Danurian ornamentation made from thin layers of blown glass.

House ~ The family name by which most Aelans associate themselves. Every House has their own color and insignia. It is by these outward displays members of nobility and the court can recognize another's importance.

House Galendrin ~ Ohlin created this House for Taryn on her crowning day. This is the highest honor anyone could hope to achieve and has only been granted once.

Kiltern River ~ A river that runs north of Paderau to Ulla.

Lan Gyllarelle (Lahn Gill-a-rell) ~ A vast lake located in the Narthvier. Its waters are rumored to hold healing properties. The Eleri often hold ceremonies on the banks of the lake.

Lake Oster ~ Located between Talaith and Paderau, Lake Oster is often used as a stopping point for travelers. Fresh water and an abundance of fish refresh stores between the two great cities.

Levon (Le-von) ~ A sleek black bird. Faster than any other birds, the levon is a favorite form of transportation for those competent in transformation.

Light ~ A strain of ShantiMari found in females born on Aelinae. Not all women exhibit traits of the power, but are able to pass on Light ShantiMari to their daughters. Eleri females have Light ShantiMari, but their powers will differ from the Fadair's in that they use nature as a catalyst and Fadair use the air and sky. The Lady of Light is able to manipulate weather and has slight control over the sea.

Light Throne ~ The ancestral court of The Lady of Light, otherwise known as the Empress of Talaith. Also referred to as the Crystal Court. The actual throne is made of ancient oak from the Narthvier. Woven into the planks of wood is a thin layer of crystal.

Mari (Mar-ee) ~ The female side of ShantiMari. Also referred to as Light.

Midvale ~ A small town located a days' ride from Ravenwood.

Mind-Speak ~ A form of communication used between two people within their minds.

Mount Nadrene (Mount Nay-dreen) ~ The holiest place on Aelinae, Mount Nadrene is where Nadra sent Taryn through a portal to Earth. It is also a cavern filled with glittering crystals and a large lake. Some believe the cavern is the birthplace of all the gods and goddesses of Aelinae.

Nadra (Nah-d-rah) ~ The Mother Goddess, she and Ohlin created Aelinae

Narthvier (Narth-veer) ~ A vast forest covering the northeast portion of Aelinae. The Eleri make their home in the Narthvier, or vier as some call it. The Eleri are protective of the forest and use veils to dissuade unwelcome visitors. Only the Eleri know how to raise the fabled veils.

Obsidian Throne ~ The ancestral home of the Lord of the Dark. The actual throne is made of the same oak planks as the Light Throne. Within the wood fibers is woven obsidian granite.

Offlander ~ Any person raised outside of the courtesies of court. The term is an insult of the highest order.

Ohlin (Oh-lynn) ~ The Great Father, he and Nadra created Aelinae

Paderau (Pah-der-oo) ~ A vast city ruled by Duke Anje.

Paderau sits between the Narthvier and Talaith, which makes it a busy port city for trading goods.

Paderau Palace ~ The home of Duke Anje and his family.

Privy Council ~ A body of advisers to the Empress of Talaith. The council is made up of senior members of the highest Houses. On occasion, as with Hayden and Duke Anje, a junior member can represent their House in council. Also included in the privy council are the High Priest, and captains of the guard or military.

Ravenwood ~ The less formal home of the Duke of Anje. When in residence, he oversees the local businesses.

Sargot (Sar-go) ~ An orange-like fruit that tastes similar to a mango.

Seal of Ardyn ~ Seals created by the Elder Gods to keep Rykoto imprisoned in the Temple of Ardyn.

Shanti (Shahn-tee) ~ The male side of ShantiMari. Also referred to as Dark.

ShantiMari (Shahn-tee Mar-ee) ~ Two halves of the same whole. ShantiMari is a power found in all things on Aelinae. Within men and women, it manifests itself in varying degrees from no visible signs, to extremely powerful. Those in positions of great power will have more ShantiMari than those born to the lesser clans or Houses. ShantiMari is often referred to as Light and Dark, or female and male. Within the confines of ShantiMari are rules, or etiquette. The power can be culled from the smallest pebble to the stars themselves. Wielding more power than one is capable of controlling often leads to a painful death.

Shadow Assassin ~ Neither alive nor dead, Shadow Assassins were the elite force of Kaldaar's army. Only a powerful Master can create the demons.

Shadow Spawn, Shadow Soul ~ Nicknames given to the Shadow Assassin.

Sheanna (Shee-ahn-a) ~ An exiled Eleri. When an Eleri is sheanna, they are required to cut their hair and live outside the borders of the Narthvier until a certain amount of time has passed. Once they return to the Narthvier, they must complete the purification ceremony before they are considered to be Eleri once more.

Silden River ~ This river runs south from Paderau to Lake Oster.

Sitari (Sit-ar-ee) ~ Blue skinned warrior women who live in a community devoid of men. Their island sits at the southernmost edge of Aelinae. It is rumored their preferred mates are Geigan males. Sitari women can be found in other kingdoms of Aelinae, usually scouting for the strongest to procreate with. Once coupling has been achieved, the Sitari return to their island. Male offspring are said to be sacrificed to their goddess.

Skirm (Sk-ur-m) ~ A banana-like fruit. The leaves of the skirm tree are broad and often used in cooking roasted meats.

Smelting Day ~ An annual celebration of Artagh to honor their god. The fires of Haversham burn brightest on Smelting Day, but no actual forging is done. Instead, the Artagh participate in dances and rousing songs around the flames.

Spine of Ohlin ~ The range of mountains stretching from the Temple of Ardyn in the far north to the Summer Seas in the south.

Summerlands ~ An island kingdom located south of Talaith in the Summer Seas.

Summer Seas ~ The body of water covering the entire southern area of Aelinae.

Sword of Ohlin ~ Also known as Ynyd Eirathnacht. Ohlin had the sword made out of godsteel for his daughter, Daknys. The bearer of the sword must be pure of heart and worthy of the weapon.

Sylthan Age (Sil-than Age) ~ The fourth century of Aelinae's time clock.

Talaith (Tal - eth) ~ The capital city of the East. Ruled by the empress, also known as The Lady of Light.

Temple of Ardyn (Ar-din) ~ Rykoto's temple and source of power. He was imprisoned here by Daknys and the Elder Gods after his defeat in the Great War.

Treplar (Treh-p-lar) ~ Round apple-like, spiky fruits from the Summerlands.

Trin ~ A form of currency in the East.

Trisp ~ A thick alcoholic drink.

Ulla (Oo-la) ~ A kingdom located in the far East of Aelinae. The Ullans are a tribal people, following their herds throughout the season. Ullan horses are of the finest stock.

Verdaine ~ (Vehr-d-ane) Daughter of Nadra and Ohlin, goddess of the Eleri.

Verdaine's Prophecy ~ When Rhoane was born, Verdaine prophesied that he would be exiled from his people until the *gyota* returned. His fate would be tied to the one who is and who is not for all time.

Veil ~ A mysterious barrier preventing outsiders from entering the Narthvier.

Vier ~ Nickname of the Narthvier.

Vorlock ~ A huge, lizard-like creature with heavy scales and a wide frill around its head. Vorlocks contain a poison that can kill a man or woman instantly.

Weirren (Weer-en) ~ The ancestral home of the Eleri King and Queen.

Weirren Court ~ The gathered nobility of the Eleri live among the many buildings interwoven through the ancient tree that makes up the Weirren.

Weirren Throne ~ Built into the oldest tree on Aelinae, the Weirren Throne is a living, breathing seat.

The West ~ Geographical area located to the west of Ohlin's Spine. Includes the kingdom of the Overlord of the West, Danuri Province, and Haversham.

Western Seas ~ The body of water located off the Western Coast of Aelinae.

Woodland Faerie ~ Faerie folk who make their home in the forests Aelinae, most commonly found in the Narthvier. Woodland faeries grow to be around three feet in height, although some are taller. They are the exception. Woodland faeries share a special bond with nature and can cultivate new species of living plants or animals.

Cast of Characters

Aislinn al Glennwoods ap Narthvier (Ay-s-lynn) ~ Queen of the Eleri. Aislinn perished in a ShantiMari accident when Rhoane was a young man.

Alasdair (Alice-dare) ~ A faerie servant in the service of Rhoane. Brother to Illanr and Carld.

Alswyth Myrddin (Alls-with Mere-din) ~ Mage with exceedingly long life. Myrddin is the advisor to Empress Lliandra and is often far from court on assignments from the crown. No known children or spouses. No known House.

Anje ap Paderau (Ann-jee ap Paw-der-oo) ~ Duke of Paderau, father to Hayden, husband to Gwyneira (now deceased). Anje is cousin to the Lord of Darkness, and third in line for the Obsidian Throne. His father was brother to Valterys's father. A prince in his own right, Anje renounced his Dark heritage to live with his wife in the Light. Descendant of House Djeba.

Aomori di Monsenti (A-more-ee di Mon-scent-ee) ~ A young Danuri lord fostering with Tinsley in Paderau. Descendant of House Monsenti.

Armando ~ Summerlander. Lover of Tarro. Whore in Nena's house. Marissa's favorite.

Ashanni (A-shawn-ee) ~ A mare Duke Anje gives to Taryn.

Baehlon de Monteferron (Bay-lohn de Mont-fair-on) ~ Danuri and Geigan knight employed by Empress Lliandra, sworn to protect Taryn and her House. Descendant of House Monteferron.

Beary ~ (Master) Unseen character in book one. Advisor to

Taryn on household matters.

Brandt Kaj Endion (Brant) ~ Aelan. High Priest of Talaith and advisor to Empress Lliandra, Brandt was commissioned with Taryn's safety when she was born. After his death, Nadra took Brandt to Dal Tara, (home of the gods), which allows Brandt to communicate with Taryn. House Arran.

Bressal ap Narthvier (Bress-all) ~ Eleri. Second Son to King Stephan and Queen Aislinn (now passed beyond the veils).

Carga ap Narthvier ~ Eleri. Daughter to King Stephan and Queen Aislinn (now passed beyond the veils). Currently exiled from the Eleri (known as *sheanna* to her clan) and working as a cook in the kitchens of Duke Anje.

Carina (Ka-reen-a) ~ Aelan. A soldier in the employ of Duke Anje, she is assigned to Taryn's personal guard.

Carld (Car-uld) ~ A faerie maid in the service of King Stephan. Sister to Illanr and Alasdair.

Celia ~ Aelan. Lady-in-waiting to Marissa and minor noble. Descendant of House Deltanna.

Cora ~ Aelan. A maid in the service of Empress Lliandra assigned to Taryn upon her arrival in Talaith.

Cynda (Sin-dah) ~ A mare Rhoane provides for Taryn.

Daknys (Dak-niss) ~ Elder Goddess. Daughter of Nadra and Ohlin, she is worshipped by the Light and Dark in the central area of Aelinae.

Ebus (Ee-bus) ~ Race unknown. Thief known to Rhoane. Becomes spy for Taryn and Rhoane. Can see the Shadow Assassin.

Eiric (Err-ic) ~ Danuri. Lover of Zakael.

Eliahnna Tjaru (Ee-lahn-ah Shar-U) ~ Aelan. Daughter of Lliandra. Her heritage is much debated since Lliandra has never publicly named her father. She is third in line to the Light Throne. Descendant of House Nadrene.

Ellie ~ Aelan. A maid in the service of Empress Lliandra assigned to Taryn upon her arrival in Talaith.

Eoghan ap Narthvier (Eee-gan) ~ Eleri. Third Son to King Stephan and Queen Aislinn (now passed beyond the veils).

Faelara Dal Arran (Fay-lara) ~ Aelan. Daughter of Brandt, Faelara is currently a lady-in-waiting to Empress Lliandra. Her Healing skills are legendary, as were her father's. House Arran.

Faisal dei Tarnovo (Fay-sal) ~ Summerlander. Sabina's father and the king of the Summerlands. House Tarnov.

Fayngaar (Fain-gar) ~ Rhoane's stallion.

Gameson ~ Aelan. (Master) Head tutor in the service of Empress Lliandra.

Gris ~ Aelan. A kitchen boy in the service of Duke Anje.

Gwyneira Tjaru ap Paderau (Gwin-eera ap Shar-U) ~ Aelan. Sister to Empress Lliandra, wife of Duke Anje, mother to Hayden. Gwyneira died after childbirth when Hayden was a young man. Houses Nadrene and Djeba.

Hayden ap Valen ~ Aelan. Lord Valen, Marquis of the province Valen, son of Anje and Gwyneira. Hayden is cousin to the heirs of the Light Throne and the Obsidian Throne. Descendant of House Djeba.

Herbret ~ Aelan. A minor noble in Talaith's court. Descendant of House Gilfroy.

Illanr (Ill-an-or) ~ A faerie maid in the service of King Stephan. Sister to Carld and Alasdair.

Janeira (Juh-nair-a) ~ An Eleri warrior of great standing, excellent skill, and deadly capabilities.

Julieta ~ Younger Goddess. Daughter of Rykoto and Daknys.

Kaida (Kay-da) ~ A grierbas Taryn rescues in the Narthvier. They become companions and have the ability to speak with each other in their minds. Kaida can track the Shadow Assassin.

Kaldaar (Cal-dar) ~ Elder God. Son of Nadra and Ohlin, worshipped by inhabitants of the Southeast until his banishment after the Great War. Kaldaar hasn't been seen in Aelinae in over five thousand seasons.

Lliandra Tjaru (Lee-on-dra Shar-U) ~ Aelan. Empress of Talaith, Lady of Light. Mother to Marissa, Taryn, Eliahnna, and Tessa. Lliandra is directly descended from the goddess Nadra. She is thought to be a just ruler who thinks of her subjects in all matters. House Nadrene.

Lorilee ~ Aelan. A maid in the service of Duke Anje. Sister to Mayla.

Marissa Tjaru (Shar-U) ~ Aelan. Crown Princess of Talaith, heir to the Light Throne, daughter of Lliandra and Esna (not named in books one or two). Descendant of House Nadrene.

Mayla ~ Aelan. A maid in the service of Duke Anje. Sister to Lorilee.

Margaret Tan ~ Geigan. Seamstress to Empress Lliandra, she often travels with the court. Her tailoring skills are said to be admired in all the kingdoms.

Nadra ~ Mother of Aelinae, Great Mother of all Creation. Along with Ohlin, Nadra created Aelinae. Mother to Daknys, Rykoto, Kaldaar, and Verdaine.

Nena ~ Race unknown. Owner of a house of prostitution in Talaith.

Ohlin (O-lynn) ~ Father of Aelinae, Great Father of all Creation. Along with Nadra, Ohlin created Aelinae. Father to to Daknys, Rykoto, Kaldaar, and Verdaine.

Oliver ~ Aelan. A servant in the service of Hayden, Lord Valen.

Phantom ~ An unknown entity manipulating Celia, Herbret, and Marissa. The phantom is thought to be an agent of Kaldaar.

Prateeni dei Tarnovo (Pruh-teen-ee) ~ Summerlander. Sabina's mother and the Queen of the Summerlands. House Tarnov.

Rhoane al Glennwoods ap Narthvier (Rone) ~ Eleri. First Son of Stephan, King of the Eleri, and Aislinn, Queen of the Eleri (now passed beyond the veils). At birth Rhoane was prophesied to be the Eirielle's protector. When he was old enough, he took an oath forsaking all others and devoting his life to upholding Verdaine's prophecy.

Rykoto (Ree-ko-toe) ~ Elder God. Son of Nadra and Ohlin, worshipped by inhabitants of the Northwest and of the Dark. Rykoto was imprisoned in the Temple of Ardyn after the Great War.

Sabina dei Tarnovo ~ Summerlander. Daughter of King Faisal and Queen Prateeni, Sabina was sent to Talaith to foster with Empress Lliandra. She was born without ShantiMari, a great disgrace to her family. Descendant of House Tarnov.

Saeko (Say-koh) ~ A maid in the service of Taryn.

Shadow Assassin ~ An unknown assailant stalking Taryn. He can 'disappear'.

Stephan ap Narthvier ~ King of the Eleri. Direct descendant from Verdaine.

Tabul (Tah-buhl) ~ Summerlander. Spice merchant from Paderau.

Tarro (Tare-O) ~ Danuri. Assistant to Margaret Tan. Lover of Armando.

Taryn Rose Galendrin (Tare-in) ~ Daughter of Lliandra, Empress of Talaith, Lady of Light and Valterys, Overlord of the West, Lord of Darkness. Raised on Earth, Taryn grew up unaware of Aelinae, believing Brandt was her grandfather and only family. House Galendrin.

Tessa Tjaru (Shar-U) ~ Aelan. Daughter of Lliandra and Razlog (not named in books one or two). She is fourth in line to the Light Throne. Descendant of House Nadrene.

Timor (Tim-or) ~ Aelan. A soldier in the employ of Duke Anje, he is assigned to Taryn's personal guard.

Tinsley Alcath (Tins-lee All-koth) ~ Aelan. A young lord with business ties to Duke Anje and is often at Paderau Palace. Descendant of House Alcath.

Tudyk (Too-dic) ~ Aelan. Sword Master in the service of

Empress Lliandra.

Valterys Djeba (Val-terr-iss D-jj-ay-ba) ~ Aelan. Overlord of the West, Lord of the Dark. Father to Taryn and Zakael. Valterys is directly descended from the god Ohlin. He rules his kingdom with a tight grasp on its economy and trade. His subjects think of him favorably. House Djeba.

Verdaine (Vare-dane) ~ Eider Goddess. Daughter of Nadra and Ohlin, she is worshipped by the Eleri in the Narthvier.

Zakael Djeba (Zah-K-ay-eel D-jj-ay-ba) ~ Aelan. Prince, heir to the Obsidian Throne. Son of Valterys and Troyanna (not named in books one or two). Descendant of House Djeba.

Acknowledgements

I find myself in the wonderful position of being able to thank those who have made this journey possible. From the first people I met at SCWC who encouraged me even when this story was a hot mess (I'm looking at you, Matt Pallamary!), to my early readers who slugged through more words than were necessary. Alexzandra Etherton, you are my sun, my moon, and my stars. You weren't afraid to tell me the truth and helped make the story stronger for it. Nicole Breton, beta reader extraordinaire! She made me realize Sabina had something to say and this book is the result of our conversations. I used to joke that she kicked my butt on the page as well as in the gym. I miss our workouts, but look forward to her opinions on my future projects. Laura Case made me think about word choice. Well, one specifically. I still used it, but not as much. Kate Wood kept me laughing with her witty and spot-on comments. He can't hurt you if he's dead! I wouldn't be here today without my HDSA's. They're always there, lurking, but never far if I need them. I love you ladies with all my heart.

My RWA Chapters of Orange County and San Diego, as well as my online chapters, again, I couldn't have done this without you! The advice, the support, the camaraderie, it's all helped shape me into the writer I am today, and this book into the book it is. Which brings me to the fabulous editors who helped whip my writing into shape. Faith DeBishop Williams, Danielle Rose Poiesz, and the incomparable Sharon Pickrel. Much love to you ladies. This book would be rubbish without the fantastic Kitty Bucholtz putting it into readable order. Thanks, Doll! I have to thank Carol Phillips for the freaking awesome cover art, sword art, dragons, and map! She never flinched from my crazy ideas and always came up with something far more amazing than I ever dreamed. To Debra Kristi, Kate Wood, and Gayle Carline, my fellow adventurers, you put up with my mischief, and keep me sane. Mostly. I love you. Truly. Madly. Deeply.

A special thank you to these four ladies who gave of their wisdom freely and inspired me not only in my writing, but through their generosity. It's a beautiful thing when I can pass on what they have shared with me. Bella Andre, Sheri Fink, Rebecca Zanetti, and my darling Steena Holmes. Thank you.

And finally, I am thankful to my family for their continued support and enthusiasm. None of this would be possible without them. David, Alexzandra, and Michael, you are my everything. Always.

Meet the Author

Rocker of sparkly tiaras, friend of dragons, and lover of all things sexy, Tameri Etherton leaves a trail of glitter in her wake as she creates and conquers new worlds and the villains who inhabit them. When not masquerading as a mom and writer, rumor has it she travels to far off places, drinking tea and finding inspiration for her kickass heroines—and the rogues who steal their hearts—with her own Prince Charming by her side.

To find out more about the author, visit her web site at www.TameriEtherton.com. Be sure to sign up for her newsletter to receive exclusives like advanced notice of upcoming releases, secret scenes, and other enticing tidbits about the Song of the Swords series.

There you'll discover the World of Aelinae where you'll find maps, glossaries, and a complete cast of characters to further your reading experience.

If you enjoyed **THE STONES OF KALDAAR: SONG OF THE SWORDS BOOK ONE**, look for **THE TEMPLE OF ARDYN: SONG OF THE SWORDS BOOK TWO** *by Tameri Etherton*

NO moon guided their way as they traveled southeast toward the Dierlin Pass. The first night of their escape, Taryn found them shelter in an abandoned shepherd's cottage. Niko munched some hay and Kaida caught several rats in the loft while Taryn and the faerie ate what crumbs they could find in the cupboard. When she sank to the floor, exhausted, a wave of emotion washed over her but she held back her tears for fear if she let one fall, a dam would burst.

They rode hard day and night. Only when she felt faint from lack of food would they stop to set snares or fish in a stream. At first, the faerie would snatch his food from her with greedy hands, taking gulping bites, afraid Taryn would take the food from him.

Very gently, as if she were speaking to a child, she would say, "You must eat slower or you'll make yourself sick." When she put a hand on his, he snarled at her, baring his teeth. "I'm not going to take your food. Slowly, that's it. Just a small bite." When she gave him another portion, he looked at her with apprehension. "You can trust me. I'm going to take care of you."

Gradually, she earned his trust and one night, under a blanket of stars, the faerie found the courage to speak. Not with his voice, but in her mind.

His name was Gian. He belonged to a clan on the western border of the Narthvier. They traded goods with several villages nearby and it was when he was out hunting for pelts that Zakael had come upon him. He bound Gian in his ShantiMari and then took him back to Caer Idris.

Beyond that Gian would say no more. When Taryn suggested she take him to the vier, he sobbed against her, his sounds muffled in his throat. He insisted over and over again that he could never return to the Narthvier.

Whatever he'd suffered while imprisoned in Zakael's dungeons had scarred Gian physically and emotionally. Taryn held him close, promising she wouldn't let anything happen to him. She stretched her ShantiMari out, pulling the shadows over them like a thick cloak.

On the sixth day of their escape, Taryn noticed a sleek black bird flying overhead. When it circled above them, her pulse quickened. Niko must've sensed the bird's presence because he pawed at the ground, snorting with angry huffs. She led him off the road and slid from the saddle, taking Gian with her.

"Go hide over there behind those trees," she told him. "Do not come out no matter what you see. Do you understand?" He nodded mutely at her and ran off to where she'd indicated. "Kaida, go with him. Zakael will be here any moment; you must keep Gian safe."

Taryn took her sword from its scabbard and stood in the center of a small clearing. The bird circled once and then swooped down, dissolving into the form of Zakael when its claws touched the ground. Her brother shook out his cloak, cracking his neck and shoulders before turning to face her. A sword appeared in his hand, its black steel glinting in the sunlight.

"You aren't making a very good escape, sister. I found you too easily. Why did you run away? It was most vexing to Father. And myself."

"I didn't run away. You and Valterys disappeared. I got bored, so I left."

"That's twice now you've left my home on short notice. Is it something I said?"

"What do you want?" Taryn flexed her fingers around the sword hilt.

"For you to return with me, what else?"

"Why—so you can ignore me? No, thanks."

"You seem to think you have a choice, dear sister, when in fact, you don't." He threw a ball of power at her and she sliced through it with her sword.

"Yes, I do." She deflected another of his attacks before swinging her sword low to catch his thigh. He danced back out of reach, laughing. The sound grated on her, like the incessant nattering of a fly too close to one's ear.

He came at her hard and fast, but she was ready.

With each of his thrusts, she parried and deflected, circling around him to slice at his knees, followed by a cut to his chest, deliberately trying to throw him off balance. The longer they fought, the more he looked astonished. He'd underestimated her skill in all things, especially with a sword. A tangle of his Shanti pulled her feet out from beneath her. She hit the ground with a thud and then immediately rolled to spring up before him.

The clash of metal rang out as they slashed and thrust at each other. Sweat ran down Taryn's face as she danced around Zakael. She saw that he, too, was dripping with exertion. She spun quickly, elbowing him in the gut and then stamping on his foot before turning to knock him on the head with the hilt of her sword. He went down on his knees, breathing heavily. She paused only a moment to gather her strength and he grabbed her with his power.

His ShantiMari whipped around her neck, lifting her from the ground. She thrashed against his power, gasping for breath. A thread of Shanti snatched her sword away while another pulled her arms above her head. She spat curses at him and herself for giving him the opportunity to restrain her.

A sharp jab to her mind sent her thoughts scattering for a heartbeat before she closed it against him. When she pulled at her ShantiMari, a barrier prevented her from reaching it. Zakael stood, one hand on his stomach, the other outstretched to her. A thread of his power ran from his fingertips to her head. Somehow he was blocking her from reaching her ShantiMari. To block another's power was strictly forbidden.

"You've no idea how much I've been looking forward to this moment." He moved a step closer. "Father wants you alive, but he didn't say by how much." His fingers twitched and the power tightened around her throat, cutting off all air.

She stopped thrashing and hung limp. Thick cords of his power wrapped around her ankles, pulling her legs wide apart. A gasp of pain came out muffled and pitiful. The exertion spent the air in her lungs.

Darennsai, shall I attack him? Kaida asked, surprising Taryn that Zakael had not cut off her thoughts as well.

Not yet. Wait for my call. Until then, keep Gian safe.

"Don't fight me, my beautiful sister." Zakael held his sword at waist level, chuckling under his breath. "You could still join me willingly. Either way, I will have you." He moved his sword to the top of her leather pants and then down to between her legs. "We were meant to rule Aelinae together, you and I." He reached out suddenly, grabbing her side, sending his power into her vorlock scar. Pain shot through her, sparking fire in her blood. Once more, she sought her ShantiMari, but found nothing. Again, she thrashed against the bonds, but they were too tight.

"I will never rule with you," she managed between breaths.

He pushed against her ribs. Searing heat, followed by icy chills, sliced to her core. She bit back a scream. "So much pride. Even this close to death, you think you have a choice. You've never had a choice, Taryn. Your fate was decided a long time ago and guess what? It's with me." He lifted her tunic, whistling at her scar. "That's really something. Marissa told me of your bravery that day and I'll confess—I did not quite believe her."

Taryn flinched when he reached out to touch it, but there was nowhere for her to hide from his grasping hands. "Oh, my sweet, after a few days in my playroom, you'll think this scar was nothing." He slid his other hand between her legs, rubbing his fingers against her above the hilt of his sword as if he meant to impale her upon it. Eyes half-closed in dreamy expectation, he bent low, his hot tongue licking from one end of her scar to the other.

Something broke in Taryn. Rage like she'd never known coursed through her. Hate. Vengeance. Images flashed in her mind, cruel and vicious in their scope. She wanted to hurt Zakael, to maim him beyond recognition so that he could never inflict pain again. A low chuckle started in her belly, working its way up until she was laughing out loud so hard that the bonds at her neck constricted, cutting off what little air she had.

He screamed at her for silence, striking her across the face with his fist. A flash of white was all Taryn saw through the stars of pain. Then Kaida was on him, snarling and snapping at his face. The unexpected attack was the break she needed to reach her power. ShantiMari flashed through her limbs, burning through Zakael's bonds.

Taryn tasted blood and sent a wave of power at Zakael, pinning him down. Gian ran forward to grab Zakael's sword, then ducked behind her, disappearing into the bushes.

Kaida, stop. See to Gian. The grierbas snarled at Zakael a final time and then loped away to join the faerie.

She pulled Zakael's power from around her neck and fell to the ground. Ynyd Eirathnacht flew to her outstretched hand, pulsing energy through her, renewing her strength. The pain in her scar thrummed and then faded. Her pendant rose in song, with the sword answering the melody. Her ShantiMari burned like a flame and she savored the sensation. Freedom, release, pure infinite pleasure coursed through her veins.

Zakael scrambled to his feet, but Taryn was on him. She punched him in the nose and then the sternum in quick succession before smashing the side of his head with the hilt of her sword. A trickle of blood oozed down his temple. She wrapped her ShantiMari around him, throwing him high in the air. During his fall, he began to transform into a bird but she pulled her power tightly against him, stopping the transformation with him as half-man, half-bird. He screamed against her bonds in a terrible cry that scattered the creatures in nearby trees.

"Become Aelan," she commanded.

"Fuck off," he spat at her.

"Very well. I'll just leave you here." She walked away.

"Wait!"

He transformed back into his Aelan form. She lowered the bubble of power until it touched the ground. His Shanti swirled within the confines of hers.

"Release me. I'll not harm you," he pleaded.

"I'm not that stupid, Zakael. As soon as I let the barrier down, you'll try to trap me again. I should leave you here in this prison at least long enough for me to return to Talaith."

His eyes grew large. "I'll starve to death."

"And I should care why? Weren't you just gloating about how close to death you could bring me?" Taryn asked, her voice cool.

"Taryn, you aren't like this. You are caring and good."

"You make me sick." Her mind screamed at her to kill him, but her bloodlust had passed.

"I'll return to Caer Idris and tell Father I couldn't find you. I swear—I won't harm you." He held up his hands, placatingly.

"Teach me to transform and I'll let you go."

He sputtered at her, shaking his head. "It isn't something you do immediately. It takes a season or more to master."

"You don't have that long. Teach me." When she put her sword at his throat, it sang a song of death and by the look on his face he heard it, too.

"Put that down. I can't think with your blade on me." His power strengthened around him.

"Don't do it, Zakael. I'll know whether you're trying to overpower me."

Indecision etched across his features and then he relaxed, drawing in a deep breath. "First, you imagine the beast you wish to become. Bird, grierbas, horse, cat—anything. Think of the lines of the animal, the musculature, the fur or feathers. All of it. You must become the animal in your thoughts and heart."

"Show me. Slowly."

"Shape shifting is very dangerous. If you get it wrong, you could stay as the animal forever. Or worse." He actually sounded concerned for her.

She touched his throat with her blade, drawing blood. "I said show me and take your time. Move by move." His arms began to change from that of a man to the long wings of a levon. His head and torso were replaced by a feathered crown and body. Finally, his legs grew scales and he stood on long claws.

Taryn watched transfixed as he changed back into Zakael once more. "Are you ever anything other than a levon?" she asked.

"No more questions. I showed you how it's done. Release me."

"I need to make sure I can do it first."

"Not on your first try. No one ever gets it right the first

time out. Practice when I'm not around."

Taryn tied off her ShantiMari so he couldn't move. She closed her eyes, thinking of a great beast, her silver scales shining in the afternoon light. Her wings flowed out from her arms and her head and body convulsed into the form of a fanged dragon. She scratched her feet against the ground, feeling her talons rake through the grass. She turned her azure gaze on Zakael. He stared back at her in absolute panic.

I am darathi vorsi, she said in Eleri and heard a great shifting of leathery wings, the scrape of a million million scales.

She beat her wings, lifting into the air. Kaida crouched low, near the edge of the clearing, and she sent a thought to her grierbas friend to not be afraid. *Stay with Gian; I'll be back shortly.* She reached out with a talon and picked up Zakael as if he were a doll. He fought against her firm grip as she beat her wings harder, rising up into the sky. Exhilaration and terror commingled within her.

Once airborne, she panicked and plummeted toward the ground.

Zakael screamed at her, "Be the dragon! Don't think like Taryn—link your mind to hers."

Taryn let her mind drift into the dragon's and gasped as everything came into sharp focus. She saw through the dragon's eyes, felt the wind across her long snout. They moved through the air at an alarming speed. Her dragon mind scanned the landscape below them and then she dove into a small canyon. Zakael cried out for her to stop, but the dragon knew what she wanted.

She sent a thought to Zakael to sleep and when he hung limp, she gently lowered herself to the canyon floor, dropping him to the ground before transforming back into a woman with ease. Despite what Zakael said, the change wasn't difficult at all. A part of her had always been a dragon. Or the dragon a part of her. After she tied several bonds around Zakael, making certain they would take most of the day to untie, she spiraled into the air, snorting a burst of flame from sheer happiness. When she returned to the clearing and transformed back into Taryn once more, it was with great reluctance.

Kaida crept forward and lay before her. *You are Darennsai.*

Gian came out from his hiding place to prostrate himself. *Great One, I am yours to command until my last dying breath. This I, Gian of the clan Brenbold, swear to you.*

Their response to her transformation unnerved her. "Get up, Gian. You cannot tell anyone of this—do you understand?" He nodded and kissed his thumb before placing it over his heart. "Good," she said as she went to find Nikosana. "Because if Rhoane knew what I just did, he'd never let me out of his sight again."

THE TEMPLE OF ARDYN *is now available in digital and print!*